THE HARE AND THE OAK

CELIA LAKE

About the Hare and the Oak

Mabyn keeps her commitments.

The land magic in Suffolk has been failing for years. When the current Lord asks the Council for help, Mabyn knows it's her obligation to see it through. Even if that means immersing herself in a role she failed at in her younger and more optimistic days decades ago. Back when she was married.

Cyrus likes a challenge.

He doesn't know Mabyn well, but Cyrus does have a gift for ritual, and a broad experience of the world. A widower with a grown daughter, he's up for tracking down a lost heir and seeing if they can learn to take up the land magics.

When they arrive at Baddock Hall, it's clear there's more going on than the current Lord's troubles. The land is boggy, the gardens are failing, the bees have fled, and there's no obvious cause. Together, Mabyn and Cyrus must face their own pasts while getting to the root of the problem and making space for the future.

The Hare and the Oak is the fifth book of the Mysterious Powers series, exploring the institutions of Albion during and after the Great War. All of Celia Lake's Albion books exploring the magical community of the British Isles can be read in any order.

It is full of land magic, a late in life romance, a failing family line, and healing old wounds to the heart and soul. Enjoy this charming romantic fantasy with a swirl of sex set in 1926 with a happily ever after ending!

ALSO BY CELIA LAKE

The Mysterious Charm Series

Outcrossing

Goblin Fruit

Magician's Hoard

Wards of the Roses

In The Cards

On The Bias

Seven Sisters

The Mysterious Powers Series

Carry On

The Fossil Door

Eclipse

Fool's Gold

Charms of Albion

Pastiche

Sailor's Jewel

Other stories

Complementary

Winter's Charms

Learn more about the world of Albion and future books at my website, celialake.com.

Sign up for my newsletter to be the first to hear about future books and learn about fascinating bits of research. Happy reading!

CHAPTER I
THE COUNCIL KEEP, SATURDAY, MARCH 6TH, 1926

"My mother doesn't know I'm here."

Mabyn looked up from the desk in the Appointments Room. She was the Council Member on duty. It was the first Saturday of the month, and they took it in turns to hear requests from people who had a particular need from the Council. To be honest, most of the interesting matters came to them in other ways. Saturday petitions tended to be grindingly tedious disagreements, like matters about surveying that needed a mediator, petty grudges that had lasted at least a decade, or people who just wanted someone to complain to.

The man standing in front of her did not fit any of those models. For one thing, he was rather young, by complaining or grudge standards. There were people who could hold a first-class grudge from their twenties, but it generally suited someone of sixty or eighty better.

This man was well-dressed, in country tweeds, but he was decidedly younger. Old enough to have fought in the War, he had that look in his eyes, which made him at least late twenties, but likely not more than thirty-five. She took the rest of his particulars in; sandy brown hair, no visible disability, pocket watch, small rimmed glasses on his nose. A little twitchy, perhaps, but that was to be expected. Most people were when they showed up here. He was a bit more of an alarmed rabbit, though, than most of their visitors.

She gestured at the chair in front of the desk. "Please have a seat. I am Council Member Mabyn Teague. You are?" More to the point, she wondered who his mother was.

"Lionel Baddock. Lord Baddock."

She, of course, knew the name without consulting the map hanging on the wall beside them. The fundamental business of the Council was the Land. She hadn't been on the Council for near thirty years for nothing.

"Lord Baddock. Tea, or refreshment, before you lay out your concern?"

"Thank you, no. I can't be gone long."

That was an equally curious statement. He was a grown man. A bit younger than her son, but also a Lord in his own right. Presumably some degree of competent, and old enough to have come through the War, besides. "Please, begin." Mabyn had never cared for Lady Baddock, but his nerves about his mother suggested there was something far larger going on here than Mabyn's personal distaste. Lady Baddock was the sort who insisted upon impossible standards, and scorned all those who didn't meet her particular benchmarks of competence. At the same time, she was primarily focused on the show, not the substance. Mabyn could respect one or the other, but both at the same time rubbed old wounds raw again.

"I inherited the title shortly after the War. My father died in 1919. A bad heart." Seven years, then. More than enough time to sort out most kinds of inheritance problems. She remembered the late Lord Baddock well enough. He'd been the sort of man who'd liked country living. He came to social events because his wife insisted, she'd rather thought. He would spend the day hunting or shooting or riding, then he would hole up in the billiards room or the smoking room, or wherever the men gathered, quietly amiable. Leaving his wife to her own devices, but that was quite a common mode.

If he'd been a town man, rather than country, he would have spent all his free hours at his club. She didn't know anything to his discredit, but she knew how easily a man could present one face in public, and an entirely different one at home.

Baddock went on. "We hold Ipswich, the land around there. Over to near Bury St Edmunds, the Alton lands."

Mabyn nodded. "And Dunwich, the school, has responsibility for the northeast." It was an odd arrangement, but the school's magic made it a logical one. After a rather alarming storm in the thirteenth century, everyone had considered it best to have strong and consistent magical attention on the coastline on a regular basis. Once the school was established, it proved much more reliable than the vagaries of a single family line.

"Exactly." He hesitated, as if he'd come to the crux. "I have done the land rites every year since Pater died. The first year, everything was all right. Within the usual range. The second year, it wasn't awful. But since then, it has gone worse every year."

Mabyn pulled a clean sheet of paper over, picking up her pen and making a few quick notes about the date and Baddock's name. "Tell me about that. The ways it got worse." She then added, "Please." People who did not know about her former life might have thought her rude. And rudeness was a tool she wielded deliberately.

"It started with a drought in 1921. That wasn't completely unusual. They do happen. And that wasn't just us." Mabyn nodded. It had been one of the first sure signs to the Council, however, that something was seriously amiss in Albion after the War. "The dead fish in the moat were more so."

"A moat?" She frowned. "Oh, Baddock Hall. Built right after the Pact, it does have that striking moat. And gardens, I remember the gardens."

Baddock looked up with a shy smile. "They are not what they were. But yes, extensive grounds. The moat, and the drawbridges. We pull them up every night, still." He hesitated, then went on.

"The dead fish were followed by a blight in the apple orchards. Ergot in the barley. A whole field of hay that went to mould. Mysteriously dead deer in the nearby forest. Two completely failed harvests on the home farm. And then the portal started having problems. They seem to have fixed that, but it needs regular checks. We've not seen badgers or foxes for at least a year. The cows and the pigs keep getting sick. Not foot-and-mouth, thank God, but bad enough. Even Mother's been ill on and off."

"Magical animals? You'd have star hares perhaps, or the nightjars?" She considered Suffolk and its environs. "The lesser silver newt, or the helical swift? Dusk-spines?"

Baddock shook his head. "Nothing like that seen, for at least a year. It's not conclusive, but." He waved one hand. "The next village over, they did report a crescent owl last month, though." They were more resilient birds, on the whole.

"And I suppose the bees aren't doing well."

Baddock looked mournful. "Not for years. We used to have excellent honey. There's one hive still struggling on, but - they're rather sad, I think."

Mabyn frowned. "And what do you want us to do about this? In as much detail as you can."

Baddock cleared his throat. "I had a bad War." He didn't explain, but Mabyn did not need the explanation. "I've tried. I've done the rites, I swear I've done them, diligently, attentively. They aren't working. Not for me."

Mabyn did not need this man having emotions at her. She wanted to manage the problem - the serious problem - he had described, not the certainly delicate dance of managing his self-esteem. She wished it were one of the men on duty. Not her, anyway. Though, she supposed, better her than Livia Fortier or even Rhoda Morwen. "What do you propose?"

He seemed a little uncertain what to do with that, as if he had expected to be fussed over. However, the practicality also seemed to settle him. "I am an only child. There are cousins, at several removes, none close. None of them have an interest in the land. I looked, I invited them, to see. They shrugged. The land shrugged." He hesitated. "I should have come to you years ago, I know."

"Likely, yes." Her voice was brisk. They had educational pamphlets and talks with enticements for attending for a reason. "But you are here now, thank you." She did not suggest any of the things currently in her head. She wanted to see what he suggested first.

He swallowed. "There is one thing. My father had a younger brother." Baddock hesitated, "Samuel Baddock. He died before the War. But I have a locket with his hair, I found it a few months ago. And one with my father's. Is it..." He clearly had thought about this, but not practised saying any of it out loud. "Is there a way to find out if there is a descendant we do not know about?"

"You would lose the title, if there is someone with a better magical claim."

Lionel straightened his shoulders. "I want what's right for the land. I can't stand to see the land dying. Not if I could do something about it. Mother will have my head, I'm sure. She likes being the Dowager Lady Baddock entirely too much. She married in, of course." Lady Baddock could have been a distant cousin of his father. People did persist in it for all that was not entirely advisable - or recommended by anyone who knew about breeding horses or hounds. "If someone else can keep the land strong, they should."

Mabyn had to admire his commitment here. She suspected the money - at least some of it - was entailed separately from the demesne lands, that often happened. Still, giving up a title was far more rare than most people realised. He should have come to them years ago, but she had to give him credit for trying to do the best he could. He was here now, and he was clearly giving his best go, despite whatever circumstances had held him back previously.

"So." She made a few more notes on the paper. "You have two lockets, one with your father's hair, one with your uncle's. You know of no other descendants they match." That at least cut down on false leads. "And if we do find someone, or can identify another potential candidate, then what? It - even if someone is suitable, it takes them time to connect with the land. To see if they can act as the..." She frowned, trying to decide whether to go with the technical ritual language or the more commonly known. "Act as the bridge to the land magics."

"Baddock Hall is quite large." Mabyn remembered that, yes. "I am the only one living there. Mother is in the Dower House." Mabyn remembered that too, as being quite substantial. Scarcely a widow's cottage. "Perhaps a candidate could stay, for some months. A full year, even, if that were required. We have staff, of course. I wouldn't want them to go without, but they, we could have a guest. More than one, if needed. A chaperone."

Mabyn half remembered there was some sort of precedent about this. But she hadn't looked at it in years, and frankly all the arguments over the past year about the examinations and teaching focus at Schola would have knocked all of it out of her head. "I would need to check what we have done in previous cases, make a proposal to the rest of the Council, and then see what is acceptable to you."

"Of course." Baddock was very willing, here. It gave her an idea of how bad things were, in his estimation. He was not holding his ground, arguing that it was his land, he had the right to decide how this went. That meant this idea might just work.

"Are you able to leave the lockets with us, or do you need to take them back?"

"Mother will miss the one of Father. She notices. Mother rarely wears it, but she notices. She is out at a tea with friends." He glanced over her shoulder at the clock. "It would be much easier if I had it back within ninety minutes."

"In that case, I will take samples of the hair. It may take us a few days, a week, to make a determination. Would your mother be concerned by a sealed letter from us?"

Baddock raised an eyebrow, and as he spoke, Mabyn decided that she liked him rather more than she'd thought.

"Any sensible person pays attention to a Council seal, Magistra. And the staff might mention it to her. But if you send it direct, it will get to me."

She grinned, despite the serious topic. "Would she know my name?" Some people kept close track of the Council Members, even the ones less in the public eye.

"Your personal seal, I suspect she would not recognise. She might know your name." That was fair.

"Let me take the samples." The room was thankfully fully stocked with the sort of basic supplies they might need. She had always rather pitied the staff who had to keep a long list of items handy and in good order. She was able to find a glassine envelope, something Alexander had recommended last year for certain kinds of samples. It was an invention from the non-magical community that was decidedly useful. Half their number had complained at dire length. But the more sensible of them - the ones with Materia expertise in particular - had taken to it with glee. Keeping one's samples free from distracting influences was a delight.

In this case she took a dozen hairs from each of the lockets. Enough for several uses, magically, not so many they would be missed. She did them one at a time, to avoid confusion, though Samuel's hair was redder and lighter, easy enough to distinguish. Grabbing a larger manilla envelope, she slipped them inside.

She glanced at the record book, and wrote the next record number on the top corner, along with her own identifying sigil. Once Baddock left, she would write up the initial report for the book, and then see what she could find in the library.

It would be her responsibility to see this to a discussion

of the Council. If they decided to act - and she expected they would in some form - it would be assigned to someone suitable. Not her, she was sure. Land magics were not her speciality, nor were the rituals involved.

CHAPTER 2
LATER THAT AFTERNOON

The library was being annoyingly unyielding. Or at least, Mabyn was having absolutely no luck finding anything that backed up her scattered memories. She had half a dozen books out, and two dozen slips of paper laid out on the work table she had claimed.

It did not help one bit that the system here was entirely idiosyncratic. To find many things, you not only had to know what they might be filed under, but who would have done the filing. She had learned a number of tricks over the decades. However, when your filing system involved thinking like someone who had been dead for four hundred years, there would always be complications.

They really ought to hire a librarian, but the library was limited to Council use. The last Council Member who had had any real talent for that kind of work had died forty years ago. Since then they'd muddled along.

And the more so since the War. It hadn't touched their ranks as much directly. The Council were too important to be thrown into battle. But the implications of war, even fought overseas, had absorbed most of their hours then and now.

It wasn't only that it affected the usual work of the Council. Not just dealing with the land magics, inheritances that touched on them, the well-being of people and plants and animals. And not just solving the various idiocies that cropped up, when people got too inventive with their magic without a thought to the consequences, or worse, breached the Pact.

But all of them, every one of them, had seen the implications of the War. New ways to kill meant new ways the land could be wounded. There had been trips to France and Belgium and Germany. The impact of death, of twisted enchantments, of the insidious nature of the magical gas attacks, each new horror was one more thing they were charged with resolving. And some, even in Albion, had expanded research into those horrors, not just during the War, but since. Without, apparently, considering the implications and consequences that flowed downhill from that.

It had meant unending research. Hours in libraries and alchemical laboratories, ritual workrooms and the spaces most injured. It had meant endless conversations, which could go from invigorating debates with people among the best in their specialities to petty squabbles. And it left almost no time for quiet reflection. There was always more to do, weighing on them and their oaths.

She wished she could at least remember which Lord it had been, where something like this had come up. She had been doing some reading about the Protectorate, she remembered that. It, like the Great War, had disrupted so many family lines and a great many of the land magics. Worse than the Tudors, which was saying rather a lot.

She was turning around to write something else down,

when she saw a movement by the doorway. "If you want a table, this one is covered in paper."

Cyrus came more fully into the room. Mabyn was relieved it was him. There were half a dozen people around the Keep today. She thought all of them were inclined to be reasonable, but there were always a couple of their number who wanted to be territorial about everything. "Cyrus. Did you need something?"

"Oh, no. I heard someone in here. Do you need a hand?"

Mabyn considered. He was certainly competent to re-shelve things, and there was a chance he might actually have some useful ideas. He was not from a landed family, but she knew his ritual magic skills were more wide-ranging than most people realised, even on the Council. And that he was a magpie for knowledge of all types.

"I was on duty this afternoon, and got handed an unusual question. Now I'm trying to find precedent. Lord Baddock - here without his mother's knowledge - concerned that the land magics are not working properly."

"Oh, if you want the charm series for those, you're in entirely the wrong shelves." Cyrus then tilted his head. "Which you know. So what's his actual question?"

Mabyn was pleased that he didn't immediately just assume he knew better. He looked just enough like her late and unlamented husband that it always gave her a start, when she started talking to him. Of course, many Englishmen of a certain social class and background tended to look and sound the same, barring some variation in the colour of their hair.

She cut to the chase. "He has two lockets with hair. And he has a desire to know whether there might be some by-blow of his father's or his uncle's out there, who the land might take to better."

Cyrus blinked at her, working through the permutations and implications like she had. She didn't rush him, there was no need for that. It didn't take him long, either. "So you'll want a ritual working to identify the location of the person or persons, if any, who meet the criteria. Map scrying will likely be most efficient, unless you have a psychic you really trust."

Mabyn shook her head. "I have a wide range of acquaintances with some ability, but alas, location of people is not in their skill set. Lost jewellery, yes. Pets, yes. People, unknown people, not so much. Also, honestly, I find that a little invasive."

Cyrus tilted his head, considering her. Mabyn knew that she was considered something of a soft touch among their colleagues on the Council, one who preferred the least invasive, least aggressive approach, given the options. At least half their number tended to attack problems rapidly and destroy them thoroughly, if given the provocation. It was necessary at times, but this was not that sort of issue. "I have some skill with map scrying. Especially if combined with a day looking at the civil records. Owners of the home, census, that sort of thing."

Mabyn blinked at that. Map scrying was not a common talent, not at all, and she'd had no idea. Though, she supposed it didn't come up terribly often even in general Council discussions. Generally, they knew where the people they were looking for were, or they didn't have a suitable sample of hair or blood to work with. And of course, if it were a legal matter, they drew on the Guard specialists for that sort of thing. She covered her surprise with a comment. "I thought getting access to the recent census records wasn't permitted."

Cyrus tapped the side of his nose and grinned. "I also

have a circle of acquaintances, the right sort of voice, and an entirely uninformative card from both Ministries. It comes in handy sometimes. We also stand and serve, who know how to search an archive."

Mabyn leaned her hands on the table, suddenly wishing she'd worn a more comfortable frock. She had dressed this morning for being soberly impressive, rather than doing extended research, and her shoes pinched and the dress pulled at her shoulders. She had, perhaps, been slightly smaller last time she'd pulled it out of her wardrobe.

And it was a sensible pale grey. Sensible, of course, unless one had been doing things with ink. The smudges on her hands and one cuff did not help the impression at all. Never mind all that. He could manage. She did not dress for his pleasure, or anyone else's. "You think that sort of search might be required?"

Cyrus spread his hands. "The scrying can tell us where to look. A map will not tell us who we will find there. I have preferred, in such cases, to go having some idea what to expect. It never survives the first few minutes, that sort of plan, but at least one can, oh, guess at the genre of the book you might find."

That was an intriguing way of putting it, and she would have to store it away. "Are you available for scrying, then?"

"We'll need to have maps on hand. Or someone to grab them. And ideally a bit of earth from the property."

Mabyn snorted. "We. You assume I'm going to take this on?"

"You will be presenting it at next week's meeting, I presume. But you are the most likely to get handed it."

She did not like the sound of that, though she had to admit, they would try. "I am still deep in the midst of the Schola committee meetings. And it looks like they're going to need to hire a new Materia teacher. The replacement for Helena Trembley isn't working out."

"Oh?" Cyrus hesitated for a moment. He moved to settle in one of the chairs in front of the table, pulling out a small notebook and making a few notations with a stub of a pencil.

"It turns out that, brave man though he was in the War, the assembled force of three hundred and fifty of Albion's best and brightest young people is too much for him. They will keep asking questions about things not on his tidily ordered syllabus. And, I admit, pranking him a bit."

"Alexander is there through this year, too. Surely he can make your committee arguments?"

"Alexander Landry will make no one else's arguments, only his own. Though he and I are largely aligned on what needs to be done. Honestly, so are most of the current staff." As opposed to certain of the previous staff. "We are mostly sorting out how to do it better, and what needs to be shifted with the tutoring houses and the exam process to make that more feasible. Which is my job."

Cyrus looked up, considered, and then reached into his breast pocket to pull out a pair of reading glasses, perching them on his nose, before making more notes. "What do we know about the father? Or the uncle?"

"The father was also a Lionel Baddock. One of those families who use two or three names in rotation for centuries. The brother was Samuel."

"Hm. Samuel sounds vaguely familiar. What happened to them?"

She had, at least, got this far in her research. "Lionel the elder died of a dicky heart in 1919, and his son Lionel inherited. The son served in the War. I haven't gone looking for his service record, obviously." That would need a trip to the

Ministry archives in Trellech, or possibly to the British ones in London. "He had a bad War, forms unspecified."

Cyrus scribbled something in his notebook, then looked up, peering at her over the top of his glasses. "His landsense."

"Gone, I think. Fractured, certainly. And that's a hard thing to heal."

"Not always impossible, but very challenging. My sister's known a few successful cases, but only a few. Not the sort of thing there are proper studies about, though." The War wasn't the only reason that sort of thing could happen, but the War had certainly vastly increased the number the Council worried about.

Mabyn grimaced. "So many of them won't admit it. And that's more and more of a problem. It is here, too. Near six years, the land's been failing, more and more each year. That's going to make it hard to fix even if we do find someone willing and able to take it on."

Seven years was about the limit, before far more direct approaches had to be taken, the kind that would involve blood of some kind. Preferably offered willingly, and not fatally, it made the magic better. People always got upset about blood mortar, or the need to build some new substantial building on their land when they already had an otherwise usable house. Possibly they'd also need animal skulls in the foundations, or bone meal before the foundation was laid. And dozens of rituals, the extended services of twenty or thirty experts. None of that came cheaply, either in terms of money, or in terms of other projects that would be delayed.

"What sort of problems? The range, I mean?"

Mabyn ran through the list. "The drought, that wasn't just there, of course. Dead fish in the moat, blight in the orchards, ergot, mouldy hay, dead deer, failed harvests, problems with the portal. And they've seen no badgers or foxes in nearly two years."

Cyrus let out a low whistle. "If they'd come and asked before that."

Mabyn nodded. "Oh, and his mother has no idea he came. Clearly, she'd disapprove."

"I am trying to remember what I know of her. She must be near enough our age, surely? If the son was of age to fight in the War?"

Mabyn looked him up and down, as she knew she had at least a few years on him in age, though he was her senior on the Council. "Look her up?" She gestured at the Gold Book, the most recent edition, on the book stand nearby. It was probably the volume used most frequently in the entire collection. "I haven't had a chance."

Cyrus got up, tucking his notebook back into his pocket automatically. She liked that; she knew too many men who left little objects all over the place, like a trail of bread-crumbs to find them by. Women, too, of course. As he flipped through the book, she began tidying some of the slips of paper into piles and clipping them together.

"Eustacia Baddock, born Wallace. The Bedfordshire Wallaces. Not a family I know well." He ran his finger down, checking the dates. "Younger than I am. I think also you?" He grinned suddenly. "I am not generally in the habit of enquiring about a lady's age."

She knew he hadn't meant the title, but it always made her mouth taste sour when someone referred to her as a lady. "What year?"

Cyrus glanced back at the book. "Born in 1876."

"A fair bit younger. Thirteen years." Putting it like that made her feel better.

"1867 for me." Before that became awkward, he went on. "Privately educated, married at twenty, her late husband was a fair bit older, into his forties." That made him young to die, but not as young as she'd been thinking. The late Lord Baddock would have done a lot better to include his son in the land rites more thoroughly.

The sensible Lords began when their heirs were children, it helped no end. Well, and the sensible Lords also tried for more than one child. She wondered, vaguely, what had happened there. It was, however, also not something she could bring up, seeing as she'd also only had the one.

"So." Mabyn cleared her throat. "What do you need to do the scrying? We have a vial of earth in the cabinet, I checked that much." They kept them stored for each of the demesne estates.

"A lot of maps. Let me go pull what we need. We'll want them handy. Though gods help us if there's someone in America or Australia. I don't think we have detailed ordnance maps for any of that readily to hand." He glanced over his shoulder at the clock. "Now?"

"If you're up for it. It would mean I could make a proper report, all written up, for Wednesday's meeting."

Cyrus glanced away, as if considering, staring off down the row of bookshelves. "I don't need to be anywhere tonight. Let me write a note, find the maps. Half an hour?"

"I'll set up a workroom." She was certainly competent for that.

CHAPTER 3
AN HOUR LATER

It took Cyrus more like forty-five minutes to find the maps he wanted. It wasn't enough to have one map. A child born twenty or thirty years ago might have ended up in all sorts of places. Canada. Australia. The United States. India. They might have to start with a world map and work their way in. Or at least, if they were outside Great Britain, they could, but perhaps they would find someone that did not require an international jaunt.

"Why do we not have detailed maps of all the places that are or were red on the map? The empire, the Commonwealth?" Cyrus brought the stacks of maps in, carrying them on a very large tray with several paperweights.

"Because that would involve a great many maps, a tremendous amount of regular filing none of us like to do, and a need to keep them updated." Mabyn was in the middle of the room, adjusting several things on the large central marble worktable. "What do you need to start?"

"This world map, to start. If there is a child, and they are somewhere else, well, that is a different sort of problem."

Mabyn nodded. "That seems entirely in your capability, mind. Or Alexander, but he's tied down at the moment. And you do have an in with Hugh Pelagius."

Cyrus glanced up and snorted. "He's off on a voyage for another three weeks, but yes." He shrugged. "I started with the travel early on in my time on the Council, and then the more transient sort of work of that kind seemed to fall to me. I don't mind much, as long as I'm back for the special occasions."

He glanced down when he felt one of the maps shift. When he looked up, Mabyn was considering him. "A widower. A grown daughter."

Cyrus nodded. "It mattered a lot more, when she was younger. To be able to take her out for a meal, when she was at the tutoring house, or Schola, or be at some performance or event or such thing. Now, we can be more flexible." He shrugged. "And my sister is fiercely independent and very busy, so we are glad to get time when we can. The journals are a great help, honestly, staying in touch without having to wait for letters."

"And your parents?" The question seemed almost idle.

"Fine people, rather hide-bound." He said it briskly. He didn't like people prying into the family situation. There was no great dramatic break, but how did one explain the problem? His parents hadn't understood anything about him for a long time, certainly not since Tanith had died, but it had gotten worse as he had gotten older. They thought he should remarry, and that he should make a bigger name for himself in the showy ways. He had a volume of passing phrases, and he was quite sure Mabyn would see through all of them.

"At any rate, there's the world map. Then I have Great Britain, in segments, and we will narrow down from there to the ordnance maps. I've grouped them with clips. One inch to the mile, then the six inches to the mile. For a few of the cities, I pulled out the twenty-five inches to the mile, or the fifty to the mile." Once they started the work, he'd have to keep going or lose the thread entirely. No time to go and pull the relevant ones.

Mabyn looked the stack up and down. "Hence your stack of maps a good few inches high. Right. Let me get a table to put them on." Before he could say anything, or offer to help, she went off to pick up a wooden table from the corner and brought it back. To be fair, it was not a terribly heavy table, and he suspected she'd used a charm to help, but it felt ungentlemanly.

On the other hand, Mabyn had long-since made it clear she had little time for men. She normally concerned herself with some of the other women on the Council, or those who might become so. Silvia Warren, for example, who had joined their number three months ago.

Cyrus had heard, from more than one source, that Silvia's success in the challenges for her seat had been more Mabyn's doing than anyone else's. Silvia's husband, Hespiridon, was head of the Council, but worked his magic in a rather different style than Sylvia. Silvia had a delicate local patience to her, while Hespiridon was all about laying out patterns for the future, over long spans of time.

Mabyn settled the table wordlessly nearby, easy to reach from the worktable. Cyrus murmured, "Thank you." He set the tray down on top, then moved the paperweights, drawing the top map off. "May I talk out the logic of this?"

She shrugged and spread her hands, looking amused, as she took up a place to one side, with the maps between them. "As you wish."

"We have two sets of hair, and we are - I believe - reasonably confident they belong to who we think?"

"His father's hair came from the locket his mother normally keeps in her dressing table. The other comes from the family vault. The hair colour matches illustrations - the uncle was more auburn. I think it is fair to assume."

"That makes it much easier. I had a very odd time once, and it turned out that our samples were not at all what we thought they were." He took his time, setting the paperweights - smooth quartz stones, worn down to have no sharp edges - at each corner.

"A particular sort of odd time?"

"Well, I found myself at the far end of an exceedingly muddy field, staring a rather toothy pony in the face. You know the sort, they're sure they're bigger than you, and are determined to prove they should get their way."

"I prefer a draught horse, honestly. They know they're huge, and they're easy-tempered because of it." Mabyn snorted. "What were you trying to find?"

"A young girl - of course, she'd had some hairs from the pony, and they were near enough a colour match for her own. We did find her, but I had to go do the ritual work again, and it started raining while I was walking back from the field."

Mabyn laughed, entirely amused. Cyrus couldn't tell if it was the image of him, sodden and muddy, or something else. "Well, no rain here."

Cyrus nodded. "Lord Baddock did not have any hint of a possible by-blow from his father?"

"I do not expect he would have told me if he did. It is not the kind of thing one tells ladies. He might have told you."

"Likely not. There's a thing, not having the title. It

divides." Cyrus came from a longstanding family, anchored firmly in Devon, but they were not Lords of the land, nor Ladies, nor had they been for a very long time. Occasional Council Members, yes, about once a century. Mostly, they went for high-ranking positions in the Ministry, the occasional Healer, like his sister. Other forms of power. Or service, as Mother would say, since she was prone to be much more self-effacing.

"Do you do the ritual twice, then?"

"Here's the thing. We will get a result for Lord Baddock himself, that we will need to rule out. Do you know, did he intend to spend the evening at home?" Cyrus frowned and finished straightening out the map one last time, making sure there were no wrinkles. He turned back to the tray and picked up the wrapped leather roll of his ritual tools. "I suppose we must start with Great Britain, then, and if we have no luck we can try the world map."

"He strongly implied that, yes. That home was where his mother expected him to be." Cyrus caught the emphasis there. It was curious, indeed, that Lady Baddock still had such influence over a grown son. There was something unhealthy there.

"Thus, logic suggests that if we get one result there, we can assume it is him. If we get two results near there, there is a local by-blow who may or may not be a candidate. If there is a result anywhere else, we may have a candidate."

Mabyn tilted her head, considering. "And if we get multiple results?"

"That is when we make notes, and narrow it down as much as we can, drawing on whatever other records we can access that are of use." He shrugged. "Did he hint at family stories, or any such thing? Often people have a sense of it, before they have certain knowledge."

"That thing where, who was it, Peter Douglas, was walking down a street, and near enough ran into himself. Only to find it was a half-brother he never knew he had?" Mabyn shook her head. "That must have been alarming, honestly." The papers had made much of the story, a few months ago.

"The very story I was thinking of." Cyrus checked one last time. "I think it is more likely - statistically, as well as my sense of the thing - that we will, if we are lucky, have two to four results from the map. A manageable number."

Mabyn nodded. "What do you need from me?" She had changed, in the interim, into ritual robes. He suspected, from some things his sister Rhoe had said, that it was as much for comfort as anything else. Even those most committed to fashion or propriety did not corset in their ritual attire.

Cyrus reached into his tools, and then drew out a single gold chain, then carefully worked the wedding ring off his finger. He only took it off for work like this, where it was a tool as much as a reminder. "Very traditional, using a ring for this. Also, honestly, more practical than a pendulum. If this works right, the ring will centre on the location." He reached for the first envelope, the late Lionel Baddock's, and drew out a single hair, then tied it around the ring. He appreciated that Mabyn had labelled things so tidily and thought about the Materia implications, but of course she would. Whatever else he knew of her, she was competent.

Mabyn nodded. "What do you need from me?" She moved smoothly around the worktable, taking up the most common secondary placement.

"Hands on the edges of the table, the corners, without touching the map. A centred presence, that makes space for the ring to move." He suspected, suddenly, that this part would be easy for her. She had all the small tells of someone who found this kind of ritual satisfying, but he'd only ever seen her in the larger communal workings of the Council. "Then think about the late Lord Baddock." They'd do him first, because there should be one result here. At least one. Unless the current Lord Baddock's mother had been keeping quite a secret.

With that, he dangled the ring from the end of the chain carefully, giving it the full length to move, so that it could tug in one direction or another. He held it above the map, and began the chant he preferred. This one had meaningless Latinate words that were utter nonsense, but somehow managed to produce far more reliable results than anything more sensical. He could feel the magic welling up from him.

This only worked for him as well as it did because of all the time he'd put in learning to draw down to the earth. How to connect himself with an entirely different sense of time and priority, how to immerse himself in the element and mingle, without losing his sense of self. He'd be exhausted tonight, but he'd sleep well and deeply, and that made it easier to work his way toward his goal.

It took only a second for the ring to start tugging on the chain, and then for it to land precisely where expected. It was centred over the Baddock estates in Suffolk, just northwest of Ipswich. He nodded once. "No tug to any other place, so let's try the local map." That was nearly on the top of his pile, since he'd expected this. He swapped out the map, rearranged the paperweights, and then repeated the chant. Again, the ring landed in exactly the right spot, and this map was in enough detail that he could be sure it was one person, in that moated manor house.

"I'm quite sure if we had a map of the house, that would be the library. I've been there, though not at all recently."

He glanced up at Mabyn. She was watching his hands steadily, not looking at his face. "I'm inclined to try the other hair, Samuel's, and come back if we need to later. I don't feel a tug anywhere off the map with this one."

At that, she glanced up. "You do this most smoothly."

"I've put in a great deal of practice. I'm tosh at most forms of divination, but someone on a trip to India - that business about returning that statue, two decades ago? She taught me how to do locational scrying properly." That was true enough, but it understated things.

They'd spent the long voyage talking through the theory, he and this woman who must have been in her seventies. Just before they'd disembarked, shehad invited him home. He had passed some sort of exam, he'd realised. When she let him into her workroom, hung with brilliantly dyed fabrics, he'd realised how limited his approach to magic had been.

She hadn't invited him to do the scrying with her, but she'd walked him through it with a brisk attention to detail that had stuck in his mind like walking into the Temple of Healing. Everything in its place, bounded by arching ceilings and glowing light through the stained glass, the scent of mingled herbs and spices in the air. It had taught him to fill the space of his magic and inhabit it in a way nothing else had.

Silently, Mabyn held out the second envelope. Cyrus cast a small cantrip to burn away the old hair on the ring, to avoid any hint of contamination, then coiled the second hair, more visibly ginger. Again, he chanted, and again he felt the decided tug of the ring. This time the ring tugged noticeably further north and west, landing firmly around the city of Manchester.

"There is no magical community there, is there?"

Mabyn pointed at the map while Cyrus turned away to rummage for a map with more detail.

"A number of individuals, but there were troubles with the portal, oh, a century ago? I'd have to look up the details. And with the industrialisation, it was hard to get another one grown. There's one a short train ride away now, people make do. Here, here's the city centre, if that doesn't work, we'll try others." He came back with a new map.

One more time, he repeated the chant. One more time, the ring tugged and landed.

"We appear to be going to there. From the shape of it, a working-class neighbourhood."

CHAPTER 4
THE COUNCIL KEEP, WEDNESDAY, MARCH 10TH

By the following Wednesday, Cyrus had been to Trellech, London, Manchester, and then to London again. Only to the registration offices, of course. He found Mabyn at five, an hour or so before their meeting would begin. There'd be the two hours of formal meeting, followed by people dividing up into groups for a late supper to pursue their own particular plots.

Cyrus came up to the door of the small room she used as a study here. They each had their own little nook. Little was the operative word. Every member of the Council came from land and money. They all had vast homes set up to their liking. However, sometimes you wanted a table and a lamp and room where you could leave your things, warded just the way you wanted. He certainly did. Certainly a place to store a set of ritual robes and whatever other accoutrements you might need for that sort of work.

Mabyn's door had been ajar, though, and so he knocked. "Have a moment? I wanted to talk about what I found."

She was sitting at her desk. Not in a chair, but on a low

padded bench hidden by her skirts. Her hair was coiled in a braid around her head as usual, and Cyrus had a flash, for a moment, of what Tanith might have looked like if she'd lived. In his memory, she was always young, the kind of young he'd left far behind now.

Her hair had been dark, like he remembered Mabyn's had been. Maybe by now Tanith would have gone to this distinguished silver. Mabyn was wearing something in a muted deep green. He thought it made her eyes shine, then he realised she had a letter in her hand, and it must be something in the letter that had done it.

"I beg pardon." He gestured, as if to withdraw. "Later?"

He'd already taken a step back when she said, "No, please. Tea? I have a pot made." It was the resolute tone, he knew it so well from the inside. When something had jarred his equilibrium, some memory, some bit of heartache, and he forged on anyway, because it was the only way to manage. She set the papers down, tucking a paperweight on top of them.

"Tea would be grand." He came all the way through the door, closing it gently behind him. Her study was pleasant. Like Cyrus, she had bookshelves against both the interior walls, covering almost the entire space. Like him, she had a reading chair in front of one set of shelves, but hers was a deep green, the same colour she was wearing. Hers was in the centre of the short wall across from the door, with a small table with her tea things off to one side. She gestured him to the chair. "Sit, please."

He had, honestly, never understood those of their number who didn't have bookshelves. Livia Fortier's study was almost bleak. Her husband Garin's had a small reference library, but his shelves were a series of apothecary cabinets. That, frankly, made little sense to Cyrus. It wasn't as if Garin would deign to do alchemical work at the Council Keep. He had his own lab, set up to his demanding preferences, at home. As Mabyn handed him a cup, she reached to tug a small sliding panel out from her desk, giving him somewhere to rest it.

"I'm sorry. I seem to have left you with all the work. You said in your note this morning you had a promising lead?"

"I thought so, and now I am less sure." He spread his hands. "This is going to take a visit, and I suspect a complicated one."

Mabyn grimaced. "I don't suppose I can talk you into it? I'm awful at this sort of thing."

Cyrus settled in the chair and sipped the tea. "You don't even know what sort of thing it is, yet." He was amused, more than anything, at how she seemed suddenly out of her element.

"What did you find, then?" Mabyn settled to face him, sitting on the bench she used as a desk chair, the teacup and saucer set on the corner in easy reach.

"I have found the owner of the current property, and the previous owner. But I am not at all certain how they connect to the Baddocks." He waved a hand. "I began by checking our Ministry for any records about the Baddocks. I found only what we expected, the usual registrations of births and marriages and deaths that the Gold Book had. And the late Lord Baddock and his wife had no other children."

"A bit odd to stop at one." Mabyn had a point, even among the landed families. Two or three were more common.

"There's no indication why, but of course, there often isn't." He shrugged. "Anyway, I confirmed all the records, and then went to Manchester, to see who owned the house."

Mabyn nodded. "And?"

"It was owned until three years ago by Poppy Martin." Cyrus waited a beat. "She was magical, she went to Alethorpe, but then disappeared into living in Manchester, not particularly connected to the magical community. Mistress Martin worked as a midwife and a local nurse. She died and left the property to Nora Martin."

"Her daughter? Is there a father?"

Cyrus shook his head. "She never registered a birth. That's what I was checking today. It took forever. And I wasn't able to trace the family back."

"Do we know how old Nora is?"

Cyrus nodded. "She's on the census records from 1901. I did get a look at the enumeration book, because I had the address. It lists her as being four at the time of the census - so born around 1896, depending on when in the year. It does say she was born in Suffolk. Stowmarket." He held up a hand. "I couldn't get to our Ministry again before they closed, I don't know if she's at all magical, or just the aunt is."

"Stowmarket is promising. But of course, the census won't have her parents listed. Blast. That's terribly frustrating, isn't it?"

Cyrus spread his hands. "That is what I found. You can see why going and asking her, as complicated as it might be, is likely our best choice."

"Does it have to be ours, though?" Mabyn grimaced. "I'm sorry. I have not thanked you enough for doing all of this. The records, how to ask for them without sounding like an idiot, I've never been good at that."

"I treat the administrative language like a ritual." Cyrus

leaned back, more comfortable. "You say the proper phrases, make the proper gestures across the form, and the wonders of the world are revealed." Then he waited to see if Mabyn would catch on to the essential problem here.

She turned, fiddling with something on her desk. "They're going to make me go and find out what's going on." She didn't look back at him.

Cyrus was torn now between offering his help and making her ask for it. Making her realise she should ask. To be fair, he knew she'd been up to her neck in every argument about how Schola should proceed with various reforms, and that was not remotely relaxing. It had likely added to her grey hairs. But she was one the one who had heard the original case, and they had customs for good reason.

"I am busy. Not make-work busy. Not endlessly writing a book that will not be published until I'm dead. Not making work for other people busy. Actually busy."

Cyrus waited it out. He'd heard this kind of complaint before. Granted, mostly from Rhoe, his sister. She tended to get tapped for every committee at the Temple of Healing that needed her particular force of will and powers of good sense. Mabyn rather reminded him of Rhoe, actually. Something in her physical presence, a rooted insistence that she was doing was important. And, like Rhoe, fairly often right about it, though he had far less experience with Mabyn on that count.

Then Mabyn looked up. "I don't suppose you'd ..." She hesitated, like asking for a favour was the last thing she wanted to do. Cyrus wasn't entirely sure why. Of course, they'd been on the Council together for over thirty years, but they'd never much come into each other's circles.

It created an odd form of intimacy and distance, all at

once. After that pause, Mabyn straightened up, like she was gathering up dignity. "Would you be willing to accompany me to talk to Nora Martin? I know you've much more experience with the non-magical."

Cyrus tilted his head, noting that she didn't use the more common phrasing among the Council, the incapable. That was promising, at least. "I've some experience. A great deal of travel, mostly, and I must often take mixed liners."

"I would appreciate it." Her voice was steady. She wasn't begging, but she did understand the magnitude of need.

Cyrus nodded. "Let us present it as a fait accompli, then, that we will investigate this. Talk to Nora Martin, see if there is a further connection to follow up. And then we can bring it back to the Council and see what to do about it."

Mabyn was relieved enough to let it show. "Are you certain?" Then she leaned an elbow on her desk. "What are our next steps?"

"You know more about the land magics than I do." He let his voice trail off. He had had hints of her background, but no one had ever laid out the personal details for him. He was certain she didn't want to. The question was whether she would.

Mabyn considered, looking him up and down for a long time, Cyrus could hear a clock on one of the shelves ticking over. Finally, she shifted to face him straight on again. "Your family isn't landed." It wasn't a question. Cyrus just shook his head. "What do you know about the land magics?"

"The kind of thing you know when you have some distance from them. I have had the pleasure of visiting a number of different rites over the years. People do like having an audience."

"And most of our number have some obligation to the land. Beyond being on the Council." Mabyn seemed to be considering where to begin. "I was Lady Teague, at one time. I married in, of course, which makes a difference for the land magics."

"Your son has the Lordship, doesn't he?" Cyrus thought that was safe enough to venture. He was sure of it, of course, he wouldn't tread here otherwise.

"He does. He inherited quite young, but he's done well with the rites. Near Exmouth."

"That must include Dartmoor. That has to be an interesting rite."

Mabyn grimaced, rather despite herself. "Challenging. Geographically speaking. I am glad to leave that entirely in his hands." She went on briskly. "You know the theory of it. I know what it is like to take up those rites, when you weren't raised with them. My late husband married for money, of course. Though Mother was delighted I'd married into a title."

Cyrus could not decide, for the life of him, if she had meant to give away as much as she had. It was generally safer to assume that when your fellow man or woman on the Council shared information, they had at least three reasons for doing so. "So you can speak to the land magics, the experience of them. I can speak to the larger potentials and obligations. And, I hope - we hope - translate between her experiences and ours."

"Assuming she is the right person. Is there a way to confirm that that we have good precedent for?"

"Oh, yes." Cyrus had looked it up on Monday night, and managed to find Rhoe to confirm it last night, right when she got off duty. "Between the hair and a drop of blood or a hair from her head with the root, we can confirm it for her. If she'll permit the magic." Which might be the trick, but they could cross that bridge when they came to it.

"And if she wants nothing to do with magic?"

"Then we bring it back to the Council. There are ..." Cyrus hesitated. "There are some theoretical methods for binding a new line to the land. None of them are pleasant. And I am not sure they would work if Lord Baddock's mother protested. Or refused to participate." He had rather more scruples about certain kinds of magical workings than many on the Council, and he was used to not letting it show.

"Mmm." Mabyn frowned, as if that had reminded her of something she would rather not think about. As she was about to say something, the gong rang to summon them to the meeting.

Cyrus murmured. "My thanks for the tea. Let me go collect a few things about that business at Dover from my study, I'll see you in the chamber." He'd give her a few moments to collect herself, that was a kindness he could offer.

Mabyn nodded, without saying anything further, leaving him to withdraw in silence. When he glanced back, she had turned back to the desk, picked up the letter from earlier, and was reading it again.

CHAPTER 5

A STREET IN MANCHESTER, FRIDAY, MARCH 12TH

Friday afternoon found them standing in the street, looking at a terraced row house. It was, much like the homes on either side, made of a ruddy brick. Wednesday's meeting had been full of four other crises, so everyone was glad enough for the two of them to investigate and sort out the next steps, just so something could be cleared off the table.

Yesterday, Mabyn had been occupied preparing materials for an offering to the Belin by way of apology for one of the crises. She'd worked for twelve hours alongside Frederica and Matthias, who would be making the actual apology with the assistance of staff from the Ministry. It had left them all exhausted.

Cyrus contemplated it. "Are you at all familiar with this sort of place?"

Mabyn was surprised he was. "Not particularly. I've not spent much time in cities, other than Trellech." It had at least been easy enough to find, after a short train trip from the portal and a walk from the station.

Cyrus nodded. "A classic home, common in many cities,

especially where there are a lot of workers. Two rooms downstairs, two up. Possibly an addition on the back, with a terrace or garden. I would recommend not using the facilities if you can avoid it. Not to our standards, as a rule."

Mabyn nodded. "And you think she will return soon?"

Cyrus pulled out a pocket watch and peered at it, just as a whistle went off. "I found some indication she might work in one of the factories. An office job, perhaps. I only got a glimpse, yesterday morning."

"Do you have some kind of plan, then? Surely we do not just introduce ourselves and say, 'Hello, we are here to spirit you away to a possible magical inheritance'. I can't imagine that going over well. And are we sure she's magical, enough for the land magics?"

"I found what I think might be her oath to the Silence, this morning, in the register, but the name was blurred. Someone of the proper age, from Manchester, first name Leonora, last name began with an M. If so, that's promising."

Mabyn crossed her arms. "That does not explain how we bring it up."

Cyrus shrugged. "I thought we'd lead with saying we have been investigating a family connection. We are wondering if she could tell us a little about her background, so we can determine if she is the person we are looking for? After all, we are fundamentally talking about an inheritance."

Mabyn eyed the house. "Does she get the income from the land, or just the land?" That had also been part of Cyrus's research this morning.

"Some of it is in the entail. If the current Lord Baddock releases his claim on the title, there should be more than sufficient to maintain the house and properties with some careful management. If the estate comes back properly, she could live comfortably, pursue whatever her interests are."

"All right. I can manage to be professionally pleasant, I suppose." Then they both stopped, seeing a figure come down the street. A woman in her mid-twenties, she wore a plain coat of a muted grey, over a deep blue skirt and a pale grey blouse. Nothing at all fussy or fancy. She had dark hair in a tight bun, and no obvious jewellery. She turned up to the house, opened the door, and went inside.

"Shall we?" Cyrus did not offer his arm, but he did gesture. Mabyn did not need the hand up, but she nodded, straightening her skirt and adjusting the angle of her hat.

They crossed the street, and then after a moment's hesitation, Cyrus knocked on the door three times, steadily. The sound resonated for a moment, and thirty seconds later, there was a quiet but firm, "I am not interested in buying anything."

Mabyn cleared her throat. This might come better from a woman. "Pardon, we're looking for Nora Martin. It's about a family matter, related to a possible inheritance."

"And you are?" Mabyn noticed, with a mix of pleasure and bemusement, that the woman didn't identify herself.

"I'm Mabyn Teague, and this is Cyrus Smythe-Clive. We represent a party involved in the inquiry. If you are Mistress Martin, we have additional information we can share."

The door cracked open, then opened wider. "I'm Nora Martin. I suppose you had better come in. The neighbours will gossip about you standing out on the street." She stood back to let them enter a tidy but plain sitting-room, with a few signs of water damage around the ceiling.

The sofa and chairs were done up in a rather faded blue fabric. There were a few books on a writing desk along the back wall, and a single flower in a vase. After Mabyn looked at it more closely, she thought it was made out of some sort of lightweight fabric, but it at least was in a more vibrant red.

"May I offer you tea?" Nora Martin glanced at the kitchen.

Cyrus read something there that Mabyn didn't, and shook his head. "We've come calling unexpectedly. If you'd like to make yourself a cup, certainly."

There was another hesitation, then Mistress Martin glanced at the other room, presumably the kitchen. "Let me make up a kettle, if you can wait a couple of minutes." When Cyrus nodded, she disappeared into the other room.

Cyrus lifted his hand, gesturing with one finger for Mabyn to stay quiet. Then he spread out his hands, palms perpendicular to the floor. It was the sort of gesture that Mabyn suspected meant he was getting a feeling for any ongoing magical workings in the home, protections and such.

There were a lot of things Mabyn didn't understand here, frankly. There were a few framed pictures on the walls, but not of people. A few were of places, a few others were of objects, still lives, at least those she could see from her seat. She rather wished that she could see the books on the desk, but she couldn't make them out.

As they heard the kettle sing, Cyrus dropped his hands, folding them politely in his lap. By the time Mistress Martin came out, they were all pleasantry and good manners. The china had once been good quality, but much used, with the flower pattern more than a little faded, and some of the gilt rubbed off. She offered a cup, already poured, to each of them, with no offer of cream or sugar or lemon.

Cyrus seemed unsurprised. The tea, Mabyn thought, had more to do with floor sweepings than the best quality tips, but it was brewed well, with an eye to making as much of the taste as one could. And having that taste not be all tannins. Cyrus sipped his solemnly, giving it as much attention as one might give the most delicate cup from the best tea shop.

When they had all satisfied the bare essentials of British hospitality, Mistress Martin cleared her throat. "I have been wondering when someone might call. The 'mistress' was a giveaway, for any future calls. That is not a term used much these days. And as a schoolteacher, I am reliably Miss Martin."

Mabyn nodded once, accepting the correction, showing no sign of what she felt about it. She felt she had mucked things up, and she let Cyrus take the lead on the next question.

"You expected someone to call? May I inquire what you expected? That may be a useful place to start."

Miss Martin considered, looking at them with blue-grey eyes, steadily. Mabyn rather liked her already. "My aunt had magic, but chose to live outside magical society." It did not, Mabyn noted, give away anything about the woman herself.

Cyrus considered, and then apparently chose honestly. "I found a record this morning that suggested you made your oath to the Silence at twelve, as we do. But you have lived entirely in the non-magical community?"

"Your schools had no interest in me. They judged I had enough magic to make the oath, but no particular potential. My aunt taught me a bit, enough to do the household things, and that was plenty." She gestured broadly, indicating the neighbourhood as much as the house. "There is not much of the overtly magical here."

Cyrus raised an eyebrow. "You think that?" Mabyn

recognised the challenge in his voice, but also the delight that he might get to talk about this.

To Mabyn's pleasure, Miss Martin lifted her chin. "You wish to make some point, I see."

Cyrus did not look cowed at all. "If you walk along the street to the park on that end, there are a number of unusually healthy flowers. Those are touched by magic, I believe a combination of attentive care from someone, and water from a suitable well or stream. If you walk two blocks that way." He gestured in the opposite direction. "There's a clockmaker who pours his magic into his work. Pocket watches and wrist watches that keep fine time, protected from passing damage. A seamstress, down toward the centre of the city."

Miss Martin raised an eyebrow. "And what does that have to do with the cost of tea in China?" She waved a hand. "I wondered if someone would notice Aunt Poppy had died. There's nothing much magical in the house, except for some simple household things. I keep the promise I made. She wanted nothing to do with your community, and she had her reasons."

Mabyn nodded. "And you?"

The young woman cleared her throat. "I have a good life. A house I own, fair and square. I have a good position for a spinster, a teacher at the local school. A steady life." She seemed to be laying down a line. "And now here you come, and I'm fairly sure it's not to leave me alone with what's been going well."

Mabyn cleared her throat. "May I ask a little more about your background. You grew up here, in this house? With your aunt?"

Miss Martin nodded. "Aunt Poppy had lived here for some years by the time I was born." She hesitated, as if she was deciding how to frame something. "My mother, her much younger sister, was on the stage, a singer, one of the Gaiety Girls, from what my aunt said. She would visit, every year or two, when I was young. She got pregnant, I was the result."

Mabyn nodded, not pressing on the question of a father yet. "And where did your family come from, do you know?"

"Oh, yes. Near Ipswich, one of the villages. Debenham. It's quite small. My grandparents had a small farm a bit outside, I'd spend summers there."

"And your aunt?"

"She was a midwife, but she was a nurse while I was little. More predictable hours, and she went back to midwifery when I was old enough to be left alone. It was considered rather daring for her to be raising a child, but she made it work. My mother was on the stage until around 1910, and then she married a Frenchman. She writes now and again, but she hasn't for a while."

Mabyn wasn't sure what she thought of such a mother, though she could scarcely be considered to be the most actively doting of parents by anyone's standards. Even if there was some reason for that.

"And - beg pardon. Do you have any idea about who your father was? Or might have been?" Cyrus pressed on.

"This would be the matter of the inheritance, then?" Miss Martin's voice was crisp.

"It would, yes. It would be a help to know what knowl-edge or documentation you have, before we discuss that."

Miss Martin frowned, and then said, "I'll be a few minutes, getting some things from upstairs." She seemed resigned, more than anything. She set her teacup and saucer down carefully on the table, and then got up, smoothing her skirts out automatically.

Once they could hear her going up the stairs, Mabyn stood, tiptoeing to the desk, to see what books were on there. They were quite a mix. What looked like a recent novel, someone had mentioned the title to Mabyn a fortnight ago. A book of fairy tales. And a book of folklore of Suffolk.

When she turned back, Cyrus had cocked his head, as if curious about what she'd found. He didn't say anything, perhaps not sure how sound would carry here. Mabyn nodded, and sat down, pulling out her small notebook and making a few notes of the titles, to remind herself later.

CHAPTER 6
NORA MARTIN'S SITTING ROOM

In another minute, they heard footsteps coming down the stairs again. Cyrus glanced over, measuring them. His sister had a theory, or rather a library of theories, about how people walked telling you a great deal about them. He wasn't sure what Rhoe would make of Nora Martin. Her movements were small, like she didn't want to take up space. Or perhaps she had been trained not to take up space.

They were precise, those footsteps, like she was putting down each foot exactly where she wanted. Of course, if she'd lived here since she was an infant, she would know each step intimately, the way it lay under her feet. Miss Martin had a steadiness to her, whatever her circumstances, that appealed to the eye and ear. It made Cyrus wonder what she was like in a classroom.

When she came back, she was holding a photo album, and a folder of papers. The whole thing was rather more tidy than some variants he'd seen at other points. She'd perched a pair of spectacles on her nose. Precisely the round ones he'd expect of a teacher.

"Auntie's papers. I've been meaning to go through them." She settled down at the desk chair, though she turned so that she could at least partly face them. "Who do you represent?"

Asked bluntly like that, Cyrus was not inclined to lie. He glanced at Mabyn, who cleared her throat and spoke. "We are both members of the Council. Did your aunt ever explain about that?"

"She didn't talk much about that sort of thing. She went to Trellech a few times, for paperwork. Aunt Poppy had magic, my mother didn't, at least not enough for anyone to care." Miss Martin's chin came up, and she was suddenly looking directly at Mabyn. "That must mean something about my father."

The woman was sharp. Cyrus nodded. "We have some thoughts on the matter. But as we said, we would prefer to hear from you." He picked up on the matter of the Council. "We have a Ministry, as everyone does in the United Kingdom. We share some records, which is how we were able to locate you, part of how."

She picked up on that 'part'. He could see that. If she'd been a hound, her ears would have pricked up. He approved, and also the way that this news, as strange as it must be, wasn't appearing to shake her out of her own priorities. Cyrus went on, smoothly. "The Council has a responsibility to the land. Once, long ago, it would have been the King's role."

"Or a queen's?"

Cyrus grinned, somewhat despite himself. "There were no ruling queens in their own right who held that role for the land before the Pact. That was Richard III, in 1484."

"Ah. Before Lady Jane Grey, Mary, and Elizabeth, then.

Or Victoria." She reeled the list off tidily. "You said ruling queens."

"There are extensive academic articles about the degree to which Eleanor of Aquitaine took on that role for either her second husband or Richard Lionheart. And there's rather a lot of debate about Margaret d'Anjou."

Miss Martin inclined her head. "Indeed. So the Council has taken it upon itself to fill that gap?"

The phrasing made Mabyn snort with laughter, an honest sound, and Cyrus waved at her to take over. "Oh, Richard III quite deliberately created the Council to take on that role. It was a tremendous amount of work, too. Much of the structure of what we still do, how we act, is laid out in our original charter. The world has changed, of course, which does lead to things that charter did not anticipate."

Miss Martin nodded. "But I do not have much land. A scrap of garden and terrace, mostly mud."

Mabyn nodded. "Your father?" She kept her voice kind.

Miss Martin opened the scrapbook. "I saw this, when I was going through things after Aunt Poppy's death, and then I got - oh, yes, Measles went round the school. We were anxious about some of the little girls. And two teachers were out, quarantined, and it was a dreadful rush."

"You teach what age?"

"Oh, it depends on what they need, which year they give me. The three Rs, of course. A bit of sewing, even to the boys. We're only required to teach it to the girls. But it's good for a boy to know how to put a button back on their coat or shirt."

Mabyn nodded. "And you've been teaching..."

"Oh, seven years now?" She shrugged. "A year of teacher's college."

"And you enjoy it?" Mabyn was circling something,

Cyrus could see that easily enough. But he had no idea what.

"I am good at it." There was pride there. "My students do well on their exams. More than that, they stand a chance at making a steady wage. I am a practical woman, Mrs Teague."

There was a flicker there. "Mistress Teague, or Council Member Teague, if you don't mind." She hesitated. "The titles I've earned. I had an unpleasant marriage to my late husband."

Again, Cyrus knew she had said that deliberately. She must have. He had not had much chance to see her on her own, without her particular allies and close associates on the Council at hand. Watching her, though, she was playing this out not like a duel, but more like a dance, revealing a deliberate vulnerability to change the positioning in her favour.

He knew she was skilled and deft, but this was not what he had expected. She had a reputation for having clear, even sharp, boundaries that a sensible man did not cross. He did pride himself on being sensible.

It worked. Cyrus could not have done it that way, and he knew it. Miss Martin peered at her, over the glasses, and then nodded. "Plenty of those around here, and plenty of women not lucky enough to be a widow. There are reasons I've never married, besides the War."

Mabyn nodded, understandingly. Miss Martin turned back to the desk, and flipped back to a page. "There was a letter. Before I was born. It had been slipped into Auntie's bible, not that she was the sort to read it often." She unfurled it, and then read, her eyes skimming from line to line. Then, silently, she handed it over to Mabyn.

Mabyn read it, and then passed it over to Cyrus. It was

one page, both sides of the paper, in a careless sort of scrawl that undercut the message. The writer - the name Felicity was in big letters at the end - was pregnant. He skimmed through what she said about the father. A young man of good birth, from Suffolk, not far from Debenham. The woman didn't give a name, just called him Wells.

They, of course, were a bit more certain of who the father had to be, but magic alone was unlikely to be convincing. Especially to someone of Miss Martin's background. "Your mother is still alive, yes?"

"Oh, yes. I get a card or letter from her once or twice a year. I have no idea where she is, though. Monte Carlo. The Riviera. New York City, last time, I believe." Again, Miss Martin seemed not to find this particularly concerning.

"And she's never mentioned your father?"

"Oh, no. By the time I was old enough she might have talked about it, she was mostly out of the country. And when I did see her, it was with her husband and it seemed rude to bring it up. Certainly, she never has." She shrugged. "I assume it was someone who, what's the term. Stage-door Johnnies."

Mabyn glanced over at Cyrus, and he gave a small nod. It was clear Miss Martin wasn't likely to have further information. They could see about following up with the mother if they needed, later. It was possible to work a blood trace in either direction, after all. Mabyn nodded. "We have an additional tool at our disposal. The way we found you is that we were looking for descendants of a family, using locks of hair from two brothers. One was the father of the man who asked for our help. The other was his brother."

Miss Martin nodded slowly. "What sort of family?"

"The Baddocks, of Suffolk. You might or might not know Baddock Hall."

Miss Martin went pale. "Oh." She put her fingers to her mouth, all the large and small signs of startlement. "What does that mean?" She clearly knew the house.

Mabyn went on, her voice clear and steady. "The man who approached us is the current Lord Baddock, who is responsible for the land magics. He has been doing his best, and the land is failing. They've had drought and floods, crop failures. There are many signs that the land is doing poorly, they've not seen badgers or foxes, the bees are dying."

"Oh." This time it was more drawn out. "Why would you come to me?"

"Because, my dear." Mabyn was brisk now, not overly sweet. "You might be able to learn how to tend the land."

Miss Martin stood, abruptly, pacing to the end of the room, into the kitchen. Cyrus had no desire to interfere. Mabyn was, in fact, going about this much as he would. But it was better coming from her. Mabyn looked serene. She held up fingers, counting silently up to fifteen, before they heard the steps coming back.

"What would be involved?"

Mabyn cleared her throat. "Ideally, that you would come to Baddock Hall, and live there for a period of time. It may become clear quickly that the land will not take to you. But more likely it may take a while to find out. A year is the usual sort of period, a full cycle of the seasons. Ideally from planting through harvest to the next year's preparations for planting."

"I do not know too much about farming - Granda was a blacksmith. But aren't we already a bit late for that?"

"A bit on the late side, but that is a reason not to delay further than needed."

"I cannot just…" She gestured at the house. "Leave my job, shut up the house, I don't even know…"

"We can help you make arrangements with your employer. That would give you options later. An entirely convincing story about a family obligation, which is entirely true, in the main. Someone to check on the house, we could hire a neighbour, or find someone for you. You would not be a prisoner, of course. You could come back here and check in every week."

"But not sleep here."

"No. Being on the land, in the land, the water, the air. That's important. It's not just the rituals, the showy ones, that there are songs and tales and customs about. It's about the day-to-day rhythm, how the light falls, or the leaves."

Miss Martin closed her eyes, leaning against the wall. "And will anyone tell me what to do?"

Mabyn grinned, suddenly. "We can arrange for someone to be with you. Had expected to."

"Why would you know? Anyone?"

"Oh, I had my time as the wife of a Lord of the land. I loved the land. And it loved me back. My late husband, not so much. I would be glad to teach you what I know, or find someone else, if needed."

Mabyn glossed over it lightly, but Cyrus now wondered, sharply, what it had meant for her to leave that land, particularly given how she spoke of it now. It wasn't the sort of thing he could ask her, they did not have that kind of trust between them. He wondered, though, who she found that space with, all of a sudden.

"And you, sir?" Miss Martin looked over at him. "You have been very quiet."

Cyrus considered and then nodded at Mabyn. "I respect skill and experience." Then he smiled, broadly, the one people generally found reassuring. "My expertise is in ritual, especially in adapting a given ritual for a particular situation or person. In this case, perhaps teaching you about that, so you can adapt things yourself. I don't know, I don't know enough about the rituals of the land there. Yet."

"And you'd both give up your time, for a year, to do that?"

They had discussed the topic briefly. Cyrus shrugged. "There are details to be sorted out. We both have other obligations, as well. But we would not leave you alone with this. As my colleague has said, we care about the land, and that it thrives. It is in our interest to help that happen, and to help you, if that is the way to do so."

Miss Martin nodded once. "I suppose you had best call me Nora. Let me find some biscuits, and you can tell me more about what is expected." She spaced the words out. "I am not agreeing, yet, but I will hear you out."

That was as good a start that Cyrus could hope for, so he nodded. "Of course. We will do our best to answer your questions. And if you permit, we do also have some methods for proving the connection before we go too much further."

Nora nodded, standing and going back into the kitchen, gathering herself before the details began like an avalanche.

CHAPTER 7
BADDOCK HALL, FRIDAY, MARCH 26TH

Mabyn arrived at Baddock Hall at ten in the morning. She stepped through the portal smartly, letting the footman who had escorted her bring her trunks through on the luggage cart.

It felt odd to have packed up. Her flat in Trellech, in one of the old houses turned pied-à-terre, would be there whenever she wanted. The housekeeper would be there to see to things. On the other hand, it made no sense to go back and forth each day, especially given how one had to wait for the Trellech portals these days. And, to be frank, she wanted Baddock Hall checked out again thoroughly before they trusted to it too much.

Lord Baddock had been most gracious in extending his hospitality not only to Nora, but to Mabyn and to Cyrus. Which presented an entirely other set of challenges. Or rather, there were several sets of challenges, overlapping in different ways.

There was the problem of the Dowager Lady Baddock, clinging with her dignity to every scrap of prestige and power that she could still claim. Mabyn had gathered, from what Lord Baddock had not said, that they had quite a row. The sort of row that in other places would be a screaming argument that lasted through three days, eighteen broken plates, a flung silver tureen, five attempts at pouting, at least three bouts of tears, and the stomping of feet.

Lionel was polite enough that he hadn't commented on the fight. He did do his best to convey filial devotion, Mabyn had noticed, for all it was a matter of show and following the expected script for that sort of thing. He had mentioned his mother had taken to her bed for three days after, refusing all food and drink except for a bit of broth. Nothing a Healer could sort, apparently, and Mabyn wondered if it were all dramatics or if there were some serious illness under the surface.

She couldn't answer that, so she turned her thoughts back to the row itself. In this case, she suspected it had been done through sniffs, the tilt of the head, and expressions of disappointment in every register. She did remember the Dowager Lady Baddock, Eustacia Baddock, from her own time in that sort of obligatory social circles. And not favourably. She had been close with Lady Jenifry Alton, still the Lady of the land by Bury St Edmunds.

The Dowager Lady Baddock was a decade younger than Mabyn, but Lady Jenifry Alton was near enough her own age. The sort of age where she could have helped, once upon a time, and had chosen not to. That did not make Mabyn feel comfortable at all. She wondered what the relationship between the two women was like. Sometimes the Lords and Ladies of connecting lands got on well. That was preferable, certainly. It made things easier along the boundaries.

Lord Carillon, for example, had done wonders by coordinating with others in and near the New Forest in the past few years. It wasn't just the land magics directly, there were all sorts of other matters about seeing to fallen trees, or washed out bridges, where cooperation went a long way. The other side of the Baddock lands, up by Dunwich, was likely to be fairly professional about the whole thing. The headmistress there had been in place for nearly thirty years, plenty of time to settle into the role.

Colchester, to the south, tended to keep itself to itself. Lord Alder was in his fifties, and had held his title since his thirties. He was doing well enough, but he'd been kept busy recently with the implications of a rapidly growing town. The military had expanded their footprint there, for one thing. The Lucas estates had been sold off, more people were moving into the town itself. It had disrupted the patterns of the magic. Nothing that could not be tended, but it meant he did not have much time to spare for things outside his own boundaries.

The larger challenges, though, had to do with the household. She had not shared a home with anyone male since her son had left school, and she had ceded the landed estates to him and his uncle. Mabyn liked it that way, frankly. She preferred her things to stay where she put them. And she was still finding herself with a great deal of work related to the curriculum review.

Lord Baddock had promised sufficient space and privacy to suit. And, she kept telling herself, if it were awful, she could always go right back to Trellech and her own tidy flat. She was an honoured, needed guest here. Not a prisoner.

By this time she had crossed the drawbridge over the moat. The house was, in the main, in good repair. But it had a dullness to the brick she did not care for, and there seemed to be few fish in the moat and rather a lot of green algae. As she reached the door on the other side, a footman bowed her in, and Lord Baddock came out to greet her.

"Council Member. May I show you through the place, and up to your rooms where you're staying?" He then added, rather conspiratorially, "Mother is still having a snit. She will likely come up from the Dower House for supper, to disapprove in person."

Mabyn nodded. "Please, call me Mabyn. It seems ridiculous to stand on formality when you are being so kind as to host us."

Lord Baddock hesitated, as if not sure what to say.

"Also, I am certain it will annoy your mother. In the order of precedent, Cyrus and I rank you - and her, of course. She cannot argue if you are simply following our polite request. Or at least, if she argues, she shows herself up."

The first part of her reply made him smile, but then he nodded. "It may take her a while to sort through that. Are you certain you don't mind?"

Mabyn shook her head. "I can hold my own. And I'm sure Cyrus can as well." The nice thing about their role, honestly, was that it was not necessary for people to like them. It was necessary for people to do as they said, at least within the area of their obligation. Being freed from needing to be liked had done wonders for Mabyn's happiness.

"In that case, please call me Lionel. I gather Council Member Smythe-Clive - I will call him by his first name when he gives me permission - was expecting to arrive around three this afternoon." That was said with a little amusement. "And Miss Martin tomorrow afternoon, once you have had a chance to look at the grounds and property."

He used the title Nora had said she preferred, she noticed. He'd been quick enough to pick that up.

"Just so. And to get a proper measure of your mother, and exactly what variety of difficult she is likely to be. There are variations, of course."

Lionel hesitated, crossing the courtyard, which was paved in pale grey stone. "When you said you preferred evening to morning, I thought we would give you the north wing. The first floor has several rooms, and a bit more privacy than the other wing, where we've put Council-Member Smythe-Clive. A bedroom, of course, your own bathing room, and a comfortable sitting room. Please ask for whatever will make you feel at home. We have set the smaller bedroom up as a study. But if you need a different chair or desk or any such thing, I'm sure we have something suitable in the attics." He added, a bit bemused. "They are very extensive attics."

Mabyn nodded. "Quiet and privacy are likely the most important, though I would appreciate a word with your housekeeper at her convenience about my preferences."

"I, um. Yes." Lionel ducked his head. "Our staff mean well, and do very well, but they are not very polished. I do hope you won't take offence."

Mabyn shook her head. "I have no objection to honest country manners. Uses strong language, does she, in some cases?"

Lionel blushed at that. "Um. Yes."

"I managed a household about this size for two decades. With more entertaining, for some of it. She is your housekeeper, not mine. And the same with the staff. If she suits you, that is what matters at the moment. Well, I do have an interest in the food and the cleaning schedule, but I am not unreasonable. Part of what I want to ask is how to avoid being so."

"We have Mrs Gotts, that's the housekeeper. Mr Orton, our butler. Then Cook and several others in the kitchen, three housemaids, three footmen, quite a few gardeners, a gamekeeper and his apprentice. A small establishment, considering. If you ride, the stables are not very good, but we have a mount or two, or can see about borrowing one from someone nearby."

"That might, if nothing else, be an easier way to get out into the countryside. I know Cyrus rides well, I'll check with him on how to handle that."

"Of course." He swept along to the far side of the courtyard, then up a staircase. He walked with the kind of stiff-leggedness that suggested a lingering injury, though he went faster than she did and had to wait at the top. It was like coming out into a wooded glade, a mix of exposed wooden beams and pale grey stonework. The curtains and fittings, though, were in a deep green that she found very relaxing.

Lionel showed her through to the corner bedroom, letting her glance around, before he nodded. "Bathing room through the small hallway there. If you come this way..."

Along the same little corridor was a modestly sized room, set up with a broad wooden desk facing the window, and with an empty bookshelf waiting to be filled. The room beside it was a pleasant sitting room, in shades of green that complemented the hallway and bedroom, but were lighter, with curtains that let in muted light.

It was not at all what she expected, and she let it show on her face.

"Not my mother's work." Lionel smiled. "Much of this wing had - well, it needed a change. I rather enjoyed refitting things from the attics, it turns out. Refinishing the woodwork, doing something tangible with my hands."

She'd heard that sort of thing from a number of men who'd come back from the War. "And a good eye for colour. Is that you?"

"Guilty. I've always rather liked the Arts and Crafts folks, the natural prints. And I think they suit here, for a house this old, but not needing tapestries on every wall. We have some, like a respectable ancient abode, but they're down in the Great Hall and a few of the other public rooms. The library is on this floor. You can go down this hall, here, or around through that one, where the other Council Member will be. In this corner are the servants."

"And your mother in the dower house. When did she move down there?" They certainly had more than enough space for her to have laid claim to her own suite.

"1921. She was hoping I would marry." Lionel seemed to be about to say something else, but shifted the topic. "Shall I ask Mrs Gotts to come up when she has a moment?"

"That would be most kind. I'll see about unpacking my books and papers. Oh, and it's not a problem to ward the study and other personal things?"

"Not a problem at all, just we'd need to make the usual sort of arrangements for cleaning or laying a fire." He half-bowed once, and then left her. Mabyn was delighted not to be fussed over.

Twenty minutes later, the housekeeper presented herself. She was a woman about Mabyn's age, and she started out exceedingly deferential.

Mabyn had snorted, and said, "It's Lord Baddock who asked for our help, and we intend to give it. I am quite easy to deal with, especially if you don't mind my being slow to get moving in the morning. A fire going in the study by ten would grand, and a light breakfast on a tray. Tea, toast, jam."

"Scones, ma'am?"

"If you have them. Raspberry, blackberry, or orange marmalade. And a good strong black tea."

"That will be no trouble at all, ma'am. Mistress. Lady?" Mrs Gotts stumbled over the proper phrase.

Mabyn smiled, though she could feel how it came out a bit more tight and compressed than she wanted. "I was Lady Teague. Council Member, or Magistra, whichever you'd prefer. I know how much work goes into a big house, even when the family is small, so please tell me if I make a request that is difficult for you."

The other woman breathed a sigh of relief. "And the other gentleman, Magistra?"

"He knows how to live in a large country house. I don't believe he will be too demanding, but he will probably also have questions, and some protections for you to sort out how to handle."

"Thank you, Magistra. Will you be needing a maid to be helping you dress for supper?"

Mabyn considered. "If someone could help with my hair tonight, but not as a general rule. For the moment, best foot forward."

CHAPTER 8
LATER THAT AFTERNOON

Cyrus looked around the study that had been set aside for his use and nodded. The furnishings were not at all new, but that was part of the charm of an old house. Nothing was musty or full of mildew. Instead, everything smelled of beeswax and a little lemon, and a hint of something evergreen.

The view out the window from the desk was quite pleasing. Distracting, honestly, looking out as it did on a large meadow across the moat. He suspected deer normally enjoyed it, possibly other animals. They would have to explore that in more depth. His fingers itched with wanting to see how far the land magics had failed, how deep the rot had gotten.

In snatched moments, he'd had a chance to look at records, both for the lands near here, and further away. It came back to the question the Council had been chewing on for years. Were the problems in the land magics due to the War, or something damaged in those who were inheriting now. It was like sand slipping through their fingers, impossible to hold down and interrogate, and yet gritty and ever-present.

It also meant pushing himself further than ideal. His morning and early afternoon had been unusually demanding, and he was, much as he did not like admitting it, not as young as he used to be. Two of his old injuries ached, but he had not had time to spare for seeing his sister to get a little help.

Also, she would have told him the same thing she always did, that rest would do more than any salve or potion. Those could take the edge off for the moment, but it was a matter of distracting his brain and senses from the discomfort more than any real healing. At least at this point.

Since he could produce the entire argument in his own mind, he had not needed to hear it from her. He knew she was right. She knew he would continue to push himself until he could no longer do so. They both drew from a deep well of service and duty, just in different causes.

On the other hand, not seeing her spared her having to figure out how to lecture him about rest when she was just as bad at it. The War had left deep marks on both their work. The Temple of Healing was only now finally recovering from draining itself to the last drops during the War and the aftermath. His road, the Council's road, had been different, but no less demanding of magic and energy and focus, over and over again.

Cyrus made a slow circuit of the room. He had set his ritual trunk in the corner, fixing it to the floor with the appropriate magics. And of course it was locked to his blood alone. The books he could leave out were unpacked. One of the maids was seeing to his clothing in the bedroom.

The housekeeper had come by to check on his prefer-ences. It seemed Mabyn did not care to be up and about early, and Cyrus had been willing enough to arrange a tray. First thing in the morning for him, but he was fine with a meal that would keep well with a stasis charm the night before. He preferred an early breakfast, followed by a walk or ride. Tomorrow, he would investigate the stables, and hopefully manage a ride the day after, once Nora was here and settling in.

There was a brief knock at the sitting-room door, a quick one unlike the housekeeper's. "Who is it?"

"Mabyn."

Cyrus strode to the door, opening it. "Come in." He had expected this. She did not seem the sort of woman to dally about her duty. No one on the Council was inclined that way, but there were variations on how one might be direct.

She came in, glancing around. "Much the same as mine, though of course a different view. I'm down that hallway, further down. The library is just past you on this side, I believe."

"I suspect we want privacy for this. Your warding or mine?"

"Better yours, really. It is your space. I suspect your preferences and mine might not carry on smoothly togeth-er." It made him wonder for a moment about her more personal preferences. He'd always seen her among women, or in mixed groups, for one, never inclined to speak to a man on on one. She glanced at the furniture and then went and settled in one of the easy chairs.

She crossed her ankles and tucked them beneath the chair. Her long skirts fell into place in the sort of practised nonchalance that Cyrus knew must have been drilled into her in her younger days. He locked the door, and then pressed his palms against it, feeling his magic twine into the warding he had already set.

He would do more tonight, of course. He had set up only the first layer. But it would do more than well enough for the moment. He had checked for any magical devices intended to overhear or affect him, of course, as soon as he had been left alone in the suite of rooms. He had not expected anything, but taking thorough precautions never hurt when one had sufficient time.

When he took his place in the other chair, he leaned back, using his own relaxed posture to indicate his ease with the conversation. "You have been here longer. What have you learned so far?"

Mabyn chuckled. "You started before I did. Tell me about your day until you came here, then I will tell you what I've gleaned."

Cyrus shook his head, amused. "Fair enough. I had those consultations with one of the analysts at the Ministry, and with that nurse."

"The Gospatricks." Mabyn offered it conversationally. "Fine establishment." When Cyrus raised an eyebrow, she added, "My nephew was there for a time."

"Why was I the one talking to them, then?" He was curious, though it had been a pleasant conversation.

"Because I do not mix family and Council business." Mabyn was brisk now, making her limits clear. "And I wanted your perspective."

"Of course, they could not comment on a specific case without a thorough examination. Nor would they venture comments on an individual without that person's permission. But we did have a detailed discussion about the impacts of the War on the landsense, and whether it might recover."

"The answer?"

"What we suspected. If it has not by now, after some years on the land, making the proper attempts, it is not likely to change. There might be options for freeing his magic in other ways, if he wished to pursue them, but it would take some active and focused work. An extended period of residence, on the order of months."

"Which he shows no signs of wanting to do. He would, if there were a chance of the land magics, I think. It is clear he loves the house."

"The house, and not the land?"

Mabyn tilted her head to the side. "The house. Ah, yes. That would be a snag, wouldn't it?"

"That will need to be handled carefully." Cyrus pulled his pocket notebook out of his breast pocket and scribbled a few notes in his personal shorthand. "What do you think of the house?"

"Ancient. I wonder about the mortar, of course, and the early warding and protections, but that's scarcely one of my areas of expertise. I've picked up a bit, talking with Isembard and Thesan, but of course, Schola is quite a different sort of enchantment. And of course, this is a bare minimum of centuries later."

"I'm sure there is a muniments room about the place, as well as the library. We're both competent at research, at least, it will go faster that way."

"You seem very sure of that." Mabyn leaned back, watching him thoughtfully.

"I know my own skills, and I am confident of yours."

Mabyn looked him up and down. "There's a fine opening. What, precisely, do you think my skills are, then? We've certainly been around each other often enough. You survived and thrived in your challenge, so you have your own expertise." She waved a hand. "And yes, I'll tell you what I think yours are, after you tell me mine."

"That has a certain bloody-minded fairness to it." Cyrus shook his head. "Drink?"

"You're stalling." Mabyn grinned. "A splash of something, if you've already sorted a decanter. I believe in many things in moderation."

Cyrus pushed himself upright and went over to a shelf behind the desk. "I opened a bottle of madeira. I'm partial to a taste while thinking. Before dinner, after. Late night." She waved a hand, agreeably, and he poured out two small glasses, bringing them back and settling down.

"Tell, then." Her voice had a teasing note to it. He hadn't expected that from her, he'd expected that cordial, crystalline distance she offered nearly everyone but her own particular allies. He liked these flashes he saw, even while they baffled him.

"You challenged for your seat after I did. But then you - mmm. Faded into the woodwork. Quite deliberately, I'm certain, and for half a dozen reasons. You are not made to be an obvious sort of power in the world, are you? Not a kingmaker, but I haven't missed how you've been mentoring. Silvia Warren, most recently of course. And the whole matter of Schola's curriculum."

"That is not - directly at least - magical. As it were. It involves many meetings, and I am grateful they've assigned a secretary to keep all the minutes so none of us have to."

"Which makes my point. You are no Livia, to make your magic a show of force and fireworks. You prefer the long game, the more subtle game. The more stable one, to my way of thinking. You take your time picking your causes, which is why this matter caught my attention. You were thinking of being involved, that first day, weren't you? Even besides the fact it came in on your watch."

"For someone who says I faded into the woodwork, you have been quite observant." Mabyn shrugged. Cyrus watched the little movements of her shoulders. She was amused, he was sure of that, rather than offended. And perhaps affected by the novelty of the conversation. "And no. I learned a long time ago that I did not care for the influence you could get only by force and fury. I would rather drop my voice and compel someone to lean forward to listen to listen than shout in their face."

Cyrus smiled at that. "Often more effective."

"Also, I am quite short, and it is really exceedingly difficult to be effective if you have to shout up at someone. It is undignified and easy to ignore."

Cyrus tilted his head, considering. "You do not seem so short as all that. A sense of presence."

"I have never needed to duck my head in any place where everyone else says 'oh, mind the ceiling'. Oh, well. Once. It was a cave up in Scotland."

"Caves do tend to produce rudely shaped roofs." Cyrus could find himself relaxing. He had been fairly sure this project would not be awful. But he was beginning to think it might be enjoyable, in the main. "I know you have extensive skills in Materia work, and in multiple classes of materials. I know you're not bad at Alchemy, especially when it comes to Materia applications. And I know that you were Lady Teague, once upon a time, and that your son has a solid connection to the land."

Mabyn inclined her head at the last. "He does." She

seemed about to say something, then took a sip of her wine. "Oh, this is quite good. Not so sweet as many."

"I prefer my wine to not be boring." Cyrus gave her the space. He did not know the details of the end of her marriage, but he had every reason to believe it had been unusually unpleasant. "And we must work together for some time. I certainly do not wish to bore you."

Mabyn snorted. "Fair enough." She set her glass down and leaned forward. "You have, of course, an excellent reputation as a ritualist. A different line of the thing than Alexander, of course, but that just means the two of you are off talking to each other every chance you get. You're not one of the best of the best, when it comes to duelling, but you hold your own. I'd expect you could match, mmm." She considered. "Garin, but probably not Livia. Not Isembard, either, at least now he's back in excellent form."

"I'd not want to try with either of them. Though I know a few tricks Livia might find difficult to deal with if it ever came to that."

"That just shows sense. I think we'll need your sense of the ritual magics, the minor magics as well as the great ones, for this. But I admit, I don't know what yet. I keep trying to come up with plans, and they all slip away into dust whenever I try to pin them down."

Cyrus tilted his head. "That is a sign, for me, at least, that there is something I am missing. I suspect seeing her here on the land, seeing what she responds to, will end up guiding us."

Mabyn nodded. "That, and figuring out what is such a block for Lionel. And how things are with his mother."

"Besides a bit of a challenge?" Cyrus couldn't resist saying it lightly.

"I had forgotten to mention you have a reputation for

understatement." At that moment, they heard the gong ring. "Will you escort me down to supper?"

"Of course." Cyrus stood up and offered his arm. There was no reason not to observe the proper formalities.

CHAPTER 9
SUPPER

The dining room was the sort of aged and ornate space that Mabyn had frankly expected of the whole house. It had been redone three decades ago, perhaps, all in that style of Ancient Olde England that she found particularly tooth-grinding.

It was not the ancient roots she objected to, not at all. She had married into one of the ancient families, but her own was entirely respectable on that count. However, there was a stuffiness in this room, as if things had been frozen in a particularly unfortunate moment in time.

Given more exposure, she was sure she would pin down exactly when it was. Mabyn suspected it was not long after Lionel's birth. That was one of the times when magic got snarled up, especially the feel of a space. It was too long ago to be the death of Lionel's father. It was some other disappointment.

She and Cyrus had arrived in the parlour to find Lionel facing his mother on the sofa. "Dowager Lady Baddock." Cyrus had bowed over her hand, his manners in full formal mode, and making a particular point about her position in relationship to the current Lord. Mabyn approved. "May I present Council Member Teague?"

Mabyn had got a brief nod, while Cyrus had received a long steady gaze. The woman was a widow, had been for some time. Cyrus was a man of a reasonable age, with his own form of power, and a widower. Mabyn had found a certain sort of woman liked to consider the potential opportunities. She suspected he would be spending the coming weeks figuring out how to set her down without causing more offence than necessary.

"Welcome to Baddock Hall." Her voice had all the plummy arched vowels of the highest ranked families. "I am not pleased in your purpose here, but of course we will be civilised about it."

Every scrap of Mabyn's precognitive ability, faint though it often was, went on high alert. She couldn't glance at Cyrus, it would be far too obvious. They would have to talk about it later, in private. There was also no good answer to that.

Mabyn saved him from trying. "I'm most interested in hearing about your experiences living here. And your neighbours."

"Ah, well, Dunwich knows their place. We've always had Schola men in the family, of course." She eyed Cyrus. "We have a few minutes before supper is served."

"And you have Lady Alton, up by Bury St Edmunds?" Mabyn kept her voice crisp and clear.

"Oh, yes, she's a delight. Of course, quite busy with the little grandchildren now. She mentioned, when I said you were coming to stay, Council Member Smythe-Clive, that she had the pleasure of an ocean voyage with you, a number of years ago?"

Mabyn caught a hint of something, the briefest flash of

a complexity. When Cyrus spoke, however, his voice was relaxed and easy. "In 1901. I was travelling with my sister, before she took up a new post at the Temple of Healing. She met her husband on that voyage, so it was quite memorable. Hugh Pelagius." Some imp of the perverse made him add, "He's a Dunwich man, of course, and all the better for it, in his line of work."

Mabyn picked up just as smoothly. "One of these days, we really must talk more about the curriculum. I'm involved in conversations about the Schola curriculum, of course, Lady Baddock. But it has been really quite informative to talk to the other schools about how they teach certain topics."

"Surely Schola has the best methods." Lady Baddock's voice was arch. "It is the best of the Five Schools."

"Schola certainly has a number of virtues, but it is a new era, as we keep learning. That means we must look at how the current teaching helps students rise to the challenges of the modern age. And how it currently holds them back."

Lady Baddock frowned at that, but before she could say anything, there was a brief knock at the door, and the butler opened it. "Dinner is served, your lordship."

Lionel stood, and nodded. "Council Member Teague, may I escort you in to supper?"

They went along, leaving Cyrus to escort Lady Baddock. Lionel was a pleasant escort, not making any assumptions about her preferences, and also not pressing. Of course, he was on his best manners with them. He might not have the landsense anymore, but he had not lost his wits. The beginning of the meal went smoothly enough, the soup course, but as the main course was brought out, Lady Baddock spoke again.

"I still do not understand why dear Lionel is somehow not good enough. Or what brings you both here." There was a note to her tone, that she was pressing a point for her own reasons, but it was not clear what it was. At the moment.

Lionel was seated diagonally across from Cyrus, next to his mother, and his eyes flared. Mabyn was suddenly sure he hadn't explained to his mother what he had asked for. Cyrus finished chewing. As mildly as he could, he asked, "You have lived on the estate for some years. Surely you have seen some matters of concern."

"I have lived on the estate long enough to see good years and bad years. The good years come around again, of course. It is a delightful place, all the history."

"You come from the Wallaces. Not a landed family - of course, the Smythe-Clives aren't either. But I have learned a bit in my time on the Council."

Mabyn pressed her napkin to her mouth, muffling what might have been a chuckle.

"That does not mean you have the right to judge Lionel's fitness, surely?" Lady Baddock's voice got a sharp note in it, though she was not, at least yet, being outright rude.

Cyrus tilted his head, keeping his voice light. "The well-being of the land, in the most basic sense, is what the Council was first made for. Lionel has welcomed us, and of course we appreciate that a great deal. Our goal - may I speak for you, Mabyn?"

Mabyn nodded. "In this matter, yes." She was pleased he'd asked, but honestly, this conversation would go better with only one of them sparring. It would give them more options later.

"Our goal is the best interest of the land, now, and going forward. That might be finding something that will help Lionel make a proper connection, so that the ancient rites serve their purpose. It may be that Miss Martin has a gift for it that should be allowed to flourish. It may involve some rituals, to resolve issues, or some approach we have not considered yet."

"And you agree with this, Mistress Teague?"

"Council Member Teague, or Magistra Teague, please, Lady Baddock." Mabyn smiled, but she was sure it was coming across a tad more aggressively than she'd like. Lady Baddock reminded her uncomfortably of her late mother-in-law, and she would have to watch herself. It would do no one any good if she lost her temper.

Aubrey, her late husband, had a great deal to answer for, but she refused to let him poison her life now. He'd done more than enough of that before he'd died. She was still pulling thorns out of scabbed-over wounds three decades later. She was older than Lady Baddock, magic came to her hand when she called. And she was certainly much happier, by all the evidence she has seen so far.

On the other hand, that was no reason to permit herself rudeness. They had every right to be here. More than a right, they had an obligation. The sooner Lady Baddock got used to that, the easier it would be for everyone.

"So formal." Lady Baddock tsked.

"So long as we are on formal terms, yes." She reached for her wine glass, considering for a moment as she took a sip. Cyrus, for a wonder, was giving her her head, apparently, he showed no signs of stepping in. "You are not from a landed family, and neither was I. But like you, I married into one."

"The Teagues are a respected family, of course. I knew Aubrey's brother rather well, at one time." Lady Baddock lifted her chin, peering down her nose. "Your point?"

"I earned my place as a Council Member the same way we all do, through a challenge that draws on skill, knowledge, and a certain commitment to fearlessness." She caught Cyrus's quick grin. "I have been called a number of things in my life, starting with Nanny's nicknames for me. But I am most fond, I think, of the titles I've earned." She spread her hands. "I am terribly plebian that way, but there we are."

Lady Baddock sniffed. "And you, Council Member Smythe-Clive?"

"Oh, the same." Cyrus had an easy drawl in his voice. Mabyn could not figure out whether he were truly at ease, the way he sounded, or whether he were simply superb at hiding his emotions. She suspected both, honestly. "All the old titles, and a fair few of the current ones, they're rooted in what one has demonstrated one can do. Or at the very least, one's ability to hold what one has claimed."

Lady Baddock peered at him, as if he had unsettled her. Cyrus went on, just as smoothly. "One of the reasons Mabyn is here is that she has experience in marrying in, combined with a mastery of Materia."

"I married in." Lady Baddock had a hint of pride in her voice. Mabyn felt that it was not the marrying in that was praiseworthy, it was what you did with it.

"You did." Cyrus was polite about that. "But I am sure you have already tried whatever skills you have to help your son tend to the estate." There was a quick jerk of Lady Baddock's face. Mabyn would have missed it if she'd blinked. Cyrus had, actually, avoided any implication of blame, that Lady Baddock had not kept up the proper standards, and yet, still, that twitch.

Cyrus sailed onward. "Mabyn, however, has earned her mastery in Materia, in several forms. And of course, has an extensive background in the related magical theory and practice. We will be relying on each other's skills."

Lionel cut in at that point. "I was, I admit, a tad surprised that both of you were willing to spend your time here."

Mabyn smiled at him. "As we explained when we were making the arrangements, we will both come and go as needed. I still am consulting with the professors at Schola, and with others at the Five Schools. We have Council obligations at various points, meetings and such. But as Cyrus said, we have different skills and talents, and we felt that both sets might well be relevant. And, as Cyrus has also said, this is our work, in the deepest and broadest sense of the word."

Lady Baddock sniffed again, but Lionel nodded. "It is an honour to put you both up, and I very much appreciate the time." Mabyn appreciated his efforts in smoothing things over, even if they'd do no good. "I do hope your rooms were comfortable? You must let me know immediately if there's any problem."

Mabyn smiled at him. "Very pleasant, and quite comfortable. You've put a good bit of attention into blocking the draughts and tending to leaks, I can see. Having lived in a house of the same vintage, and visited quite a few others, I always appreciate that particular detail. There is no need to suffer for history, I always think."

Lionel lit up, for a moment, before his mother glared at him and he subsided, like a hare freezing when it saw a fox waiting to pounce. He swallowed, then said, muted, "I am very glad it meets your standards."

Cyrus regarded him, the sort of long steady glance that made Mabyn glad he didn't turn that sort of thing on her. It was not menacing, but he was taking in every detail, filing them away. It was necessary, of course. There was something deeply wrong here, in the relationship between Lionel and his mother. Or at least in his mother's reactions. One might almost think she wanted him to fail.

When Cyrus spoke, he was entirely pleasant. "On that note, you needn't feel you must entertain us. We have brought books, as well as our various ongoing work, and you've already encouraged us to make free use of your library. We do not need to get in your way. And my compliments to your staff, for making settling in so smooth."

That note of praise made Lady Baddock raise her hackles again, but Lionel smiled, shyly. Then he launched into some comments about other parts of the house, offering a brief tour of the downstairs before they went their separate ways for the night.

CHAPTER 10

LATER THAT EVENING, MABYN'S SITTING ROOM

"I have had worse starts." Cyrus grunted as he settled in the chair. After the tour of the public rooms downstairs, they had silently agreed further discussion was called for. Mabyn had shown a preference for her own rooms, and he had been curious to see what they were like. She nodded, then hesitated, her hand on the back of the other chair, before sitting down. "Do you mind if I let my hair down? Literally, in this case."

"No, do go ahead. Can I pour you a drink?"

"Please. There's brandy in the decanter, the glasses are next to it. And help yourself. I'll just be a minute or two."

Cyrus desperately wanted to explore the room, but he had more sense than to do that. For one thing, it was rude, and being rude would do no good. For another, he was quite sure Mabyn had her own protections. He couldn't feel them, not like his own warding, but that just made him both more curious and more cautious. He went to the decanter on the sideboard she'd indicated, pouring two glasses, and then brought them back to the chairs before circling back over to the window.

It was dark now, though the moon was near enough full that he could at least see shapes outside. An ancient oak towered over the landscape. He thought, for a moment, he could see something under the tree, but when he looked more closely, it seemed to just be a shadow. That was a pity, it might have indicated the land was in better shape than they feared. He'd know more when he could get out onto the property in the coming days, but there was indeed something wrong here.

He stared out the window longer than he intended, and only turned around when he heard footsteps. Mabyn had indeed let her hair down; it was now in a long braid down her back. She normally wore a braided crown around her head, but tonight it had been up in tightly pinned puffs. She'd also changed into what his sister referred to as artistic dress, comfortable and uncorseted. It allowed her to sweep along in a flow of skirts, and settle down, claiming the chair.

"Well. Supper posed a whole new set of challenges. I saw to the warding as I came back in, add what you like."

Cyrus reached out, brushing his fingers against the window sill, where he could feel a faint tingle of the magic settling into place. He considered, then cupped his hands, chanting a well-worn ritual until a white rose appeared in his hands. He flung it upwards, as it took flight, before it settled in the centre of the ceiling. "Sub rosa. It'll wear off..." He glanced at his pocket watch. "About two in the morning."

"Well, I certainly don't expect to be up that late tonight. That will do well." She glanced upwards. "Not my usual method, but I understand that's one of your preferred modes?"

Cyrus nodded as he came back, settling in the chair

opposite her. He'd not worked closely with someone else on the Council in quite a while, and it was a pleasure to be able to share references so quickly and easily. "Now is the time, if you have questions for me."

"And you are not demanding answers from me?" She arched an eyebrow.

"I am exceedingly clear that demanding anything from you would end badly. On my part, at least. I try to be more sensible than that."

She raised her glass, and took a sip. "Not the usual thing I hear." She cut off, suddenly, and Cyrus was sure she had been tempted to say more.

"Men, you mean? Men on the Council, in particular?"

Mabyn's lips quirked. "Insulting men who might be your particular associates seemed a poor opening move. I am not much of a chess player, but even I can see that coming."

"You have struck me, in what I have seen so far, as more interested in collaboration than competition, certainly. Which comes with its own assumptions."

Mabyn nodded. "That's the woman's lot, isn't it? To mend the breach in the world with her body or her soul or her future."

"Too often all three." Cyrus agreed, watching her closely now. He'd seen the hints at supper, of threads in her past she did not want to talk about.

She glanced up, taking him in. "Your sister trained you well, didn't she?"

Cyrus inclined her head. "She believes I am up to her standards." He considers. "You'd not have known her at school. We barely overlapped."

Mabyn snorted. "There are whole worlds since our

schooling. Let's just say I'm quite sure you don't know the half of who I know."

"Oh, I have no doubt of it." He flicked his hand. "Materia, Alchemy. Agreeably competent by my standards in ritual work, though in rather different styles from what little I've seen outside the Council forms. Where I have an interest in ritual, and near as much of one in logistics. Hugh has had something to do with that."

She looked at him, thoughtfully. "You did something with logistics in the War, didn't you?"

"I had a place I could get free from when needed for Council business. They couldn't send me overseas, or at least not for long."

"And there are still a fair number of our rituals that rely on the fertile pairing, at least in symbol. I'm entirely unwilling these days." Cyrus thought that was an interesting way to put it. He'd never much cared for them, but he'd been told he was not able to bow out. At least some of those forms didn't care much what one thought or felt while doing them, just that they were done properly. That unpleasant thought made him fall into silence until she cleared her throat. "You were saying?"

Cyrus looked up, then took a sip from his own glass. "I was thinking, beg pardon." He didn't much want to discuss that with her, not tonight. Nor the War, either.

"Are we going to keep circling around essential matters, feeling each other out? Or are we going to make some progress forward?"

Cyrus snorted. "Begin as we mean to go on, as it were? And we haven't had much time to sort that out." He hesitated. "If being here at the house is not the thing, please tell me. I gather there's some complex history."

Mabyn lifted her drink, in a silent toast, then took a sip of it. "And you. Lady Jenifry Alton's a widow again."

"Wait, she is?" Cyrus had missed that. "And Lady Baddock."

"See? You may need to scurry off to some piece of urgent Council business. Much easier if I cover for you, mind." Mabyn shrugged. "A year ago. You were travelling, I believe. Missed the funeral, and all the announcements, certainly." Lady Jenifry's late husband had been ill for some time, so not seeing him around wouldn't have been informative. And she'd been the one who held the land magics, so there hadn't needed to be a formal declaration at Winter Solstice.

Cyrus let out a sigh. "I'd appreciate that. Please. I know how to do the dance and disengage, but a certain sort of woman will keep trying."

She looked him up and down. "You are certainly more promising than a number of people. Not a Lord of the land, but that's not necessarily a problem. Council does nicely, for them as don't understand it, just the show of power. You have a grown daughter, who if she is not married yet, is certainly settled into adult life. No little ones to have to pretend to adore. And likely you'd not pressure a woman your own age to attempt to have more."

Cyrus couldn't quite repress the shiver. Mabyn had laid it out, almost surgically, but it was the last part that got him. People so rarely spelled it out. He took a long sip of his own brandy, then said. "My wife, Tanith, died having Gemma. I barely made it through my sister's pregnancies with my wits intact. She had the best care the Temple of Healing could provide, and an excellent and extremely reassuring midwife."

"You're very close to your sister, yes?" Mabyn had lowered her glass, and was watching him carefully.

"We don't always get to see each other often. Busy with our own work and our own lives and duties. But yes. A meal every couple of weeks, a few days together here or there. It's been easier since things settled down after the War, her schedule's more regular again. My nephew did well at Schola, he's taking after her and apprenticing in a different line of healing. My niece is about to finish up at Dunwich. She has quite a knack for locational magics, and I'm fairly sure she'll be doing something for her father's side of the family promptly."

"Hugh Pelagius. Very pleasant, the times I've seen him at parties. Not at all grabby." She said it amiably.

Cyrus considered. "Do you have that problem as a rule? People making assumptions about what you must want? As, um, as Lady Alton and Lady Baddock may wish for me?"

"Not so much since the rumours about my having a hand in my husband's death got well and truly started." She said it so dryly that Cyrus almost didn't register the content for a moment.

When it hit, he blinked and set his glass down. "Any particular reason, beyond the usual gossip people get up to? You've heard what they say about Lady Alton. That's not why I have trouble with her, for the record."

"My husband was an utter bastard in every sense except the legal one. I have no desire to allow anyone that kind of power over me ever again." Her voice took on a fierce and sharp note, though not one that clarified whether or not she had taken some permanent action to stop him. "Your sister speaks well of you. Not in the obvious ways, when someone tries to convince you. In the small ways, the stories she's told over the years."

Cyrus leaned back, considering all of this. He had heard a few rumours about Mabyn's late husband, and he knew all too well how successful fury and raw need could propel someone through the Council trials. "I have no desire for power over you. Or most anyone, frankly. For the record." He flipped his hand palm up. "You must be a member of Many Are The Waters. Like Rhoe."

Mabyn nodded. "Sharing the mysteries with someone does form a bond. Stronger with some than others, but she has a flow to her. More since she took up with the healing baths. Or just before. That trip you took, the one Lady Alton was on."

Cyrus nodded. "It was memorable. As I said earlier, her meeting Hugh." He waved a hand, thinking with affection about that part of it. "I'm glad she found happiness, even if my road has been very different." Then he considered, choosing his words carefully. "And of course, your situation was clearly rather worse."

Mabyn snorted, but didn't comment. "So. How do we go forward tomorrow. Nora should be arriving around eleven, and that will take her through luncheon. A walk through part of the estate after that? Tea?"

"A walk. I would prefer to give her a few options and see what she is drawn to. It may well be informative. Do you ride?"

"Not by preference, though I can stay on a well-behaved mount. Were you thinking of going out in the morning?"

Cyrus nodded. "An hour or two, enough to get a sense of the spaces nearest the house, a circuit. I'd like to know where things are worse. And better, if there's a better."'

"In that case, I will spend the morning making sure her rooms are welcoming, and talk to whichever housemaid will be seeing to things. I suspect the idea of staff will be rather a challenge to her."

Cyrus blinked. "I'd not thought about that, but of

course, yes. I suspect she and her aunt might have had a cleaning woman or sent the laundry out, but that would be about the limit." He tapped his fingers on the glass as he picked it up again. "I'd also like to find out more about her grandparents, in Debenham. It's about ten miles, that's not a bad ride. Or a carriage drive, if you'd want to come. Or, I suppose, automobile." He was dubious about those, but they were efficient.

"See what our options are for a carriage, if you're able to drive one." Mabyn was gloriously decisive, at least. Cyrus appreciated that already, and expected he was going to appreciate it more and more as things went on. "And Lionel mentioned his mother would be dining on her own tomorrow, so that at least gives us a bit to sort out things with Nora."

"And for the rest, we have to see how she reacts to the place, and how the place reacts to her. So." Cyrus nodded, then caught himself yawning. "I should find my own bed, I think. Not as young as I was."

Mabyn snorted, and stood, moving to the door to do something to the warding. "See you - oh, ten-thirty? Or were you going to go meet her to take the portal?"

"Half-ten it is. She said she'd prefer to come on her own."

CHAPTER II
SATURDAY, MARCH 27TH

Nora had arrived promptly, with a trunk. Mabyn had already had a word with Mrs Gotts about having a seamstress come out. Nora wouldn't need anything terribly fancy yet, but she'd want some outfits for being out on the land; sturdy shoes and tweeds and split skirts. Very practical, tweeds. Possibly riding gear, if she was willing to give learning equestrian skills a try. At least no one was going to make her learn how to ride sidesaddle, as Mabyn had had to do. The modern age had several recommendations, really.

They had let Nora have an hour to settle in before luncheon. By the time Mabyn retrieved her, she was looking more than a little overwhelmed. Mabyn considered her, now, looking at her as Albion would see her, not England. She had long hair, that was excellent for integrating into magical society, currently tucked up in a tight bun at the back of her head.

She wore a plain blouse of pale blue and a darker blue skirt, both unremarkable in cut but without the charmed embroidery or jewellery common to a woman with magic.

She was tidy, in the sort of clothing that was defensive and unremarkable. One might think her a minor craftswoman, perhaps an apothecary, not risking her better clothing to stains or spills.

That showed good sense, honestly. It was not wrong clothing for the place. Nora clearly had some native instincts about that. And, Mabyn supposed, it was unlikely her wardrobe ran to either flapper frocks or the loose trousers becoming fashionable in some circles.

Mabyn had suggested a simple lunch, the sort of soup and sandwiches that suited a somewhat chilly day, and would be reasonably familiar to someone of Nora's background.

At the end of the meal, Cyrus made a couple of gestures. They really were going to have to agree on which form of signalling they were going to use. She was quite certain she almost misinterpreted one. Then he stretched. "It's not actually raining, so I think I might continue my circuit of the grounds, but there's no reason you ladies should go out in it. I haven't discovered where all the boggy bits are yet." His tone implied he kept finding them, which she'd have to ask about.

Mabyn nodded. "Shall we go up to your rooms, Nora, and chat for a little? Lionel thought he could give you a proper tour of the house before tea."

Nora spread her hands and gathered herself. Mabyn thought that being a teacher had done excellent things for her. She had a sense of presence, of understanding the limits of her influence that many people never gained. "You have a plan for me, I'm sure. Better to hear the syllabus first thing."

"Not very much like school learning, but yes, we have a

plan and some pieces to talk to you about. Your rooms, or would you prefer mine?"

There was a minute hesitation. "Yours, please."

Five minutes later, Mabyn was settling in the chair she had claimed as her own, after promising the staff they would ring for tea if they needed refreshment. Nora had not yet sat down. She was looking out the window much as Cyrus had last night. "That's a grand oak."

Interesting that that was the first thing she was drawn to. Mabyn had noted her solidness in their previous conversations. She took up space on the earth, that might be a way to put it, for all Nora wasn't physically a large woman in any dimension. Someone with a taste in shallow metaphor might have likened her to a bird, which was entirely incorrect.

Mabyn glanced up. "You spent summers near to here, yes? You must know something about the local flora and fauna."

"Oaks. Yews. The deer. My grandparents had a den of foxes, down at the end of the garden. And there were badgers, down along the hedgerow, nearer the fields. They were out on the edge of the village. Never anything terribly dangerous."

"There are old tales about how the hedgerow is the liminal space. Where you move from the outer world, the wildwood, to the settled lands."

Nora turned, looking over her shoulder. "And then I would go back to a city, and what's a city?"

Oh, this was going to be fun. Mabyn hadn't been sure, not until just this moment, but Nora had a fine mind, if perhaps decidedly untutored in a number of areas. But she was quick to learn, willing to comment, aware of the limits of her knowledge and current ignorance. "A city is alive. Not just with animals and plants, though those too, but the way people are in a city, they form patterns around each other. The rhythms of it. Bells or whistles might be different from birdsong, but they have their own cycles."

Nora turned fully around now. "You don't live in a city."

"Trellech's not like Manchester, but it's a city. Healers and the Ministry and the Guard. Primary schools, and people apprenticing. Quite a lot of people apprenticing, we had a ruckus last week, some sort of prank from the Fullers' Guild. They were streaking down the main street wearing next to nothing and a lot of historically inaccurate blue paint."

Nora blinked several times. "Good grief, are you people so behind that you don't have mills? Fulling machines? Why on earth do you have fullers? Never mind, why are they blue? I'm not sure I want to know." She shook her head. "Also, Wales. Not Scotland."

Mabyn laughed outright. "Magical cloth needs to be made by hand in many cases. Spinning, weaving, fulling, cutting, sewing. Not that we do that for everything, of course, it's an absurd amount of labour." It was.

She went on. "But, oh, I'm sure whatever Cyrus is wearing out in the woods right now, is a proper enchanted cloak. Something full of weaving to keep the rain from soaking it, to keep it from staining, runes or sigils or alchemical symbols or something of the kind that mean he'll be warm and comfortable inside it. His boots will be the same, I'm sure. Perhaps not his clothing, not for this, but I'm sure he has a suit for that, and breeches, and so on."

Nora shook her head. "Just when I begin to think I have the measure of it." She took several steps forward, almost instinctively, before making a decision and coming to claim the chair opposite Mabyn's. "You can't imagine I can learn all this."

"First, many things can be learned. And you needn't master them all now. Or even this year. If you finish your time here with a sense of the scope, what magic can do and can't do, that will be a grand start. And have a list of experts to consult when you need something more detailed. And, before you comment, we have experts to introduce you to. Besides being two ourselves."

"It's clear you have some..." Nora gestured. "Some influence. The way the staff treat you."

"We explained about the Council, and the staff here, they know enough of what that means. Though most people don't have a good sense of the full scope of the implications, they know we did something terrifying and must be competent. And Lionel - Lord Baddock - has been very clear he approves of our being here."

"You call him Lionel." Nora chewed on her lip. "Do I call him Lionel? And his mother? And I don't even know. What do I call, there was a housemaid earlier." There she was. Mabyn had been sure that at some point this afternoon, all of this would rush in. All the things Nora didn't know, or perhaps knew only from the sort of novels that had you believing that England had thirty-odd eligible and unmarried dukes roaming the countryside at any given time. Though Nora did not seem inclined to the more inaccurate of that kind of thing.

"It is the same as in your school. Names are about power. Magically, of course, but also socially. The first name shows intimacy, a title indicates distance, either respectful or disdainful. There's nothing quite like a woman saying 'Oh, Lady So-and-So' in a particular tone of voice to make the disdain clear."

"Or a man?" The example made Nora smile and relax a little. That was excellent.

"Men do it differently. I'm fairly sure. That is part of why Cyrus is here as well. There are things he can explain better than I can, and vice versa, and not all of them are about our particular specialities in magic."

"The names, please." Nora seemed about to ask something else. "So I am Nora to you, and you are Mabyn and Cyrus to me, even if that feels most peculiar. But as you said, begin as we mean to go on."

"Also, saying Council Member Smythe-Clive every other sentence is terribly awkward." Mabyn was about to go on when Nora hesitated. "Yes?"

"Council Member seems rather unwieldy. To the uninformed ear. Especially if one says it all the time."

"Ah, that is a grand historical argument. The original model was the Council of the North, if you know your history, and all of them had other titles. Around a century later, in the late 16th century, there was quite a fuss about people using Councillor."

"Why would people fuss about that?" Nora was relaxing a little, puzzling through it.

"We have a particular role, and within that role - the land magics - our word is absolute. We bow to no king, nor queen. It is an imperfect system, and we are decidedly imperfect people, but when it comes to the land magics of Albion, we rule. We do not counsel, we do not implore, we do not encourage. There's even a Latin motto, 'Non admonemus, agimus.' We do not advise, we act."

"And that means..." Nora worked through it. "You're choosing to go gently here. You could insist on things, and you aren't. Not yet. Even with me."

"Well, this will go rather better if we have your willing

cooperation. We can't force people to take on a commitment to the Land. We can, however, act if they don't, or won't."

Nora nodded, her fingers worrying at a fold of her skirt. "Oh." She swallowed. "I beg pardon, you were going to say something else when I asked?"

Mabyn thought back. "Oh, about the formality? Cyrus does not stand a great deal on formality, he has the breeding where he doesn't need to."

Nora tilted her head. "And you have had to?"

Oh, that was sharp of her. Mabyn grinned, a bit toothily. "I have no worries about your ability to learn - or observe - for the record." She tapped the arm of her chair, letting Nora see her little tells of thinking deliberately. "I married a Lord of the land and tried to do my best by the land and our son."

She had said it that way deliberately, and she both hoped and feared Nora would pick up on it. "But not him? Was it like that from the beginning?" When Mabyn hesitated, Nora went on, her voice now gentler but precise. "I was a schoolteacher in a factory town, with people in the middle of grinding poverty. I could hear the arguments, see what people were like the next morning. The flinches, the bruises they couldn't hide. All the saints know I heard stories from my students, including all the things they didn't realise they were telling me."

Mabyn nodded. "It was not a good marriage. I don't talk about it."

"I understand. So magic doesn't spare someone that."

That was an interesting way to put it. Mabyn considered and chose her next words carefully. "Magic doesn't make a hard man kind, or an angry one calm. But I could protect myself, in ways other women can't. Most of the time. And I had a sense of my own worth. If I could hold on to it. That's the worst thing they take, in some ways, I've always thought."

Nora nodded. "People are going to expect me to marry, aren't they?" She gestured. "If this works. Which I'm none too sure it will."

"That is what we are here to find out. If it doesn't, you will go back to your job, or we will find you a job you'd prefer. We have some influence, even in the places where no one would admit to magic. As to marriage, you would be in a very different position. People would court you. You could have your pick. If you are the one who can hold the land, if the land rituals work for you, then you'll have property. Both physical - this estate, among them. But also money."

Nora blinked and then froze. "Wait. Lord Baddock."

"You know about entails, yes?" Nora nodded. "There are properties entailed with the title. If that is you, he will have a place to live, money to live on. You would not be turning him out onto the streets. And honestly, it would be up to you, even with this house. If you decide you like having a cousin around, he could live here, or in the dower house, or somewhere else on the property. That would be your choice."

"I am not at all sure it's proper for one person to have that much power. Property." Nora looked up. "That makes me unfit, surely."

"Honestly, I think it makes you exceedingly fit for the work. The best of the Lords and Ladies of the land think of the land and the people on it, long before they think of themselves. Lionel has enough of it that he came to us, rather than let things get worse. He knew what he was choosing."

"And his mother? What do I call his mother?"

"You call Lord Baddock - well, you are cousins. There is no reason you might not be Lionel and Nora, if you wish. He does not seem to stand on the title. As to his mother, I suppose." Mabyn took her time thinking about how to put this.

"I gather his mother is likely to be difficult. What do I call someone who does not wish me here, who is of a higher social station? Dowager Lady Baddock?"

"Oh, just Lady Baddock. If you take the title, then others might need to disambiguate. I admit, I do not expect any of us will be calling her Eustacia any time soon."

Nora nodded. "All right." She hesitated. "Before we dive into the estate, can you tell me how things work in general. The framework of it? I do better working from the broad to the specific, as a rule."

Mabyn nodded. "Let me make some tea, and do that."

CHAPTER 12
SUNDAY, LATE MORNING

Cyrus settled on the folding stool they'd brought out. It was not actually raining at the moment, which was a blessing. It had this morning, it likely would again after lunch. For now, though, they were under the branches of the great oak tree. Nora perched on the stool opposite him, and she looked very dubious. A light mist had settled in, making the house across the lawn a gesture at the shape of a building.

Lionel had lent her a cloak, at least, which would keep her comfortably dry. Mabyn was seeing about a seamstress and sorting out a list of likely clothing and the order Nora would need it in. Cyrus could probably have managed that, at least with some consultation with Mrs Gotts, but it was decidedly not his forte.

"What is the lesson here?" She looked as if she would be much happier if she had a notebook and pencil in hand. Cyrus made a mental note to make sure she had both provided.

"To learn about the land. Or rather, to begin with this tree."

"Why this tree and not some other?" Nora looked up. "It is a grand old tree, but there are others." She gestured across at the small cluster of trees near the portal. Then she looked back to the oak, as if drawn to it.

"This is a grand old tree, two hundred years old. But it is still living memory, this tree. The trees by the portal were planted to support the portal, and those are, those are serving a different purpose."

"I do not understand the portal. Honestly, a train seems vastly more logical, or a road." Nora glanced over in that direction, twisting around on the stool as if she could make the trees make sense by sheer force of will. Perhaps she would.

Cyrus laughed. "We take trains, too. Or roads, or horses, or even automobiles these days. Though I am rather baffled by automobiles, honestly. Not my area of expertise, but I'm willing enough to ride in them. Rather like an ocean liner."

Nora tilted her head. "You are a strange man. Are they all like you and Lionel?"

"Mabyn is just as strange." Cyrus pointed out.

"Mabyn is strange like Aunt Poppy was strange. I am entirely used to that. Or rather, differently strange, but I at least see how she might fit into things."

Cyrus considered this. "Lionel is currently in a peculiar position, being willing to cede a thing he was raised to tend, but not knowing if you can take it over properly. Also, I do not know the story of his War, but I suspect it was particularly unkind in places."

Nora glanced back at the house, as if expecting Lionel to appear out of the mist. "How can you tell?" Cyrus liked how she didn't argue with him, or even with the premise. She just wanted to understand what he was seeing, so she could decide for herself.

"We've only had a day or so more with him than you have, but there are the various signs. He keeps an eye on where everyone is. He wants his back to a wall, if he can. Always wondering what might happen next." Nora was about to say something and Cyrus raised his hand. "You have not yet seen him with his mother, and certainly some of it comes from that. But also the War."

"What did you do, then? Do they send members of the Council to fight?"

"Some. The colleague Mabyn has been working with closely, he did. Several others you might meet sometime this summer. I worked in logistics. The Council needed to have my skills handy on short notice for a number of ritual workings. Quite manageable from an office in London, to take a portal to where I needed to be for the evening or the dawn, rather more difficult from overseas." He waved a hand. "And I'm old enough not to have been conscripted. I turned fifty at the end of 1917, just before they raised the limit."

Nora frowned, thinking about that. She stood up, abruptly, going to touch the broad bark of the tree, pressing her hand to it, then her other, as if she were listening to it. It was an excellent instinct. She stood there for a good two minutes before she turned around and came back. "What gives you the right to judge someone else's War?"

There were two ways he could answer that. Far more than two, but they boiled down to answering one of two questions. Why him, and what made him qualified.

"You don't trust power, do you?" Or, of course, he could use all his applied knowledge and go in a new direction.

Nora blinked, but she settled onto the stool and folded her hands in her lap, under the cloak, before she peered at him. "No sensible person does."

It made him snort. "The power is there." He gestured at the tree. "The tree does not care what we think of it. The land does not. The river does not care. The sun certainly does not care, or the stars in their places. And yet, all of them have power."

"That's different, and you know it." Excellent, he'd pushed her about as far as he wanted to. This would work so much better, the more actively she engaged with it, with him and Mabyn.

"I am not perfect. Mabyn is not." He flicked his fingers. "I don't want power over people. I never have. But I want to understand that dance, how we can align ourselves with it. That is the heart of the ritual magics, whichever of their infinite forms they take. Bringing us into relationship with the tree, the portal, the sun, the stars, the moon, the land."

Nora peered back at the tree again, as if she expected it to give her some answer. "My grandparents had dozens of customs. Around Christmastide, making the pudding, and Granda always took part in the mumming plays. Aunt Poppy swore that was some of where my mother got it from, performing." She waved a hand. "Setting things out for the farisees."

That was an unfamiliar word for Cyrus. "For who?"

"The farisees. Local word for fairies. Small, with sandy hair and blue eyes." She gestured with her hands. "Sounds quite odd to the ear for anyone who knows their Bible." She then peered at him. "Do you?"

Cyrus snorted. "Fair bit of ritual magic in the Roman Church, one way and another, and a fair bit more in various customs. There's a whole set of places that recite psalms for protection or healing or what have you. I'm not a Christian, though. Not much of anything. Honestly, I leave religious commitments to my sister."

If her comment had made him blink, his did the same. "Is that common among you folk?"

"There's a wide mix." He then added, by way of explanation. "My sister is a Healer at the Temple of Healing. Healers and nurses usually make their oaths to a particular deity associated with healing. That might be Jesus or the Christian trinity, but a fair number swear to one or the other gods or goddesses of healing. Apollo, Asclepius, and so on."

He waited until Nora nodded. Clearly she knew a bit of her mythology. "My sister's role at the Temple means she must also be a sworn priestess, and she's sworn to Belisama. I don't mind a religious ritual. There's something beautiful in them, the pageantry. But I've not much desire to go looking for that kind of thing myself."

"And you don't care about what happens when you die?"

In almost any other circumstance, Cyrus would have brushed it off, as he always did. Now, though, sitting here, with the work at hand right in front of him, he paused. "I think how I live matters more than whether I swear my life to a particular deity or belief." Then, more carefully, he continued. "And I challenged for the Council because I needed something full of awe and terror to pledge myself to. One, however, is more than enough for my lifetime."

Nora looked him up and down, then asked, her voice clear, though she had other signs of nerves. "What brought you to that, then?"

"My wife died." The three words always felt heavy enough to sink through the planet, and sharp enough to cut everything in their pass. "In childbirth, with our daughter Gemma. She's near three years older than you."

Nora didn't press, and Cyrus was suddenly terribly

grateful, as well as feeling this conversation had entirely got away from him. Instead, she said, "And you did something useful enough with it. Instead of getting lost in a bottle or angry."

"Oh, I was plenty angry when I was younger. Raging at the heavens and the hells and everything in between. But I was a lot younger then. I had the energy for it." He was often tired these days. It wasn't just the War, it had begun before that. The same arguments, the same foolishness, the old patterns that trapped the wary and unwary alike. Himself included.

She looked at him, thinking, but shook her head, as if not willing to engage. "So, the land. How do I learn that? You said there are rituals. Do I do the rituals?"

Cyrus waved a hand. "There are rituals. Customarily for May Day, for Summer Solstice, for harvest, and often something in the winter. Different places have others. As you say, your grandparents."

"And that's something more than the dancing and all that in the villages? We went once, when I was little. Aunt Poppy had to be away for some reason. I was six or seven."

Cyrus nods. "Offerings to the land, and to the waters of the land. I've chatted a bit with Lionel, of course, and he's lent me the various books that talk about the specifics. It's not..." He hesitated. "The form of the ritual matters. It helps shape what you're doing. But the form matters less than that it works. If you come to the moment and feel it needs something, an addition, a change. Going faster or slower, or more or less. That's more important than following the form. Do you bake?"

The question came out of nowhere, but it made her snort. "Of course I bake. How else would we have bread in the house?"

"This kind of ritual is like baking bread. Every loaf is a little different, depending on how much water the flour soaks up. What the oven's like. But you get a feel for it. My apprentice mistress walked me through it over and over again. Not my best skill, but I can make a more than passable loaf, even now."

Nora tilted her head. "I have trouble seeing you in a kitchen, your hands all over flour."

Cyrus shrugged. "Some rituals, you want the offering cakes and such to be something you made a particular way. She was a ferociously accurate ritualist, but she also believed in the old customs like that working best. I've not found any reason to do otherwise."

"So you people apprentice, normally?"

Cyrus nodded. "Mine was unconventional. Tanith - my wife - and I married while we were still both apprentices. Not the usual thing. She was apprenticing in Flora, what we call herbology or herbalism, with an eye to use for ritual and application uses. So she didn't have to interrupt it for her, when Tanith was expecting." He caught the stumble and went on. "And after - after the immediate aftermath, I flung myself into training for the Council Seat. It changed my apprenticeship, but it worked out well enough."

He remembered Mistress Belling - she'd always preferred that to Magistra, as a title - most fondly. She'd been a grand dame with formal ritual, but Cyrus had long blessed the fact she wasn't just interested in the formalities. He'd treasured those afternoons in the kitchen or out in the gardens. Mistress Belling hadn't had a maternal bone in her body, but her firm attention and raw presence had carried him through the worst days. She hadn't exactly approved of his going for the Council, but once he'd made it clear he would, she'd taught him all he could learn.

"You - it sounds like you were young?"

"Quite young. Twenty-five by the time I went for the seat, a year from the end of my apprenticeship. I was another four years earning my proper mastery."

Nora snorted. "And how'd you do that, then? Not sleep?"

"Not sleep, training or studying dawn to well past dusk, except for time with Gemma. And she was a good sleeper from early on, so I'd come home, and check with Nanny, and find myself with another hour or three to work."

Nora nodded, then glanced at the tree one more time. "All right. How do I make this bread, then?" It was an abrupt change of topic, but Cyrus smiled. Forging ahead, that he knew all about.

CHAPTER 13
TUESDAY MORNING

Two days later, it was raining. More than raining, it was a solid soaking downpour.

Apparently, the water wasn't settling right. Mabyn thought a fair bit of it was going into the moat, which was a perfectly reasonable place for water to be. Cyrus, though, had been unhappy about something. He had put on the best rain gear available to go have a look. He'd mentioned he kept finding scattered odd sinkholes, muddy unpleasant messes that had no apparent rhyme or reason. Cyrus had thought seeing them in the rain might show up some of what was going on better.

Lionel, for his part, had gone off to his mother's house to deal with a complaint about a leaking roof, brought by Lady Baddock's maid. The poor woman had been half-drenched by the time she got to the main house. Mabyn had felt sorry for her, and sorry for Lionel, and sorry for the house. She had not felt very sorry for Lady Baddock.

That lady had continued to be difficult. There had been a stilted lunch, where every topic Lady Baddock brought up was difficult. It was entirely intentional. Mabyn knew it.

Cyrus knew it. Lionel, poor man, knew it. Nora had done very well with it, but she had tried to treat it seriously and kindly. And she had therefore stubbed her toe on half a dozen submerged conversational rocks.

Mabyn turned the metaphor over in her mind and decided it more or less worked. Then she frowned. Nora had disappeared after lunch. By now, they had a plan for giving her some of the framework she needed. Cyrus had been working with her this morning, on things you could do with magic. They were focusing on the little cantrips and charms young people usually learned at tutoring school, if not earlier.

There were a whole set that made lights of different colours, or sounds, or shapes. Mabyn knew a few for smells, so you could create something that smelled like baking cookies with the sugar and vanilla and spices. Cyrus had been surprisingly good at sounds, creating a set of chiming bells or birdsong.

Nora had looked them up and down, and pointed out it was a ridiculous way to teach anyone anything. Looking at it that way, Mabyn supposed she had something of a point. The charms, while fine, did not particularly connect to anything else. And they were awkward. Unless you were very good, the colours weren't quite right; the sounds were hollow.

More to the point, it had not seemed to help any in connecting Nora to the land and the land magics. Of course, it was still early days yet. The weather, even before the downpour, had not been very cooperative. Nora needed boots and skirts for tromping around the grounds. Those were in progress, but it would be the end of the week, at least.

Mabyn thought the bigger issue was that they barely

had a sense of what Nora was like. The woman had been pleasant with both of them. She wasn't sulky or standoffish. But she was reserved, like there was a wall around her that kept everyone out. If she had grown up magical, fully in the community, Mabyn would have expected some training. The kind people who were more sensitive to the flows of magic got.

Instead, she'd learned to pull in everything around her. It was like a quiet place in a pond, the place you didn't look. Cyrus had wondered about it last night, when they'd retreated to his sitting-room to make plans for the next few days.

She supposed it made a certain amount of sense. Living in amongst the terraced houses, so close to the neighbours, or working in a crowded school near a factory. Nora had commented more than once about being close enough to hear arguments, the outbreaks of intimate violence on the other side of the wall or across the street.

Trellech was a busy small city, but people with magic had learned to respect a certain amount of space. Flats tended to be well-insulated, cushioned in sound muffling charms. Sharing a room - even a bed - was not uncommon in London, between siblings or children or family. It must be the same in Manchester.

In Albion, anyone much over the age of fifteen was accustomed to sleeping in their own room if they possibly could, with charms to mute noise and light. Too many people found it terribly distracting. Most made an eventual exception for a beloved spouse or partner. Plenty of others kept separate bedrooms, or at least separate beds, with curtains to anchor the charms in.

Mabyn had not had that choice. Aubrey had refused to permit her to have her own rooms, or even her own bed. He had always felt it was his right to be wherever he wanted to be. Most of the time, he didn't touch her. He didn't need to. His just being there, noisily, demandingly, was awful enough. It was constant. It was unyielding, and it was often painful. It was like a squeaking piece of chalk on a chalkboard, eternally there, eternally annoying.

When Aubrey had died, it had been the blessed silence that had been a relief. The chance to be alone with her thoughts, to let her magic pool and flow rather than form spikes of brambles and thorns. For years, she had thought she had solved something, only to turn around and find another snare, another place things had pulled entirely out of place. It wasn't just the obvious mental scars. She'd mapped those out long ago. They were as healed as they were likely to be. The problem was all the places she'd ducked around to avoid another problem, and that had become habitual.

It had been that, more than anything else, that had led her deeper into the Council. Wanting to hunt those things out, figure out what they were. She had fundamentally wanted to know and understand them, not hide them.

And now that meant she needed to go find Nora, clearly. It took a full circuit of the ground floor, and then tracking down one of the housemaids who was cleaning the library. Finally she got pointed to the stairs to the attic. They were quite wide and well-dusted, as attic stairs went, and the door was cracked open at the top.

The attics stretched the length of this wing. Mabyn suspected that at least one of the other wings had bedrooms, set under the slanting roof, for the maids and the footmen. Here, though, there were lumps of furniture, covered by clean white sheets. There were wardrobes and desks and trunks. Quite a few things that had that tickle of magic, too. Mirrors. Mabyn felt all mirrors had a bit of magic, but some had a lot more than others. Desks. Lamps. Lamps could be charmed to do quite a range of things. She'd have to investigate that.

It made her realise that there was not all that much magic in the furniture currently downstairs. That was more than a little curious, in a house of this kind of age and prestige. It made her wonder who had decided that. Was it Lady Baddock? The late Lord Baddock? Some older generation? Many of the pieces here looked to date more to the 18th century than the 19th. Not even Victorian. She saw the figure across at the other end, and called out, "Nora? Found anything interesting?"

There was a moment as Nora turned around where Mabyn had a hint of something. If she were a sensitive sort, she might think it some whisper of a ghost or a memory. She, however, knew better than that. Ghosts existed, though she had never seen one, and was unlikely to. And this house, unlike so many stately homes, had relatively few ghost stories. Certainly none about some newly wed bride getting locked in a chest or wardrobe, only for her skeleton to be discovered centuries later. Mabyn had checked, like a sensible person would.

Nora waved her over. "I've never seen so much furniture in my life. What's this supposed to be?"

Mabyn made her way across, through the aisle between the various items. She came up beside Nora to find her peering at an unusual chair. It had a seat, but narrower than one might expect, arching into an even narrower back. Two curved arms came out, and a large flat board was mounted on what one might think was the back of the chair.

"Georgian." Mabyn said cheerfully. "We used to have

one. The - um. My son still does, I suspect. It's a reading and cockfighting chair. Quite popular for a time."

"Reading and wait." Nora's voice trailed off. "Those are not two things that go together."

"Well, these days, they rarely use the chairs. Cockfighting's been illegal for ages. Not that that stops people doing it, but it does mean they do less hauling out solid wood chairs to watch it with. It is awfully hard to deny that you were there for an illegal match when you have coordinating furniture."

Nora snorted. "How do you know it's not just for reading? For men, clearly."

"Here." Mabyn reached to the latch that held the broad reading ledge in place. "If it were just for reading, you'd not need that to fold down nearly so much. And here, there's a cabinet under here, for you to tuck your winnings or your betting slip or what have you. I'm sure that's a blood lock, Cyrus could tell us for certain."

"A blood lock." Nora sounded uncertain. "Isn't that - a wrong sort of magic?"

"There are all sorts of magazines, aren't there? Penny-dreadfuls, I think they're called? Something else?"

"Pulp magazines. Half-penny periodicals. Very popular with a number of students, and I will admit a certain inducement to learn to read from time to time." Nora was smiling now. "Yes? I assume the tales about evil magic and Hellfire clubs and all that are, in fact, fictional?"

"Oh, any time a group of men of a certain age with too much free time on their hands gets bored, there's something like a Hellfire club. Many names over the years. Fortunately, most of them are sufficiently dilettantes that they don't cause more than a strictly local sort of trouble."

Nora nodded, turning to look around the room, then

stopped, stock still. Mabyn caught the shift before she realised what Nora was looking at. Set into the side of one of the dormer windows was a striking painting. It was striking enough that Mabyn had to take a breath and consciously remind herself of where her feet were and how her lungs worked.

It looked entirely too much like Aubrey for comfort. Certainly the features did, though the clothing was early Regency. Something about the smile, though, as well, the little twist to the mouth that hinted at something deeply unpleasant. She found herself reaching for Nora's hand. "Tell me, why does that catch you."

"It has you too." Nora didn't turn around, but her hand fumbled to grab for Mabyn's.

"He looks very much like my late husband. I didn't realise there was a family connection, but there must be." Mabyn did her best to keep her voice even and relaxed. It really wasn't working, and they both knew it. "You?"

"Granda's brother. Not a nice man." Nora furrowed her forehead, thinking back. "Stubborn man. Didn't look much like Granda, actually." She considers. "Doesn't look much like Lionel, either, but more like his mother?"

That suggested quite a number of things, none of them entirely surprising, but none of them at all pleasant. Mabyn swallowed and said, "Downstairs for a warm drink with a bit of brandy. And then perhaps a look at the family tree?"

Nora did not want to turn away, but Mabyn took a step, then another, tugging her along by the hand. It was only when they were halfway back to the stairs that Nora spoke again. "Was that magic? I don't like it."

Mabyn let out her breath slowly. "Do you mean, is the painting magical? Probably not. It would feel different to me if it were." She realised as she spoke, that was true. "I can check, a moment." She wanted to check now, to make sure, to know that little twist of discomfort was her own history, not something larger.

She left Nora standing there, and went back to do the simple charm that would tell her. Nothing flashed, nothing shifted. Mabyn came back to Nora, both relieved and puzzled. "Nothing but an unpleasant man."

CHAPTER 14
BEFORE SUPPER THAT AFTERNOON

Cyrus settled into the chair in the library with a groan. Despite a reasonably hot bath and changing into dry clothes, he still felt chilly. It was about an hour to supper. At least someone had lit a fire, and it was pleasantly toasty.

That just brought home the differences. The house itself was well-managed, considering. Old homes, especially over four centuries old, like this one, tended to be draughty and leak. The floors sagged, and things creaked. There were spots worn down in the stone steps and lintels. Here, though, things were quite cosy.

No, the problems were outside the house, so far as he could tell. Oh, it was early days yet, he supposed. Architectural magic was subtle, if also often somewhat manipulative. He'd not had time to do a full exploration of the house. There were certain spaces he wouldn't get a look at. Lionel's rooms, for example. Or Nora's. Not without some better reason than his curiosity.

The land, though, that was a conundrum. He hadn't

expected there to be a simple, obvious answer. Lionel might be hiding something. Well, was likely hiding a dozen things. Most people were, that was to be expected. The question was, what kinds of things, and what about. And how many of them had to do with the house or the land magic in specific.

None of which made it easier to figure out what was going on with the land. Cyrus was no expert here, but it wasn't as if experts were thick on the ground. Oh, there were places in Albion doing better than others. But the places that seemed steadiest right now, in terms of the land magics, were mostly those where the Lord had held the land since well before the War. Where they had not served in the trenches, and ideally where they had named their Heir before the War as well.

If they couldn't figure out what was going so wrong here, perhaps they'd have to call in favours with one of those places. It was, perhaps, more than past time to do a survey of the demesne lands, all of them, and how they were currently doing. Cyrus had a growing fear that more of them were in trouble than the Council realised.

He was deep in thought when the door opened, and Lionel came in, then stopped. "Oh, beg pardon."

Typically British. The man's own house, his own library, and he was apologising for coming in. Though he'd noticed that Lionel had more than the usual twitchiness, even for a veteran. It was like a hare darting away at some noise in the underbrush.

"Please, no. I was just enjoying the fire. If you wanted the library, I could go elsewhere." Two could play at the apology game. Or dance. It really was more of a dance, a gesture and response in stylised form.

As Cyrus had expected, Lionel shook his head. "I was

looking for the fire. Nothing wrong with sharing the space. How did things go today?"

"I was out on the land most of it, and got soaked through despite the rain gear, or near enough. There's something very odd about your water runoff, you know. I took a fair number of notes, but I'm not sure how to make sense of them."

"Not a good sign, then."

Cyrus shook his head. "Things flow towards the moat more than they should. You - I sincerely hope you do - must have some records about the construction of the place? Significant additions, repairs, that sort of thing?"

Lionel nodded. "Muniments room. Where all such things are stored. They're in an awful state, though, and whole swaths of them are in awful handwriting. I think a form of - what's it called? Chancery hand. Is that the term?"

"I've got a fair bit of experience with all that. I suspect Mabyn might have a bit more. Definitely a learned skill, though. If we could settle down to have a look in the next week, that would be grand." Cyrus leaned back.

"What are your plans other than that?" Lionel settled down in the other chair nearest the fire.

"We're still feeling our way through the best options. It's a very individual process, of course. The land, the person, the history. We've had more reports like yours - people who served in the War in the trenches, in particular. However, we don't have nearly enough to have a solid idea of the best approach yet."

"Wait, I'm not the only one?" Lionel pushed himself upright. "I didn't realise."

Cyrus frowned and considered how to go about this bit of explanation. "You understand, first, that it is a slow rolling process. The Lords of the land - and the Ladies - are of all sorts of ages and states of health. There are quite a few who were too old to enlist, but still quite hale. Those estates are doing fairly well right now."

"And the Heirs?" Lionel stood, abruptly. "Drink before supper?" When Cyrus nodded, Lionel went to the decanter and poured out two glasses of brandy, then brought them back. It gave Cyrus a chance to think about how to put this.

"The Heirs are where it gets complicated. It is not true of everyone, we know that. But a fair number of men who served, especially those in the trenches, or near them, seem to struggle in the same way you have been. It is hard to tell what that means until they inherit. Some have worked themselves around to managing, given some time. Carillon, down in the New Forest, seems to be doing fairly well, and he never expected to inherit. Though he always preferred the demesne lands at Ytene, rather than their other estates."

"Do you know why he's doing better than the others?"

Cyrus spreads his hands. "Therein lies the mystery. The man's got a pleasant reputation, but nothing terribly out of the ordinary. Plenty of travel, a love of horses, a fondness for incunabula. I've talked with him in passing, like you do, but I can't say I've ever had a deeper conversation with him. Neither of those being particular passions."

"You're a fine rider, though." Lionel tipped his glass. "I saw you when you were out on Map."

Map was a fine chestnut gelding, getting on in years, but still up for a solid walk around the property. "Map's an easy ride. Bit leggy."

"His dam's a hunter. His sire was a Suffolk Punch. An attempt to do some crossbreeding, in my father's generation of the stable. The Suffolk Punch is the local draught breed, always some shade of chesnut, and they're even tempered." He waved a hand. "Traditionally spelled without the middle t, by the by, should you need to write it down. C-h-e-s-n-u-t."

Cyrus grinned. "You, clearly, have a fondness for a horse? As well as precision of language?

"Oh, enough of one. You know where you are with a horse, generally speaking. I'm not gifted at it."

The discussion of a breeding program reminded Cyrus of something he'd been meaning to ask. Perhaps this was the moment - man to man, just the two of them. "I had a question - about the land, not the horses."

Lionel raised an eyebrow. "I am sure you have far more than one question."

"True enough." Cyrus paused. "If you knew the land wasn't responding to you, why didn't you consider marrying and seeing if it would respond to the child?"

Lionel looked up sharply, then back toward the fire. He wasn't particularly good at covering his feelings. Cyrus let him take all the time he wanted. Eventually, without looking back, Lionel said, "I think I am unlikely to ever marry. Acknowledging that, doing what is right for the land, that matters more. I haven't explained the matter to Mother."

Cyrus mentally sorted through the potential reasons. There might well be more than one. He knew that well enough. "Are there reasons you're able to share at the moment?"

There was another long silence while Lionel stared at the fire. "Providing an heir the traditional way, a child of my body, will not happen. Even before the War, women did not provoke an attraction. Since, however, the idea of permitting anyone so close..." He let his voice trail off. "If you perceive?"

"Quite." Cyrus considered that. A preference for men over women could be managed, sometimes. It certainly had been in the past. By kings before the Pact, even, if you believed some of the histories. But someone who could not tolerate the briefest intimacy, that would complicate matters quite a lot. Less for a man than a woman, from what he'd heard from Rhoe about the more mechanical methods of encouraging children, but still a degree of intimate assumption.

Lionel murmured, "I am sure it disgusts you."

Cyrus looked up at that. "Beg pardon?" That was the safest way to go here until he could figure out what Lionel meant by that.

"It's unnatural. Mother's certainly lectured about it enough. In a general sense, she does not know about my preferences. And given that they are an entirely academic question these days, no reason she should ever know."

It was difficult to know where to start with that. "It is not unnatural, you realise. Animals, which we also are, form all sorts of configurations."

"But the - " Lionel rubbed his face. "The implications of the land magics."

"They do best when there's a blood connection between Lord and Heir. When the Heir is long-familiar with the land. But there are other ways to manage that." Cyrus wondered how much of those wrong-headed assumptions had poisoned this place long before the late Lord died. "Your preferences are not the problem here, though they may suggest different resolutions than in other situations."

"Mother would be furious. If she knew about..." Lionel cut off. He was visibly still deeply uncomfortable with it. "She has been very determined about getting me married off. So much so it's driven her into ill-health."

"It is certainly not a thing I would dream of telling her. I may, beg pardon, need to mention it to Mabyn, should it become relevant in our planning."

Lionel shrugged, a rather defeated shrug. "I assumed."

Cyrus chose his words carefully, wanting to drive the point home as far as he could. To see if he could get Lionel to see it as a known variation. Shame didn't do anyone any good. "In my line of work, I have come across a number of ways people choose to live their lives. My sister is a Healer, and has seen many more. You are aware of your choices, you are taking steps to manage the implications, in terms of how they affect others and your responsibilities." He gestured at himself. "The reason your humble servant is here to have awkward conversations with."

The last made Lionel snort, and raise his glass in acknowledgement before draining it. "Still. Not the done thing."

"More common than you'd think." Cyrus waved his hand. "There are traditional solutions, as I said. Adoption, among them, including from a cadet line. Though there doesn't seem to be much of that, does there?"

Lionel shook his head. "We run to one or two children a generation, and often only one has had children. Or, of course, daughters married out of the family line. And no one knew Nora existed until you found her. We did not know at all. I'm not sure that Uncle Samuel did, though there's a trunk of letters somewhere to Pater. I suppose that might give an idea if anyone went through them."

"We might want to do that." Cyrus hesitated. "I'm beginning to wonder if the root of the problem isn't rather older than you. Certainly before the War. I'm not at all sure, though. Mind, this is on first glance, without trying several rituals that might be informative. I'd be interested in looking more at the family history."

Lionel waved a hand. "The skeletons in the closets are yours to examine, if you wish. I can hunt up that trunk of letters, the family tree. We're an ancient family, married into most of the other aristocratic lines of any historical note. It's all rather hard to untangle."

Cyrus nodded. "Any of recent interest? The past two or three generations?"

"Mother's grandfather was a Teague. A younger son, something of a wastrel. I didn't much want to bring it up around Mabyn." Lionel gestured. "Not a kind man, I gather, though Mother rather doted on him. She was his pet as a girl, he died a few years after my parents married. They only had a daughter, so the name didn't carry on in her line."

Cyrus coughed. "I can see the - well. The delicacy of bringing it up with Mabyn. I would like a look at all of that, please. Which brings us back to the rituals and the land. And whether this is an older problem than the War."

Lionel waved his hand. "Granted." Then he swallowed. "What makes you feel that?"

"There's a sense to it. Have you seen a landslide, or the collapse of a bit of a cliff? There's a long slow shift, and then suddenly, everything slides downhill. I feel you have had a long slow slide over decades, and then here we are, and we're sliding down the cliff, or about to."

"Oh, that sounds hopeless. Like everything else. I don't have an idea. And I'm sure Mother wouldn't be forthcoming."

Cyrus shook his head. "We can do quite a lot to stop it. Unlike a landslide. There are all sorts of nets, ritual actions. Some materia choices, perhaps pillars at certain resonant locations. Mabyn has some expertise there. Or using the existing flora, perhaps." He hesitated, then added the joke. "You can use the fauna too, but they do like to move about."

Lionel grunted. He looked into the fire again. "You think there's a chance?"

"I think we will give our best to finding that chance and making the most of it." At that point, the going rang for dinner. "I expect the ladies will be down shortly. I appreciate your candour, as difficult as it was."

Lionel nodded. "I appreciate that you did not turn away in horror." Before he could say more, there was the sound of people outside the library. They both settled into the overtly relaxed pose that denied any vulnerable conversation had taken place here.

CHAPTER 15
IN THE GARDENS, TUESDAY, APRIL 6TH

A week later, they were out in the formal knotwork gardens that stood between the moat and the kitchen gardens. The size of the gardens was impressive, but they were currently rather dowdy. There were spring bulbs coming up, but the whole effect was iffy. It was as if a quarter of the plantings, scattered through the garden, had died. The established bushes and larger plants were more or less coping, but more of the annuals and smaller perennials were struggling.

It was another sign of whatever was affecting the property. At the same time, it was not terribly informative, in terms of how to resolve it. Barring, of course, the larger question of resolution, of helping Nora open her hands to the land magics, and send them flowing as they should.

Mabyn took a circuit around the garden while Cyrus was setting up for the exercises he planned. It involved a series of modestly sized stones, a compass, and a bowl of water. That was some approach she didn't know well herself, though she certainly knew the kind of thing he had in mind. Last night, when he'd been laying it out, he'd pointed out that they did not yet know of Nora's particular preferences.

Each person sensed their magic in their own way. For Mabyn, it had always been rather like light through stained glass, a shift of colours and shapes that she could sometimes sketch but rarely articulate. She reached for the energy that matched a particular hue or saturation, and she could thread them together into patterns and overlays. Or at least she could now. When she was younger, first learning, it had been all she could do to have two or three contrasting shades in play at one time, all distinct from each other.

It explained, perhaps, one reason she had long favoured Materia work, the magics inherent in different materials and how human attention could shape or form them into something new. She preferred oils and salves and tinctures, the distillation of the magic of the plant into that could be stored and carried. She did well enough with metals, better with woods, not so well with stones. And, of course, there were all sorts of things shaped by men and women.

Cyrus, she gathered, favoured a more elemental method, at least for this kind of work. She got the impression that he had begun with a preference for formal ritual. He seemed the sort to favour the sort of thing involving chalk lines in a prepared workroom, that you laid out precisely and did at the proper time guided by the stars. A few references she'd found in the Council library suggested he had spent much of the past twenty-five years broadening out from that, into a more situational approach.

Aubrey had been a stickler for the proper form, done as expected. Mabyn had often wondered if that was why his magic had been far more fragmentary than hers, coming in fits and starts. Their son Davin certainly had struggled in his schooling, until he had found a place for himself in alchemy. Alchemy, of all the magical arts, rewarded precision of measurement and method. At least in the more elaborate forms. Mabyn's simples and salves were not the same thing at all, as both Aubrey and Davin had told her repeatedly.

Cyrus seemed to have the table arranged now, and one footman was gathering up long poles meant for hanging flower baskets. Cyrus was gesturing with a flutter of brightly coloured ribbons in his hands. One set was reds and oranges, another shades of yellow, a third was blues and purples, and the last was greens and perhaps browns.

That made her curious enough to come over, and risk him grumbling at her or worse. Aubrey had wanted no one near him when he was preparing for some working. And by near, he meant she should sit in the corner of the second library, so he could bother her whenever he wanted, but not move near him or away. Or do any of the things she'd rather be doing.

She made her way halfway back down the long path down the centre of the garden, then hesitated. Cyrus turned to glance at her, then waved her closer, grinning broadly. She swallowed, fighting down the still painfully strong instinctive desire to retreat. But he had been clear enough, and Nora was right there. Nora was, frankly, looking very sceptical, and that made Mabyn smile.

"Mabyn! Here we are." Cyrus was decidedly genial. "Nora isn't sure what to make of all this foolishness."

"You said that magic was inherent in the land." Nora gestured. "And then you have things to put on poles, and what is that, there, then?" She gestured at a piece of parchment on the table at the centre, a diagram.

"We are cheerfully bodging together several approaches

into one. Philosophically speaking. Now, you remember I was saying the other day that ritual magic has many forms? There is a workroom, a proper magical workroom, in the house, though it needs some care and attention. Lionel and I have talked about that. We'll be getting someone out to have a look at the stonework, but we shouldn't use it until then."

Nora nodded, raising an eyebrow.

"So instead, we are going to play with the natural alignments, and see whether that gets us anything interesting." Cyrus waved a hand. "Or rather, we are going to impose some very human choices on the landscape, and see what happens."

"I would have thought a house and gardens in tidily lined beds would be rather a human imposition. The moat did not put itself there, surely." Nora was finding her feet, Mabyn thought. Or rather, she had - unlike Mabyn - always had them under her, well-rooted. The woman had a clear sense of herself, and her values, and Mabyn found that both fascinating and charming.

"Ritually speaking, the house and garden are, these days, established in the landscape. That is an entirely different discussion, Nora, dear."

Nora snorted at that. "Which I am sure I will get sometime."

"Oh, certainly." Cyrus grinned. "The form we're using today arguably dates back to some of the work from Agrippa in the 1500s. Not the forms that survived in the non-magical community." Mabyn noted with pleasure that he also used that term. She might not spend much time with those without magic, but they were certainly capable of many things. Curious, and also more courteous; she approved. "We are laying a map of our own on the world, aligned along the compass points. Now, you saw me marking that out earlier."

Nora nodded again. "And the garden seems - more or less aligned?"

"It is!" Cyrus looked truly delighted at this. "A number of the great halls aren't, and that's always an interesting question. This one, however, having been in magical hands from the beginning, is well-aligned for our purposes. Not that there aren't some quirks. You can see how this area is planted differently? I gather there's a sandiness in the soil that keeps returning."

"Why does that matter, the alignment?" Nora had settled into asking questions now. That was excellent.

"Well, it makes things much easier. You understand that in ritual terms, we could, in certain forms of ritual, declare that up is down, left is right." His eyes twinkled. "And that lambs and wolves should lie down next to each other in utter peace and contentment."

Nora, if anything, looked even more sceptical. "You're having me on, surely."

"There are - oh, at least a dozen reasons for ritual, distinct ones. But that is one reason for magical ritual, to create a space in which things that seem impossible are made possible. What else is magic, or at least some forms of it? Come on, Nora, you know your tales about Merlin and Morgan le Fay well enough, I'm sure."

"The tales did not talk about that kind of thing. Not the ones I know."

"Well, no. Merlin was rather more fond of waving wand and staff and clapping hands and the show of magic. But that show comes from ritual, generally speaking. Or a miracle, and we do not expect miracles. Proper preparation is ever so much more reliable."

Nora laughed at that. "So what are we doing if not a miracle?"

"One method of ritual construction is to align a space to the compass directions. The compass draws on the natural magnetism of the earth, and it places us in space and time. If you had gone to Schola, or perhaps one of the other schools, you'd have learned something of astronomy. In our circles, that is the art of knowing where and when we are. And then perhaps creating some other opportunity, if we're skilled at that particular magic."

"And why are we doing that today?" Nora glanced around again.

"It gives us a structure. Not only for our own work, the immediate moment, but this is a core form and a structure used by thousands of people over the centuries. That gives the whole thing weight. You're Church of England, I think you said?"

Nora nodded, then considered. "Going to services is an important way to know what's going on. For a midwife, and for a teacher."

"Ah, but you're not entirely sure what you believe?" Cyrus grinned. "That's fairly common, even among the devout, honestly. My sister says faith should be a verb, it is in Greek. It is something you do, not something you have."

That made Nora blink a dozen times before she said weakly, "You do know you are rather strange, correct?"

Mabyn laughed at that. "He is aware, or should be. But in this he has a point." She glanced at Cyrus. "The methods we repeat, over and over again, generation to generation, they gather their own weight, becoming more substantial in the process. A talented ritualist..." She gestured at Cyrus, who bowed. "Can come up with a ritual in the moment and have it work. They might gather fragments from other rituals, planned and structured, but they take the pieces and stitch them into something new and astonishing. A patchwork coat. When it works, the thing holds together and is transformed."

"And if it does not work, you are cold and embarrassed, and possibly worse?" Nora suggested.

"Exactly. Which is why knowing your limits as a ritualist is a large part of our training, as well as learning those established and customary rituals. Some of them are obligatory - the oath you made to the Silence at the age of twelve. That is a ritual that has not changed much, other than the pronunciation of the words, since it began."

"And this?" Nora glanced around again.

"Somewhere in the middle. Here, we are using the framework. The four directions, with the elemental associations for each direction. These are somewhat arbitrary, but they give us spaces to work with. Rather like deciding to group books on shelves in our personal library. A system that makes some sense, but could be done differently in any number of ways."

"That may be the first truly sensible thing you've said so far. And what am I supposed to do in this?"

"See if there is a direction, a shelf of items or materials, you find that draws you. It might be a plant, it might be one stone we've set out, it might be some feature in the garden that catches your attention. We are hoping to learn if there is anything like that, and then follow that inclination further."

"I suppose there are worse ideas." Nora looked around the space. "None of this is going to hurt me or damage me or be a risk, is it?"

"Oh, no. That is why I am here." Cyrus was firm now. "And what we are doing is - oh, a child of five might do it, depending on her parents. Think of it like browsing in a library or a shop, seeing which things you are drawn to, and which do not hold any interest."

"What will you be doing, then?" Nora stretched a little, as if beginning to brace herself.

"I will be creating the ritual space, the threads of connection. And then ensuring you have time to explore."

CHAPTER 16
THAT AFTERNOON

Cyrus let Nora circle around the space once, without rushing her. Mabyn came up next to him. "Anything I should know?"

He shrugged. "This is fairly routine, honestly. I'm not expecting sparks and flourishes, but I'm hoping it gives us some sense of what direction to explore first. Or second or third."

Mabyn nodded. "Something like the early exercises at Schola. I have some articles you might like, especially after we figure out what she's most intrigued by. Do you have any early theories?"

Cyrus laughed and tapped his nose. "That's for me to know and not talk about. I don't want to prejudice your observations. Basically, though, I want to chime the space, and then see what draws her attention." He gestured at the bell on the table. Cyrus presumed she knew the term, for all it was awful ritualist slang. It was, however, an effective method of clearing the space, drawing the mind to items in new ways, and generally starting off on the right foot, as it were.

Mabyn spent a moment watching Nora move around the circle, then cross back. "If you intend to do more ritual work with her, someone will have to discuss proper directions with her."

"That is, I believe, a more advanced lesson." Cyrus hoped this would at least give them something to work with. He had felt like he was in a river, barely able to keep his footing against the current and the slickness of the riverbed. Oh, he could fake certainty and confidence with the best of them, and he had, but that didn't make him feel relaxed about the whole thing. Not at all.

"What's my role here?" Mabyn took a step back to glance at the items on the central altar table. "Follow your lead, tell you what I notice afterwards?"

Cyrus nodded. "Exactly so. Down the road, we might want something different, but I'd not ask you to step into that without conversation, first."

Mabyn smiled, a bit toothily, suddenly showing an edge of fierceness. "Negotiation, yes. And agreement. All right. Ready when you both are."

It gave Cyrus time to go through his plans mentally one more time, before Nora came back a minute later. "It's all baffling, but it will not change because I'm staring at it. Why don't you do whatever you're doing." She waved a hand at it.

"Right, then. I'll be ringing the bell, and you'll hear some chanting in Latin. It's basically all about aligning what we're doing. It's not very good Latin, even." Once Mabyn and Nora were both waiting patiently, he settled into doing the necessary ritual steps. He'd done them so long and so often that he could likely do them in his sleep, for all this wasn't an approach he used regularly.

He had finished the ritual, stepping back to the centre

and gesturing for Nora to explore. Mabyn was perhaps five or six feet away. Nora began at the east, pausing for a long moment in the corner, peering at a plant, then moving south and toward the west.

Out of the corner of his eye, Cyrus could see Mabyn suddenly pivot. At exactly the same moment, he felt a twinge in the magic. He'd set up the whole thing. All of it was connected through him, as intimately as a ritual could be. It clutched at him suddenly, grabbing at his body in a way that made his muscles seize for a moment. Everything went black for three or four seconds.

When he could see again, Mabyn had her feet braced, her hands facing toward the ground, one of the classic postures for gathering up potential. Nora was behind them and whatever the thing was, that was a help. He was doing all the analysis almost as fast as thought, and then he twisted, his hand going immediately to the polished wooden wand he'd set out. His blade would have been better, but that was locked in the trunk in his rooms.

The wand came up, all the instinctive memory. He reached up, the centre point of the circle, and down to the bottom of it, and opened what could only be described as a tunnel between them, with him caught between both poles. He let that magic fill him, the grace of the stars and the patient shattering power of the deep earth.

Once he did, he could near enough see the threads of what was being done. The roar of anger deep inside his head that someone was trying to disrupt this space he had made made him vibrate. Creating a ritual space involved an act of arrogance, at some fundamental level, putting on a cloak of power.

He spoke a single word, a Word of Command, that coiled those threads and pulled the person at the other end towards him. His eyes were half closed, and the figure was in shadow. It wasn't until they were ten feet away that he realised it was Lady Baddock.

"Stool, please, Mabyn." He knew it was coming out terse and hard, but he couldn't spare energy for that yet. She was fighting against the limits he'd given her, repeatedly. Utterly ineffectively, of course. Cyrus knew the range of his skill. Few people could match him, not in this.

Mabyn, thankfully, hadn't argued. She'd gone to pull a stool out from under the main table, and placed it where Lady Baddock could sit on it. Cyrus said, clearly. "Sit." Once she had obeyed that, he added an order that meant she could not stand until he gave permission.

It was, on one hand, a tremendous use and potential abuse of power. On the other hand, it was meant for just this kind of situation, where someone's unwarranted inter- ference could be dangerous to others. If they'd been using Theobold's Second Iteration, the way he'd been originally thinking, it might have done irreparable damage to the land, and quite possibly to one or more people.

And it was one of those things that only some of the Council had at their command. He knew he wasn't the only one, but he suspected Mabyn wasn't one of that select company. She, though, was a picture of calm. She'd gestured for Nora to come join her. The two of them were standing about ten feet away, to the side, well out of the line of any likely problem.

"Explain yourself, Eustacia Baddock." He could see her eyes flare at the deliberate refusal to use her title. He didn't reinforce it with the Word of Command. If he needed to, it really should be a matter for the Guard at that point.

Lady Baddock was silent for a moment, staring at him, as if staring at him would make him yield. She might be fierce and stubborn, but he had faced down far worse in the past, and probably again in the future. She certainly wasn't a pinch on his mother, who knew exactly how to make him feel guilty. She was a stranger, and it gave her vastly less leverage. When she didn't speak, he added, "Now."

Grudgingly, she nodded. "That one." She nodded at Nora, the sort of tight, dismissive nod. "Has no right to be here. Lionel refuses to do anything properly, so of course, the work falls to me."

"What work would that be?" Mabyn had slipped an arm around Nora's shoulders. He could see that out of the corner of his eye. "And where is Lionel?"

"In the dower house, checking on the leaks and all. He thinks I'm having a little afternoon nap. As if." Cyrus made a mental note to make it clear to Lionel that his mother was clearly up to quite a few things. Perhaps especially when he thought she was otherwise occupied.

"What did you plan to do?" Cyrus asked her again.

"The girl has no idea what she's doing. It's easy enough to make that clear." Eustacia's voice had a coldness to it, a ruthlessness. He'd heard it from the Council before, of course. Decisions that needed razor-sharp logic, without letting too much empathy get in the way, were one of their duties. But to hear it here shook him more than he showed.

He wasn't exactly surprised she was being difficult. He'd honestly expected that, from the first moment when Mabyn had explained Lionel had come without alerting his mother. His mother would want to cling to her pride of position. Being the widow of a Lord wasn't nearly as potent or powerful as being the mother of one. But this was something else. It had roots that went much deeper, that went back much further than Lionel's request or their arrival.

"And what were you going to do?" Cyrus was trying to be patient.

"Oh, just pull the magic so she'd fall. Fail." Eustacia waved a hand. "It's no matter to me what happens to her. And it shouldn't be to either of you. I don't know why Lionel's tolerating your presence."

Cyrus glanced at Mabyn, to see if she had any particular thoughts. She pulled away from Nora, coming to join Cyrus. "Whatever your opinions are, Eustacia," she used the first name too, like a weapon. "You may not interfere with our work here. This is proper Council business, for the good of the land. We have all the right we need - including the welcome of the current Lord - to be here and do this work."

Eustacia opened her mouth, as if she wanted to pour out something. Excuses. Blame. Nastiness. Mabyn lifted her hand, murmured a Word that Cyrus didn't know, and there was silence. "Much better." Mabyn turned to Cyrus. "I do believe this is a matter for an oath."

If Cyrus had been Lord of the land, he could have forced truth-telling. He could have used a far more thorough version than he'd just done, and got a complete sense of her current and future intentions. If he were a magistrate, he could have done the same. He didn't wish to ask Lionel to take the Lord's part.

For one thing, he was not at all sure it would work, given how the land magics were reacting. And for the second, it was rather cruel to ask someone to do that to their mother. Not that it hadn't been necessary at some points, historically, but that didn't make it a good idea.

Cyrus nodded slowly. "I would be glad to handle that matter now as soon as we settle on wording." He glanced up and saw Eustacia struggle to try and stand. "A moment, please."

Mabyn turned back to Nora. "Nora, dear. There's no reason to keep you out here. Cyrus, would you open up the space for her, and Nora, if you'd see about having some tea - sandwiches and something warm in the library would be grand. We'll be back in about half an hour at the outside." She then nodded at Cyrus. He gathered up the threads that made the ritual space, turning in place, then stomping his foot three times, to anchor it.

Sorting out the wording for the oath was a matter of mutters and whispers. Mabyn had cogent suggestions, tweaking the wording here and there. They made Eustacia wait a good twenty minutes before they were both satisfied, then Cyrus turned around. "You can make the oath, or you can be held until the Guard can come pick you up. Your choice."

Eustacia sneered, the corner of her mouth twisting. "The oath."

Mabyn came and held it where she could read it. Cyrus planted both feet, feeling the magic enfold him, bending his knees just slightly for the flexibility to flow with the pull of the magic. He opened himself to it, the way it always felt a little like opening a faucet and letting the universe flow through him. Not for the first time, he felt like his metaphors were inadequate to his life.

He coached her through it, listening as she spoke. "I, Eustacia Carlotta Wallace Baddock, swear by the Silence that I will take no magical or physical action against Nora Martin, Council Member Smythe-Clive or Council Member Teague, or any who are aiding in mending the land magics on this estate. I swear I will treat all on the estate with courtesy."

It was bare in places, but it should cover the essentials. Cyrus wondered what the housemaid assigned to the dower house was going to think about her new experiences.

"Excellent. I will walk you back to the dower house now. I want a word with Lionel. Mabyn, if you'd see how Nora is doing, I'll be up for tea promptly."

Mabyn nodded. "Shall I clean up for you?"

Cyrus had nearly forgotten that. He glanced around. None of the items were unduly personal, bar that one case that held his wand and a set of stones for the directions. "A moment." He gathered them into the case, closed it, and pressed his thumb against the lock. "If you'd keep an eye on that until I reclaim it?"

"Done."

That left Cyrus with an uncomfortable walk down the lane, toward the dower house.

CHAPTER 17
LATER THAT AFTERNOON IN THE LIBRARY

"My mother did what?"

They had reconvened in the library in the main house. It was a soothing space, at least to Mabyn. It had more than enough room for everyone to spread out. And it had a drinks cabinet. Cyrus turned around and handed Lionel the glass he'd just poured, some dark liquid. The maid had already brought in a simple tea spread, sandwiches and scones.

Lionel grasped at the glass, not looking, then drank about half of it in one long gulp, before holding it out again to Cyrus. He was all twitches again, and flicks of checking the world around him as he folded himself into a chair, cupping the glass in his hands, and falling silent. Cyrus considered, then topped it up. He turned back to pour a glass for himself and set the decanter down.

Mabyn wasn't able to read him, now. He was contained, controlled, every movement measured. That was exactly what she'd expected. He'd shown his hand more than she'd expected, actually. He'd come back from the dower house with Lionel, all his movements with that tight edge to them. It reminded her far too much of Aubrey.

Then, somehow, as if he had changed his spots entirely, he had taken a breath and all that simmering tension and fury had turned into a resolute steadiness. She'd have thought it some sort of charm or enchantment, but she was almost certain he hadn't cast anything like that. Instead, he'd shown Lionel through into the library.

There was no smooth and polished way to say someone's mother had committed a nearly criminal act. It was the nearly that was the trick. It wasn't just interfering with the ritual work, though that was decidedly not approved of. By anyone. It was the interference, the planned interference, with Council work.

And, of course, it was not precisely safe. If Eustacia had managed it, she might have done some harm to Cyrus. To Nora. Probably not to Mabyn, who had not been so intimately tied into the working. Certainly Eustacia might have done further harm to the land magic.

"What did she say?" Lionel was grasping at any faint hope now. "Maybe she didn't mean it."

"Lionel." Cyrus was clear now. It wasn't exactly a paternal tone. Mabyn rather suspected that would not go over well. She suspected Lionel had got on well enough in his way with his father. But it would have been the distant closeness of men of their class. It would have been made up of conversation about shared interests, the land, the house, perhaps a piece in the newspaper.

Lionel buried his head in his hands again, setting the glass down blindly on the table. Mabyn reached out to make sure it wouldn't tip over. No need to waste the brandy or stain the rug. She cleared her throat. "When you came to the Council, you said she did not know you were there."

Nora stood up. "I should let you talk."

Mabyn shook her head. "I'd prefer you stayed and heard this out. You should know."

Lionel looked up. "Please stay. I'd rather explain it once, but you have every right to hear." As Nora settled back again, Cyrus moved to take up a place at the other end of the couch from Mabyn. After a moment, Lionel went on. "Mother has always liked the status. She's not from a landed family. The title appealed. The, the cloak of the magic." He gestured vaguely, making a circle with one hand before he picked up his glass again.

"How did your parents get on?" Mabyn thought she saw some of the patterns here. "You told me some of it."

"Not just separate rooms, but separate wings. Not that that's challenging here. Opposite corners of the house. From just after I was born, I gather."

He was about to go on, when Mabyn asked, "Was there a particular reason that you know of? Or have guesses at?" She wished she could ask the staff, but even those who had been here then would be unlikely to tell her. They'd have their own loyalties, and their own concerns about who information might harm.

Lionel shook his head. "Just hints. Some divination went badly, I think. I've come across a very occasional reference to a line of something unpleasant in the Wallaces, mother's family. But surely Pater would have sorted that out before they married, if there was anything."

Mabyn had thought the same thing about her parents and Aubrey's family and she knew all too well how wrong that had been. Families had secrets, and their own lines of magic. She began to wonder if the Wallaces had some sort of family magic, their own set of rites and practises, around getting what they wanted. It wasn't at all uncommon. She set aside the uncomfortable thought of whether the Wallaces were related to the Teagues for some later, more private time. She certainly hadn't had time to research that portrait upstairs.

Cyrus cleared his throat. "We can follow up on that, certainly. Using our own methods, not asking your mother. It's very clear how badly that would go."

Mabyn thought that was understating it entirely. "And she stayed there. Did your parents spend any time together, other than the social obligations?"

"No, Pater had his own life. Mother wanted to go to Trellech, I think, and he wouldn't. Wouldn't let her gad about in town, either. I mean, to be fair, she'd have spent all the money and taken a lover, and it might have improved her mood, but it would have been bad for the estate." Lionel looked down at his glass, as if it had loosened his tongue far more than he intended, and set it aside.

"Which rooms did she have?" Mabyn did him the kindness of a much simpler sort of question.

"Mother was where you are right now, Mabyn, and further along. I've completely redone those rooms. Down to the wallpaper and plaster being stripped." He grimaced. "It was an awful green. And one of the other rooms was mauve."

Mabyn considered. Then something caught her memory. "And she moved to the dower house. That's unusual, given you're not married yet." It was far more common for the dowager to move only once the new Lord or Lady had established their own household. Which meant, by convention, getting married.

"She did. Almost as soon as Father died." Lionel grimaced. "That is curious, isn't it? I would have thought she'd have clung to the house. Or decided to go to Trellech, finally."

"What else changed around that time?" Cyrus was leaning forward, listening intently.

"Besides everything?" Lionel was wry. "We had some problems with the house. A few mice, a few leaks, nothing unusual."

Mabyn tilted her head. "Your housekeeper said you don't have ghosts. But do you?" Cyrus looked up sharply, but Mabyn forged on. "Especially the familial sort?"

"There are a few stories about a grey or white lady. But everyone has those. Um. Nothing in the house, that's more than that sort of tale. Someone seen wandering past the oak, on moonlit rainy nights."

"So quite often, then." Mabyn let the humour show in her voice.

Lionel snorted, perhaps despite himself. "We've far fewer people on the estate than we used to. But the second gamekeeper, before the War - whoever it was, there are reports from five over a couple of decades - reported it regularly. That cottage faces that way."

Cyrus nods. "That might be worth some further investigation. No cold spots, or unusually warm spots, or anything like that?"

"No, no. And nothing odd that turned up in the renovations, either."

Mabyn nodded. "Tell me about the renovations." Lionel opened his mouth, and she added quickly, "Not all the interior decorating details. We can do that some other time. Why you set about doing them, what your goals were, how your mother took it."

"I wanted to make it more, more flowing." Lionel gestured broadly, almost spilling his glass. "It was all very late Victorian. Mother's heyday, as a bride, when they were entertaining a good deal more. Father lost patience with it, even before the War."

"And that is when your mother moved to the dower house. Did she throw a snit, or was it planned?"

Lionel looked up sharply. "She was visibly disappointed in me and all my choices. That was, however, nothing particularly new."

Mabyn snorted. "She has a particular mode, doesn't she? Was she pressing you to marry?" She assumed that had been part of it. Lionel was visibly whole, a man of property and magic. He'd have been a good catch even before the War.

She noticed immediately that Lionel went still. Cyrus spoke, instead. "You know the sort, Mabyn, I'm sure." He then went on. "Your mother took oath on the Silence, Lionel, to take no magical or physical action against Nora, either of us, or anyone else aiding in mending the land magics. And to treat those on the estate with courtesy."

Lionel snorted, visibly surprising himself. "That will be interesting. She's particular with maids."

"Particular and awful or just very demanding?" Mabyn leaned forward.

"Very demanding, mostly. Once someone is trained to her specifications, I gather it's all right. Mostly. I make sure whoever that is is paid very well."

Nora ventured, "That only helps for so long, I suppose."

Lionel seemed to have forgotten she was still there. "I beg pardon, Cousin Nora. This is not a kind introduction to the family."

"It is an honest one. And that is probably more important, if I have to choose." Nora swallowed. "What does that mean, the oath? No one ever really explained when I was young."

Mabyn caught Cyrus's slight nod. "We've talked a bit about the Pact, the agreements made by Richard III in 1484. The Silence is how's enforced, put in place by the Fatae. Honestly, likely to make sure we kept our end of the bargain. It's twined around with your magic, as part of the core of who you are. Think of it like - oh, ivy on the walls here. If you make an oath on the Silence, you'll feel a brush of the consequences. If you begin to overstep that oath, you'll feel it press back."

"What does it feel like?" Nora cupped her hand around her cup.

"Your greatest fear." It was a simple phrase to say, but far more complex in reality. "People don't often talk about what that is. Or if they do, it's an intimate conversation. One might tell a beloved, or one's best friend."

She wasn't likely to tell anyone, ever. It was far too easy to use against her. "Most of the time, someone feels that discomfort. They know to stop, even if they might not know why. The oath you take at twelve, for example, you might be about to do magic around someone who doesn't know about it, without realising."

"And if you went ahead and did it anyway?" Nora was weighing this.

"Usually the fear gets to be so much you can't do anything but be terrified. If you stop, if you don't keep pressing, trying to do whatever it was or say whatever it was, it will ease off without damage." Mabyn paused. "People have died, but it's quite rare."

"And you have children make that oath." Nora's voice was sharp and fierce now. "Really?"

Cyrus cut in, and Mabyn didn't mind at all. "It was an

oath made in different times, when twelve was on the cusp of adult expectations. And it is self-maintaining, which is kinder, on the whole, than any other form. Less prone to manipulation by others, certainly."

Nora chewed on that. "I suppose." She was not at all convinced, of course, but Mabyn liked how she would listen and then think it through herself. "What was it you said before that? To make her come over when she interfered. Or, Mabyn, you said something different?"

"That was a Word of Command. There are different Words. They won't stay in your mind if you haven't had them gifted properly." He glanced at Mabyn. "And a Word of Silence, yes?"

Mabyn nodded. "I learned mine during my Council trial, which is relatively common. About one person in eight or ten." She didn't inquire about Cyrus, who showed no signs of wanting to comment on this point. "They do what they say. Word of Command is, admittedly, more flexible, since of course, one could command silence."

Nora grimaced. "More ways you can control someone else."

"It's a fair concern. The hope is that people whose magic is strong enough to do the things that might be the greatest problem will, well, be trained up not to do that. Or go into fields where they are bound by an oath that limits some of what they can do. The Guard, for example, make oaths keeping them from abuse of power. The magistrates can compel truth-telling in the right circumstance, but only if certain conditions are met. I have some things you could read, from various perspectives."

Nora nodded, and pushed her glasses up her nose. "I would like that, yes. And to talk about it after."

"That is the best sort of learning." Mabyn agreed. "And you have good reason to want to ask many questions."

"Do you mind if I go up to my rooms for a bit?" Nora was suddenly a bit withdrawn. "It was rather tiring, all told."

"Dealing with difficult relatives often is, and this was particularly so. I'll let Mrs Gotts know you might want to ring for some soup or a meal in your rooms. How's that?" Frankly, Mabyn wasn't entirely sure she was up to a formal meal in that dining room at the moment either.

Nora looked relieved. "Thank you." Then she stood. "Later."

Lionel stood - as did Cyrus. Both of them well-mannered, in the ways of gentlemen. But when Cyrus sat back down, Lionel remained standing. "I, perhaps I should do the same. I have a lot to think about."

Mabyn glanced at Cyrus. "How about we go up to one of our sitting rooms, and leave you the library? There's plenty of room, no need to crowd you out." When he looked just as relieved as Nora had, Cyrus nodded and stood again.

"My rooms or yours?" Clearly, they were going to have more to talk about.

Mabyn considered. "Mine, if you don't have a preference. Let me go see about a meal later as well. Meet you up there in five minutes?"

"I'll get a few things from my rooms."

CHAPTER 18
MABYN'S ROOMS

"I do beg your apology." Cyrus had, in fact, beaten Mabyn back to her rooms, and was waiting by the sitting-room door when she opened it, about eight minutes later.

Mabyn stepped back, gesturing him in, giving him no hint what she thought of that. "There will be a meal brought up around six. Soup and sandwiches, nothing heavy. Tea?"

He nodded and then claimed what had become his chair. She was not giving him much to work with here, but he really was apologetic. Once she had set the kettle going and taken her own chair while it boiled, he repeated. "I honestly am sorry. I was rather high-handed, earlier. In the garden."

Mabyn leaned forward, considering him. She didn't say anything, she barely moved. Instead, she was observing him like some new item of Materia. Or perhaps more the way Gemma would examine some new alchemical process. "It was your ritual, at heart. Not mine."

That was true, and that was fair, but it was also not how many others would have taken it. "Still."

She waved a hand at him, leaning back, amused. "What would you do if I were upset?" She seemed to be posing it as an entirely academic question. He had suspected for some time that she had got through her own challenge for the Council seat on something other than duelling skill. But it wasn't something one could ask about. Or did ask about.

Cyrus considered that, giving it due diligence. "That would depend a bit on what you were actually offended by. My acting, responding, without consulting. My reacting without leaving much space for your own action, rather shouldering you aside. My demand for a stool. The Word of Command. My leaving you to deal with Nora."

She inclined her head at each point. "You did not know how urgent the threat was, and it was your ritual. You were better placed to take action. You consulted once that was feasible. As to the stool, I recall you said please, quite politely, and it was a reasonable request. Nora is easy enough to deal with, thankfully, and not prone to hysterics."

"And the Word?" Cyrus wasn't sure to think of the fact she'd left that one out.

Mabyn shrugged. "We have neither of us laid out all the magics that come to our hands and our lips. Blaming you for caution would be hypocritical. I do try not to do that, it's so terribly boring, for one thing."

"And we can't be boring." Cyrus agreed. "All right. How do we go forward?"

Mabyn opened her mouth, then closed it, thinking through things. He was, frankly, surprised that she let him see that indecision. She had always seemed self-contained to him. It went beyond what he had said, when they had been feeling each other out on the first night here, about blending into the woodwork. It was, in point of fact, more like becoming a tree. Something there, and solid, but not at all demanding attention, much of the time. It made him want to come closer, too, though that wasn't something he'd permit himself unless she were clear it was welcome.

"Two things. The first, and likely the simpler, on some level, is that I think it would be good for Nora to meet others near enough her own age. I am not, however, sure how best to arrange that. Silvia is busy, and a bit old for the purpose. We want people in their mid-twenties to early thirties."

Cyrus leaned back, tapping his fingers against each other, his hands steepled. "What exactly are you thinking of, in terms of numbers?"

"I am thinking a modest number, but enough variety. I am interested in where she migrates, where she finds herself most at ease, given a bit of time. Isembard and Thesan might do well enough though Isembard's on the older side for what I had in mind. I have a little leverage with them to ask a favour, but they won't host during term. Sensibly. Perhaps later this summer. But that gives you a sense of the thing."

Cyrus nodded thoughtfully. "I could see if Gemma was up for a garden party. You know the sort of thing, twenty or thirty people, a mix of couples and otherwise. Decent food, a bit of alcohol, pleasant environs."

"She has her own work, surely?" Mabyn hesitated. "I would not wish to put her out." That was exceedingly interesting. Gemma was indeed busy. She was always busy, never bored.

"She's at the family estate. Near Exeter." He paused, weighing whether to ask her about more. "If she doesn't want to, I'm sure she'll tell me. Is there a reason you're worried about putting her out?"

"Silvia thinks well of her. And I think well of Silvia's opinions, on the whole."

Cyrus nodded. "I'll ask. If that isn't an option, she'll tell us quickly, and we can consider who else owes us a favour."

Mabyn snorted. "Since neither of us - apparently otherwise competent mature adults - is quite able to host such a thing?"

"I am a widower of some years. Quite a few years. No one expects me to host anything more complex than a supper at one of my clubs. I have a flat in Trellech, I have rooms at the estate, but I let Gemma make it her own years ago. She has use for the lab, and if I actually need the full workroom, it's easy enough to arrange."

"And men get away with not needing to host things. People assume I will, and do not think about what it means to host in a small flat. Or rather, a moderately sized flat, but two of the rooms are filled with books."

"I would find that quite excellent hosting, honestly. But I agree, other people do want food and amusements not found between the pages, in my experience."

Mabyn leaned back, considering him. Cyrus forced himself not to stiffen. Two could play at this game of easy conversation that hid a dozen other things. As they were, in fact, both doing. "May I ask a personal question?"

"You may ask, if you don't mind that I may choose not to answer."

She waved a hand, amused. "Shall we take it as read that either of us may refuse to answer something? Otherwise, we will be endlessly asking permission, I suspect, and that will get quite tedious."

It was a particular sort of offer, not of intimacy or trust, but of a key step in the working relationship. He'd found it with a handful of others in the Council, over the years, but not many. They were, as a group, wary of trust, of any show of weakness or imperfection. And of course, what one said and how one said it tended to reveal things.

After a pause for proper consideration, he nodded. "Agreed. Please, ask."

"Why did you challenge for a seat?" Of course, she wouldn't ask about the challenge itself. He'd never talked about all of it with anyone, though he'd compared a couple of elements with those he was most comfortable with. This question was not entirely unexpected. Before he could think about answering, she went on. "I ask because I am thinking about what draws us to a particular type of magic, or use for magic. The Schola staff have all sorts of theories and data, and I suspect they're on to something, but that doesn't help here." She considered, then added, "I'm also thinking about Nora's questions about power and its uses and abuses."

That put a focus on it. At that point, the kettle sang, and Cyrus waited for her to pour hot water into the pot and bring it back. "My wife, Tanith, died in childbirth with Gemma." It had been haemorrhage, everything changing far too fast. "It - I loved her with all my heart, and then she was gone."

"Not an arranged match, then." Mabyn's voice was dry. "Mine was."

"One of those where we were in love, and socially well suited. We were supposed to have a golden future together. Instead, there I was with Gemma and a wet nurse. Rhoe was a great steady pillar, of course." His parents had been rather less help. Tanith's parents had been shocked and then very distant, before arguing that he was a poor choice to raise his daughter and trying to take her away.

"And the Council seat?"

Cyrus shrugged. "I needed something to aim myself at. Hone myself for. There was a risk, but Gemma was so small. If I'd died, well. It would have made Tanith's parents happier."

Mabyn considered him, and she must have heard the fatalistic streak that had run through him down to the bone in those years. "My husband insisted I challenge for it. I've since become certain he felt he would win either way. Either I would succeed, and he would control a Council Member. Or I would die, and he would be free of his commitments."

That was far more than Cyrus had expected to hear. So far beyond that, it made him blink and come up short for words. Mabyn met his gaze easily when he looked up at her, before saying, "Cream or sugar?" and gesturing at the tea.

He was sure she was giving him a chance to gather his thoughts, but he replied to the immediate question. "One sugar and a splash of cream, please." Once she handed the cup over and settled back with her own, he nodded once. "That is not a story you share often, I gather."

"No." It could have been flat and final, but her tone left the topic open. "I always wonder, honestly, what people have heard. There was a fair bit of gossip that I'd killed him at the time."

Cyrus considered saying the first thing that came to mind, wondered if he should restrain himself, and then gave in to that sharp pull of temptation and intuition. "Personally, I think your late husband must have been a rather stupidly short-sighted man."

Mabyn blinked at him then grinned and lifted her teacup in a toast. "Do, please, go on?"

"The base logic is rather compelling. You were competent enough to earn a seat on the Council." He hesitated again, feeling his way through this. "He must have assumed he'd be able to control your decisions. Not understanding about the oaths and fortifications."

"Do you see them as fortifications? We really must discuss at some point. Quite, though. He thought I would continue to be under his direction. He was most unhappy when he pressed hard enough that the Silence exerted itself to protect me." There was a shadow in her eyes. Cyrus expected that while that moment had come at some significant personal cost, even if it had also brought a fair bit of delight in private.

After a moment, he realised what he wanted to say. "I am very glad that he is no longer an issue for you, whatever the cause. And that it has left you free to pursue your own interests at last." Then he went on, surprising himself a bit. "I was travelling for some of that time, but the gossip I heard was more about how he had little sense of how to handle power. His own or other people's." Cyrus was deeply curious now about the cause of death. He'd have to ask Rhoe if she'd heard anything.

Mabyn inclined her head. "Appreciated." Then she took a sip of her tea. "We should probably consider the functional fortifications here." She sounded slightly regretful.

It was a necessary task, and one that would mean several hours of focused work. Cyrus stretched. "We have food coming. And you're right. It must be done. Neither of us is inclined to shirk doing what needs to be done. I like that very much."

She grinned quickly at him before saying, "Would you like some paper? I suspect you may prefer to diagram. And I have a few copies of the layout of the place, as well."

CHAPTER 19
THE NEXT DAY

"Come along over here." Mabyn gestured at Nora. They were in the walled garden, beyond the formal gardens on the west side of the house. It was neglected, but still had a great deal of charm.

"There's a children's book - very popular with girls in my classes. About a secret garden. Though I suppose this isn't terribly secret."

"I suspect it was a bower, in former centuries. You could walk out along the path there, under those trees, and then come through that gate, see how it's hidden by the ivy? And come through onto these benches. That tree must have had a swing or something of the kind." Mabyn tilted her head. "What happens in the story?" She'd not had cause to explore the sort of stories young girls liked these days, not as a mother, nor as an aunt. And she was not permitted to give her grandchildren books, Davin was clearly suspicious of what attitudes she might share that way.

"A girl comes from India, an orphan, taken in by her uncle. It's rather gothic, honestly, a vast manor house with secrets and mysteries. She finds her cousin, who is an invalid. Another local boy with a gift for animals helps her. They restore the garden, and there's a happy ending." Nora glanced around, looking at the work that would be needed here. "I can't stop thinking, now, about those young men ten years later, and the War. They'd have been old enough to fight."

"That's the thing, isn't it, as a teacher? You teach them, and they go off. And the world asks too much of them." Mabyn tried to keep her voice calm and clear, but some note of something much darker crept in.

Nora glanced over. "You're not a teacher, are you? You haven't been? Other than something like this." She gestured. "Whatever this is."

"Apprenticeship is common, in Albion." To distinguish it from Great Britain, the far larger non-magical population. "I've had my share. My most recent, ah, she's a gem. She was a grown woman with a half-grown son when she came to me and asked for help, but she's been a joy. As you have, so far, mind you. If in a different way."

"What did you teach her?" Nora reached, her fingers almost brushing a plant.

"Oh, dear. Don't touch that, Nora, it wouldn't do you any favours. Though that's one of the things I came out here looking for." Mabyn lifted the small harvesting basket she was carrying and pulled out a pair of lined gloves. "That's Solomon's Seal. The root is used medicinally. The rest of it is lovely but could make you rather ill. The berries, for anyone, but many magical folk react to something in the sap."

"Oh." Nora backed up, folding her hands behind her back. "Some parts of Manchester, people have nice gardens. I've only ever - Auntie only ever - had window boxes. Not the same things. And an allotment garden for vegetables, of course."

"Not the same kind of garden, no. Though also excellent." Mabyn gestured. "I'm going to snip these, and put them in this special wrapper here. It's silk on one side, sewn to waxed cloth. That protects everything and you can bend the waxed cloth to keep the clippings from falling out or moving around."

"If it's so dangerous, why are we cutting some?" Nora leaned over the basket to peer at it. "And why are you teaching me?"

"My particular speciality is what we call Materia - the magical nature of physical things. That might be plants or trees or stones or metal. Any number of the modern chemical elements, though we're still figuring out what that means, magically, some of them. Every Materia expert I know has been dubious about radium, for example, for all it was used as a health tonic by many people. They're starting to learn just how wrong that was."

Nora nodded sharply. "I remember the news stories about that from America." She shivered, delicately, and Mabyn decided to move on. Nora was a sensible woman, clearly able to extrapolate safety considerations. There was no need to terrify her, like she might have needed to with fearless young men who were sure they'd live forever.

"This isn't so dangerous a touch would be deadly. But it might be unpleasant, and it's best to have good habits about that sort of thing. Silvia - my most recent apprentice - is a specialist in Alchemy. She came up with a new method for encapsulating the plant, so that we can use the magical tendencies without handling it. It's rather novel, as a technique, and few people know it."

Nora nodded. "Are there other plants?"

Mabyn nodded. "The other one I wanted is stock - see those brightly coloured flowers there? They're safe to handle. Purple, blue, yellow, or orange would work best for what I have in mind, whichever most takes your fancy." Mabyn wanted, more than anything else, to give Nora choices in this. Not simply the salve, but all it implied.

"You have something specific for us to do?" Nora turned, rather like one of the flowers would turn towards the sunlight.

"I do. I want to create an oil - a magical oil - that will hold the potential for a bit of protection, and a great deal of joy and blessing. For you, as you figure out your role here. We'll be combining these with other things in the laboratory equipment that I brought. It's often best to have one or two items from a place, when you're working somewhere specific."

Nora looked up sharply. "Is that all there is to it? Mixing some things together?"

"Oh, goodness, no. It's an art, a science, a craft. We'll only be touching on the basics today." Mabyn gestured. "Which of the stocks do you like?"

While Nora was brushing her fingers through flowers, looking for the most beautiful one, she asked another question. "You seem to know a lot about teaching."

"I've been working with the professors at Schola on curriculum changes and changes to the examinations to get in. I'm no teacher, but I've been listening to people there, and at the other of the Five Schools."

"There are only five? Or are there more but only five are posh?" Nora lingered by a golden yellow one. "Could we do one gold and one blue?"

Mabyn had been noticing that fondness for blue. "We could. And there are five schools for Albion - England,

Wales, and Scotland. Most people apprentice. There's a whole network of village schools, and then tutoring houses for children who will go off to the Five Schools when they're a little older. The people who apprentice continue learning their reading and writing and geography and history and what have you, from their apprentice master or mistress. Or sometimes a travelling tutor will come one day a week. It's worked well enough for a long time, but that doesn't mean it's the best thing going forward."

Nora frowned. "And that's true for both men and women?"

"Oh, yes. None of those schools where for five years or more, boys never see a woman. Or never see one who isn't the wife of a teacher or the vicar or the woman who runs the tea shoppe in the village, at any rate." Mabyn considered that. "Albion is kinder to women than Great Britain, on the whole. We've had equal rights all along, though with the various limits by class. A woman with strong magic, if it's not trained properly, is dangerous to everyone around her, you see. So is a man, mind you."

Nora contemplated that. "So there's some enlightened self-interest at work then. And not bias?"

"Oh, there's plenty of bias, still. And there are some kinds of magical work that aren't safe during pregnancy, and taking the portals often is not advised, and so on. But there are options for managing much of that." Mabyn clipped the flowers that Nora had selected. "Come along, let's go back to the stillroom and see what we can do with these."

Nora was quiet as they walked back through the kitchen garden, and then across the small drawbridge, then along to the stillroom on the ground floor. "Here we are. I laid everything else out already. It's safe to touch, and the containers have labels. You explore that while I set up what we're doing with Solomon's Seal."

Most of what they needed for this salve was simple, a selection of dried herbs and infused oils, some beeswax, and some additional oil to soften everything. The Solomon's Seal, however, needed a proper alchemical kit, and she'd set that up on the stone surface to the side. Safer that way, and easier to fully cleanse after. She took a minute to check that everything was still as it ought to be.

"Do you want to watch? This is actually fairly quick. We're looking for a magical reaction, not calcination or distillation."

"Of course. Where should I stand?" Nora came over to Mabyn's side.

"If you're here, you should have a good view. I am going to take our sample, place it in this glass bottle, cork it with this cork that is attached to this glass tube, and then attach that up. I'll be adding this liquid here to the vial, and then drops of this one here. The reaction, what's the right word for it. Catalyst."

Nora leaned forward as Mabyn explained, following the rather convoluted tubing. "And that gives us something we can use?"

"Once it is filtered, yes. We don't need much for what we'll be making." Mabyn checked one more time, then set everything going. She opened the valve that permitted the preservation liquid to fill the sample vial. It gave off little pops of blue and purple sparks as the liquid made contact, then settled down to a slightly effervescent agitation.

Once the vial was completely filled, Mabyn closed the initial valve. Once she was sure it was clear, she added a measured amount to a second tube, waiting for it to settle before she opened that valve. As the two finally mixed, the liquid in the vial turned a vivid indigo blue. Beside her, Nora gasped. Mabyn laughed. "That's magic for you. Very striking, isn't it? Now we let it sit for twenty minutes, here's the clock."

Guiding Nora back to the main table, Mabyn worked through preparing the other materials. Nora was an comfortable companion for it. She was glad to help, within her ability. Most usefully, she didn't complain when asked to grind the lavender to a finer powder, or to break down an acorn. That one, Mabyn gave a bit of help with, using a charm that would begin to shatter it into pieces to get her going.

"We won't use much of that. We don't want things gritty, but it's from the tree you like, the one that Cyrus started you with."

"That's a grand tree. So old, and so tall and sturdy. I can see why people go on about oaks now. I don't think I ever paid proper attention before."

Mabyn heard a note in her voice, that dance of curiosity. "That's your work for the year. Learning about trees. And streams and gardens and roses and apple trees and elder-flowers. And whatever wildlife we can find."

Nora worked with the pestle a bit in silence. "It feels wasteful. Focusing all this time and attention on me. Even this. I know there must be people who do this kind of work all day, and here I am, dabbling in it."

"You were not made to be a dabbler, I expect. If you were twelve, and about to go to one of the Five Schools, you'd have a clear sense of what people would ask you to learn. You'd know your family who'd gone there, or they'd know people who had. As it is, you have the entire range of magical learning spread out in front of you, too many choices, and no idea what you're choosing between."

"It's like a fantastical banquet in a storybook, where I don't even know the names for the foods, never mind what they taste like. And yet, knowing there are consequences to the choice, beyond the moment." Nora nodded, as Mabyn took the last of the grinding from her, and then dumped a spoonful into the bowl. "Here we go. Now we mix this with the oil in this bowl. Do you want an oil or a salve?"

"Can we do both?" Mabyn grinned, inside her head, at least. That curiosity, that desire to learn, that would do very well. Even more importantly, she had evidence now for her theory that Nora would do best getting her hands a bit dirty.

"Both it is. Oil first, then I'll show you how to make a salve."

CHAPTER 20
THE SMYTHE-CLIVE FAMILY HOME,
SUNDAY, APRIL 18TH

Cyrus had found a spot on one side of the terrace. The height made it easy to see the people spread out on the lawn, and the various tables that were laid with treats and bountiful bouquets of spring flowers. He had to admit that the gardens looked lovely. Gemma had done a tremendous job tending to them, in and around everything else she was involved with.

The invitation list had been varied, too. It was a mix of people around Nora's age or a few years older. He and Mabyn had come to the conclusion that she'd likely do better with people who were a few years older. People who were fully settled into adult lives, rather than those finishing apprenticeships and still finding their feet.

Lionel was escorting her, of course. Quite proper, as her cousin, introducing her to magical society. He was doing it well, not hovering too much. Cyrus had caught him earlier, explaining to Nora what the different food items were. Someone - Cyrus expected Mabyn, honestly - would need to walk Nora through all the etiquette for less trustworthy circumstances. It was part of why they'd started with Gemma hosting. It was far easier to control the situation.

He felt, more than saw, someone come up near enough behind him. A moment later, Gemma leaned down to kiss his cheek. "You're all alone, dear papa." Emphasis on the second syllable, drawing it out. She looked especially lovely today, with her hair pinned up in a set of curls and puffs, and a green dress that was all about the blossoming spring-time. More than that, she looked entirely confident as a hostess.

Cyrus snorted. "Whenever you sound like a Victorian children's book, I know I'm in trouble. What do you want now?"

Gemma laughed and settled into the chair in a swirl of pale green silk skirt. "Your thoughts on how it's going." She held up a hand. "I do like Nora. She's charming."

"I am glad you think so. I admit, there's something to her attitude that is both seasonal and refreshing. She asks excellent questions, too."

"You always do like the people with questions. I've noticed." Gemma leaned back, taking it in. "If I do say so myself, it's a rather well-run party."

Cyrus waved a hand. "I was thinking the gardens look lovely. Don't think I haven't noticed the poison garden flourishing." They were a recent addition, put in last fall and this spring.

"You know perfectly well it's a viable method of protec-tive warding. Besides, so many of them really are beautiful. And I laid things out so that if there are children here, sometime, it will be easy to manage." She then raised a finger. "Don't you start, papa."

"I would not say a thing." Largely because he had learned that doing so was entirely futile. Gemma had been known to point out that if marriage was a virtue beyond all others, he should have remarried long since. Since he had shown no desire for married bliss, again, she saw no reason she should interrupt her work for the demands of a hypothetical husband.

And Gemma's work was, in fact, both brilliant and much needed. She had a deft hand figuring out antidotes to poisons and what the non-magical referred to as chemical damage, as well as her other line in complex alchemical potion design for specific purposes. Cyrus was sure his theory was not up to understanding a good third of what she was working on these days. He'd have to remember to ask her for a supplemental reading list and endure the teasing that went with the request.

Most of the people here were, in fact, coupled up, which might have felt awkward to others. Gemma, however, seemed to sail through it. She occasionally borrowed one or another gentleman as an escort, but mostly she avoided the sort of parties where that was obligatory. Barring Council events, of course, which she attended on his arm for the formalities. On the other hand, it meant she'd been able to put together a gathering that mixed people from varying circles.

"Good." Gemma looked out across the lawn. "Nora will get along brilliantly with Isembard and Thesan when they're free. I can host a dinner."

Cyrus raised an eyebrow. He agreed, but he was amused that Gemma would extend herself that far, on short acquaintance. "And why do you want to do that?"

"All the glorious debate about educational theory? How much has Council Member Teague talked about that?" Gemma was in a fine mood, then. He'd been a little worried about her, recently, that she was getting too lost in her work. Not that he could throw stones from glass houses about that.

A new voice behind Cyrus caught them both off-guard. "Under the circumstances, do call me Mabyn." Mabyn was dressed in a dark blue that suited her, mature without being severe. Cyrus was saved from that particular sort of challenge of figuring out how to impress through clothing. He had suits that fit well, and normally a man to see to them at home.

Gemma beamed. "Mabyn." She leaned forward, all glee. Cyrus was sure she was up to something now. Likely several somethings, she was his daughter. And Tanith's, which did not help one bit. "I was just saying I will be hosting a party sometime this summer with Isembard and Thesan. For Nora, of course."

"If you can talk them into it, I think that would be a fine thing. Or you might convince them to host, even."

Gemma nodded. "We'll see how persuasive I can be. I can't threaten to tell Thesan his childhood secrets, worse luck. He's already told her all the ones I've tried."

Cyrus burst out laughing. "Serves you right, imp." He gestured out at the lawn. "What do you think about things so far?"

"I wasn't entirely sure about the Edgartons. They both work rather relentless hours, and they keep their social circle rather bohemian." Gemma nodded at the small knot of people that currently included the Edgartons, Nora, Lionel, and several others.

Magister Edgarton was his father's Heir, to lands in Kent, and worked as a Penelope, investigating various criminal and magical matters. However, he wasn't someone Cyrus had worked with much directly. His wife stood out like a jewel. She was wearing a vibrant emerald green sari that complemented her brown skin and black hair, a contrast to her husband's dark blond hair and brown suit.

"There was a bit of scandal at that, wasn't there?" Mabyn considered. "I was busy with something at the time, I can't remember what. Thesan found her very helpful for our current project, however. About some of the preparation people get when they're plucked out of the non-magical community and put into one of our schools. I gather Magistra Edgarton was a year ahead of her in school, and often up in the Astronomy rooms."

"Surprise, more than anything. Scandal requires being known, don't you think?" It was a curious way to put things, but Gemma had a point there. "She's known to be quite fierce about philanthropy now, as well as her professional work. Both of them are. But no, I invited them because Gabriel Edgarton's known to have quite a strong connection to the land. His father's not terribly old yet, not like dear papa here."

"He's eight years younger! That's not a vast difference, you." Cyrus protested, knowing it would do very little good. Gemma had the bit between her teeth now.

"Anyway, his father's in fine fettle, but Magister Edgarton, there, all cheerful and chipper, didn't fight in the War. Came of age that March, had a bad injury of some kind, didn't recover in time. So whatever the War did to people, it didn't affect him the same way."

Mabyn leaned forward. "And how did you find that out?"

"Papa checked the records for me. And there were several pieces around their wedding, too, of course. People tried to dig up scandal, whether he should have been showered in white feathers for cowardice. I gather he doesn't have many close friends, at least not in these circles. But he has rather a lot of people who don't want to be his enemy?"

Cyrus considered the young man thoughtfully. "Fitz-Alan raised the idea of the younger Edgarton challenging for a seat," he said to Mabyn. "I gather the response was that it would become obvious why he wasn't in a few months. During which time they became very public about their betrothal."

Mabyn pursed her lips. "And there are some people who'd make things terribly difficult. Sensible of him, but I suspect that's our loss." She looked out over the groupings. "Who else, then?"

"The usual set. The Fortescues, there. The Appellines." Those were a man and woman who were both preternaturally blonde, but in very different styles. They must be cousins of some sort. Gemma added, "They've an interest in bees. Papa mentioned you might need someone who could consult, but they're quite picky about where their bees go."

"And you expected Nora to impress?" Mabyn sounded curious.

Gemma grinned. "They can be enticed by novelty. And Nora is certainly pleasantly novel at the moment. We're taking advantage of that while we can. And a selection of men, near enough her age. That's Darius Gallagher and his sister Antonia. Their father's a solicitor, working mostly with the Ministry offices." Which was an interesting threading of the social needle. Nora was legally speaking illegitimate. Which would not matter one bit in terms of inheritance if the land accepted her as Lady.

It did, however, mean the better families would likely not permit a son to marry in. Both because of her birth, and because marrying in ceded all sorts of rights to the other family. One did it in times of extremis, but the Gold Book families did not approve. Finding a potential suitor from the professional class would likely be both easier for Nora and socially simpler.

"What does he do?" Mabyn gestured at Darius.

"Just finishing an apprenticeship in his father's chambers. A different speciality, I believe, but he has a head for precedent and a deep respect for the details of history. His sister's delightful, she's a bit older. I met her while I was doing the research to improve the gardens here. She's a Flora specialist, mostly based in Trellech. Some work with the Temple of Healing." Which suggested her competence in the field.

Cyrus shook his head. "And what are our next steps, then? Since you have so many possible ideas laid out here to choose from?"

"Well, that depends on how well you do your part, Papa."

"You see what I put up with." Cyrus wasn't entirely sure what Mabyn made of this. Gemma was being notably informal, in a way she usually wasn't with his colleagues.

Mabyn snorted, decidedly amused. "It was not what I expected of the day. But seeing the way you're fond, that's something I needed." She gestured. "Lionel and his mother are - well. About what you'd expect. He's still mortified, she's still being awful. Taken to her bed, as well, though I'm honestly not at all sure how much of that is real and how much is show."

Cyrus nodded. "And it isn't as if we can ask, we must leave that up to Lionel and his filial duties." He shook his head. "I am sure there are things below the surface we're not seeing. Yet."

"Well, if you judge people by the company they keep, I

was already inclined not to like Lady Baddock." Gemma sounded utterly certain.

"I didn't know you'd spent much time talking to her. When?"

"Oh, Papa. I heard about Lady Jenifry. Auntie Rhoe mentioned that liner trip. We had lunch last week, and I was trying to figure out who else was in that part of the world. My second year at the tutoring house, I was quite put out I couldn't go with you."

Cyrus murmured to Mabyn, "That jewel." She nodded, though a bit vaguely. It had been a while, and her specialities did not touch entirely on that particular problem. "On the whole, I was quite glad you weren't with us. And it would have limited Rhoe, I suspect."

"And since Uncle Hugh still brings me all the best books..." Gemma let her voice trail off, laughing cheerfully. Then she brushed her hands together. "I should circulate again. Papa, you are staying after everyone else goes home?" It was not a question, more a command performance.

Cyrus waved a hand. "Estate business?"

Gemma nodded. "If you don't mind. I've already given up doing anything useful in the laboratory today."

"We can't be interfering with your work. You don't mind, Mabyn? If you'd rather wait, we can find you a library to sit in."

"Oh, no, I'll go back with Nora and Lionel. I believe you can be trusted to take a portal by yourself."

Gemma chortled and then bent to kiss Cyrus on the cheek. "Later, Papa." She went cheerfully off, taking unfashionably long steps, and waving to attract someone's attention.

CHAPTER 21
THE GARDEN PARTY

Mabyn watched Gemma go. She wished a number of things had been different about her life, really. Most things about her marriage. Most things about her current relationship with her son. If one could call their distant civility a relationship. Mabyn had a closer relationship with the distant cousin she met once a year for tea, scones, and discussion of the current birding season.

Seeing Cyrus with Gemma just brought all those failings back in a rush. In her more rational moments, Mabyn knew it wasn't anything like entirely her fault. But she was the one alive, she was the parent; she was supposed to know what she was doing.

It made her wonder, though, what he was like with colleagues when he relaxed. She suspected, now, that was mostly Alexander. They had an ease with each other that had this flavour. Knowing what the other could be trusted with. She'd had her own occasional moment with him, fleetingly. It made her want to see more of it, to see if she could figure out what let him open that door to someone else.

The silence dragged on uncomfortably long until Mabyn forced herself to stop ruminating on things that couldn't be changed. "Gemma's here by herself?"

Cyrus glanced over at the house, which was a pleasant manor house, likely Georgian. It was substantial, though perhaps only half the size of Baddock Hall. The front, where the portal lay in a grove of middle-aged horse chestnut trees, had a pleasant drive lined in oaks. These gardens were expansive, with a swooping terrace that cupped the central lawn area. He then nodded. "Largely. The staff, of course, and I have an elderly aunt who lives here half the year. She's out for the day, I believe."

"And your parents are in Trellech?" Mabyn was trying to figure out how this fit together.

"They have a flat. I have a flat. Rhoe keeps a room in my flat there, though these days she usually makes it back home at night. She and Hugh have a home near Romsey, close to Southampton. She doesn't mind the portal trip, and it means he can get the portal or the train, whichever makes more sense. And I have rooms here, of course, though obviously I'm not using them at the moment."

"Do you miss seeing Gemma regularly?"

Cyrus blinked at her, and then he began to laugh, whole-heartedly, his eyes crinkling up. It could have felt isolating, like he was laughing at her, but it didn't somehow. He let himself laugh, easily. She envied that, too. When the laughter subsided, she tilted her head, waiting for an answer.

"In the average week, when we're both here, I might see her two or three times, at least one of them for a bare few minutes in the breakfast room. We keep rather different schedules, and we're both horrifically busy." Then he sobered a little and gestured toward where Gemma stood. "She gave me quite a telling off, oh, a decade ago, about how I was hovering."

"And yet you're very fond." Mabyn tried to keep her voice neutral.

"Exceedingly. My sister is wonderful. But for most of Gemma's life, she had an even worse schedule. It was just the two of us in a wing of this house, my parents often elsewhere. And a nanny, of course." Cyrus looked off across the lawn. "I worry about whether she's happy enough. She tells me I'm fussing too much." He added, his tone amused. "Mind, we do our best to have lunch together once a week, whenever possible. Now Nora's settling in, I'll see about picking that up again."

"We can certainly spare you for a lunch. And we'll both need to be at the next Council meeting. I have my suspicions there will be another seat empty before too long."

Cyrus tilted his head. "What do you know that I don't?"

"Many things." Mabyn grinned at him, broadly. She enjoyed the way he asked, too, giving her space to decide how to answer.

Cyrus snorted at her after his initial bemusement faded. "Granted, granted. In this particular case, however?"

"Silvia mentioned something about a couple of people noticeably preparing. You know the signs."

"Additional duelling training, with certain instructors. Orders for potions and alchemical supplies beyond their usual. The sort of robes that look impressive and are much less use than they think." Cyrus nodded.

"Introductions to Imbert and Sons being hard to come by on short notice." Mabyn gestured at his own robes, which came from there.

Cyrus shrugged. "They do good work, and I've found myself going from a leisurely afternoon to some minor crisis often enough to appreciate not needing to change. You must have it a bit harder?"

"Women can get away with wearing more jewellery. And the sort of enchantments that make pocketwatches grumpy." Mabyn waved a hand. "At any rate, I've a guess or two about which seat."

Cyrus glanced off across the lawn, then he said, "Are you telling me as a step in a closer alliance, or something else?"

He didn't look back, just paid attention to Mabyn with a wide soft focus, out of the side of his gaze. She let her hands fall into her lap. "Oh, do look at me, we can admit we're having this conversation."

He swivelled in his chair to better focus on her. "The point remains."

Mabyn shrugged one shoulder, making sure she remained relaxed, and letting her hand fall open as if she were holding a ball. Making a container for the conversation, a trick Silvia had taught her. "I find myself intrigued."

"Any particular reason why, at this moment?"

Mabyn considered. "Ask me again when we're in private tonight. Your rooms, this time?" She honestly preferred his warding and protections. Hers worked well, she didn't permit carelessness in that sort of thing. But his were more like trees, well-rooted, but with an ability to flex and change that she found both compelling and useful. A bit like Nora was coming to be, now she thought about it that way.

"Fair enough." It was the sort of reply that she'd come to expect from him, for all it shocked her every time. He didn't barge into her thoughts like men so often did. He let it be, patiently assuming he'd hear when she decided to tell him. And it was not the place for it. Sooner or later, someone would want to talk to one or the other of them again. Even if the younger generations seemed entirely occupied. A few people had got up a demonstration of some of the bohort puzzles. Someone had a croquet set out, with some charmed hoops that added additional challenges.

Mabyn kept looking out toward them, watching Gemma. Granted, Gemma was intriguing to watch. "Is she much like her mother?"

Mabyn could see him stiffen, the way his shoulders tightened, bracing against the memory. She should not have surprised him with it, for all it was absolutely a logical and timely question. Gemma seemed to be everywhere, a flow of grace and attention and curiosity. "Yes and no. I suppose that's true of most children." He hesitated. "She looked very like Tanith in her twenties. And of course, neither of us got to see what Tanith would have looked like in her thirties. It's a nose to grow into, and cheekbones, Tanith said."

Mabyn snorted, but nodded. "It must be a challenge to see her grow past that age. She has a confidence I find rather compelling, honestly. It was that more than the physical features I was thinking about."

"Tanith was fearless. Sharp and perceptive. Far more active in the pursuit of knowledge than I was, at that point." Cyrus spread out his hands, looking thoughtful, perhaps wistful.

"I have not thought you to be slow to act." Mabyn was thoughtful now.

"I changed." It came out flat and sharp, and Cyrus immediately winced, holding up his hand. "I beg pardon, that's not your fault. But I needed to set a more well-rounded example for Gemma, as much as I could. Give her all the things her mother would have wanted, as well as those things that were mine to begin with."

Mabyn nodded slowly. She thought about what it would have been to have a father like Cyrus was. Or at least appeared to be. "I know enough of her alchemical work to be impressed, though I gather much of it is still in the developmental stages. Was that your wife's interest, alchemy?"

Cyrus nodded. "Flora, but with an eye to alchemical applications. Both practical and theoretical - she'd been focusing on the Flora while she was expecting, of course." Experimental alchemy had a number of possible risks. "I've long thought that experimental alchemy takes a quick mind. I know the basics to a reasonable level - Master Norton considered me competent, but not inspired. But I was never half as good as Tanith was, or as Gemma is."

Mabyn nodded. She was about to ask him more about that, but at that point they both noticed the figure crossing the lawn, to the steps near their seats on the terrace.

Nora came over. "Pardon, I just needed a bit of a pause." She looked embarrassed.

Cyrus gestured at the chair Gemma had used. "Please, sit down. Do you need someone to fetch a drink?"

Nora shook her head. "Just, the conversation got complicated. Someone asked about my mother. They ... they meant well. I think? I'm honestly not sure, now I've said that."

"Who was it?" Mabyn kept her voice casual, but she wanted to know if someone had been difficult. Cyrus straightened a bit, suddenly fully focused.

"The Fortescues? It was a pleasant enough conversation, I thought. And I gather they knew the basic circumstances. But I explained my mother had given me over to her sister to raise, and I considered Aunt Poppy my mother in all the ways that mattered." Nora frowned. "I suspect my mother being on the stage didn't help."

Mabyn glanced over at Cyrus and waved a hand at him. He considered how to phrase this. "The stage connection is - well, people look down on performers in magical circles, much as they do in non-magical ones. Or at least some people do. Others can't get enough of them, of course."

Nora nods. "So they were being rude?"

"Rude and a tad demanding." Mabyn spoke before Cyrus could. "Do you know why Gemma asked the Fortescues?"

Cyrus contemplated that. "They're about the right age, and they have connections to other social circles. I'm afraid that's not my usual network, though. We could ask Gemma later. Have other people been—" He stopped, and began again. "I hope other people have been kinder?"

"Oh, several of them, yes." Nora smiled. "Antonia and Darius made me laugh, and they asked very interesting questions about living in Manchester. I enjoyed talking to them. I feel like I was missing half the conversation with the Edgartons, but not in a way that I minded? Just that they're so used to talking to people who pick up some of their references?"

"I don't know them very well, but I gather they're both highly respected in their fields. And unlike some people, I believe they can be nudged into explanations."

Nora nodded. "The Appellines were - they do like bees an awful lot, don't they?" She glanced back across the lawn. "I suppose it's good people do. They were telling me more about the bee lore. I know about telling them about a death, of course, but there are apparently quite a lot of other things."

"I'm glad. Gemma was thinking getting their interest might be a help. They approve of our hives here, and she's very proud of that. And those were the Mallorns you were talking to? Sister and brother and cousin?"

"Yes." Nora sounded a little more hesitant. "I'm not as sure what I thought about them. It felt like they were testing me, and I wasn't doing terribly well? Like being quizzed on a chapter no one had told me to read."

Mabyn grimaced. "That is an uncomfortable feeling. Here, how about I come out and circulate with you a bit? If you've not talked to Alice Langford, you might like her company. You don't mind, Cyrus?"

"Not at all. I might even sneak off to grab a few things from the library here. Nora, do write up your questions when you get home, and your impressions, and we'll talk about them tomorrow."

CHAPTER 22
BADDOCK HALL, LATE THAT EVENING

They were not back at Baddock Hall until rather later in the evening than Cyrus had expected. Gemma had given a tour of the gardens after everyone else had left. Nora had taken quite a lot of interest, in the historical plantings, especially, and the idea of a working garden. It had thrilled Gemma to explain the layout of the materials she used for some of her alchemical work, even though other parts came from specialists. Mabyn and Nora had ended up exploring the long gallery and the family portraits while Gemma and Cyrus saw to the necessary estate paperwork.

Now they had come from the portal back across the drawbridge and split up to their various rooms. Mabyn had murmured that she would be along once she'd changed into something more comfortable. Cyrus, after a moment's consideration, went to change into a smoking jacket before returning to his sitting room and pouring out some brandy. By the time Mabyn knocked, the room was comfortably lit, the wards were ready, and he felt sufficiently hospitable.

"Come in." Once she had her chair, he raised an eyebrow. "Food to go with the drink?"

"Goodness, no. I am very well fed. I got the impression your cook there was glad of the chance to extend herself. A garden party is rather tricky to cater for in some ways. So dependent on the weather."

"We were quite lucky there, weren't we? No sign of a shower, no bother with insects. And I think it was very informative, in terms of the social patterns." Since they wouldn't need to wait for food, Cyrus called the warding into action with a twist of one hand. He let the shimmer of light cascade from that central point in the ceiling and fade away.

Mabyn nodded. "Quite. I assume you'll be sending something along to Gemma? I'll have a note to go with it."

"Of course. Normally we use the journals, but I had a few clippings to send along to her, from some of our research, or copies, at any rate. Whenever you like, no rush on my end."

Mabyn hesitated, then said, "I suppose that brings us to the more private conversation. Though I had something before that. Related."

"Related?" Cyrus honestly felt he had no idea where this was going. Discussing an alliance was one thing, but what else?

"It was seeing you with Gemma." Mabyn made that little gesture with her hand, as if she were cupping something. "Seeing you together. I'm a tad envious, actually."

Cyrus was not sure what to do with that. Faced with this particular challenge, he could do one of two things. He could force his thoughts along the lines of reason and logic, going along cautiously. Or he could trust that thread through the labyrinth would guide him. He flung himself into trust, hoping he was right. "Exactly how irritated are you at Lady Baddock?"

Mabyn's bark of a laugh told him he'd chosen well. "Very. And with myself. And not just for the obvious reasons. Lionel's quiet and reserved, but he's a reasonable young man. He has a care for his responsibilities, and he's doing his best. There's a great deal to respect in that." She had retreated to the more distant question of Lionel, rather than the more personal one she'd just brushed past.

"And his mother..." Cyrus wanted to see what she'd say now.

"And his mother has no respect for him." Mabyn pursed her lips. "She got her son back, sufficiently in one piece. But none of her reactions make sense. She pushes him away, discourages his interest in the house and lands. I also am deeply curious about why she moved into the dower house when she did. Still. Was she pressing him to marry? She must have been."

Cyrus hesitated, "In confidence, he made it clear to me that he would never marry. A matter of inclination, before the War, and now, well. He said he cannot bear someone else close, whatever else he might have wanted at one time."

Mabyn considered that. Cyrus waited for her to sort through the implications, he was sure she would. They all knew the codes and hidden references.

"Does she know, do you think, or only suspect?" Mabyn waved a hand. "Or how long?"

"It wasn't something I could ask him directly, all things as they are." Cyrus shrugged. "If I had to lay a bet, it would be on some mess when she first pressed him to marry. If I were feeling generous - or thought she were - I'd think she moved to give him room to find what pleasure he could.

Hire a steward or secretary or some such, as a cover for whoever he preferred. I know more than one family where that permitted the sort of marriage for mutual benefit that saw to the next generation and the land."

"But we do not grant that she has that kind of generous heart." Mabyn agreed. "And the house?"

"Lionel was exerting himself, in a way she did not approve of." Cyrus had a deep familiarity with that, and he chose to let enough of that show in his voice. "And he's got - well, he has some shame about his inclinations, and that came from somewhere. I made it clear I didn't think less of him."

Mabyn caught that first part, as he had known she would. "How often do you see your parents?"

"Once a month, on average, in Trellech. I don't dislike them, but we have remarkably little in common. It's tiring. It's more complicated than that for Lionel, I suspect."

"I got the impression that your parents ran to benign neglect rather than actively undermining, yes." Mabyn shrugged. "The question is what we do about it. Besides the oath." She was definitely dodging around another topic, but Cyrus would not push. Yet. This direction deserved to be explored as well.

"The oath was, as such things go, fairly broad. While not limiting a wide range of perfectly reasonable actions. And yet, I'm worried too. That small nagging voice over one's shoulder that suggests something has been missed."

"The finely honed voice, quite." Mabyn hesitated. "Do we discuss Lady Jenifry first? Or an alliance?"

Cyrus grunted. "Lady Jenifry was on that ocean liner trip to Boston. You remember the report, about a rather bodged together ritual to pacify the One Below. On the one hand, it threw my sister and her now husband together in a mutually delightful way. On the other hand, we had to redesign half a dozen Council plans when I got home and it meant..." He paused, counting off on his fingers. "Fourteen additional trips and diplomatic negotiations over the next few years."

"And Lady Jenifry?"

"She set her cap at me, and when I did not oblige - and Hugh did not oblige - she told tales about how she'd had time with me in private." He shrugged. "It wasn't the sort of thing that did damage to me."

"Anyone who actually knows you knows you've been celibate since your wife died. Virtuous." Mabyn shrugged. "We do chat, from time to time. I've had a couple of people ask me if your preferences were true, if they had any chance."

Cyrus shrugged. "Tanith was beautiful. Whirling. Engaging, more than classic beauty, incredibly alive." Until she wasn't. "I always felt I'd stumbled into some extraordinary gift I couldn't possibly have earned."

"Gifts aren't earned. Or owed. That's why they're gifts." Mabyn's voice was quiet now, but there was weight in her words. Cyrus looked up and then lifted his glass in a mute toast. "What did you do about the gossip?"

"Resolutely refused to be seen with a woman on my arm besides my sister for the next decade? Thankfully, Rhoe was able to help with the Council dances. A bit grudgingly, but she helped."

"I was an only child." Mabyn spoke slowly. "And my parents arranged my marriage."

Cyrus was instantly alert. There was a note in her voice. It was one he'd heard before, from time to time, of someone talking about a thing they'd rarely discussed. He didn't jostle her, didn't press. He just nodded. "It was not a kind one, I gather."

Mabyn shook her head. "Demanding. Full of expectations I never could meet. Bar producing a son as a first child, he couldn't find much complaint with that. But..." She shrugged. "Seeing you with Gemma, it brought back to me how far I failed Davin. My son."

Cyrus felt there was nothing useful he could say here. For one thing, he'd never seen them together. Which, now he thought about it, was telling. One might normally expect a son to escort his widowed mother on some occasions. Mabyn had always paired up with one of the male Council members for the required dancing that opened their Solstice ball. On the other hand, his relationship with Gemma was very good, not least because he'd done his best to make it so.

Not that she hadn't pitched a screaming fit with him toward the end of her apprenticeship. It was that fight which had driven his parents to their flat in Trellech for good. Gemma had been right. Cyrus had known it almost as soon as she began. He had been far too protective, and he'd let his fears begin to fence her in. That was not kindness, it was not love, and he had done everything he could to avoid doing it again.

That memory, however, gave him somewhere to go forward. "Tell me about him, if you would?"

Mabyn glanced up. She was certain he was up to something. He was, so that was fair. She took her time in answering, clucking her tongue once and taking a sip of brandy before she spoke. "He believes in doing things properly, like his father. And he's done well by the land magic, from what I can tell." She flicked her fingers. "At a distance."

"You've not been back there, then?"

"No." It was flat and sharp. "Not since he was in his third year at school. His uncle - his father's brother, of course - has lived there with him. They get on well. There's another brother, with his cousins."

Cyrus was not sure where to begin with what was implied in those few spare sentences. As the silence continued, Mabyn watched him. "You must think I am a horrible mother. Parent."

It would have been easy, politic, to protest and deny it. She deserved better. "Is your son happy?"

Whatever she expected, it was not that question. "What?" Mabyn set her glass down, and Cyrus heard more than saw the clank as it settled unevenly on the side table.

"I know the land magics are well tended. I do not know awful gossip of truly distasteful habits, and I hear a fair bit of that sort of thing. There's no apparent scandal. Something about a marriage, before the War?" Which raised the interesting question of what he did during the War.

"He is married. I was there, of course. We are not feuding so publicly as all that." Mabyn shrugged. "His wife is..." She paused, as if trying to find a way to say something that was otherwise insulting. "She is a pleasant woman. Not inclined to want complicated things. I have a grandson and a granddaughter. She will bring them to tea with me every so often. I may indulge them from a distance, from a list of permitted items."

Cyrus was getting a clear idea. "The way things work, among a certain class. I presume they have separate lives, then?"

"Yes. Aubrey insisted I be present, available. Davin does not, thankfully. But Celtine has not shown many desires to do more than be a socialite. The usual philanthropy, she's a committee member for the Albion Inheritance. She is quite fond of gardens, though not in a way I consider very systematic." She wrinkled her nose. "I admit I am rather a snob about that."

"You asked some delightful questions this evening. Gemma was thrilled you appreciated her work. She went at it the other way around, of course, from Alchemy to Materia and Flora." Cyrus hesitated, then asked, because it was relevant. "What did your son do in the War?"

Mabyn waved a hand. "His son was a baby. He has a questionable heart, according to the healers. I'm fairly sure he bribed someone, actually, but I could not see a way to push for the answer without an abuse of power on my part."

Cyrus frowned. "It must be very difficult to think of your son like that. Whatever else has got in the middle."

"I am glad he was born. I did my best to love him when I could, and I don't have the foggiest idea what to do now." Mabyn said. "And I am sure you must think the less of me for it."

Again, Cyrus took his time. "I think I know nothing but the barest outline of your marriage, but that you were put in a difficult position. You know how the saying goes. Either Aristotle or Ignatius of Loyola, depending on who you believe as the source. Give me a boy until he is seven, and I will show you the man." He let that sit a moment before he went on. "I am presuming, but with some evidence, that you were not permitted much choice in how your son was raised, other than the physical requirements."

"Barely even that. There was a wet nurse installed immediately. Aubrey didn't consider it ladylike." She lifted a hand. "Yes, that's ridiculous. I think he just didn't want any other claim on my time or attention."

Cyrus had known other men like that. It required a

degree of insecurity he could not permit himself, and frankly found baffling. He nodded. "Certainly whatever blame there is should be proportionate to the amount of influence." He hesitated. "Is it something you would like to change now?"

"If wishes were horses, beggars would ride." Mabyn half-smiled as she quoted the old saying. "And even the most deft with chronological magic can't change the past." A moment later, she shook her head. "I am, I think, going to grow maudlin, and you needn't put up with me in that mood. Tomorrow, we'll see about what Nora made of the party."

Cyrus wanted to object, but he knew it would be fruitless. And also rude, honestly. He could scarcely think one moment that a woman knew her own mind and then argue he knew best. He did not permit himself to become a hypocrite, either.

"As you wish. Tomorrow morning once we're all up and about."

CHAPTER 23
MONDAY MORNING

"Where's Cyrus this time?" Nora was peering around along the edge of the meadow.

"Council business. The sort of thing that's far more his line than mine." Mabyn let Nora poke around. It wasn't as if she had a firm idea of how to move things forward.

The request had come in early that morning. Mabyn had got the notification in her own journal, the soft chime she'd set with a charm to alert her to anything with urgency. She'd pulled on a dressing gown, and made it halfway to Cyrus's room, to find him coming to meet her.

In this case, someone had tried the sort of magic that was forbidden by the Pact, and someone from the Council had to go deal with it. Three someones, in this case, the sort of problem that might be solved in a few hours or a few weeks, if they were lucky. Months or years if they were not. Alexander was in the last part of the Schola term. They wouldn't drag him out if they could avoid it, and this was not the sort of thing where they wanted Lucas's experimentation. Which meant Cyrus needed to be one of the three.

It had at least been a way to avoid the awkwardness of last night. She was sure she'd said entirely too much, and that he thought less of her now. Forever. She was just as sure - uncomfortably so - that she didn't like that idea. Having an imminent crisis was helpful on that front. For values of being helpful.

"No one's really explained that properly." Nora looked up, then lifted a hand. "Beyond what you told me when you were convincing me to come here. I realise now you must have glossed over quite a lot." She turned. "Tell me. Please."

Mabyn frowned. Where did one even start, explaining something so vast? It was like being asked to explain the stars in the sky. Did you talk about them as stars in the scientific sense? About the myths of constellations, the stories that people had told over centuries or millennia? Or did you start with talking about the universe and how tiny this one planet was?

Mabyn delayed trying to answer that for a moment, turning to spread out the picnic blanket she'd brought out. One it was laid out, with a charm at each corner to keep it in place. She pulled out the two flasks of tea in the bag and set them where they'd be handy. "What do you know about magic?"

"That is an unfair question." Nora came over and settled down. She was not elegant, not the way many of the women of the Great Families were. Though, of course, those women had been trained in elegance from before they could sit unassisted. "There are stories. I'm sure most of the ones I've heard are not at all accurate."

"Stories hold a lot of truth." Mabyn cast around, trying to figure out where to start. Then, suddenly, she glimpsed movement about fifteen feet away. "There - don't move quickly. In the bush there."

It was a grown hare, the shading of her coat shifting in the dappled shade from the leaves above her.

Nora leaned forward. "Oh, she's lovely. And so close."

"There are stories about hares and magic. Quite a few of them. And not just the star hares." Mabyn watched the hare for a moment, who hopped forward once and nibbled cautiously at some grass.

"There's - oh, I came across it in some old book. Scotland, something in Scotland. Something about witches and hares."

"Isobel Gowdie." She was a curious artefact of history. "She wasn't part of the magical community, at least so far as we can tell. We're fairly sure she never made her oath to the Silence. Well, that part is fairly obvious."

"She confessed to witchcraft, didn't she? That part, you explained clearly. If she'd made the oath, she wouldn't have been able to confess like that." Nora seemed rather pleased by the logic of this. It was rather tidy. Of course, that bit was designed to be as tidy as magic could ever be.

Mabyn nodded. "She confessed, and she talked about all sorts of things. Going off to lavish feasts with the Devil, spoiling crops, stealing a child's body out of a grave. Sexual escapades. Planning to kill a laird's son. Gatherings with the Queen of Elphame at her grand home." Mabyn hesitated there. Nora had a certain reticence about the topic.

"And which of those things are not like what you do?" Nora's voice shook a little in the middle.

"Aside from the sex? People being people, no matter whether or not they have magic? None of that. We do like our feasts, but the Devil does not get invited to any I've been to."

"And the Queen of Elphame? Or doing harm with magic? Or the hare, you left out the hare."

"Three different topics, that. It is possible to do harm with magic, of course. Many tools can be used in a range of ways. The classic but somewhat cliche example is fire, of course. We need it to keep warm in the winter and cook our food. We've needed it for light. And yet it can also burn down a house, or kill someone."

Nora snorted. "Fairly simplistic example too. But I take your point. Magic can do many things. Some undeniably good, some undeniably horrible, most somewhere in the middle."

"And as we said, part of the work of the Council is taking action, on behalf of the land, when it's needed. Which as you can imagine, can be broadly interpreted."

"That's the kind of thing that leads to people grabbing for power of their own. What stops you all from doing that? Though I admit, you haven't... seemed inclined to do a lot of that."

"The most, mmm. Powerful thing you've seen so far that's obvious is Cyrus reacting to Eustacia Baddock's invasion."

Nora's chin came up. "You're not using her title. Any title."

"She acted against the good of the land, directly and unambiguously. We'd have been within rights to bring her to a judge or a tribunal or some other sort of legal arrangement." Mabyn paused. She and Cyrus hadn't really talked about that, but she knew that they agreed about why. "We're not, because magic doesn't actually solve all the problems. It often creates more. We do not actually have good evidence of what she intended beyond knowing she wanted to make you go away."

"And magic doesn't solve that?" Nora frowned. "That doesn't seem useful."

Mabyn snorted. "Oh, there are rituals to compel someone to tell the truth. They're rather fiddly, by my standards, though I suspect Cyrus thinks that's an average Tuesday. But they involve being able to ask the right questions, and then having consequences that suit. We are, societally speaking, unwilling to pull them out for every small thing. Truth is hard to hear, after all."

She hesitated, gathering her thoughts, laying out what she thought Nora needed most right now. "We do when it tears the fabric of society. Treason, murder, large-scale harm. We might for someone who, oh, falsified building records in a way that put dozens of people at risk. We also don't have a wide range of punishments. People can be confined to their home, or have their magic bound, or pay a fine. But prisons are complicated to manage and usually end badly. Not just for the prisoner."

"That seems both sensible and frustrating."

"Quite." Mabyn shook her head. "We use the truth rituals more often for people who aren't fighting a compulsion. Someone who wants to give evidence, for example, can use that ritual to make it clear they are telling the truth, and clear their name."

"The Queen of Elphame?"

Mabyn nodded. She'd save the hare for last. "You've heard tales of the fair folk, the good folk. Whether that's fairies down at the end of the garden, or whatever."

"Those - I mean, I saw the issue of *The Strand*. I couldn't decide what to make of them."

"Whatever the Fatae look like, it's not much like that. There are some who look much like any other person." Mabyn knew there had been descendents, born of the Fatae and men and women, but she would not get into that. Entirely too complicated, and likely not terribly relevant.

"But the main agreement of the Pact was that the Fatae would withdraw into their own places. It would be safer for people in Albion - in England and Wales, and later Scotland - who had magic, or who didn't have magic."

Nora was chewing on that, rather visibly, but she nodded.

Mabyn went on. "Oh, there are some exceptions. It's not like there's a solid wall between their places and ours that never gets crossed. And some of the Fatae, they're part of the fabric of how we do things. The Belin, who deal in stone and the deep earth. The custos dragons in the banks. Trees who talk, and guard certain places. But most people, even among the magical community, never see them. Probably think they're mythical, honestly."

"Huh." Nora snorted. "And you know better? Because you're on the Council?"

"Exactly. I've met all three. A few others, too. But none of them looked like those photographs. And honestly, we'd have known if something went against the Pact. They're not supposed to meddle with people."

"Was there a lot of that? The meddling?"

Mabyn let out a beleaguered sigh. "Oh, was there! We have records from before the Council existed. All the things that could go wrong when people went through a gate the wrong way, or left the wrong seasonal offering, or did something that offended. We've shelves and shelves of notes, gathered up over centuries. And people would go making promises - usually about finding true love or trea-sure - and they'd get answered in bizarre ways, ones that hurt people much more."

"So why did anyone even want to talk to the Fatae? They sound, they sound scary." Nora was frowning now.

"They're not like us. The Fatae live a long time, most of them. A big part of it is that they care about different things. The Belin care about a well-tended mine, about how the stone feels, things I don't have the first clue about. If you think about it like the land here, where there are trees, and hares, and sheep, and barley, and the fish in the moat, it makes more sense. All those things are in the same space, near each other, but quite different. But they also interact. The hare eats the grass, maybe some of the fallen grain, the bees get pollen from the flowers, and so on."

Nora nodded. "And you said most people never interact with them. I wouldn't have to? I'd be scared of doing something rude. Wrong."

"Very unlikely indeed. Honestly, if you're ever not sure, there are some ritual phrases that are safe. Don't accept gifts or give them, unless you're sure who you're giving them to. Cyrus has a potted lecture, I suspect, he does some of the training around that for the new Council members."

"You have training?" Nora lit up at that. "That's a sensible thing. Like learning to be a teacher?"

Mabyn laughed. "Oh, yes. Anyone who earns a Council seat - and no, I'm not telling you what goes into that. Beyond that there's a complicated magical challenge. We're sworn on the Silence not to. And mostly we don't talk about it with other people, even on the Council."

"You haven't with Cyrus?" Nora leaned back on one hand. "Do you get on with him?"

That was an awkward question. "Quite pleasantly, in what we're doing here. Though we're both quite capable of focusing on our work, and doing what needs to be done." Then she said briskly. "The hare."

Nora snorted. "I can tell you want to change the

subject." Mabyn felt it was a challenge she hadn't expected, teaching someone who was new to magic and this world. But also someone who had a well-developed sense of who she was and what she would tolerate. "Go on?"

"One more kind of magic - and I swear this one is real - is shape-shifting. There are different reasons, sometimes it's a curse, sometimes it's a family thing, passed down. Sometimes someone learns how." Mabyn hesitated. "It's very useful, I suppose, but people are also rather suspicious of people who can. So, if you're around, oh, one hundred people who are fairly competent magically, chances are good one of them might be, but you would probably never know."

"Is there a way to tell? What do people turn into? Is it wolves or something else?" Nora shook her head. "Now listen to me. What I'm asking. This can't be real, can it? You're pulling my leg."

"Quite real. It can be any animal. Though some of the curses are about wolves, yes, the best known ones. Or the berserker tales of people turning into bears, that can be a family trait. But what Isobel Gowdie said about going into a hare, that's a reasonably common one, from what we know. A bit of a risk, any small prey animal is, but hares can take surprisingly good care of themselves."

Nora frowned. "So the other things from folklore, there might be some truth to that?"

"Depends on the folklore. Don't trust to iron to keep you safe from anything, unless it's been designed to. But the tales about gifts, and being cautious? About animals that can change form and carry you off to your doom? Rare, but real." Mabyn waved a hand. "For now, let's consider the tree some more. They wander about quite a lot less, trees."

Nora laughed and then twisted to peer up at the tree. "The oak."

Mabyn settled in to begin the discussion she'd intended for today, about how Materia - the magic of materials - and folklore intertwined. And in particular, to talk about how the oak was a useful example of both.

Cyrus found himself making circles of the workroom, with no real purpose.

He had got Lionel's permission to set up in it for a few days. Now he was trying to figure out how best to proceed. His preference, left to his own devices, was for an elemental focus to this ritual. That was what had come most naturally to him for years, and it was also flexible. However, it was draining to do on one's own and he'd feel it for days. He wasn't sure of Mabyn's preferences, or even how to ask.

She might be willing. She might find it presumptuous. She might not be any good at this form of magic. Mabyn had proclaimed herself not a ritual magician by preference, for all she knew the basics. But then, anyone on the Council knew the basic expectations. Or they learned them, by the time they'd made it through a few years on the Council.

Out in the garden, she had followed what he was doing, but she'd made no attempt to step in, other than when Eustacia Baddock had appeared. He'd meant to discuss it more with her, and then a dozen other things had got in the way. Which left him restlessly circling the workroom, trying to decide what to chalk out on the floor.

In the end, he decided to trust that nagging instinct. Or habit. It might just be habit. It was a deliberately chosen habit, however, and one that should not cause offence here, even if it turned out not to be the optimal approach. Once he'd made the decision, he felt a bit better. Going to the trunk by the doorway with his working tools, he took the box of chalks from the top tray and the cord measure. He fixed one end to the centre point of the workroom and used the knot in the cord that would give him a nine-foot diameter. Plenty of space to work, even if it would only take up half the workroom.

While he worked at tracing the outline he wanted, from longstanding memory, he thought again about Lionel. Cyrus had to respect his honourable nature, but there were ongoing questions, even mysteries. Lionel had come to them, but not as quickly as he ought to, even allowing for a difficult mother. The house itself seemed sound, and magically, it felt sound. But the surrounding land was not, in subtle ways and more obvious ones. Cyrus half expected to find the great oaks shattered in the next storm, or the banks of the stream and moat overflowing. Or perhaps run dry, leaving the fish flopping uselessly into death.

Automatically, he made the little hand gesture to avert evil, the one he'd had trained into him during his apprenticeship. Everything could be part of a ritual, in this stage of preparation. He'd been trained to be cautious. More than cautious, if at all possible.

He turned his attention back to the chalk lines and symbols. Cyrus knelt on one knee by each, making sure they were clear and precise, before touching fingers to them, chanting the charm for colour under his breath. He had just finished the last, in the north, when he heard a careful knock on the door. He had not yet locked it, nor had he cast the charms that would muffle everything from outside until he was done.

Cyrus stood, going to the table by the other side of the door, and brushing his hands off, then cleaning them on a linen hand-towel. One Rhoe had given him, of course, made of simply hemmed linen with a single neat line of coloured thread along each end. Once his hands were clean, he opened the door.

Mabyn was standing there, patiently. He'd expected, honestly, Lionel or perhaps one of the staff. He wasn't sure what to do with Mabyn. "Mabyn?" Her name was a good place to start, rather than asking what she was doing there. He was afraid it would come out accusatory or difficult.

"I didn't want to interrupt you." Which did not explain why she'd knocked.

He gestured. "I was almost done setting up." The chalking was done, the altars at each quarter were set up with their various objects. He was not sure whether to ask her to come in, or to stand here awkwardly in the doorway.

"I had a thought. Can I come in for a minute?" That made it easier. He nodded, and stood back to let her come in. She was wearing a quite simple dress this time, in a deep green, and slippers on her feet. "Nora said something earlier, after you'd left. And I couldn't stop thinking about it."

He'd had a follow up meeting from the business two days ago. Tedious, complicated, delicate, and largely boring. But it was the sort of meeting he'd needed to be at in case it had become interesting. There had been disruptions in the magic near Cardiff, and they still did not know why, only that it did not seem to be ongoing.

There had been a sudden flowering meadow filled to the brim with rare orchids. And nearby, a slick of oily, pearlescent liquid in a pond that disappeared a few hours later. They'd had to call out one of the Penelopes with particular investigative skills, as well as three of the Council.

Nothing any of them had found had showed the cause. That it had come from within fifty miles, probably twenty-five, but that was not a great deal of help. He was wool-gathering again and rather rudely. He closed the door behind Mabyn, and said, "I'd offer you a chair, but I'm afraid there aren't any."

She laughed, apparently in good humour, despite whatever had brought her down so urgently. Then she sobered. "She asked whether there was a curse on the land. She's read stories, of course. And I couldn't tell her it was foolish. But is that what we should be worrying about?"

"They are certainly not common, though I'd have to consult the books. It's more common to curse, oh, someone else's cows or sheep or fields. This is, this is everything. The water, the land, the wildlife, the domesticated animals, the wilder places. And who would do that? Who would be capable of it? A single bad harvest, I'd believe, but an ongoing blight would need near constant renewal and a powerful will behind it."

Cyrus felt better laying things out. "And it doesn't seem to have much affected the house itself, which is curious. The land nearest here, but not the house. No unusual leaks or bits of stone falling off, for one thing."

"That is an excellent question, isn't it? Do we think Lionel has particular enemies? Enemies who are magically quite competent, or able to hire someone who is?" Mabyn frowned, as if she were thinking through the possibilities.

"It is, of course, hard to tell. It's not the sort of thing people talk about to strangers. Even strangers you've asked for help." Cyrus had an awful thought. "Do we think he's the one who's doing it? Consciously, I mean. The subtle effects of a miserable Lord are more complicated to untangle."

Mabyn didn't answer for a long moment. Instead, she walked the edge of the ritual circle. "Twetherton's Fourth?" The geometric cut stones were a giveaway for that, if you knew the form in the first place. It wasn't commonly used. Then she turned back. "I don't think he's consciously doing anything to harm the land. I believe he's sincere about wanting it healthy. But I also know I could be very wrong."

"That is about where I had got to. Though being here with your company is better." He made a small bow. Then Cyrus nodded. "I prefer Twetherton's for personal workings." He hadn't intended to say anything further but then he found himself going on. "Would you like to join me?"

Mabyn turned back toward the altars, then looked at him, as if trying to decide if he were serious. He felt rather like a hare or a squirrel, caught out in the open, observed by something or someone that might be a threat. Then her expression shifted, as she worked through whatever her own personal equations were. Finally, she nodded. "It's been at least a decade."

"You needn't do the speaking parts, but I admit I'd appreciate a second set of eyes on what happens." This particular ritual worked well to petition for information. Most often, Cyrus got a flash of insight into the question, anchored by one or more of the Platonic elements. "Do you have a preference for where to stand?"

Mabyn shrugged. "I prefer earth, if you don't mind. Northwest?"

Cyrus nodded, unsurprised. Most of the more skilled Materia specialists found earth the easiest to connect with. He himself had found air easiest at first, and now the meditative aspects of water. He waited for Mabyn to leave her slippers by the door, leaving her in bare feet, while he made one final check that everything was as it should be.

The Twetherton approach to these rituals involved invocations to each element, which he had long-since memorised. The trick, always, was to keep them fresh while holding onto the essence of the invocation. It was rather like singing a piece of music that had been familiar for decades, and yet making the performance hold something new and living. Filling the space, as he'd learned that day in India, making it real in every way.

This time, apparently, that meant that he leaned into the imagery that was about sound and about touch. That was not usually what grabbed his attention, the phrases about echoes of bells or the light of a thousand candles and the smell of the wax.

One never stepped in the same river twice. Mistress Belling had drilled that into his head, over and over. And no ritual was ever the same twice, even if you did it three times a day for your entire life. This time, though, it had a flow to it that pleased him.

Even better, Mabyn joined him on the call and response, between each invocation to the elements. He had said the first one, not expecting she would, then there was her voice. There she was, her magic open.

In the larger rituals they'd done, the ones that called on all the Council or a substantial portion of them, she had been more guarded. Here, it was more like a well with a bucket ready, or perhaps ivy, stretching out over sun-warmed brick. Available, that was the word he wanted.

He reached for that magic after gathering his own, trusting to his training and skill to weave it into the work at hand. As he finished the last invocation, the one to the earth, he could feel everything coming together and shifting into something well beyond the physical world.

He braced his feet, then felt himself going down to one knee, as images washed over him. He could see - could feel - the way there was a lack in the soil and the water. They were there, but they were not living as they should be. As if they'd been drained of vitality, of the spark that made life, and now they were just a seeming.

It wasn't just one place; it was dozens. That made him more sure it was not a singular curse. It was like a flood of water, with momentary glimpses floating by him, and he did his best to remember them all. The oak was still surprisingly strong, it had a luminous quality to it that spoke of life, but even it could only last so long. There were glimpses of a cauldron, with flowers in it, but he could not quite see which ones hinted at a possible aid.

Finally, at last, there was a glimpse of Nora, standing at the edge of the meadow. Her skirts were blowing behind her, as if she had planted herself like a sapling tree. Supple enough to move in the gusts of wind buffeting her, but sturdy and strong enough to stay upright. It was, on the whole, a hopeful note. That they had not guessed horribly wrong in bringing her here. But the visions did not grant him, at least, a clear idea of what had caused this.

When they finally receded, he took in a breath, then another, before opening his eyes. Mabyn had gone to her knees, her hands pressed down against the marble of the workroom floor. If she was cold or uncomfortable, she showed no sign of it. He didn't want to disturb her, so he waited a good minute, perhaps two, until she pressed her hands deliberately down, then brushed them off, before she looked up. When he opened his mouth, she shook her head.

Instead, he silently held out his hand, helping her to her feet. Still without saying a word, she let him light the incense and waft it over her, over himself, and then over the altars. She picked up the candle and paraded it around, offering the light to each direction and those who dwelled there. He offered the cup the same way, before coming back to the centre and offering it to her to drink. She took a sip and handed it back. When he set it down, she had picked up the honey cake. A moment later, he was opening his mouth, and she placed a pinch of it on his tongue before he took the plate to offer it to her.

That, more than anything else, felt intimate. He had not done this, not with one other person and only one, other than with Tanith and more recently with Rhoe or Gemma. He almost fumbled the plate, but she took it smoothly, leaving him to make the final thanks and farewells.

When the elements had returned to their homes and the ritual was truly done, he turned. She smiled once, and murmured, "Later." Before he could think of what to say that would not break the moment, she was sliding her feet into the slippers and leaving him alone in the workroom, to clean everything up and make his final libation outside, under the oak.

He wanted desperately to know what she'd seen.

CHAPTER 25
THURSDAY EVENING

"Start from the outside and work in, for both the knives and forks." Mabyn leaned over. She was sitting next to Nora at the moment. Nora was peering at the cutlery set out in front of her. She had been invited to a small, more intimate supper with Darius and Antonia Gallagher and a handful of friends, as well as their parents. It would be properly supervised, but Nora, of course, wanted to make the best impression she could.

"If I get it wrong, they'll laugh." Nora frowned.

Cyrus settled back in his chair. "The other tip is to wait for someone else to pick up a utensil and follow their lead. Mistress Gallagher or Antonia would both be safe choices here."

Nora raised an eyebrow. "You've never been unsure what to do at a meal, I'm sure."

Cyrus cut a fine figure, honestly. Mabyn had to admit that. He looked like a man who enjoyed his food. He laughed. "Oh, here in Albion, I don't have any concerns. I can manage everything from a pub in the back of beyond to full formal Council meals with all the precautions. But I took a trip to Japan, on Council business, once, and that's an entirely different way of eating. They use chopsticks, or their fingers, but there are many specific customs."

Nora blinked. She seemed about to say something, then caught herself. "Wait, all the precautions?"

Mabyn had known they were going to have to discuss this sometime. "Magic can do a great many things, as we said. Not all of them kind."

Nora turned to her, raising one eyebrow. "Go on. Please."

"You might have noticed, at the garden party, about half the women were wearing light-weight shawls or jackets over their frocks? There are potions that can be applied to the skin in passing. A layer of fabric is enough to disrupt almost all of them, especially if the fabric is charmed to repel liquids." Mabyn said it as evenly as she could.

"Wait, you what now? That's a thing you all think about? And you think that's normal?" Nora half rose from her chair. Lionel, seated across from her, looked startled, and about to consider running himself.

Mabyn spread her hands. "Only in some circles. The very posh ones, usually, who make the manipulation of power their primary hobby and interest, whatever form it takes. Most commonly it's not poison, anything lasting. But it might make your tongue looser, make you more inclined to let something slip that others could use. So yes, it is a thing I think about, at every formal gathering. Cyrus as well. But not at others. The garden party, for example, was a smaller group and chosen for pleasure rather than politics."

"You said you'd invited a number of people I might like." Nora settled back into her chair, but she was still visibly on edge.

"Selected in part because they would not..." Mabyn wasn't sure how to put this.

Cyrus didn't step on her metaphorical toes, but when her voice trailed off, he spoke up. "They would not take advantage. We selected them for being interesting, from a range of backgrounds, and not interested in those particular status games."

Nora frowned. "Even the other people with titles? Or who will, I guess?"

"The Edgartons are because Gabriel Edgarton has an unusually strong connection to the land, and he and his wife are interested in the world, broadly speaking. The Gallaghers don't have a land connection, but they value education and learning. They don't move in the sort of circles where you'd need to worry."

Nora nodded and subsided a bit. The silence left Mabyn time to reflect again. The ritual yesterday had left her suddenly uncertain. She'd spent the morning cleaning the stillroom and setting up some additional distillation. The afternoon had been given over to talking through frocks for this dinner invitation, and what the different options would signal.

That had been rather pleasant, on the one hand. On the other, it brought home to Mabyn how unfashionable her own frocks tended to be. She dressed appropriately, of course, for whatever the gathering was, but she had given up dressing to look particularly smart or fashionable long ago. At Aubrey's death, more or less. Being in formal mourning had been an excellent excuse to stop.

And yet, talking with Nora today, she had become suddenly aware she had spent yesterday evening with Cyrus, wearing an old frock. One that had a hole in the pocket and was five years out of date, in a colour that suited her but a shape that did not flatter.

It wasn't just the clothing, of course. Mabyn knew perfectly well the clothing was standing in for a whole host of other feelings. Being in the workroom with him - and just with him - had brought up memories and dashed hopes. At the end, when they had made the offerings, she had found that brush of intimacy, of care, startlingly real. And tender, as if some part of her was not as protected as she'd expected.

The meal had proceeded on without her. Lionel was talking about upcoming summer fetes and fairs, open gardens, about whether Nora might like to attend anything in particular. That had got them into a rousing discussion about the Suffolk Show, the local agricultural fair, and favourite moments from their respective childhoods. That carried them through the next two courses. Nora had preferred watching the horses, while Lionel had a fondness for sheep, including sheep herding trials.

Once they had finished the meal, Mabyn was still sitting at the table when Cyrus cleared his throat. "Drink? Wherever you prefer?"

She startled. "Pardon, I was lost in thought. Anything in particular on your mind?"

"I'd like to talk through the ritual work yesterday. Now I've had a chance to think about some of it. If you're will-ing?" His voice might be described as diffident, but she thought that cautious might be more accurate. As if he were afraid he'd overstepped somehow.

"My room, shall we? Though if you want to bring your brandy, I wouldn't object." Mabyn stood, and he pulled the chair out neatly as she did. She had come to like his brandy, despite not having started with much of a preference for it.

Five minutes later, she let him into her sitting room. He had the brandy bottle in one hand as she gathered up glasses. She gestured at the chairs, and he settled down. As he did, she was struck again by how things had shifted last night.

He didn't speak. He simply poured her a glass of brandy and handed it to her. Then he took his own chair, crossing one ankle over his knee, letting her set the pace. Of course, she had no idea how to begin.

How did you say that you'd been up far into the night, thinking? She'd thought, of course, about what she'd heard and felt in the ritual. But more than that, she kept coming back to him, in a way that made her feel deeply uncomfortable. As if she had crossed some bridge of intimacy he had not offered and she had not wanted.

Or at least, if you had asked her yesterday at lunch, she would have said she did not want such a thing, would never want such a thing, thank you. And yet, here she was. Aware of what it was like to be in a ritual circle with one other person, who treated her as a competent ritualist, without any apparent question.

Last night had been one of the best experiences of magic in her life. It had come close to those moments in the midst of her trials, when her blood was afire with it. When she knew Aubrey would never touch her again if she did not choose. That she had power and choice and ability, no matter what his words said, no matter how his voice tried to cut those things away from her. She was made of vines and thorns and deep roots that went down to unshakeable bedrock.

The ritual had brought all of that back. She flashed to the feel of sun on the earth, the scent of verdant loam where things grew easily, the light all living things turned towards, whether it came from the sun or a hearth fire or a candle. She had felt tall and competent and like she was doing what she had always been meant to do. Oh, she'd had flickers of that feeling through the years. But this had been like diving into it, letting it surround her and fill her and heal her in a way she had refused to admit she needed.

As the silence dragged on, she cleared her throat. "That must be a ritual you do often?"

"In the simpler form, a few times a month, on average. I've had periods when it's been nearly every day. Others when it's weeks between. As we did last night? A few times a year." He hesitated, then visibly decided. "I began when I started planning to challenge for the Council seat. I didn't have people I could ask, not really. No patrons or allies. I had some of my great-great-grandmother's journals. She was the last to hold a seat in our family line." He spoke slowly, as if he were feeling his way through the conversation, much as she was.

Her chin came up, and she couldn't help leaning forward. "And you succeeded. The first time."

One of his shoulders twitched. "I was driven by grief and needing to control something in my life. Not exactly the best reasons." He looked out toward the window, to the dark outside. "And then, of course, I wanted to do the thing properly."

Mabyn hesitated, then girded herself to ask. "What was it like, your trial?"

His attention snapped back to her. When he spoke, it seemed he wasn't answering the question. "In the end, I went back to the old records. Before the Pact, around the time of the Pact. The threads of tales that we've lost to myth and legend." He gestured vaguely down toward the workroom. "Last night, that is an outgrowth. The elements are eternal, and the elements are ever changing. Plants change. Animals change. The ways people live change. But fire is fire, and water is water, and air is air, and earth is earth."

Mabyn had never heard of someone going so far into that sort of fundamental elemental approach. Oh, plenty of people used the ritual forms he'd used last night. She did herself. Plenty had an affinity for one element or the other, and drew on it in their magic, taking the path of greatest ease and confidence. What Cyrus was talking about was something different.

He looked away again. "That trip, the one where Rhoe met her husband. You remember there was an issue with one of the Ones Below? This bit wasn't so much in the later discussions."

He'd brought it up before. She had been present for the discussions about that, though she had been very junior on the Council at the time, and Aubrey had still been alive. The combination meant she was not at all inclined to speak up and ask. "I remember the outline, yes."

"We had to sort out the ritual work on the fly, middle of the ocean, no workroom, just what we could find on the ship. Something in that changed things for me. I've never found a good way to put it into words, but the experience of ritual, especially elemental ritual, shifted for me. It had more colours, more sounds, more tastes, more textures. There are days when I open the gates, and I say my hello, and I can near enough see a salamander on the workroom floor. Real, and yet not solid. Or a gnome, peeking out from behind the table." He glanced up. "You know what others would say."

Some would mock him. Some would say he was going batty. A fair number would say he'd been drunk - though, she'd never actually seen him drink until he was even tipsy. It made her brave enough to share something of her own. "Last night, it was much more vivid than I've had before. You are the ritualist. I would expect it to be clearer for you. I usually need some sort of physical focus. Materia, Alchemy. You know the sort of thing."

"I was wondering why you don't wear a focal pendant routinely, actually. You wear your pendant, but you don't use it as a focus." He gestured at the pendant hanging from her neck on a sturdy rope chain.

She found herself reaching for it. "It's -" She then blinked up at him. "what I've always worn."

"And I suspect it's not a stone that particularly speaks to you? A family stone, perhaps?"

Mabyn nodded. Without looking back up, she found herself saying, "I feel idiotic now."

"Don't." His voice was kind, but it had a fierceness to it. "It's the kind of thing we all trip over. The choice made long ago, that's become part of us." There was something here, underneath his words, that was more personal, and she did not know how to ask.

He went on. "Tomorrow, I can pull out books, make some suggestions, if you like? By which I mean I suspect I will list off several dozen stones, perhaps hand you a few. You will refuse most of them and know deep in your heart when you figure out the right one."

That made her laugh, despite everything. "You don't dismiss intuition?"

"Oh, goodness, no. I know ritualists have a reputation

for being all about precise words and measured angles and thinking everything out in advance. But I have always left space for inspiration. Alexander does too, for the record, if you'd not noticed, for all his ancient forms of magic."

CHAPTER 26
THURSDAY EVENING

Mabyn was watching him extremely carefully now. Cyrus leaned back, at least trying to show he was at ease. It was strange. He wasn't uncomfortable, exactly. But he had the sense of weight rolling downhill behind him. That something in the conversation, or perhaps the coming days, would matter a great deal.

She reached for her glass, taking a measured sip before she set it down. She more or less matched his posture, though she nudged off her slippers and tucked her foot under her knee instead of over it. "You asked, a while back, if I were proposing a closer alliance in the Council. Among our fellows. Would you be interested?"

Cyrus tilted his head, letting his amusement show. This was not where he had expected her to start, but he had to admit it made sense. "I'm not one to leap without looking. But I admit, I am intrigued. What do you have in mind?"

"You know we are a net of connections. People of similar preferences and specialities. People with similar goals. At various places those intersect."

"Teach your grandmother to suck eggs." Cyrus said, amiably. "And you have been moving in rather different circles than I have. Given the relatively small numbers."

"How would you define those circles?" She lifted a hand. "I'm actually rather curious about how we do and don't overlap in how we see things."

Cyrus supposed it was a fair question. "Only if you promise to tell me too."

"Fair." Mabyn waved a hand. "Gentlemen first."

"You're right that it's layers of groupings. I spend time with the other ritualists, of course, the people who enjoy talking through it. Alexander, now he's back in the country. Philomena, though her stamina isn't what it used to be, her memory is still sharp as a trap. Lucas and Frederica less so, though they're certainly competent." He made little gestures, pointing out their usual seats in the Council hall, scattered through the room. "Then there are the family connections and alliances. I needn't spell those out?"

"No, you needn't." Mabyn sounded amused.

"Then there are the people who have particular interests. I do more interaction with the Healers, because of Rhoe and her connections. Lenox has picked up what Fitz-Alan used to do with the Guard. You and Alexander have an interest in Schola and in the other schools. Silvia, too, these days."

"And Hesperidon?"

Cyrus snorted. "Hesperidon wishes his son to be properly educated and apprenticed, he is less concerned with the process that makes that happen." Then he shrugged. "You have, thus far, appeared to spend your time with others who have a focus on Materia. Some of those interested in Alchemy. But you notably prefer the company of other women on the Council. Some of them."

"Some of them." Mabyn agreed. "The ones who believe there are more approaches to a given problem than, mm, shall we say, aggressive applications of magic? Of course, that leaves out a certain number of men. One reason I enjoy Materia so much is that it is a more subtle art." She flicked her pendant. "You should not have needed to call out the fact my pendant does not suit me as a working focus."

Cyrus spread his hands. "I will not apologise for saying a true thing. You deserve the best I have on offer."

Something about how he said that went horribly wrong. He could see it happening, like a glass about to topple from a sideboard and shatter. He held up his hands immediately. "May I restate that?"

Her eyes closed for a long moment, one that seemed like it lasted forever. She took a shallow breath, then a slightly deeper one, then she nodded once.

Cyrus gathered all his wits and his skill. He had to get this right. "I find I want to give you my best. You are thoughtful, disciplined. You give of yourself freely to the causes you choose. I find all of that admirable, if a tad difficult to live up to. You make me, in short, think of my sister and my late wife, to whom I have long compared myself. And found myself wanting."

Once he came to the end, he closed his mouth, nodded once to show he was done, and closed his own eyes, counting out three breaths. When he looked at Mabyn again, she was watching him, the slightly wary look of a fox caught out in an open field. She did not speak, not until she had drained her glass and reached to refill it.

"We have rather different ideas of my potential value." Her voice was quiet. "But you are right about the discipline. It has taken me through dozens of challenging times." Then she cleared her throat. "I see roughly the same web in the

Council as you do. But I also see ancestral connections, not just current ones. Patterns people have fallen into. Assumptions. Sometimes they are obvious, sometimes they are very subtle."

Cyrus frowned. "I am curious. I also expect that is a long conversation, and perhaps not for tonight." He flicked his fingers. "We really should talk about the ritual."

Mabyn let out a long breath, as if it freed her from steeling herself to a different task. "You said you have done that ritual many times. That you'd gone back to some of the ancient roots in your preparation. I - it is not how I go about things. I'll be honest and say that a lot of formal ritual leaves me cold."

"That is true for many people. Sometimes that works well enough, but I find I prefer the rituals where you are supposed to feel something." Cyrus leaned back again.

She snorted. "It cast things in a new light, that might be a way to put it." She waved a hand. "You're different, in that kind of ritual space. Do you let other people see you there, often?"

His head came up, and he knew immediately he'd given a fair bit away. "Not terribly often. Other than my particular connections." He considered. "In the ritual last night, I got strong visual impressions. That's common for me, more than hearing or smelling or touching. The last part, the piece that gives me hope, was seeing Nora standing in the meadow, a breeze blowing her skirt and her hair, but standing strong."

Mabyn leaned forward now. "And before that?"

"Glimpses, flashes. I don't believe it was one curse. It felt like the magic had been draining all over, pockmarked, like a measles rash spreading over skin. I saw different corners of the estate, and perhaps some of the surrounding countryside. Those boggy spots, for one, though not just that. The way things are faded out of proportion. It didn't give me answers - our lives would be much easier if ritual managed that reliably. But it gives me ideas of where to check. And I would appreciate your help in figuring out how best to investigate."

"And it was raining today, so you haven't gone looking."

Cyrus shook his head. "May I ask what the ritual gave you?" He suddenly felt like he was on very tenuous ground, and he did not want to press her.

Mabyn hesitated, her fingers brushing the curve of her glass on the table. "How often have you done that ritual with someone else? Or any ritual with offerings?"

"I was thinking, yesterday, how long it had been since I'd done it with anyone other than Rhoe or Gemma or Tanith." He spread his hands. "You fit smoothly into the work, as if you knew exactly how to proceed. Not just the steps of the dance, but the musicality of it."

Mabyn glanced up at him, then looked away, towards the dark window. "I was thinking about how strong the sensations were. The smells, the touch. Warm sun on the earth, how it feels on your hands digging in the garden. The way plants turn towards the light and the warmth."

Cyrus nodded, and he knew that was true, deep down in his bones. It was the way she'd said it, the quietness. The greatest magic, he'd come to think, was the quiet magic, the magic you knew without shouting and fireworks. He watched her and then trusted that flash of intuition. "That wasn't all of it, was it?"

Her chin came up, her eyes widening. Then she must have realised how much she'd revealed. She stood, going over to the window, and looking out into the dark, as if she weren't sure how to say anything.

Cyrus waited. He would go if she suggested he should. Otherwise, he could sit here in silence perfectly well.

She spoke, without turning back to look at him. "I felt like I did after my trial. Like I could do anything. The world was open to me. It would come to my hands. Delicate, fragile - a hummingbird, a butterfly, a skittish fox. I had forgotten what it felt like to have it so solidly that I could not argue with it. Could not possibly forget it."

He had no idea what to do with that. It was not his doing that she felt that. Not his doing she had not felt that. But he had, last night, perhaps made it easier to open a door to that feeling. Or maybe they had both simply been particularly blessed. "I am glad. That you could feel that. I wish that was what magic always did."

She turned at that and smiled. "Our lives would be very different, wouldn't they? If everyone lived like they'd never been hurt."

Cyrus swallowed. "Have you ever talked to anyone about your trial?" He had danced around the edges, with Rhoe, but never more than that.

"Oh, no. Silvia talked through hers, afterwards, but she wasn't ready to hear about mine. Other people? No."

Cyrus nodded. "You feel strongly about her." He'd not had an apprentice like that, where there was that depth of feeling. He'd thought himself, honestly, incapable of having that again with anyone other than Rhoe and Gemma, and they were different.

It was that which made Mabyn come back toward the chairs. "I wanted to make sure she didn't end up like me. And she isn't, in all the ways I cared about. Her husband treats her well. They are fond of each other. Her son loves her. Her magic comes to her hand, like a puppy looking for praise."

"She was very fortunate to have you. And you were just as fortunate in her." Cyrus shook his head. "I've helped various people over the years, but I've never had a close apprentice. Competent, yes. Inventive, yes. Close, no."

Mabyn frowned. "You present yourself as rather solitary. With your daughter, orbiting. Glaring at people who might upset you."

"She what?" He had not noticed this about Gemma.

Mabyn laughed. "She noticed, quite quickly at the party, if you might be unhappy or bored or needing any small thing. She worries about your happiness as much as, I am sure, you worry about hers."

"I feel it is my duty to worry rather more than she does. I wish she wouldn't. Worry, that is. I am happy enough, I have work I love, and there is always more to learn." Cyrus could feel, as he said it, that he was protesting too much.

"As you say." Mabyn tilted her head, but she didn't go on. Then, she changed the subject. "I won't ask you to pull out stones tonight, but do you have some theories on what might be worth trying? Or preferences in approach?"

CHAPTER 27
THE APPLE ORCHARD, THURSDAY, MAY 5TH

"Again, please." Cyrus perched on a canvas stool, looking entirely composed. They were out in the apple orchard, which seemed to have been less touched by whatever was causing the difficulties. The apple trees were certainly flowering profusely. Mabyn had never been one for frills and flourishes, but there was something abundantly joyful about an apple tree in full bloom.

They'd at least made it through the May Day offerings without catastrophe. On one hand, there had been no great rush of magic restoring all that had failed. On the other hand, nothing had been blighted. There were small signs, at least, that the land was starting to respond. Nora's offering had burned well, the libation had sunk into a thirsty ground, the wreath of fresh flowers had flourished for a full three days.

Nora sighed, and moved to a space between three trees, planted her feet, and inhaled, before beginning to chant a simple chant for blessing the fruit. It was one Mabyn had done in her childhood, a pleasant wassail tune. And unlike the January apple wassail, good any time of the year. Well, any time there might be fruit, anyway.

Mabyn settled more comfortably on her own stool, nodding. "She's getting better at it. I can feel things stirring. The right sort of stirring, not jostling."

Cyrus looked over at her, then back at Nora. "You've more than a bit of a touch for the earth, I've noticed. Do feel free to comment?"

"It's not a thing I'm used to teaching. That wasn't part of what Silvia and I did."

"Silvia," Cyrus pointed out, "Had a well-trained governess and one of the best tutoring houses. She has all the wealth of Schola's resources and marrying into one of the foremost magical houses of the country behind her. She did not need tutoring in the basics."

Mabyn had to laugh, then she waved a hand at Nora. "You'll like this, come over, get some tea."

Nora came over, amiably enough, sinking down onto the third stool. They were sturdy - magically sturdy, Mabyn was sure. Cyrus had produced them this morning, saying that while they were learning and studying, they might as well be comfortable. He'd said something else Mabyn wanted to follow up on, but she'd wanted Nora to hear it.

Mabyn explained, "We were talking about Silvia, and about how she had all this training, before she and I ever really talked."

"You've mentioned her several times. She's the wife of the head of the Council. I did memorise the charts. Her husband's, um, Hesperidon Warren, he's been head for decades, she's rather younger, and they've got a son named Claudio. And she's on the Council now herself." Nora was a quick study, which was very rewarding.

"Exactly so." Mabyn beamed at her. "And Silvia's very

good - a different flavour of alchemist than Gemma is, but just as skilled. There are three things we worked on. First, she had to unlearn a lot of things. She'd had excellent training, but it turned out to be head-excellent. Not heart-excellent. And that matters, when we're talking about the levels of power and the range of skill."

Nora frowned. "You mean she knew things, but they weren't working as well for her as they should be?"

"Yes. Partly because our ideas of what best looks like - well, it mostly means men, and it mostly means a certain range of skills. Duelling is favoured, for example. Alchemy or Ritual work, rather than Materia or Flora or say, Astronomy."

"So you're saying there are proper masculine magics that the lords and masters of the realm prefer, and they look down on the others? And that even though Silvia was good at Alchemy, that was different?"

"Well, for one thing, for women who are aiming at having children, Alchemy and Ritual have a few more risks. Materia and Flora and some of the other magics have risks too, but they're easier to contain or spot, unless you're mucking around with completely unknown items."

"But people do. Try dangerous things." Nora grimaced, as if trying to work things out.

Mabyn glanced at Cyrus, and when he lifted one of his fingers, nodded to let him take over. He didn't start where she expected. "Some people are always looking for innovation. The next thing, the new thing. Some of our ritual methods are millennia old. They have tried and perfected over centuries. You could think of it rather like recipes, though, tastes change, over time."

Nora nodded. "And so people combine things, or try

something new. Or I suppose someone does the equivalent of importing the tomato or potato?"

Cyrus beamed. "Exactly so. We go somewhere, we learn something, we have a conversation, and it inspires innovation. Sometimes the useful sort, sometimes the destructive sort."

"What happens then?" Nora frowned. "That can't be simple."

Cyrus shrugged. "Sometimes the Council cleans it up. Often, it's the Penelopes. That unweaving of magic, especially unintended effects, is how they started, originally. For all they now work closely with the Guard to deal with criminal cases and gather evidence."

Nora nodded. Mabyn gave her a moment and then picked up. "Silvia had a lot of the most prestigious sort of education, but that wasn't what she turned out to need. Our work together was more about figuring out what suited her." Mabyn considered. "Fashion might be a good enough example here. You know the sort of women who wear the most fashionable design, no matter that it suits their particular body poorly? Or is uncomfortable for them? It's like that."

"Huh." Nora tilted her head. "And you're doing the other thing with me. Several other things."

"We are." Mabyn grinned. "Though it's taken us a bit of experimentation to figure out what that might be."

Nora nodded. She glanced behind her, at the apple trees, then looked back at both of them. "And you're putting in all this effort. Putting aside other things you were doing. What happens if I can't learn it? Or if I decide I don't want to?"

This time, Mabyn caught the flick of a finger from Cyrus, encouraging her to take this on. She supposed she was better suited to it. "Are you feeling you can't, or you won't? Or is more about figuring out the map, so you know where you are on it?"

"The second." Nora was clear about it. "Part of me wants to run back to what I know. Fairly regularly at three in the morning."

"Three in the morning is the worst time, isn't it?" Mabyn had all the sympathy. "I wake up then, and I'm sure the world's ending. Everything is bleak at three in the morning."

Cyrus nodded. "More like just before dawn for me, but the same theory."

Nora looked amused. "Oh. Well. All right then." She paused, looking from Cyrus to Mabyn and back again, as if weighing once again the fact magic didn't mend everything. Then she forged on. "Other times, I'm - it's an amazing thing, this magic."

"Oh, and we haven't even shown you more than a glimpse. Later this summer, there's an agricultural fair, sponsored by the Council, with all sorts of performances and magical devices and illusion work. We'll have to make sure you get time there."

"All those things?" Nora was bemused.

"Also all the ordinary things at a fair. Biggest marrow, horse racing and showing. Sheep. Lionel likes the sheep, as we've talked about." Cyrus gestured. "I'm fairly sure Mabyn knows more of the interesting gossip about who's exhibiting than I do."

"You must sit around and drink and watch the horses?" Mabyn ventured, teasing him a little.

She was rewarded with a broad grin. "I like watching people be good at things. And the pavo matches are usually fantastic." He added to Nora. "We explained bohort, I remember. That's the puzzle-based game played on the ground. Pavo is the same, but played on horseback. At any rate, we'll book tickets and make sure we have a tent to retreat to. Much more civilised."

"Are there traditional drinks?" Nora was looking impish now.

"Oh, there are always traditional drinks. With fruit, and little charms that make the alcohol sparkle. It's very festive and a tad ridiculous. And there's always some new food or drink or charm that's all the fad." Mabyn honestly rather liked that part. It was a cheerful outing, even if some of it was very big business indeed. "It's finally been picking up properly after the War again."

Nora nodded, then returned to the earlier question. "What happens if I decide not to do this?"

Cyrus said, "We - by which I mean the Council and Lionel - would figure something out. A cadet line, a more distant relative. Possibly quite distant. We'd see what we could do. It's much easier, if there's an attenuated line, to fix it earlier. Have a younger cousin or nephew or niece or something come to live on the estate from the time they're ten or so. They'll have a far easier time connecting with the magic."

"Does that make a difference, then?" Nora's voice had an odd note to it now, not quite hollow, but as if she were suppressing something.

"Often, yes. You met Gabriel Edgarton. He's got a notably strong connection to it. His father had him out all over the estate from the time he was old enough to stay on a round little pony. It certainly doesn't hurt."

Nora hesitated. "I told you I used to stay with my grandparents in the summer. Not too far from here. Until they died. Did that, would that have..." Her voice trailed off.

Mabyn nodded. "That would be a help. We could go to the village, if you wanted?" She hesitated, not sure how Nora would take that.

"I'd like that." Nora's answer was immediate. "The trees there. And I - there were foxes who lived down at the edge of the woods. I miss the foxes, watching the kits play on the grass."

Cyrus smiled. "There's nothing quite like it, is there? So that answers two of your questions. And you're ducking around the first one, whether you can. I think it's likely you can. We're not testing you with it, because - failing, well. It changes how you see yourself, doesn't it? You know that better than we do. So we're going to wait on that until we're fairly certain you'll succeed. And that also means you have plenty of time to decide that you're willing."

Nora glanced back at the apple trees. "Why ... why do people choose to do this thing?"

Mabyn gestured at Cyrus. "You get to answer that one, Cyrus. I just got married into it. Entirely different problem."

Cyrus leaned a little, thinking. Mabyn liked how he didn't just roll into an all-knowing explanation. "Now, bearing in mind, I've never taken on this particular obligation. We can talk all we like about honour and duty. All the virtues of a proper English man or woman, if you read some of the more gung-ho empire-building literature."

Nora shook her head. "Built on the backs and lives of far too many people who couldn't say no."

"Exactly. The more so in the War. And certainly, I think people who take the work on do feel some sense of duty. But I think there is often an honest sort of hedonism in it. Pleasure. Connecting with the land, when it works, it should be a joy. It won't always be easy - there will be storms and drought and tragic deaths of people and animals and trees before their time. But it should be a relationship like others, with joy and opportunity in the mix as well."

Mabyn was not sure what she thought about that. Or rather, the woman she had been as a new bride would have wanted that, would have flung herself into it. The woman she was now, all these years later, was far too cynical. Far too scarred. Nora must have caught something in her expression, because she glanced at Cyrus. "You are far too optimistic, I think. Idealistic."

Cyrus spread his hands. "I know I am. That is the luxury of this not being my particular task or duty. Nor, in the general run of things, is teaching. You are something of a unique combination."

That made Nora laugh and ease back. "So why do people do the work?"

"Because they feel called to it. Because they think they can do it better than the other options. Anyone can turn down a Lordship. Very few people do, of course, but they can. Slightly more often, we get someone like Lionel, who recognises that he can not do the work justice. And we'll help him figure out some other thing to do, if he wishes. If there is a resolution here."

"All right." Nora swallowed. "Let me have a little tea, and we'll try again."

CHAPTER 28
DEBENHAM, THURSDAY, MAY 19TH

" **I** haven't been back here since my grandparents died. Well. Fifteen years, give or take." Nora was looking around.

"You must know the lore of the place better than I do. Where did they live?" Cyrus had a cane with him, more for show than anything else, though it had a fair number of protective charms imbued in the wood. They were in the Debenham churchyard, admiring the architecture. They'd taken a carriage out for the trip, and the groom was clearly glad to wait at the pub until they were done.

"About a mile and a half that way, north of the village. A small farm - chickens, sheep, nothing that took a lot of space." Nora nodded. She was looking more like a schoolmistress than usual, her hair up in a coiled braid on the crown of her head, as Mabyn wore hers. "Why are we here?"

"Seeing what the local area is like. It's a help that you're familiar with it. This would be much harder otherwise." Cyrus kept his voice low. You never knew in a churchyard when you might come across someone tending a grave or polishing brass or doing a tomb rubbing, or some such thing. The bell-ringers at least announced themselves.

Nora circled around a set of tombstones, as if looking for something specific. "Can I ask you some questions? Since we won't be interrupted by anyone?"

Cyrus nodded. "Here? In the church? A walk down the lane?"

Nora hesitated. "A turn around the church, then we could walk down toward the farm? Is that too much." She nodded at the cane.

"Oh, no. Mostly for show." Cyrus could explain it later. "Were you in here, as a child?"

"Not often. Grandmum helped with the flowers sometimes, but we only came to services about one week in three. And of course, I didn't know about the architecture then, or some of the history." She led the way into the church. "That's called a Galilee porch - quite rare in England, it was used for confessions and penitence. Also sometimes for weddings."

Cyrus snorted. "I'm not entirely sure what I think of that juxtaposition. The ... my, this looks quite old. The tower, I mean."

"I think very early Norman, but I might be misremembering." Nora turned into the main nave. It was an impressive building, by village church standards. Cyrus had been dragged around a fair number of them by his mother, who was partial to visiting them for the art and architecture. The most interesting glasswork was in that Galilee porch. The church itself was the usual mix of memorials and carvings, and a large effigy on a tomb. Certainly lovely and historic.

Cyrus was, however, more interested in a few hints he felt of older magic. He circled to find a spot in the south aisle, where there was a tomb set into the floor. Cyrus could feel the charms that had been set in the brass, but the carvings had faded. He could only read "the famous physician".

A healer, then, he suspected. After the Pact, so someone who had taken his magical talents and cloaked them in science. Or perhaps who had been brilliant at the science and didn't even realise the magic was in play. It could be hard to tell that far back. What he was sure of, however, was that magic infused that tomb.

Nora took his arm as he turned back, and he nodded. "Let's walk down the lane." Once they were well out of the churchyard, he asked, "You mentioned you go to services in Manchester. Do you miss it, at the house?"

"I thought you all didn't much go in for religion?" Nora let go of his arm, now they were down the lane.

"I don't particularly. Mabyn doesn't, I believe. My sister, though, she's a sworn priestess of Belisama, like I said before." When Nora looked blank, Cyrus grinned. "Don't worry, most people haven't heard of her. Gallic goddess of, as Rhoe says, fire and water and the space between them. Her best assistant is Christian, though of a more mystical bent than many."

"That doesn't really answer the question." Nora sounded amused, more than anything.

"The thing about magic - I'll answer you, just a moment - is that people are still people. I think you've been wondering what foreign land you've wandered into. We have all these customs. Some, as you rightly point out, are entirely ridiculous. Or awful. Why should we have to guard ourselves against potions and poisons at a social event? Why should we have so many peculiar customs and rituals?"

"Many customs." Nora agreed. "You had a point, I'm sure."

"In some cases, we know exactly how the magic works. It is, in that case, a science. You do this thing, you get this known reaction. As with science, there might be some variation - fresher materials, stronger materials." Cyrus waved a hand. "That's the easy part."

"That implies a harder part." Nora hesitated. "I remember that tree." She gestured. "It's a bit further now."

"The rest of magic is somewhere between a craft and an art form. A craft is repeatable, usually, but it has a lot more of the personal in it, especially in how you go about the work. An art form - well, those tend to vary from person to person. Even if you're an artist learning to make copies. It is a great deal more intimate." He gestured back toward the church. "That kind of magic permeates things, like the tomb I was looking at in the church floor."

"And the religion?" Nora paused, looking at a patch of wildflowers as if something had caught her attention more generally.

"The point is, there are as many ways to use magic as there are people. Rather more, probably, since it's not as if a person is limited to just one. For some people, religion is part of that. For some, it's something else. Or nothing else, I suppose."

Nora let her hand brush along a flower. "And for you?"

"The ancient magics, elemental ones, are what caught my attention. Not at first, I'm not one of those people who has known exactly what magic he wanted from the earliest I can remember. But certainly by the time I got to Schola, I knew I wanted to understand some of that. The fire, the water, the air, the earth. The rituals give us a framework for talking to beings who aren't human. Sometimes not remotely like humans. And then I had other experiences. The particular ocean trip that has come up, it ended up making me a great deal more aware of water than I had been."

"And what does that mean for me? This?" Nora gestured with her other hand.

Cyrus grinned. "I think you're going to do fine. Take a look there, the field?" He'd noticed them while he was talking. Four glowing red shapes, a vixen and her kits, rolling around in the grass.

Nora stepped back, putting her hand to her mouth. "Oh. Oh!"

It was charming, really, how caught up she was in it. He let her watch. Well, he let himself watch too - for several minutes, until the vixen bundled her little ones off toward the tree line. "I was curious about something, and that's suggestive."

"Suggestive?" Nora gestured. "The farm was just up here. I'm sure it's in ruins now." They turned down a small lane, branching off the main road. Certainly, the ground was overgrown by now, a fair number of wildflowers beginning to grow and bloom. The house, when it came into view, was indeed falling to pieces, and Nora put her hand up to her mouth. "Oh."

Cyrus came up, and after a moment's consideration, put an arm around her shoulder. "Hard to see. Hard to have it be real to you."

She sniffed, once. "You're going to say it's a thing to learn. You keep doing that."

"It keeps being relevant." He gestured. "The magic that was your grandparents in this land, that isn't here anymore. The magic of tending the chickens and the sheep, and the leak in the roof. Or the window pane that needs fixing. No one to weed the garden, or fill in a hole in the lane. The magic of the land, it's like that. It needs tending. What this tells me is that whatever the problem is, it's somewhere closer to the estate. The land here is doing well. Energetically, even."

"You can't tell that just from looking."

"No, but I looked at the harvest records for the past few years, radiating out from the manor. A sample set, of course, there are too many villages to look at every one. Certainly too many villages to look at every one without calling too much attention to myself."

Nora snorted. She had appreciated that sort of humour from him, he'd noticed. Which was part of why he leaned into it now. "And closer to the estate?"

"Not doing as well. It appears to be spreading out, but it hasn't gone as far as I thought it might. That's very promising. And it strongly suggests that a large part of the issue is something on the estate."

Nora grimaced. "That doesn't sound good. I mean."

Cyrus dropped his hand from her shoulder. "Gemma's doing some analysis for me. And passing some along to a few friends who do other things. To see if there's any consistency. It occurred to me that many of the issues Lionel's described have to do with imbalance, especially excess. If this were the 17th century, and the land were a person, I suspect I'd be suggesting bleeding or applying leeches."

That modest joke made Nora laugh out loud. "That image. I'm fairly sure the marshier bits already have leeches, though."

Cyrus grinned. "So. We are making progress. Assuming, of course, you continue to be willing."

That made Nora turn and look at him, a long, slow look.

"You don't seem to have a lot of other choices. Not likely ones, at any rate." She then gestured back to the cottage. "And this. Well. I do love the land, it turns out. I remember how hard it is to work the land. But I love it."

"The land rites are not, thankfully, the same as doing the farming yourself. Generally, fewer chickens are involved. Except perhaps for supper."

Nora shook her head. "You are in a mood. You're more relaxed out here."

She was right. He'd been feeling it. More like when he'd stopped at home for tea with Gemma. Or gone back to Dinas Emrys, the Council keep, for a look at other records. "You know. That's an interesting thing to note."

"And you're easier with me than Mabyn is. Oh, she's been very kind, and she's a grand teacher. Takes one to know one." Nora grinned at that, also rather more relaxed out here. At least now she'd got over the shock of seeing the way the cottage was turning into a ruin.

Cyrus shrugged. "You are younger than Gemma, and younger than her son. But I have a much better relationship with Gemma." He hesitated. "Also, Gemma gave me a lecture when we were setting this up. That you were a grown woman who'd handled your life well up to this point, and we should treat you like a sensible woman. You don't know some things, but no one knows everything. And besides, we're not here to have you be amazed by our wisdom and skill. We're here to see if you can come home to the land."

"Come home to the land." The phrase caught her attention. "Can I have a few minutes? On my own?" She glanced toward the house. "I won't go in. I know it's likely not safe. But I'd like to walk around it."

Cyrus nodded. "I'll go lean on the fence there." He did

so, giving her the privacy he could while being close enough he'd hear if she called out in need of help. She was at it for twenty, perhaps thirty minutes, before she almost startled him, popping up next to him with no warning.

"Thank you. This was a help." There was something in her tone that forbade him from asking. So he just nodded and offered his arm.

"Drink at the pub before we head back, then?"

"Let's."

CHAPTER 29
IN THE GARDEN, MONDAY, MAY 23RD

"I have a question." Nora came over to the table in the garden where Mabyn and Cyrus had settled with their tea.

"We are often at your disposal for questions." Cyrus said. He had come back from his outing with Nora rather more relaxed than Mabyn had expected. In the three days since, she'd noticed that he had a lighter touch with teasing Nora. And more to the point, that Nora was responding to it well.

He had, Mabyn realised, been making a point of an outing here or there every day since. They were all reasonable errands to the Council keep, or to the family home and Gemma, or to a library. None of them took very long, an hour or two at most. She wondered what he was up to, and more to the point, if he would ever tell her. Probably not. She didn't have the right to pry.

Nora snorted, then settled down in the fourth chair. Lionel had been off peering at some of the roses, which were just starting to bloom, but he came back as Nora sat. "Afternoon, Nora."

"Lionel." They seemed amiable enough with each other, though still unsure. It was a bit like cats, newly in the same home, circling each other.

"I enjoyed my supper with Darius - and his sister - a great deal. Is the proper thing to do now to extend an invitation? Is that - is that something I could do here?" The end of Nora's question came out all in a rush. She had asked dozens of questions over the past weeks, but this was the first time she'd had that sort of desire in her voice.

Mabyn glanced at Lionel, catching that Cyrus immediately did the same thing. Lionel leaned forward. "For my part, you are certainly welcome to invite a few guests to supper. With some conversation with the staff, of course, in case there's something already planned."

"The mysteries of who has a half day, and such. I don't think there's anything scheduled for a few weeks, though we'll have some commitments around solstice. Both the land offerings and the fair." Mabyn offered that as a bit of reassurance.

Nora blinked. "It's that easy?"

Mabyn waved a hand. "Well, there is deciding on the menu and the guest list. But we can help with that." She considered Cyrus. "How do you arrange a dinner party?" She knew most of the answer, but it would do both Nora and Lionel good to hear it.

Cyrus laughed. "These days? I leave it to Gemma or host it at one of my clubs. Depending on the invitation list."

"Gemma, for the people you feel you need to invite, and the club for the people you want to see?" Mabyn wanted to see what he said to that.

"A hit, a palpable hit." Now Cyrus was laughing. "Honestly, I know I show well at a larger gathering, but I prefer a smaller one. Four to six guests, when you can have a proper conversation, and not worry too much about treading on other people's conversational toes."

Mabyn winced. "You must have been at a number of awful formal dinner parties. The ones where you are matched up with someone horrid, and then you have to talk to them for a course, then turn the table."

Nora looked a mix between horrified and baffled, so Mabyn explained. "At a formal party, you have a seat assigned by the hostess. It's usually paired by social status, but of course you never sit with your spouse. It is more relaxed these days, thankfully. Also, not everyone throws a dinner party, or only for their intimates. A tea time gathering or a ball can both be far more fluid. Or a garden party. Garden parties are, in terms of social expectations, a joy. You just have to worry about the flowers behaving. And the weather."

Nora shook her head. "You're all potty. You do know that? So, what do I do?"

Mabyn waved a hand. "We'll sit down with our diaries and talk to the staff about a suitable date. You may have us there if you prefer, or you may ask us to go eat somewhere else. There are certainly plenty of options. Or we could go out for an evening. For this, you probably wish to invite at least one other pair, possibly two. Six is a good number, small but not entirely intimate. We can talk through combinations."

Nora nodded, then glanced at Lionel. "If you'd be willing, I'd be glad to include you."

Lionel was caught out, and he opened his mouth, then closed it silently before saying, "I appreciate that, a great deal. May I think about it?"

"Of course." Nora was about to say something further, when they all heard a pair of women's voices - Eustacia

Baddock and someone else. A moment later, they came round the corner into the garden. Mabyn caught the way Cyrus immediately stiffened. Then he and Lionel were both standing, showing good manners.

There was something in him, a twitch of his hand, that Mabyn noticed, filing it away to investigate later. Then he nodded. "Lady Baddock. Lady Jenifry Alton. You remain memorable, Lady Jenifry."

The other woman was rather tall, the sort of woman who went angular with age. Mabyn was put in mind of a greyhound or an Afghan hound, something made of legs and the potential for frenetic movement.

She was blonde, though Mabyn suspected it was charm-coloured. It had that particular flatness of tone that often happened, and she was perhaps five years younger than Cyrus. Her robes were an aggressively mature sky blue, a shade that did not pretend to be an ingenue. She had the sharpness of a woman dressing to cut her way through any gathering.

"I had heard you were here, Cyrus. Such a pleasure to see you again, after we had such a grand time together on that trip. Oh, I was just a strip of a girl, wasn't I? And you've grown into yourself." That was rather a particular approach. Mabyn was competent enough to avoid glancing at Cyrus to see his reaction.

Cyrus made a slight bow. "May I present Council Member Mabyn Teague? And this is Mistress Nora Martin. You must know Lionel, of course." His voice had dropped back to that quiet and resolute neutrality, the tone she'd heard from him all the time, before they had come here.

"Oh, yes. I had hopes that Lionel and my daughter might make a match, once upon a time. She is happily married now, to Alaisdair, Lord Farrell."

He was a cousin of Aubrey's, and Mabyn suddenly wondered what sort of man he was, what sort of husband. Whether this daughter was in the same dire straits she had been in. She wasn't sure if she could ever find out. These were not her usual social circles, not anymore.

Lady Jenifry continued to advance. "This is so quaint, out here. I've heard all about your little project." She made it sound like they were in some cottage somewhere, full of chintz and bundles of herbs. Not that there was anything wrong with either of those, though Mabyn drew a line at covering every flat surface with a lace doily.

Something about that put Mabyn's hackles up. She could feel herself reacting, before she reminded herself to take a breath. Lady Jenifry advanced, then reached to touch Cyrus's cheek. "May I take your seat, Cyrus, dear?"

It was one long stroke of her finger along his skin. Cyrus did not pull away, did not react, other than to gesture with one hand. Lionel stood aside to offer his mother his chair. Men were ruled by the formalities of etiquette.

There was something in the set of Cyrus's shoulders Mabyn did not much like. As Lady Jenifry sat down, he pushed the chair in, then took several steps to the side to come closer to Mabyn. "We were talking about the Midsummer Faire, and some other plans for the summer."

"You expect to be here so long?" Lady Jenifry looked around cooly. "That is grand for us. You really must come to supper sometime, Cyrus." Mabyn could have sworn she saw his hand flick closed and then open slowly. The offer was clearly aimed at Cyrus, not the rest of them.

"I'm quite committed to my plans here. And of course, various Council and family events. I take my duty seriously. I know you found that - what was the word? Quaint of me, across the Atlantic." He added to Mabyn, conversationally.

"Besides making sure Rhoe had a grand time, as I'd been glad to arrange, I had some projects for the Council. It took up rather all of my time, other than a few pleasant duelling bouts with a few of the Scali men, and a night of card playing."

"Do you win at cards?" Mabyn cursed herself for the inanity.

Curiously, Cyrus lit up, and laughed, a moment of the ease he'd shown before Lady Baddock and Lady Alton had shown up coming back. "I won and took my sister and Hugh out to a fine supper on the winnings once we arrived in Boston. And a tour of a bookshop followed by quite a few purchases." He nodded at Lady Alton. "Lady Jenifry thought her quite a bluestocking, I know. Not her sort of person at all."

Which made it clear that Lady Alton was not Rhoe's sort of person. Or Cyrus's, she was sure now.

Lady Jenifry pouted, the sort of expression that often made men willing to do quite a lot to make it stop, and reached for Cyrus's hand. "You must have some time to come round. It's been so lonely since my late husband died."

Cyrus raised an eyebrow. "I've heard quite a few tales about your house parties, I recall. You've never struck me as someone alone in a crowd." He shrugged. "As I said, a strictly limited number of outside social engagements, while on Council business. I'm declining most other invitations at the moment."

"Oh, pah." Lady Jenifry looked discomfited for a moment. Only a moment. "You must tell me all about what you've been up to, though. That's the proper country thing to do, sharing the news and the gossip."

She had, Mabyn realised, entirely been ignoring Mabyn

herself. "Cyrus is quite right." She reached out, a sudden impulse to touch his hand, and felt his fingers shift and squeeze hers for a quick moment. "We have obligations here. They have turned out to be quite pleasant, as it happens, but they must have our first attention. Our time is not our own, that's one of the first things anyone on the Council learns."

"Oh, pish." As a direct form of address went, it wasn't much. "And your role in all this? Taking notes?"

Mabyn blinked, then she laughed at the insult. She could sense Cyrus, next to her, shifting position, as if he were going to take a step forward, but as soon as she spoke, he eased back, minutely. "Goodness, no. I have a perfectly competent shorthand - I read four languages, it uses all of them - but I use it for my Materia and Alchemy work. Cyrus is perfectly capable of his own paperwork. Better than I am at it, I'm beginning to suspect."

"And your people?" This got Lady Baddock leaning over to murmur something. The dowager had kept quiet, through this, which was also rather suspicious.

Mabyn answered with a twitch of her shoulder. "Oh, I'm quite sure you know, you've already dissected my apparent failings between you." Part of her wanted to point out that Cyrus freely gave her his time, was a charming and intelligent partner at every meal she ate in company. "I don't play that game. Not anymore."

CHAPTER 30
INSIDE THE HOUSE

Cyrus blinked at that, then he grinned slowly. "You will find both of us quite set in our ways and on our proper course." He then shrugged. "If you both would prefer the garden, Mabyn, may I escort you inside? I'd very much appreciate your advice on that next bit of research we were thinking of tackling."

Mabyn picked up smoothly, thankfully, given that Cyrus was making this up out of whole cloth. "Quite, yes. You were thinking about the implications of materials that would wash away. I had a thought about powdered flower petals, actually, I found a reference this morning. We could get some lovely strong colours that way."

Cyrus nodded. "Nora? Lionel? You're both welcome, of course."

Lionel looked rather as if he wanted to come along, but his mother promptly said, "Stay, Lionel." It was rather the sort of command one gave a dog, and Lionel subsided.

Nora nodded. "I have that reading you wanted me to do to finish." She stood. "Lady Baddock, Lady Alton." Very polite, indeed. Cyrus entirely approved. He offered his other arm to Nora and escorted both women back across the drawbridge into the courtyard, where Nora immediately broke off. She kissed his cheek lightly. "Very gallant. I'll be up in my rooms."

That left Cyrus alone with Mabyn, and at a loss for words. She turned, moving to face him, and then she reached up to touch his cheek for a moment, just the way Lady Jenifry had, before she lowered her hand. "She doesn't know you at all, does she?"

Cyrus held still through the touch, though he followed her hand down with his eyes before looking back to meet Mabyn's. "What was your first clue?" He was, in all honesty, feeling rather more shaky about the whole thing than he wanted to admit, even to himself.

Mabyn looked him up and down. "Come along. Upstairs. Drinks. It's a bit early, but entirely called for." When he hesitated, she reached out and took his hand, tugging him along behind her. He felt a little like a small child dragged along while someone was out shopping, but he didn't object.

She led him to her sitting room, and nudged him into a chair, before going to pour them both drinks. When his hands were cupped around the glass, she settled down in the chair facing him. A moment later, she'd reached into her pocket, and she'd pulled out a small smoothed stone, tossing it up in her hand, then catching it, over and over.

Cyrus found the movement curiously soothing. He leaned back, closing his eyes and rubbing the bridge of his nose. "She put it around the ship she'd slept with me." It came out before he was entirely aware he was speaking out loud.

Mabyn's snort made him open his eyes. "You'd implied that, before. You are very restrained, not embarrassing her in public." She then considered, and said, "You able to catch?" He nodded. "Three, two, one." She tossed the stone in a tidy arc, and he caught it easily. Good thing, too. He suspected dropping it would have been both horribly rude and possibly dangerous.

He knew for certain it would have been both when he got it in his hand. It was a hag stone, with a natural hole in it, but it wasn't the usual sort of river stone. He lifted it up. The glossiness of the surface, the way it felt almost waxy under his fingers. "Flint?"

Mabyn nodded. "I've had it since I was a girl. I found it when I was five."

Cyrus looked up sharply. "And - here." He made as if to give it back.

She shook her head. "I gave it to you for a reason. You keep it safe, give it back in a bit."

That made him consider the other ways the stone felt. There was nothing engraved on it, no obvious enchantments or charms. Not that he could give it a full run of testing sitting here. He was exceedingly competent, but not that kind of gifted, to know the magic of a thing, just by touch. It made him feel better, in some indefinable way. More balanced, more himself. Less buffeted by the expectations.

She must have seen something shift in him, because after a few minutes of silence, she spoke again. "Of all the things I brought into my trials, that's the one I didn't expect I'd need."

Cyrus looked up, blinking, his fingers still wandering over the surface. "Hag stones for protection, for scrying. There are certain application for the Fatae, I came across a reference about their use when creating or repairing portals..." His voice trailed off. "You surely know this."

"You explain so well, though. It's a pleasure to listen to you." She was smiling at him. It was a compliment, naturally, but it felt like a very honest one. Then she added, her grin getting broader. "Also, I've noticed you like to think out loud. I certainly don't mind."

That made him wrinkle his nose. "A bad habit. An early one. I'd talk things through with Tanith. And then, when I was preparing for the Council trial, I'd go practice, after I'd done my apprentice duties, and then come and stand over Gemma's crib and tell her. It sorts things out in my head."

Mabyn nodded. "I'd tell the stone. There's lore that a hole in a stone will keep secrets for you. Certainly, it's never told anyone what I whispered into it."

Cyrus considered for a long moment. "And it's enchanted. Properly, I mean. Not by any method I know."

"Well. Rather, let's say it's enchanted by every method I've ever learned, all on top of each other. Starting when I was six, and wished on stars."

He considered that, and then rummaged in his inside jacket pocket, pulling out the small rectangle of ebony wood he kept there. Cyrus ran his finger down the back, loosening the charms that held it in one long piece, and then folded it to make a square instead. He ran his fingers over the stones set in the wood. They made a square now, or properly a diamond, one stone for each direction, for each element, for each point. "Here." Cyrus stood briefly, to hand it to her.

She said nothing, taking her time examining it. He knew exactly what she'd notice. The four stones, amethyst, ruby, aquamarine, and jade. "I had an opal in there, originally, for water. It shattered, and I replaced it with an aquamarine."

"After that particular trip? I recall it was an aquamarine,

that project to connect the different continents for urgent messages." Mabyn, of course, would have read up on it by now.

Cyrus waited, just a moment, and then said, his voice as even as he could make it. "During. The night we made the offering to the One Below."

Mabyn looked up at him, then down again at the stone. "Fine repair work." When she looked up again, she said, cheerfully. "May I presume on your permission to ask more questions?"

"Long since given. I'm not so far gone I can't manage to refuse." Even if Cyrus were still rather more wobbly, mentally speaking, than he wanted to be.

"What did you bring in with you?" To the trials. That sort of question, without a proper antecedent, for them, always would mean Council business.

"My self, dressed in robes embroidered with a dozen different protection charms. A fair number of potion vials, Rhoe was still early in her apprenticeship, but she made friends with three different and talented apothecaries once she realised what I was up to. A variety of prepared charm stones, absolutely none of which I used in the end."

"Did she try to talk you out of it?" Mabyn had wondered that.

"Goodness, no. My parents did. She just..." He shrugged. "She rearranged the shape of me in her head, made space for that madness, and saw me through it with as much help as she could offer."

He looked up to meet Mabyn's eyes. "My trial was not like anything I expected. Even though we never talk about it, most any of us, I gather that's fairly common. We spend all this time preparing for what we think it will be, and it is something entirely other. Rhoe has a few stories of what we might call visions, knowing there was something she was trying to reach. My experiences were not nearly so tidy."

"That's a mystery, you know. In the oldest sense." She hadn't stopped examining the stones. Mabyn didn't look up, but after a moment, she went on. "Mine was like walking into a forest, a garden, a mix of places. The wealth of materia, at my fingertips, like I could pluck anything out of the world I could ever want."

Cyrus considered this, watching her. "Did you? Take anything? Reach for it?"

She looked up, and there was something wild in her eyes, a great storm. "Oh, I'd been trained out of wanting things. By my parents. By my husband, particularly. Wanting was dangerous, wanting was forbidden. I was supposed to do what I was told. Small steps, slight movements, shallow breaths. I wanted to do differently. Incoherently, but that was the thing I wanted."

"My sister entirely agrees on thinking there should be something different. As did Tanith."

It didn't ease the storm, but Mabyn smiled. It was like a crack of sunlight, through a cloudy day, sharp and startling and beautiful. "I thought about all the stories, of what is forbidden. The apple, in Eden. Orpheus turning back to look at Eurydice. Any number of geasa, in lore."

Cyrus nodded, not entirely sure where she was going with this. Or rather, how much she might say.

"The trick is, what do you reach for?" She shrugged, then reached into her pocket and pulled something else out. She didn't toss this one. She held it out on her palm, two panes of amber, with something between them. A leaf, a single leaf, still glowing with the vivid green of life. "It was like that when I took it from the floor of the tower."

He didn't touch it, just came and stood, bending over it. "That is a blessing and a challenge, isn't it?"

"The amber holds. It's a stasis. But the leaf insists on life." She let him look and tucked it back in her pocket. After a moment, he offered her the hag stone back. He found it tremendously soothing, and yet he could not borrow that comfort for long. It was not his to ask for.

She took it, settling it back in its proper place, then offering him his small stones. They were far tamer stones, he realised, in their setting, than hers were. For all she seemed settled and mannerly, fully of the civilised places, there was clearly a wildness in her that no one noticed. Certainly her increasingly unlamented husband had not.

"Mine wasn't like that. It...." He hesitated. "I'd spent all this time immersed in the elements. Flinging myself into the experience, over and over again. Like it would burn or wash or blow or bury everything I was feeling that I didn't want to feel. When it came to the trial itself, it was more like I was all alone, in a featureless plain. Oh, there were challenges, though honestly, they faded from my mind almost immediately. I remember the shape of them, a puzzle, the sort of conversation where one wrong word will bring everything down."

Mabyn snorted. "We're a fine pair, aren't we? Me, too afraid to want anything, you having thrown yourself into the experience so much there was nothing left."

Cyrus nodded. He was not sure, honestly, what that meant. What that might mean. He hesitated, then asked the question he'd really wanted to know. "Are you glad you did it?"

CHAPTER 31
TUESDAY

Mabyn was still thinking about Cyrus's question the next day as she sat out at the table in the garden, considering their next steps. In the moment, she had gone quiet. Glad was the wrong emotion, certainly. Proud, terrified, awestruck, determined, those all fit better than glad. All she'd been able to do was nod.

And yet, she kept coming back to that word. Cyrus had not pressed her for an answer. Her silent reaction had apparently told him enough, the expressions on her face that leaked through her control. He had turned the conversation smoothly to stories about his apprenticeship, how his burning drive for the Council had alternately bemused and frustrated his apprentice mistress.

Cyrus seemed to have had a good relationship with her. One that involved a certain amount of teasing and informality, certainly. He'd told several stories of pranks, and not just the ones where he came out better. Mabyn had felt that with Silvia, and with two or three others before her, but it was not how things usually went. Much more commonly it was made up of formality and enforced intimacy, but the kind that did not last long past the moment.

It made her sad, honestly. She had been a romantic when she was young. That there would be these tremendous life-changing relationships in her life. With her apprentice master, with her husband, with his family, with the family they would make together. With whatever apprentices she might take on later in life. Instead, she all too often felt like she was in a formal dance, all the steps laid out. People might touch and brush hands briefly, but it didn't last, it didn't deepen.

She was lost in thought when she heard Nora behind her. "Mabyn."

"Nora. You're not interrupting, I wasn't getting much done, anyway." She gestured at the chair.

"Is that what they're all like? The ladies and lords?" Mabyn had expected a question somewhat like that.

"Not all of them. Oh, there's plenty who value how up to the mode a frock is, or whether you picked exactly the right flowers for a gathering. But there are, in fact, people who are experts in fashion and flowers and any other skill, and it is possible to hire them. I have a little black book for such needs. I will be glad to share recommendations."

"How many of them?" It was a sticking point.

"About half." Mabyn had to admit that. "The other half, mostly, have professions they care for, or some other passion, and they do not fuss as much about the flourishes."

"I couldn't be a teacher." Nora leaned forward, her elbows on the table.

"Yes and no. Not like you were in a classroom, all the time, likely not. The seasonal offerings and the obligations don't fall at holiday times anymore, in your world. Though some people manage something near enough."

Mabyn shrugged. "But you could run a tutoring school. Perhaps especially for people who didn't come from the sorts of families who went to Schola or Dunwich or Alethorpe. You could do some work with the Ministry, around education and opportunities. You aren't forbidden from working, so long as you are available for the seasonal rites, and manage whatever tenants there are."

"Is that actually required?" Nora peered at Mabyn.

"Well, it's encouraged. And it's often seen, traditionally, as part of the land rites. A good Lord - or Lady - can't abuse the tenants too far."

Nora nodded, then looked back off down the length of the garden. "And Lady Alton?"

"Lady Alton is a particular type, and you do not need to do things that way. We can introduce you to some of the others, the current Lords or Ladies, or their Heirs. You've met the younger Edgartons already. I expect you'd quite like Gabriel's mother. I also expect she'd like you, honestly."

Nora nodded. "And these people will - welcome me?" Ah, that was the crux of the question, and a complicated crux at that. "How do I know who to trust?"

Mabyn considered. "How did you decide it before? We are still people. Some of us have power or position or strong magic, or something else that gives an edge. All right, quite possibly several things that give an edge. But that is not so different than the world you've grown up in."

"And yet, you have the same issues. Unpleasantness. I didn't care for how Lady Alton was with Cyrus."

Mabyn hadn't either. She wasn't sure about what to say to that.

Nora glanced over at her. "And you didn't like it either. Why didn't one of you do something about it?"

Mabyn shrugged a shoulder. "We are both highly trained and competent magicians, in our own rights. He does not need my protection, and I do not need his. But we are still bound by social niceties. If we throw that power around, we do not get cooperation. We might get fear, we might get obedience, but it might well not last. And unleashing that magic is the wrong tool for a social difficulty." She tilted her head. "Mind, I suspect that's how Cyrus ended up in the original problem with her, all those years ago."

Nora hesitated. "And you and your late husband."

That was a very direct hit. Mabyn went still, but then she nodded. "Just so." She hesitated. "There's a woman I know, younger than I am, the same sort of awful marriage. Well, not exactly the same sort, but near enough. There isn't an easy way out. The binding portion of the magical oaths makes it complicated, unless the other person actively breaks them."

Nora glanced over, now leaning on the table. "And?"

"And Lady Edgarton - Alysoun - was helpful. She and other people she knew, not titled. She's done the same for a handful since. Alysoun wasn't able to save me, she's a decade younger. But there are options. More to the point, those don't apply to you. Whatever marriage contract you make, whatever oaths you swear, if you take on the title, you will have protections."

"Would anyone?"

"Anyone the Council favoured. Cyrus doesn't bring it out to the surface all that often, but he and Alexander are two of the best with ritual language among us. They know the solicitors who can work with that, to build a contract that fits the oath. They know the loopholes."

Nora was quiet before standing to walk out into the garden itself. She walked to the edge of the nearest bed, by several flowering herbs, bending to brush her fingers along leaves.

Mabyn let her take her time. There was no rush to this. Urgency, yes, but not right in this moment, this afternoon. Nora had been introduced to the land at May Day, and at solstice, they'd see if the land began to respond to her directly in the rites. If the response was bad, they were in trouble. If it was subtle and quiet, or was fairly mild, they were likely doing well enough.

When Nora turned, she looked resolute, but she came all the way back to the chair, settling her skirt before she spoke. "It all seems too perfect. Even with what you've said about people being difficult."

"We're people. We have those who want to gather all the power to themselves. And honestly, you should be dubious of the Council there too, though at the moment, we're mostly grabbing at influence, rather than raw power. But there are people who want money, who want control, who don't care what they have to do to others to get it. We aren't perfect. We're still people."

"And the magic?"

Mabyn shrugged. "Magic makes the range of what people can do to each other wider. Though it varies. Most people don't have incredibly powerful magic. I don't partic-ularly. I'm, oh, around the two third mark, as we measure it. That's not a thing most people know, for the record. I got a chance to look at my educational records."

"And Cyrus?" Nora was frowning at this.

"Stronger than I am in terms of raw ability. We're about

equal, I think, in how adept we are at using what we have." Mabyn frowned.

"You say that, but now you're not sure."

"We were doing a ritual, and - that's not about power. It's about something else, most of the time. Using the power you have well. Intelligently, sensibly. Whatever the word is." Mabyn settled back in her chair, not entirely satisfied with her explanation. Nora nodded, and let the conversation end, before she asked about some of the newly blooming flowers.

CHAPTER 32
TUESDAY LATER AFTERNOON

Cyrus hesitated at the door to the library. He could see Mabyn there, her head bent over the book she was reading. Her hair had come out in small curling wisps, softening the line of her neck.

He was still trying to decide whether to interrupt when she looked up. "For Nimue's sake, don't hover."

Cyrus snorted. "I'm across the room. I thought hovering required closer proximity."

"That's looming. Don't loom, either. It strains my neck. And my neck is reminding me I am not as young as I was."

He came forward, settling down in a chair on the other side of the table. She didn't cover up her notes. Instead she moved one hand to reveal part of them. She had a map of the grounds with several layers of tracing paper over it, showing different things.

"You weren't at tea." Cyrus offered it carefully.

"And you were, what?" There was a note of defensiveness in her voice, he thought.

"I caught a glimpse when you were talking with Nora. A difficult conversation?"

"Nora wasn't difficult at all. She isn't. I'm sure she could be if she put her mind to it." Mabyn's comments flowed out, immediately, directly.

Cyrus inclined his head. "I didn't say Nora was a problem." He set both his hands on the table, palms up. "If you tell me to stop asking, I will."

She kept looking down at the papers in front of her for a long moment, then she looked up. "I almost believe you would." She turned her head, looking towards the window.

Cyrus waited, patiently. He applied all the skills in waiting he had learned for ritual. Waiting for the person leading it to be ready. Waiting for other people to sort themselves out. Waiting for the right moment to begin. Each ritual had its own timing, its own pacing. That was, in truth, where he excelled. Being able to feel what was needed.

And right now, this ritual of conversation needed his silence and his patience.

The silence went on, and he simply breathed in it, letting the stillness continue. It must have been a good two minutes before she turned back to look at him, then carefully reached across the table, putting her right hand in his left. "I am teaching Nora to take on something I failed at. The hubris of it is getting to me. And the hypocrisy." Her voice was quiet and tight, but not small.

"I would think your experience makes you a better teacher, rather than a worse one." Cyrus spoke before he consciously thought through the implications, but they were, for all that, the words he needed to say in this moment.

He felt her fingertips shift, as if moving to dig in, before she deliberately took a breath and let it out. "Explain that to me. Would you?"

Cyrus took a breath in his turn, holding it for a count of four and letting it out. "You know a number of ways it can go wrong. You know why it matters." He gestured with his right hand. "You have said very little about your marriage, but I am clear it was nothing like mine. In the middle of that, you held your own. You did your best by your son. And while I am clear you are not close, he takes his responsibilities seriously. The land is doing well. The people on the land are doing well."

He heard her inhale before he saw the change in her expression. "How do you know?"

"I looked at the records. Both the Council records, and the Ministry ones. Nothing you haven't done for others. Though I understand why you wouldn't want to ask in this case."

"Looking at the records would either imply I didn't trust him, or make plain that we do not talk." Mabyn grimaced. "Neither is palatable."

Cyrus considered. "I would be glad to show you my notes. Do you want to know how people talk about you and him?"

Again, there was that clench of fingers, for just an instant. "Please." Then she was bracing herself. He could feel the tension from her fingers, and see the way her shoulders shifted, her breathing.

He tugged her hand between his, enclosing it. "People mock me for how close Gemma and I are. They have mentioned you and your son. That you have let him grow up, you let his uncle have a role. That there is a proper British distance there."

She grimaced, opening her mouth and then closing it.

He went on. "The people I have overheard - and I have no illusions. A number of them wished to be overheard, but not all of them. The ones I have heard, they consider the way you and your son are to be far more the done thing. As they consider your marriage to have been far more the done thing. I am far too given to sentimentality to be entirely trustworthy."

"No one thinks you're soft." Mabyn's response was quick. Too quick, the way Cyrus got when someone put him on the defensive.

"They don't know what to do with me. Not when it comes to that sort of conversation. No one can deny Gemma's competence. People admit, sometimes grudgingly, that I did well by her. But it is not a form they understand."

"Where does that leave me, then?"

"A dutiful mother, raising a son who does what is expected of him." Cyrus tilted his head. "But it bothers you, doesn't it, that he does what he ought, but no more."

Mabyn let out her breath in a rush. "Blood and bone." Then she nodded. "That is on the nose."

"I'm sorry." Cyrus let the emotion come through in his voice. "He is a responsible man. There are many worse things in the world. But that's not what you wanted for him, was it?"

She shook her head, a tiny shift. "I wanted so much more for Davin. And I didn't know how to give it to him."

"He trained in Alchemy, didn't he?" He knew the answer. He wouldn't have gone down this conversational road without knowing it.

Mabyn nodded, slowly. "What are you aiming at?"

"Tell me about his alchemical work. You know I'll follow enough of the details."

"Honestly, he's a bit plodding. More than a bit. He is very capable at following directions, someone else's work or procedure. But he's not at all inventive. He considers it a waste of energy, going haring off after ideas that might not work out. Also, he points out frequently, whenever he wheedles information about my expenses out of me, a needless waste of coin."

"I never did like your brother-in-law." Cyrus offered it as a gift. "I didn't know your husband well at all, but I suspect I'd have thought much the same."

"Oh, Aubrey was far worse." She tilted her head. "You overlapped fairly closely with Gerold, didn't you? At school?"

"He was the year behind me. Fox House." He tilted his head. "You're probably lucky to have been spared us, honestly. We were an awful lot at the time."

"You as well? I have a bit of difficulty imagining you as a feckless youth." Mabyn did smile at that image, and Cyrus was pleased. He did not like how tension made her coil into herself.

"Ah, I was somewhat redeemed by my desire to impress Tanith. And have her not think me an idiot." He smiled. "Gerold kept trying to get her attention."

"So he disliked you. Rather intensely, I suspect."

"Entirely valid. I was blessed, and I know it." Cyrus shrugged. This was coming rather near the heart for him, but having started this conversation, he would not allow himself to back away. "But while I do think that moderation in spending is a sensible fiscal policy on the whole, it is not the only thing to factor into your life."

Mabyn opened her mouth, then closed it. She glanced down at their hands - hers was still between his. "Explain that, please?"

"This is a theory I've not talked about much. Some with Gemma. A little with Alexander, last year, he was thinking of teaching something that made it relevant. I would appreciate your help finding gaps in it, actually."

She nodded once. "Go on."

"When does a ritual begin? When does it end?" Cyrus laid out the bare questions without biassing her.

Mabyn pursed her lips. "It begins when you begin the steps of the ritual." Before he could say anything further, she caught herself. "But that leaves out the planning, the preparation you do. Laying out the space, having a purifying bath, whatever it is."

Cyrus could feel himself start grinning. "For the record, that's as fast as Alexander was about it. And he'd had a little priming, technically."

"And it ends not with the last steps of the ritual proper, but sometime later. Though that isn't as tidy, is it? Does the ritual end when it stops having a meaningful effect? Goodness, when I wake up in the middle of the night, I have something to chew on."

Cyrus nodded. "Roughly speaking, I feel that the ritual begins when you start considering that you want to do one, and that the active portion continues until you have set the work of the ritual fully on its way. Concluding the ritual, directing the magic appropriately, tidying up loose ends. Personally, I think it runs at least until you've slept, and rather longer for more complex things that have ongoing actions on the physical level. But I am willing to be argued with about that."

Mabyn snorted. "Fair enough. I will not argue it now without a good and specific example. What does that have to do with Gerold?"

"I see the scope of the ritual being rather like a Gaussian curve. A bell curve, swelling up in the middle, tapering off on either side. Some people like to make it a triangle, or something that looks a bit like a child's drawing of a mountain range, all little spiky peaks. It begins in a small way, grows bigger, has more influence and weight, and then it begins to steadily decline in impact. No single point is clearly vastly up or down from the one before or after it, but at some point you can recognise the rise, and the fall."

"A flow, instead of, as you say, mountains." Mabyn nodded. "And Gerold?"

"He has struck me as being prone to dualism. A thing is good, or it is bad, and there is no middle ground. You are climbing the peak, with all its challenges, or descending in supposed glory. Presumably not failure. Such men do not like to think about failure."

Mabyn considered. "And so you think better to build a life that rises and falls like waves. Naturally, moving, changing, rising to the next goal. Rather than something rigidly aligned." Cyrus nodded, and she went on. "And you think Gerold and Davin are rigid."

"Our world rewards predictable rigidity. It's seen as safer. Being a known man, a respectable man, doing the intended thing. Rotating between one's duties, one's club, perhaps a match or a race or two." Cyrus shrugged. "That is not where genius dwells, as a rule. Some people, even many, are happy there. And for all I know, that includes Davin and his uncle. But it is not, I think, a place where you could be happy at all."

Mabyn hesitated for just a moment. "Aubrey, my husband, was exceedingly rigid. And he demanded I become so. He never left me alone, because he did not trust I would do what he wanted. Always at his beck and call. Always where he knew where I was." She squeezed Cyrus's hand once, then drew her hand back. "It felt awful."

Cyrus swallowed, closing his eyes, trying to imagine

what that must have been like, and failing. When he opened them again, she was there, waiting, like a hare spotted too far away from safety, with that trembling anticipation of the danger about to come. "You hated it." It wasn't a question. "And then he died, and you were free. And now..."

Mabyn stood, suddenly. "Now, I need to think." She came around the table, leaving the papers. "Look at those." Then, as if she did it without thinking to stop, she bent to kiss his cheek. "Thank you."

With that, she was gone, and Cyrus was not at all sure what had just happened.

CHAPTER 33
WEDNESDAY MORNING

"Tell me." Nora had come out to the garden, looking fierce. Cyrus had been out there all morning, collaborating with Mabyn on a tricky bit of testing the earth, to see what magical blessings or taints might be lingering.

"Tell you what?" Mabyn took over easily, and Cyrus let her. She liked that about him, for all it still kept her awake at night. He didn't grab at power, like many men she'd known. Cyrus was glad enough to share it, generously. He did his share of the actual work, too, which was perhaps even more peculiar. She'd had him moving things around for hours, and he'd made no complaint at all.

"What you think is going on. You have some idea." Nora put both her hands on her hips. It reminded Mabyn of what she'd been like as a girl, though she'd never had the courage to be so openly defiant.

"Can you pack up here and meet us in my sitting room?" Cyrus asked her easily, but gave her the space to suggest something else.

Mabyn raised an eyebrow. But she got what he meant,

that he wanted his warding around them, tight and close. "Lionel?"

"If you see him, let him know we're talking. Might be a bit? We should be down for tea. But I think he might be out at one of the tenant farms, checking on that roof."

Nora nodded. "He offered to take me, but it's a long ride for me yet."

"Well, that makes it easier for us to chat. Come along up. Mabyn, are you all set?" Mabyn felt an odd itch between her shoulder blades.

She nodded. "I'll be fifteen or twenty minutes. Tea would be grand, if you could put on the kettle."

He nodded and stood, offering his arm to Nora. Mabyn didn't rush packing up, but by the time she was done, that itch was definitely more annoyingly noticeable.

"Ready?" Cyrus turned to Mabyn without preamble.

She tilted her head. "Add the other?"

Cyrus laughed. "As if I'd forget." He then stood in the centre of the room, just under that rose, and called his magic to him. It was the first time he'd done something quite so visible around Nora, and he clearly knew it looked impressive. It was a shimmer of light and almost tactile power, thrumming for a moment until it settled.

They'd had a pleasant wrangle about it a few weeks ago. People thought that a magic like that was like calling a well-trained dog to heel, certain of obedience. She and Cyrus both knew better. It was more like luring a cat with a bit of fish and hoping the cat would deign to do as you wished. Still, whatever else it was, it was a spectacular bit of a show.

It put her in mind of one of the cards of the Howard Tarot. Not the Lord of Wands, though there was some physical resemblance there. Instead, she thought of the Lord of

Swords. That was a nobleman taking his ease on his throne with sword and pen to hand, an owl perching on the back of the intricately carved chair. There was a precision there, that was far more about air than fire, in the end.

When he looked down at Nora, she was blinking. "You've not done that before. That's nothing like..." She gestured out the window at the outdoors.

"Walls make a difference, it's a different structure for the magic to dwell in." Cyrus settled back in his chair with a flick of one hand to pull his robes out of the way.

"Do you think it's a dwelling? Mistress Elling always thought it was more like decoration. Though Master Ottson argued it was more like a container, as in cooking or baking." Mabyn settled back. She never could resist a good bit of theory natter. Especially with Cyrus, who had turned out to be as widely-read as he appeared to be. Not how that usually went for her, either. Too many people pretended to have read more than they actually had.

Cyrus laughed. "Different kinds of buildings have different sorts of uses and spaces. Some are temples or cathedrals." He added, as an aside to Nora. "I'm in and out of the Temple of Healing a fair bit, just meeting my sister for meals. We should take you sometime. The gardens are coming into their most showy form."

Mabyn said, amiably, "The gardens are restorative, and they also grow a number of plants used in the healing. Not in apothecary quantities, but there are a number of healing charms that work better with, oh, a spring of rosemary in the room. A bit of lavender under the pillow, a bit of hyssop in a cleansing bath."

Cyrus grinned at Mabyn. "There are more kinds of magic in the world, dear Nora, than are dreamt of in your philosophy."

Nora grimaced. "Please, do not abuse the Bard of Avon to make your point. Honestly." She then frowned. "Which raises the question of what he knew about magic, doesn't it?"

Cyrus spread his hands wide. "That's an entirely different conversation, you're right. A fairly agreeable one for supper, honestly." He then sobered. "You asked what we thought was going on."

Nora straightened, her shoulders shifting back into that determined set. "I did."

Mabyn glanced at him, and he waved his hand. She could do this better than he could, most likely. "The conclusion we've come to is that it must be something that Eustacia is doing. However, we haven't figured out what, exactly. Or why. Or even whether it's deliberate. Asking her is unlikely to be a help, unless we could bring the court into it."

Nora frowned. "You said something about being able to make sure someone told the truth."

Cyrus nodded. "There's a particular ritual that some people can do. A Lord of the land, if their magic is strong enough and well-trained enough and they're on their own land. A magistrate with the proper arrangements. A judge in the courtroom. Certain of the Guard in specific circumstances, with the local Lord's permission. It is not easy - truth isn't, is it? But it works. On the other hand, it is easy to see how it can be abused, and so we have limits on how it is called down. And it is not easy, so most of the people who can don't do it idly."

Nora considered. "So you would need evidence, something compelling. More than being sure it must be her."

"Exactly." Mabyn settled back in her chair. "And honestly, I can't tell if she knows she's doing it or not. I'm not sure how to find out, without someone following her all the time."

"If we were in certain novels, someone would be bribing her maid around now." Nora said it matter-of-factly.

Cyrus blinked. "I have read some of those novels, and I admit, the thought had occurred to me, though I would have asked Mabyn to do the bribing. But in this case, the maid is entirely loyal. A local girl, grown up here, she's never known anyone other than Eustacia as Lady Baddock. It's why she's the one down at the dower house. She doesn't mind being ordered about as much as the others."

"Aren't they also local?" Nora frowned. "Someone said?" She seemed about to chase it back through her memory, then she visibly set it aside.

"Also local." Mabyn offered the information. "But a bit older and wiser. And I believe all of them had either served in other houses, or been here under Lionel's father." She shrugged. "A wider experience of the world."

Nora nodded. "So what are you going to do?" She seemed so sure that they had a plan, and Cyrus hated to disappoint her.

"That is an excellent question. She will not simply tell us, that ship sailed long ago. Around when we arrived, honestly, if not years before." Cyrus frowned. "I'm not sure, honestly."

Mabyn looked up, tilting her head. It wasn't like him to be this uncertain. Or, if he were, to let it show. Then she took a breath. "I'm not either, honestly. Do you have thoughts?"

Cyrus shook his head. "A nagging, teasing idea that won't let itself be seen. Most frustrating. What would be ideal, of course, would be to catch her doing something unambiguously a problem."

Nora looked from Cyrus to Mabyn and back to Cyrus. "What - no, wait, I have a different question. Likely a silly one."

"No sincere question is silly." Mabyn replied promptly.

"You've talked about the oaths that the Lord takes. Or the Lady, the one sworn to the land. And I saw the one you made her take." Nora hesitated. "But did, I mean, how does that work if you marry?"

Cyrus looked up, and Mabyn realised he wanted to know if this was too much for her. It was delicately done, a raised eyebrow, a tiny tilt of the head. She smiled at him more than anything. "Let me start, and Cyrus, you can fill in anything else?"

He nodded, settling back and picking up his teacup. Mabyn gathered her thoughts. "First, some parts depend on the timing. If someone is the Heir when they marry, or the Lord or Lady. How long they've been any of those, if they are."

Nora considered. "Because someone could be the Lord - or Lady - and marry. Or they could be the Heir. And they could have been the Heir for ages, or they could have just become one."

Mabyn nodded. "Exactly. And there are different ways of being someone's Heir. An eldest son, who doesn't yet have a child, their younger brother or sister might be their heir, but it's expected that will change sometime. It doesn't cling as tightly, from what I've heard." She waved a hand. "I can give a few examples?"

"Please." Nora leaned forward. "I do better with examples."

"You've met Gabriel Edgarton. He was formally

inducted as Heir when he was eleven, and everyone was sure he'd manage the magic. He's lived and breathed that land since he was born, near enough. The land magic, the connection to it, is very strong. I'm fairly sure that by now, he knows any time a tree falls in their woods and causes more than the usual amount of damage. His father, it came out differently, from what I've heard, but he also was Heir from an early age, and it shows in the cleanness, the clarity of the connection."

"That makes some sense. So that is how it goes when it's easy." Nora hesitated. "Was it like that for Lionel before the War?"

Cyrus considered. "I didn't know him well, more than in passing. That makes me wonder, though, how he experienced it. Does he feel the sense of loss? Or was he always distant from the connection? It's hardly the sort of thing you can just ask about."

Nora said softly. "You can't. I probably can. He tells me things. Did you know he did all the decorating of the house himself? Very deliberately? He was showing me his sketchbooks where he worked it all out. He didn't hire anyone in."

Mabyn filed that tidbit away, but nodded. "If you happen to get him talking about it, it might be a help to know. At any rate, some people are more distant. Especially if they didn't expect to inherit. The awful sort of thing where you have a run of deaths all at once, or in a row."

Cyrus nodded. "And then we're all scrambling to figure out how to help someone, well, do what you're learning."

Nora shook her head. "I'm glad it's not, that I'm not the only one like that." She then pressed the point. "And someone who marries in?"

Mabyn took that on again. "The oaths are lighter. She's not the one responsible - usually she. If a man marries in, he usually has to take her family name, and for some reason men refuse to do that remarkably often. Or their families do. At any rate, the one marrying in isn't responsible for the land rites. It's more about not interfering with them, with what needs to be done."

She tapped her fingers on the arm of her chair. "But I am wondering whether that's why Eustacia has been ill this spring. And before this spring, on and off. It's hard to tell, damnably hard. She could be making a point of her disapproval and retiring to her own house in disdain. She could honestly be unwell. It could be somewhere in between. It could have nothing to do with the land."

"Does it go the other way? The land affecting someone tied to it?"

Mabyn was about to say something when she saw Cyrus put his hand to his mouth. She quickly said, "Ah, that's a whole other line of theory. How well do you know your more obscure Arthuriana?"

CHAPTER 34

Cyrus stood up on top of the hill. There had been a chapel here, once, before the English Civil War, and the cemetery had remained long after the rest of it had fallen into ruin. It was a fine and traditional place, with a yew shading many of the graves. They were not ruins at all, he made sure one of the gardeners from the house had a full day to keep things tidy here every fortnight.

In that first awful year, he had come out every day, whether it was rain or shine. Including the day after his Council trial, when he could barely drag himself out of bed. It hadn't mattered if he'd only had five minutes to spare after Gemma was truly asleep. Those five minutes were Tanith's.

Cyrus settled down on both knees in front of her tomb. Her parents had wanted her buried in one of the newly fashionable cemeteries. One of those in London or the garden cemetery curving around the outskirts of Trellech, looking for all the world like a sheltered park, carefully landscaped and treated as a garden for memories. He had refused, and he had kept refusing until Tanith's small mausoleum was complete. He'd done the final warding himself, layering every protective charm he could, anchoring it into the stone.

Thirty years later, the stone had weathered into a softness that he hadn't expected at the time. He had been pleased with the carving from the beginning. Curved benches drew the eye to the central monument, standing a foot taller than Cyrus himself. There was a copper plaque, a bas relief, added on the anniversary of Tanith's death. Tanith leaned on one hand on a table full of alchemical materials, all the glassware and bottles and an alembic. And stacks of books, of course. It wouldn't be Tanith without stacks of books.

He had insisted on the benches, too. Her parents - and his - had considered it too sentimental. The cemetery was close to the main house, but tucked away behind a row of trees. It was supposed to be a place everyone quietly ignored, except during funerals or tidy, polite forms of grief.

Cyrus had refused that. He had come out here, as Gemma grew older, to tell Tanith the news. He told the news to the bees, and he told Tanith. That was just how it was. Somewhere in that first decade, he had found himself thinking of her as the queen of some distant land. He'd had a single bee, of the same copper, added to the back of her monument. The metal was shiny from where he'd rubbed it with a kiss carried on his fingers, every visit.

These days, it was part of his regular routine to walk along here, whenever he was at home, and tell Tanith good morning or good evening. To pass along the news, to talk out loud about what his mind had snared on.

He came wanting some sort of peace in his heart, and today he wasn't finding it, not at all. The birds, the rustle of the grass, the smell of the damp earth, those were all as they should be. Nothing had changed there.

But something had changed in him, or was changing. He didn't know, he didn't begin to know how to name it. It had been so long since he'd worked closely with any woman beside his sister or Gemma. Cyrus knew others considered him odd, to be so single-hearted, especially when Gemma had been young. Most men in his position would have remarried for her sake, if not for his own, and he'd never wanted to.

And now, he had begun, somehow, to live with another woman again. To look forward to her comments, to seeing her over the breakfast table. To having a nightcap with her before they went to their beds. Separate beds, on opposite ends of a large house, but he had honestly enjoyed the ebb and flow of their days. Mabyn was thoughtful, clever, and she no longer treated him warily, as she had in the beginning.

He also couldn't deny what it was like to do ritual with her, the intimate rituals of the elemental work, or the wardings they had done. Or for that matter, figuring out the different approaches to exploring what worked best for Nora's learning.

She wasn't Tanith. No one was Tanith, even Gemma. Mabyn was herself. But it was as if he had passed from one room, decorated a certain way, into another room in the same house where he felt safe. One with a different purpose, different decorations and colours, but still part of some larger comforting whole.

He had no idea how to describe that, what emotion that was, never mind what he should do with it.

Cyrus was, in fact, so lost in thought that when he heard a cough behind his shoulder, he jumped a good foot.

He heard the laugh before he turned. Gemma. He took a breath, standing up and brushing off his knees. "Warn an old man."

"I was whistling, coming across. If you didn't hear me, that's your own lookout." Then she stopped and peered at him, before sitting down on the bench and gesturing at the other. It put them within a few feet of each other. "What is the matter, papa?"

Cyrus closed his eyes. It wouldn't fool her at all. He didn't know how to put any of what he was feeling into words. Especially to Gemma, who would rightfully have all her own feelings about the topic.

When he opened them again, she was leaning forward. "May I tell you?" Her voice was quiet, but suddenly insistent.

His eyebrow went up, and then he nodded. It might not be pleasant, but Gemma loved him. She would be as kind as she could. And it would be quick, rather like removing a sticking plaster all in one go. He had always appreciated that about her. Cyrus himself tended to circle a topic until he was ready to discuss it, and Gemma strode in fearlessly.

"You enjoy Mabyn's company. In a way you haven't in a long time. You're a bit like you are with Auntie Rhoe. Teasing. Smiling, the proper one that makes your eyes crinkle." It was crisp, but said softly, and she was watching him intently now.

Cyrus let out his breath. He nodded once, then spread his hands, palms up. "The first part of that is true enough. I don't have the proper perspective to judge the rest, but I trust you as my mirror." He settled his left hand on the bench beside him, leaning into it.

She grinned at that, an old habit between them of her

saying what she saw, that he might notice. "She likes your company too." That was less expected.

"You can't possibly be sure of that. Unless. She hasn't talked to you, I'd have known."

"In fact, she has, when you had that Council meeting a few weeks ago. After that. Oh, not about her feelings for you, whatever they might be, though I do have observations, papa. Rather, about some of her interests."

"Alchemical or otherwise?" Cyrus felt on slightly more solid ground when it came to a more academic discussion.

"The more esoteric applications of alchemy, all that about perfecting the self. She wanted to invite me to some regular discussions with Silvia and perhaps one or two others. No one I'd hate to be in the same room with, she was asking me first."

Cyrus considered. "Suggesting she particularly wanted you - and Silvia - more than the others."

"Exactly." Gemma beamed at him. "I am delighted to be so high in her estimation. It promises to be an interesting discussion. She sent round the reading list and I'm a third through it."

Cyrus snorted. "Whatever amuses." He hesitated, then asked, "And the rest of your observations?"

"Has she told you much about her personal life? Her marriage? Any of that?"

"Her marriage was the sort of thing you are bound and determined to avoid, and then some. Rather awful, and for a decade or so before her husband died. But there's a core of her self that she never lost. The fool man thought he could push her into a Council trial, and still control her when she came out the other side."

Gemma let out a long, decidedly unladylike whistle through her pursed lips. "Not that you have ever explained the specifics, and I know better than to ask you. But that strikes me as decidedly small-minded on his part."

"To put it plainly, yes. I have been trying to understand why she didn't take more active measures against him. Her son, mostly."

"Have you asked her?" Gemma leaned on one hand, mirroring his position now.

Cyrus shook his head. "We've talked a bit about her son, how she feels about him." He tilted his head. "She said she rather envied us. I didn't know how to explain what we'd done. What we'd had the chance to do."

"You rearranged your life for me, over and over again. Don't think I haven't realised." They hadn't talked much about what it was like when Gemma was young. About which assignments he chose, and the ones he'd declined because they would keep him away from home too long at a time. How he hadn't wanted to miss the first time she did something, or at least the first day she did. "What do you feel like with her?"

Cyrus sucked in a breath through his teeth. He knew that would show, and he knew that Gemma had meant to push him into some reaction. He could not exactly complain. He was the one who had taught her much of that art.

"I came out here because I enjoy her company. I am still trying to figure out what that means. And I do not know how to name what else I feel." He gestured at the memorial. "I envy the people who had time to talk about the future, when their beloved died. We were so young, we'd never talked about any of that."

"I suppose people do." Gemma sounded thoughtful.

"Your Aunt Rhoe and Uncle Hugh did, early on. She told me about it sometime later. He was - well, he still is - on the ocean near a third of the year. And while the Pelagius ships are as safe as any ship can be, that is an imperfect protection. Especially during the War years. She said, rather primly, actually, that they both knew that whenever he left, it might be the last time she saw him. And that like sensible people, they had discussed what they cared about. What they wanted for their children, for the future."

"I have difficulty imagining Auntie Rhoe as prim. And yet." Gemma nodded. She let out her breath slowly. "And you never had that with Mama."

"No. Which means I sit here, and I wonder what she would say, and I fancy I know it, and I don't know how much of that is wishful thinking." Cyrus shrugged. "You see the problem."

"You never have been one for idle daydreaming, Papa. Or for making plans when you don't have enough information or understanding."

Cyrus nodded. "And I - nothing in her life has inclined her to the pleasures of marriage. Just the duties and obligations."

There was a long pause. Then Gemma looked at the memorial, then back at him. "You are putting the cart before the horse. You are grown adults. You can find out what you think about each other without expectations of marriage or setting up a home together. I would like to know if you intend to invite her back here, but that's mostly so I can be prepared for a proper alchemy conversation over breakfast."

Cyrus blinked at her, speechless. Not a mode she got to see from him very often. Then, picking his words carefully, he asked, "Are you certain?"

"She makes you smile. You make her smile. And I'm a grown woman who understands you could never replace

Mama. But that perhaps, she wouldn't want you lonely forever." In a rustle of fabric and skirts, she stood, then bent to kiss his forehead. "I'll go see about tea. Take your time, but don't make me come fetch you."

He watched her go, before turning back to his contemplation of the tombstone.

CHAPTER 35
EARLY AFTERNOON AT BADDOCK HALL

Mabyn had been reading in the library for an hour or so when Nora found her. "Mabyn?"

"Yes?" She'd thought Nora was going out for a ride, a gentle one, along the lane. But here she was, not in riding clothes. "I thought you were going out?"

"The mare I was going to ride came up a little lame, and Wykeham doesn't trust me on the others yet. Rightfully so." Nora took a step in, and then stopped. "Do you know where Lionel is?"

Mabyn shook her head. "I don't. I haven't seen him since I came in here. Why, is something wrong?"

It was at that point when one of the maids came in without knocking, then stopped suddenly. "Pardon, mistress, please, do you know where his Lordship is?"

"Nora just asked this. I haven't seen him. Is there a problem?"

"Yes'm. Lady Baddock, Alice just found her in the Dower House, oh, and she looked awful poorly. He should come right away."

Mabyn stood. "Nora, can you go look for Lionel with the

rest of the staff? I will go right down there. I have enough healer training to be useful. Has someone gone to the Temple of Healing yet?"

The maid bobbed and said, "One of the footmen, mistress." Mabyn rather wished Cyrus were back already. He would have a better sense of whom to talk to at the Temple. It was a Friday afternoon in pleasant weather. She suspected that a number of Healers had found other places to be for the afternoon, unless they had to be on call.

Nora went off, dividing up the space with the maid as she went. Mabyn went down the stairs and out across the small drawbridge directly to the Dower House. She had her satchel with her. Her more complex tools were in her rooms. But she suspected that whatever the problem was would either respond to what she had in her bag, or it would need something very specialised indeed.

By the time she walked into the open door of the Dower House, she could hear someone talking quietly and rapidly to someone else. As she turned the corner into the parlour, she found Lady Baddock stretched out on a chaise longue, her maid perched beside her on the stool. The woman was breathing, but not at all sensible to the world.

"May I ask what happened? And perhaps have a look?"

That second question provoked a flurry of glances and murmurs, but after a moment the butler nodded. "If you would, Council Member."

Her training in healing matters ran more to alchemy and its various products than to diagnosis, but there was something of the woman's pallor that made her curious. She ran the simple charms - heart beat was there, if a bit shaky, she was breathing, but she did not respond when tapped gently or spoken to.

Something in that stillness made Mabyn frown again

and try another charm. As soon as she saw the flare of deep purple magic, twining like tendrils up Lady Baddock's fingers and wrists, she whistled. "Immediately. Someone needs to go find Nora and Lionel, and get them out of the main house. Right now. Everyone else too, as soon as possible. Take pots off the fire, anything that might cause a danger if it were left, but get everyone out."

The butler froze for only a second, and then he was striding out, bellowing orders as he went. Mabyn heard him send the footman waiting outside to gather help and go room by room.

Only the maid by Lady Baddock remained. "Pardon, Mistress, will she be all right?"

Mabyn stood, grimacing. "It's a matter of the Pact." She gestured. "Keep her warm and tend her. I'll wait by the portal for the Healer and tell him. They'll need to take her to the Temple, you should gather up anything you or she will need for the day, at least. Change of clothing, a night-gown and robe for her, something that will soothe you if you need to wait, a book or knitting or what have you." Then she waited only a moment for the maid's nod, before making her way briskly to the portal. Once there, she pulled out her journal to write Cyrus a note.

In the end, he made it back just after the Healers. "What happened?"

Mabyn explained succinctly, ending with, "We'll need to search the house. I've already written the Penelopes. Will you?"

"Much more my line than yours, yes." Cyrus nodded absently, considering his options. She let him sort through them without interruption as they walked up to the front of the house. Lionel and Nora met them as they came up to the drawbridge. "Is Mother all right?"

Mabyn shook her head. "There are strong signs that she tried to break her oath, the one made to the Silence. The healer is with her, I'm sure he is making arrangements to move her to the Temple."

Cyrus said, absently. "More than one oath. I suspect it may also be the one she took at her marriage." He was looking up, scanning the house. "We will need to check the house thoroughly."

"Check the house?" Nora was baffled, and not unreasonably.

"There must be some proximate cause of the oath - well, we say biting, most commonly. Simply thinking of something that goes against the oath might cause some discomfort, but not a lasting effect. Acting on it, and acting in a way that was decisive and could not be simply undone, that would produce something like we're seeing. Something given to a maid, or even dropped into someone's pocket, meant to cause you harm, or the Land."

"What, um, what do we do?" Lionel swallowed. "Do I need to go with her?"

Mabyn glanced over at him and offered a smile. "Your duty is here. That comes before filial obligation. She'll be in good hands with the Healers, as much as with anyone. And her maid can go with her. Unless you truly want to go."

Lionel looked distinctly relieved, then did his best to hide it. "And the searching?"

"We'll want to question all the staff, but best to wait for the Penelopes." Cyrus was still distracted. "Nora, we explained them?"

"You did. Or at least as much as any explanation makes sense. They investigate things. Gabriel Edgarton is one. He told a few stories at the garden party."

Cyrus glanced up, still somewhat distracted. "It won't

be him. I'm fairly sure he's on another case. We'll see who we get. I know most of them by sight. It shouldn't be long."

He went back to making a few notes, before pulling a copy of the floor plan of the house out of the back of his journal. He cast the charm to make half a dozen copies, one after the other. He divided each neatly into sections - the public rooms, Lionel's rooms, Nora's, their own, the household staff spaces - using another charm to layer what looked like a watercolour wash. Cyrus asked Lionel a question or two to clarify, but he had an excellent sense of the house. Mabyn left that in his very capable hands and focused on identifying the staff who would be most familiar with each area. Lionel and Nora stood together rather forlornly on the lawn.

It was only another ten minutes before a group of people came out of the portal and toward them. The one leading was a woman in her middle forties with dark hair pulled into a tight bun at the back of her head. She was trailed by two younger women and a younger man with apprentice badges. Trotting along next to them were five Guards, in full uniform.

"Council Members. Lord Baddock. Mistress." It was all very brisk and precise. "I am Penelope Doyle. Lucy Doyle. We came in sufficient number for a search of a large house."

"Penelope Doyle." Cyrus nodded and then introduced Nora. "The floor plan, here. Let me make a few more copies."

Mabyn cleared her throat. "Allow me." Cyrus promptly handed over the papers. Mabyn gestured. "I've had a word with the staff about who knows which area best. They have taken Lady Baddock off to the Temple of Healing, but I can confirm that it looks very much like a broken oath. Some definitive act, likely linked to some object."

Penelope Doyle nodded briskly, taking one of the sheets and looking at it, all three floors. "Your thoughts, please, Council Members?"

Lionel cleared his throat, then glanced at Nora. "Pardon, may I ask what you are going to do?"

Her posture shifted. Mabyn found that most intriguing, or would, if the situation had been not so dire. She'd seen Penelope Doyle in action a few times before, usually in matters that required precision. "Lord Baddock." She didn't soften, exactly, but she allowed space for the question. "With your permission, we wish to conduct a thorough search of all spaces in the house. That must include private rooms and any belongings that would be accessible to a member of staff."

She then hesitated for just a moment before going on. "The Council Members suggest it is likely that your lady mother pressed against her oaths in an unmistakably deliberate way. I agree with their analysis that it is most likely that she asked a member of staff to place something in one of your rooms. Or perhaps in a room where you - especially Mistress Martin - spend a great deal of time. However, it is also possible the item was placed in, for example, the kitchen. Or that there is more than one."

Lionel sucked in a breath, and Nora tucked her hand into his arm. She then squared her shoulders. "How will you know you've found everything?"

Penelope Doyle grinned, a toothy smile. "We can identify certain kinds of magic and then examine them. It is, pardon, an invasion of privacy."

Lionel shook his head. "I don't mind that. In this case."

Cyrus nodded. "I would wish to be present for a search of my sitting room, but everything else of concern is currently in my locked trunk. Mabyn?"

Mabyn nodded. "The same, and we should be present for the stillroom and the ritual workroom. Do you wish us to help, or would you work more smoothly without us?"

That amused smile got turned on Mabyn now. "The latter, and I appreciate your asking. I would prefer you both fresh to deal with what we find, when we find it. It would be a help if you stayed here. If we may?"

Mabyn handed over the clean copies, one to each of the Penelopes and the Guards. Penelope Doyle drew them away, dividing the house up into four. One of the Guards split off to go talk to the staff, and the others paired up, before trotting off to the entrance of the house.

Nora let out a long breath. "They seem very efficient?" Her voice shook a little on the last word, and Lionel patted her hand. It did him good, Mabyn thought, to have someone else to focus on.

"Let us see about bringing over some chairs from the garden." Cyrus said. "The Penelopes are skilled at this - even the apprentices. They'll know how to handle anything they find, or when they need to call in an expert. It will take a while, though."

"What do you think happened?" That was Nora, still hesitant.

"I suspect that there is some item, cursed and charmed to avoid notice, that has been placed somewhere in the house. Possibly it's still in something one of the maids was carrying. A book in the library, something loaned to you, a flower arrangement in a vase."

"Oh." Nora's voice got very small. "People can do that?"

"I expect Lady Baddock hired it out. There are people who will do that sort of work, but I expect it took her some effort to find one. Mabyn and I could do it. We know how to. Because we know how to find such things and make them safe. Money can be a powerful incentive."

"But she's so ill now. Surely she'd have known..." Nora glanced from Mabyn and Cyrus to Lionel, who honestly looked like he needed a stiff drink.

Mabyn shook her head. "Many people don't swear to the Silence often. They forget how it can bite. Especially if they overstep as far as this."

CHAPTER 36
LATER ON FRIDAY

In the end, they were waiting for an hour and a half after they'd been brought through for the search of their private rooms before one of the Guards could be seen coming back toward them at a loping, ground-covering pace. She pulled up neatly in front of the table and chairs they had arranged, with the staff scattered nearby on the lawn.

"Penelope Doyle requests your presence, Council Members, if it please you." It was the formal phrasing, it wasn't like she could order them in the ordinary way of things.

Cyrus was already standing. "You've found something, then, excellent. Can you say where?"

"Sir, Penelope Doyle preferred not." The Guard backed up a step.

Cyrus went to pull back Mabyn's chair, speaking to Nora and Lionel as he did so. "Stay here, please, where we can find you if we need you."

Mabyn nodded. "They may want to know what you know about wherever it's been found, or if an item is yours." Then, to the Guard, she said, "Lead on, please. And your name?"

"Guard Stephens, Magistra." The woman looked unsure for a moment, then relaxed when Mabyn smiled at her. "Harriet Stephens." It was rather like Mabyn, even in a moment like this, to want to know who she was working with, and provide appropriate praise. She led them back across the drawbridge, up the stairs, and toward Nora's rooms.

Penelope Doyle was standing in the middle of the room, pivoting slowly. There was a charm cast that laid out a grid, mirroring along the floors and the walls. The building had settled at some point, so that the floor sagged in one corner, and Penelope Doyle frowned at it, as if it displeased her.

"Ah. These are Mistress Martin's rooms, I gather? Are either of you familiar with what should be here?"

"I've been in here a few times, discussing clothing, consulting with the dressmaker." Mabyn said briskly. "There should be very little magical here, among her things. A boar bristle hairbrush. That was her aunt's. We did get her one of the journals, but I believe she has it with her."

Cyrus murmured, "She had it in the library when I left earlier at lunchtime."

"Before we go further, I must ask for your witnessed oaths that you have not been in this room today, nor altered anything in the underlying magics. Please also state your activities for the day, briefly."

Mabyn glanced at him, and she must have seen something in his face, because she went briskly on. "By the Silence, I swear I have not been in this room today, and I have neither altered the room's magic nor caused enchantment to be placed on any object. I spent the morning working with Nora in the stillroom, and after luncheon settled in the library to read. Nora found me just as one of the maids was looking for Lionel Baddock to attend his mother. I went to check on her, alerted the Guard as well as the Healers, and wrote to Cyrus. So I swear, so it is." Cyrus could see the brush of the oath tightening against her, a single tremor, before she took a breath.

"Well sworn, Council Member." Then Penelope Doyle looked at Cyrus, just waiting.

"By the Silence, I swear I have not been in this room today, nor have I affected this space by magic or caused to be placed in it any object today. I spent the morning evaluating a ritual working to manage the energies of the fields, with Lionel, about a mile from the house. At luncheon, I went back to my family home, for a meal with my daughter." He hesitated, but he could feel the insistent pull of the oath. "I spent some time at my wife's grave, and we were partway through the meal when Mabyn wrote. As I have said it, so it was, is, and shall be."

As he finished, that pull sharpened into something painful enough to make him grunt with it. Most of the time, it did not hit him quite so hard, but the combination of talking to Tanith, and then to Gemma, brought that fear into sharp focus. Gemma, dying like her mother had, gone so pale and still, all the vibrancy bleeding out. He could not look at anyone in the room for a long moment, but when he did glance at Mabyn, the corner of her mouth lifted slightly.

"Well sworn." Penelope Doyle took a breath, then forged on. He appreciated that, not dwelling. "Let me show you what we found."

She clapped her hands, then cast a charm, wordlessly. It was a matter of a few specific gestures, an exhaled breath, and then something in a vase lit up in a sickly green.

"Flowers from Lady Baddock's garden." Mabyn frowned, her eyes narrowing. "They don't grow anywhere else near the house." She glanced at Cyrus, then added. "Not poisonous in and of themselves. That would have been too obvious, I expect, but that's Vervain, the Enchanter's Herb, tucked in among the others, to anchor whatever charm. I can't say I think much of her magical theory. Something in the vase, then?"

Penelope Doyle nodded. "I wanted witnesses when we removed it. Would you prefer somewhere else?"

"The workroom is clean. Perhaps better there." It would also give him a minute or two to gather himself. "Easier to clean up. I admit I don't much like the idea of Nora being exposed to that more than necessary."

"Quite." Penelope Doyle's voice was dry. "If one of you would get your ritual tools - I have my own - and the other show me down?"

Silently, Mabyn nodded downstairs, and Cyrus peeled off to go collect his tools, the full set in the wooden case from his warded trunk. By the time he got down to the workroom, someone had adjusted the lighting. There was a single large marble-topped table in the centre, suitable for working and easy to fully clean afterwards.

Mabyn was just moving a smaller table into place. "For your tools." She looked him up and down. "More your line than mine."

Cyrus smiled a little. "I want your eyes on it, though. You will spot things I don't, I'm sure." He had, in the interval, managed to shove his personal feelings back down where they wouldn't bother him unduly. "Do you have a suggestion on how to proceed, Penelope Doyle?"

The back-and-forth discussion about their options and mutual preferences took a few minutes. Mabyn stood back, amused, while Cyrus and the Penelopes wrangled through the choices. Malgantis's Wreck was discarded as too likely to damage the object. Reginald's Remedy might not be protective enough. They had several other more experimental ideas. But when Cyrus proposed a solid and reliable standard, Occitan Illumination, even Penelope Doyle nodded. "If you're confident with it, which I'm sure you are, since you suggested it. You'll need two assistants."

Cyrus raised an eyebrow at Mabyn, who nodded. "I know it. Penelope Doyle, if you would? And if the rest of you would watch closely, especially the colour changes?" Her comment made it clear that she knew exactly what to expect.

Penelope Doyle indicated where the others should stand, with a specific instruction or two along the way for a particular thing to monitor or observe. Cyrus pulled out the tools he would need. Between them they laid out a stack of silk cloths. Penelope Doyle added an insulated box to place the cursed token in for later investigation, an evidence case, and a variety of long-handled tongs and utensils. Cyrus was quite sure he didn't want to touch this thing by accident.

The working itself went smoothly. Cyrus was glad he'd done so much other work with Mabyn. He had forgotten how much easier it made things, to have someone you knew well enough to judge how they would be following along. Mabyn was always right there, anticipating what he or Penelope Doyle might need.

That didn't mean it was simple, however. The vase narrowed at the neck, so they began by carefully removing the flowers, handling them with tongs and laying them aside where they were well out of the way. Then he and Mabyn worked together to somehow get the cursed item out of the vase. Breaking it would have been a pity. For all her other flaws, Lady Baddock had an eye for ceramics.

The cursed talisman, when they finally eased it through the neck of the vase, seemed unprepossessing at first. It was a dark stone, but as Cyrus held it with the tongs, he could see the shimmer of magical engraving on it. When he set it down, he said, "I know who made it. He's been in trouble before."

"Daniel Rollings." Penelope Doyle nodded. "He should have known better. That's a nasty piece of work. Let's find out how." There was a note in her voice of disdain, but also unrepentant curiosity.

Some of the investigation would take longer. It would need to be teased out by someone looking at the engraving under a magnifying glass, possibly even a microscope. But the core of it was obvious enough. It would have caused Nora to become ill. It would have sucked her magic away.

Much as, Cyrus realised, the land had been. "She's done something like this before. It feels like the land does. Which may help us undo some of the damage here, if we're lucky." He glanced at Penelope Doyle. "We can leave the further investigation in your hands? Can someone confirm Nora's rooms are safe?"

"Already done. We're finishing with a search of the rest of the house, but we think this was the thing."

Mabyn nodded. She was helping put things away. "I'd be glad to come to the Guard Hall and do whatever further work you like. I suspect I speak for Cyrus as well." Cyrus nodded absently, feeling the rush of the magic ebb away from him. He felt hollow now, and he could only hope it did not show. At least not too much.

Before he realised it, the Penelopes had packed up. "With his Lordship's permission, I would like to leave

Apprentice Williams, here." That was the oldest of the apprentices, who was likely nearly done with her apprenticeship. "And one of the Guards. They'll just need a place to sleep, and to be handy, while we continue investigating. I'll go see about that. I can find my own way." It was a tidy dismissal, really.

Cyrus finished cleaning things up, packing up his tools. "I can't imagine he'll object." He cleared his throat as he closed the latches on his kit. "I should take this upstairs."

"I very much appreciate your expertise, Council Members. Both. It has been a pleasure in that regard." There was a brief moment where she smiled, and Cyrus could see her true delight in resolving a complicated problem well. He liked that she wasn't jealous or grasping about her role in it.

"Likewise. I'll send a note round to the Guard Hall. You have been as efficient and thorough as anyone might wish." They all knew how this game was played. She'd earned a commendation and the bragging rights that came with it, and Cyrus was glad to do his part in that.

She grinned once, more broadly, and made a small bow, then bustled off to see to her next tasks. Cyrus turned to go up to his rooms, vaguely aware that Mabyn had come along behind him.

Once he had deposited it in his trunk, checking the protective warding three times, he came back out into his sitting room to find her leaning against the sofa. "I find I do not want to be alone tonight."

He stood, flatfooted and tongue-tied, unsure what she meant. She took a step towards him and took his hand. "Come with me? It's late."

Cyrus let her take his hand. He didn't pull away. He didn't want to pull away, but he didn't know what to do. It was clear, in this moment, that she was offering to proposition him. Or something of the kind, at least. To offer more intimacy of some sort, to be mutually agreed on.

She waited for him to think through it, then she spoke again, quiet and intent. "Will you come with me?"

He took a breath and let it out. "Yes. But…" He swallowed and didn't know how to ask what she wanted.

"We'll talk. In my rooms." With that, she threaded her fingers through his, not the more formal way of tucking her arm through his. "Please."

Cyrus found he wanted to find out what she wanted. What she had in mind.

CHAPTER 37
FRIDAY EVENING

Mabyn was not sure this was a good idea. But she was also sure that if they did not talk about this now, tonight, when they were both a bit off-balance and in need of understanding company, they never would.

If she left Cyrus alone, tomorrow morning he would have put all his walls up. He'd have put each and every emotion and memory tidily in place, where they could be taken out only when he wished. That had worked for him for many years, and probably would work for him for many years to come. That did not mean it was good for him.

And it did not mean that it was good for the Council or for the Land. Mabyn could not decide which of those three mattered most, but she didn't have to. In this case, the thing that would help all three was the same. She did not need to choose between them. She squeezed his hand. She might have suggested he bring a dressing gown, but she had been afraid that any pause would have let him put up all those civil diplomatic distances again.

Mabyn tugged him along, gently but unyielding, to the door to her rooms. She pressed her hand on the door, feeling the wards welcome her, and then opened the door, steering him inside. Mabyn thought for a moment about pausing in the sitting room, but then forged on. Something in her was burning now, a steady fire. The kind of fire you built for cooking or for a great alchemical work that took over an entire stone hearth and several tables.

Mabyn expected him to protest, but he didn't, even when she steered him to her bed. "Sit. Please. Shoes off, if you would."

Something in her tone - amused, no-nonsense, prag-matic - made him blink. And do what she asked, which was promising. She did not want to trick him or rule him or order him. She wanted him to be happy, and none of those things would bring happiness for either of them. But she wanted him to talk, and that was the challenge before them both.

He perched on the edge of the bed for a moment, then pushed back until the bed was properly under his thighs. Mabyn smiled at him, bending to kiss his forehead. She moved to the wardrobe to slip her own shoes off, then take off the loose linen jacket she'd had on over her dress for the day. She came back to the bed and settled beside him. The bed was low enough she did not have to do an undignified hop to sit, not like the bed Aubrey had kept uncomfortably high. But once she was seated, her own stockinged feet didn't touch the ground.

Cyrus blinked at her, then carefully asked, "Are you all right? The ritual, I mean."

"The ritual was a pleasure." Mabyn was clear on that and wanted him to be just as certain. "Doing ritual with you has reliably been a pleasure." She hesitated for only a moment, then slipped her hand into his again. "You're not used to having a partner anymore, are you?"

He stopped breathing for a moment, and Mabyn wasn't sure if she'd broken any future they might have had, in whatever way they might have had it. Then he shook his head. Just a quick movement, but she saw it.

"Your sister isn't the same. Or your daughter." She considered, then asked, carefully. "What is it like, having a wife you miss so much?"

She knew what she was asking, enough. She wasn't sure, though, that he understood why she was asking. What it would be like to be missed that much by another person. If she died tomorrow, she knew she would be missed. She knew her funeral would be full of people who appreciated her and her work. But she was fairly sure none of them would be making a point of coming to her grave and talking to her thirty years later. Even Silvia.

Cyrus squeezed her hand once, but took his time in making any other response. "I always miss her. I thought, once, that it would get better. Wanting to turn over my shoulder and tell her something. Being away and finding things in the bookstores she would have loved. I give them to Gemma, we add them to the library, but that's not the same as talking about them with her."

He shrugged. "It's a different kind of pain. The first few years, it was shattering, over and over again. Now it aches, it's more bearable. I've built up calluses about it, like you do when you handle hot pans often enough."

Mabyn lifted her free hand and held it up. Her hands were roughened, indeed, from a mix of the alchemy lab, the stillroom, and the garden. "My maid despairs, but it's helpful, isn't it? To have a bit of a buffer against the fires of the world."

Cyrus's mouth quirked. "That's a way to think of it, yes." He took a breath and Mabyn could tell he was on the edge of something, something that swept off into a complex landscape she couldn't see. "I was thinking about you, actually."

"About me?" Mabyn was not sure how to take that.

"You." He was smiling a little now. "And then Gemma had a few things to say. She mentioned, first of all, that she is delighted to be so high in your esteem, that you'd set up a gathering especially to her interest."

"You know perfectly well your daughter is brilliant. And charming, she has all your charm. And I do feel an interest in the next generation. Perhaps even more after talking to Isembard and Thesan, and a few others of their age. The way the War broke apart the foundations they had expected."

"Ah, a strategic decision." Cyrus's eyes were dancing now, with amusement.

Mabyn nudged his arm with her free hand. "Also, your daughter is a delight. I have to work to keep up with her, and that's the best sort of conversation."

Cyrus smiled, and this time it didn't quite wrinkle his eyes. "And me?"

He was nervous then. Mabyn twisted to look at him straight on. "You know your own skills as much as any man I have ever known, or any woman. You are also a delight to talk to. I have enjoyed our conversations a great deal. That would be part of why we are sitting here now."

He raised an eyebrow. "What changed, then?"

"You have been, you have given me." She stopped, then

tried again. "Aubrey never let me be alone. Never gave me space. You do, you trust that I will do my own work well, without needing to be checked on. And yet, when we talk, you pay attention, you listen, you ask useful questions. My work is better because of you. Not something I must hedge around with thorns."

The smile lit up his eyes this time. "Good. That is what I hoped for. You have every right to that space and my attention."

"Right?" Mabyn would not have put it that way, would not have expected it.

"You are an expert. You know hundreds of things I do not. Probably thousands. You have your own way of looking at the world. What sort of man would I be to make you smaller because I felt threatened by that?"

"A very common sort of man." Mabyn snorted. "You are rare, you know."

Cyrus shrugged slightly. "I am as I am, and I want to know more of what you know. Enlightened self-interest, at the very least, suggests that listening to you might be worthwhile."

"Is that what you're calling it now?" Mabyn was teasing, but his expression changed again into something more sober. She thought, for a moment, that she'd offended him, but he shifted to take her hand in both of his.

"Not just that." He took a deep breath and let it out. "Gemma says you make my eyes crinkle up properly."

Mabyn smiled and risked reaching up to touch his temple. He didn't pull away, just meeting her gaze.

"And she says Tanith wouldn't have wanted me lonely forever." He then hesitated. "That we're grown adults, with grown children. We don't need to decide what anything means just yet, or what we want in specific. Though she would like to know if she can expect you at the breakfast table for a proper alchemical debate."

Mabyn inhaled sharply. She had a dozen things she wanted to say, but it all came down to two words. "And you?"

He didn't look away, still watching her with that open ritual gaze that took everything in. "I am exceedingly out of practice with everything. But I find, for the first time since Tanith died, I might like to be in practice again. In a limited way."

"You are a handsome and intelligent man of property. Surely other people have been interested? Beyond the sorts like Lady Jenifry Alton."

"Some of them had interesting minds, or skills, or knowledge. I did not want to go to bed with them."

"And you want to with me?"

He moved then, reaching to cup her cheek, echoing and reflecting her movement. "Not tonight, not that way. We're too new to each other, to this. If we do that, I want it to be a time when we can be at our leisure. When we will not be interrupted. When we have privacy. And yes, eventually my daughter at some meal, probably."

"I have a townhouse, and it is entirely lacking in daughters." Mabyn said this with some dignity. "And it has a very comfortable bed, for the record." Also, to be honest, the idea of bedding him in a home he'd shared with Tanith was a tad much. At least right now.

Cyrus laughed, and the sound filled the room, richly echoing. "Well. Let us see about strolling together in that direction."

Mabyn laughed. He didn't move his hand, and after a

moment, he tapped her cheek once with her thumb. "Also, before we go to bed, before we do anything too intimate, I want to understand more of how your husband hurt you. How your son has hurt you. I would like, very much, to ease some of that if I can. To convince you that for all my flaws - and I have quite a few - I will not hurt you those ways."

Mabyn closed her eyes, and she could feel her body tensing. He didn't pull away, didn't withdraw, he was just there and steady, one hand on her cheek, the other holding her fingers gently in his. "It feels stupid and small to talk about it. He didn't hit me, he didn't curse me, he didn't injure me. Not the way people mean when they ask about a bad marriage. He didn't leave bruises."

"He didn't leave bruises that could be seen." Cyrus's voice was firm now. He went on, unrelentingly. "When someone is injured during a duel, they learn to protect the injury later. It changes everything, even after they heal as much as they are going to. They take a shorter stride, they favour that leg or arm, they avoid whatever it was caused them pain. As a general rule. Your husband fenced you in, over and over, so that wherever you turned, you limited yourself. You have broken away from that, in so many ways." His voice caught.

"Yes?" She leaned forward a little, not sure how to respond to any of that, but wanting him to keep talking.

"I let my grief keep me safe. You let your distance protect you. Fine choices, given the options, but they are - they are not the things that bring us joy now, now that we have changed again."

Mabyn let out her breath. "How do we begin? I - I still do not want to be alone tonight."

Cyrus closed his eyes for a long moment. "I used to read

to Gemma. Perhaps we take turns reading aloud to each other. You could get under the covers."

Mabyn frowned. "That seems unfair."

"I can sit. And hold your hand. We seem to be doing well enough with that." He glanced down, then back up at her face.

This might just work, in their slow and uncertain way.

CHAPTER 38
MABYN'S ROOMS, SATURDAY MORNING

Cyrus woke rather early, shifting with a start, and realising he'd fallen asleep leaning on the end of the bed, his head pillowed on his arms. His back was complaining rather loudly. He was not nearly so young as he had been.

He'd thought Mabyn was asleep, but just as he moved, she reached a hand down toward him. "What time is it?" Her voice was quiet, a bit blurry.

"Not too long after dawn." He stretched and heard his neck pop.

As he grimaced, she pushed herself up on one elbow. "You must be terribly stiff. I'm sorry. Well. I'm not entirely sorry."

"Not entirely?" Despite the minor aches and pains, he smiled.

She smiled back at him, then stretched herself. "I'd like to talk a bit more, but you must want to wash up and change clothes and..." Her voice trailed off.

Cyrus considered. He found himself enjoying this quiet intimacy, but yes, he wanted to wash and do all the usual morning ablutions. "Come along to my rooms in half an hour? I get a good view of the fields at this time of day? I can order breakfast up, we can eat..." He hesitated for a moment. "In bed?" Before she could say anything, he added hurriedly, "In whatever form you'd prefer."

She was silent for a long moment. "I think I might like to try kissing you when we are both washed and sorted for the day. Let's say forty-five minutes? I'd like to wash my hair."

"Of course. I'll see about breakfast." He then pushed himself upright, hesitating for a moment. "Soon." Then he made himself turn and walk out the door, carefully letting himself out. She'd set the wards so he could, he could feel that easily, and he'd have to leave his own open for her. Well, and for the breakfast.

He made it back to his rooms without running into any of the maids, ruffled his own bedding, and then rang. A maid came along promptly. Cyrus requested breakfast for himself and Mabyn, asking her to leave it on a cart in the sitting room, and let Lionel know they'd be busy for at least some of the morning. Then he went off to run his own bath, bathing efficiently and then getting dressed in loose trousers, a simple linen shirt, and a dressing gown over it. He charm-dried his hair, brushing it out so it lay suitably flat, and then he had twenty minutes to wait.

It was no use settling down to do anything. He kept looking up at every small noise, wondering if it was Mabyn, and it wasn't. As soon as the maid left the food, he brought it into the bedroom, then he pulled the sheets back appealingly. He wanted flowers, but he certainly couldn't go down to the garden.

He stood by the cart for a moment, then gathered his magic. He had learned the art of illusion flowers a long time ago, to amuse Tanith and then to delight Gemma. When she was small, she'd demand all manner of them, squealing with delight whenever he produced one. On the days he'd be out all the time she was awake, he'd leave them on her pillow.

Cyrus wondered for a moment if Mabyn would think them too childish or too insubstantial, but - well. He could tell her the story, if nothing else, and perhaps that would make her smile. It had been a long time since he'd called one into being, though, and it took him a moment to gather his magic and shape it. As he'd often done, he let the shape take form without consciously directing it. Safer, honestly, since his inclination often shaped a better flower than trying to make each element perfect.

This time it came out as a blowsy cheerful peony, a glowing red bundle of petals. He rummaged for a spare toothbrushing glass, and set the peony into water on the cart with the food, then arranged everything. He had a table in his bed for a meal there. They'd just left it after he'd had a leisurely meal or two that way last month. It looked rather smart, really.

He had some nagging sort of memory of what partic-ular flowers meant, but that had never been one of his better strengths. His mother considered it a woman's art. Rhoe had refused to learn it, being far more interested in the healing applications of whatever plant happened to be handy. And Cyrus had not felt strongly enough about it to make a study of it.

He went back to the sitting room to wait, jumping when he heard Mabyn's knock. When he opened it, she was more dressed than he was. She wore a simple sage-green frock, with her hair loose over her shoulders, a definite concession to some sort of intimacy. She looked lovely, and undeniably certain of herself. Cyrus offered his hand and escorted her back to the bedroom.

He got her settled in half of the broad bed, bringing over the tray, when she blinked at him. "Did they bring the flower?"

Cyrus shook his head. "It's an illusion-flower. I made them for Tanith…" He hesitated. She perhaps did not want to hear about his much loved late wife at such a time. It certainly seemed a tad rude. "And for Gemma."

"Did you pick the flower?" Her voice had an odd note to it now.

"I usually let it take whatever form suits. I did with that." He flicked his fingers at it. "Why?"

She laughed, an easy warm laugh that included him. "You don't know your language of flowers then, or at least not the peony? It is not so obvious as a red rose, but they're - oh, love and passion and prosperity. A happy marriage. Also, sometimes, bashfulness."

Cyrus could feel his cheeks flush. "I didn't mean to imply."

"Oh, come here, you ridiculous man. Don't hover, you're too tall to talk to properly when you hover." She patted the bed next to her. "I'm not upset. Very amused, but not upset. And I am hungry."

"Right. Here. Toast and eggs and there's some sausage, and I remembered you like marmalade in the morning." Cyrus settled carefully into the other side of the bed, waiting for her to sort out her own plate, then adding things to his own. "This feels like a midnight feast at school, somehow."

"It does, doesn't it? Like we're getting away with something, even though first, it's no one's business. Not yet. And also, it's breakfast."

Cyrus smiled, then he gestured at the flower. "And is that presumptuous?"

"Knowing what your heart offers, when you don't even realise you are, I'd say that's actually rather useful. Otherwise, I'm sure we could have circled around this question for months, between us."

It made him laugh. "We are good at prevaricating. And not talking about how we feel. Decades of practice."

"Decades upon decades. I've never been very good at talking about feelings. You seem rather better. You'll have to teach me. Give me plenty of personal tutoring." She said it lightly, but it had a layer of gentle, welcoming flirtation to it that made him shiver and close his eyes.

When Cyrus looked at her, she was watching him carefully. The way you watched a skittish foal or kitten, while they were deciding if you were friend or foe or utterly unknown. "That's new for you?" He offered it just as gently.

"Rather." The comment had broken the tension, and she smiled more easily again. "I do not know how to do this. Do you?"

Cyrus shrugged. "I was - well. I only had eyes for Tanith, honestly. I got to watch Rhoe and Hugh fall in love, but I'm not sure that they're entirely the best model. Both rather singular."

"We, also, are singular. Unique in all the world." There was a note in her voice now that bubbled like champagne.

He lifted his teacup. "You sound giddy. I like that."

Mabyn snorted and lifted her cup in a toast. "To trying new things. Together. And not minding a bit of foolishness."

Cyrus took a breath. "I like that we can. I don't know how things are with us. But ever since the elemental ritual, I've felt at ease with you. Comfortable being close with you. Before that, probably, but I couldn't begin to say when."

"I've felt the same." Her voice had a warm burr to it now. "My logic tells me something awful will go wrong now."

"Look." Cyrus laid out what he'd been thinking about during his bath. "Everyone expects us to spend a lot of time together. Certainly through to the autumn, if not longer. Though perhaps Nora will make more rapid progress now."

"And perhaps Lionel will settle. Though I suppose that depends on the specifics of his mother."

Cyrus snorted. "Yes." He shook his head. "I suppose I ought to be sympathetic, but."

"She brought it on herself. We're all taught, over and over again, about the power of the Silence. The fact it so rarely goes so far makes people forget."

"There's a project for the Council, how to remind people of the oaths they've made and the way it can bite. I suppose it would be tacky and inappropriate to have an object lesson." Cyrus flicked his fingers.

"Are you always so ruthless?" Mabyn wasn't judging, just considering him.

He shrugged. "Pragmatic. I don't..." He swallowed. "Look. Before we talk much more, I'm - I'm going to keep bringing up Tanith. And I realise that's rude, and puts you in an awful position, and yet..."

"And yet, she's been part of your life since you were, what, fourteen? Whatever this is, it's not a competition. For one thing, I'm sure I'd lose." Before he could say anything, she went on.

"I care that Gemma approves, or at least does not object. I care about what your sister thinks, as a sister in the mysteries. You clearly trust her judgement, and she adores you. I care what Silvia and a few others think, but honestly, Hesperidon won't care unless we have such a vast falling out we can't be in the same room. Let's not, that seems exhausting, we are neither of us young enough for that sort of thing."

Cyrus laughed. "It does, yes. And Hesperidon has certainly coped through a dozen affairs between our colleagues, where everyone had to pretend in public it wasn't happening." He took a bite more of his food. "So how do we handle this?" Then something occurred to him. "The summer solstice gathering is next week. Would you do me the honour of partnering me?"

"My. That will cause talk." She grinned. "Gemma won't mind? Or Rhoe?"

"Goodness, no. Gemma would rather watch, honestly. And Rhoe will tease, but only in private."

"And everyone else?" Mabyn was pressing the point.

"Everyone else can gossip, and lay bets, and we will eventually be more obvious and amuse people in the process. But in all truth, solstice - the summer one - is easy. We are doing shared work, of course we are spending time with each other." Cyrus shrugged. "Besides, we do our duty. How we find our pleasure is largely not anyone else's concern."

"My son will be horribly offended." Mabyn's voice had gone soft.

"I cannot speak to him. Or what he'll do. But if that's what he chooses, he's choosing. Continuing to choose. You gave him all you could. He is a grown man. If he can't have a conversation with you about it, well. He's choosing that too." He turned his palm up. "I know. I'm making light of it. It would destroy me if Gemma objected. But - whatever there is with your son, this is a symptom of it, not a cause of the distance there is."

Mabyn closed her eyes as he watched her. Then she nodded. "You are right about that. I'll, I'll find time to speak with him privately this week. He deserves not to be surprised with it in public."

"There. We have a plan. About this, at least." He hesitated, clearly weighing whether to bring something up or not.

"Go on, ask." She could see him grimace at her catching it.

"It's not pleasant." Cyrus turned his hand palm up. "The rumours about your husband. Would you tell me what you know of the truth, so that I may be of use with them?"

It was a curious way to put it. But of course, it was strategic and sensible. As soon as they made their affections more obvious, there would be gossip. That gossip would enfold him, whether or not there was any logic to doing so. And honestly, he had some right to know.

"What have you found out on your own, then?" She was quite sure he'd done some investigating. She certainly would have, around the time they began working closely together, and he had better resources for that sort of thing.

He coughed. "I did consult Rhoe. She was not directly involved in the case - which made it easier, there was more she could share. She heard a fair bit of the gossip, both that the Healers were asked to look for evidence of some sort of foul play, and that none was found."

Mabyn let out a puff of breath. "I did not kill him." She hesitated. "I did not cause him to die." This was harder to say. "He had sent me to the second library, told me to wait until he called. Teatime came and went. Supper. I slept there. I can still remember the awful sofa, the scratchy lumpiness of the horsehair." Cyrus nodded, not interrupting the flow of whatever she wished to say. "He was found in the morning, a heart attack or apoplexy. If someone had found him earlier, perhaps he would still be alive."

When she came to a stop, he squeezed her hand, his mind whirling with what he wanted to make sure she heard. "You did as he ordered. After a lifetime of learning what pain he would send your way if you stepped out of line." Then he added, more bemused. "The staff too, I'm sure." He was certain that more than one other person in the house had been glad of Lord Teague's death.

"I wondered, later, if they'd known. But I would never ask." She would have had to do something about the answer. The Guard had asked, he was sure.

"And you had the cloak of expected mourning." He had had the reality of it, but the show of it could be a ward and a protection, and she'd earned and needed that. "That tells me what I needed to know. If you want to talk about it, you have only to ask. But only as you choose."

Mabyn leaned into his shoulder. "You have a knack for finding that line."

"While I am being your conscience, we should, like the dutiful and responsible bearers of our oaths, figure out what we're going to say to Lionel and Nora today." Cyrus wanted to shift the conversation for her sake, to something less treacherous.

"We should. First, though, breakfast." She reached for one of the small bowls of early strawberries, then eyed him. "May I feed you this?"

Cyrus inhaled, then nodded. "Yes." Yes to that, and to many more things to come.

CHAPTER 39
SUNDAY LUNCHEON OUT IN THE GARDEN

The next morning was clear, and they had luncheon out in the garden.

"Your mother?" Mabyn knew the answer. This was Council business, and so they'd had the report from the Temple of Healing late last night. But she wanted to see what Lionel said.

Lionel went still. Nora patted his hand once, reassuringly. "It's hard to find the words." he said, finally. "On a practical level, well. If she doesn't die in the next day, she'll go to a care home. From there, they'll have to see, how much care she needs. Even if she could come back here, it's likely destroyed her magic."

"Breaking your oaths will do that. And oaths at least twice over." Mabyn didn't want to be cruel, but she did feel someone ought to be clear.

"Twice?" Lionel looked up, blinking.

"Her oath as Lady, to the land. And then the oaths we bound her to, after her more obvious interference. Over there." She gestured at the spot.

Lionel let out a long breath. "Twice over. And you

warned her." He seemed to find some comfort in that. Even while his new freedom was a complicated tangle of new choices in front of him.

"We're fairly sure, though it will take more evidence to be certain, that she's been undermining the land magics for years. It's not clear why, and she's in no state to be questioned, and may never be." Mabyn paused. "Would you prefer to hear about that now, or wait?"

Lionel hesitated, closing his eyes. Nora shifted her hand to cover his. "Now, I mean." His shoulders twitched. "There's no good time."

Mabyn nodded. "Nora, you remember that we talked about different uses of magic. That painting, up in the attics, made me wonder about the relationships. The family magics. Your mother's grandfather, Lionel, was related to my husband's people. Which makes me wonder about other patterns."

Cytus coughed. "We know that there's a thread of - making people do things the way you want them to, that runs in that line. But also a host of unspoken expectations, bounded by punishment for stepping out of place." Mabyn wasn't entirely sure what she thought about Cyrus using 'punishment' there, but it was true, and not more than she'd strongly implied to Nora, if not Lionel.

Lionel flinched at that. "She was very clear about her expectations, yes. And in this case?"

Mabyn picked up. "I think she thought to force you to marry. First by making space in the house, and then more directly. That if the land did worse, you would feel more pressure. That you would turn to her for help, that she would help you make a match. It may have started unconsciously, but at some point she became deliberate. Around the time you turned down Lady Jenifry's daughter, perhaps."

Lionel went still and silent, the sort of silence that spoke volumes in a man of his class.

Mabyn hesitated, and added, "Families are complicated and family magic moreso. Cyrus and I are pursuing some options for investigation, but I gather she didn't keep a personal journal of anything important. And it's not as if we can ask Lady Jenifry or another friend of hers, though I know a few people who might give it a try."

Lionel made one small nod. No one spoke until he raised his eyes. "Your sister came by, sir. Yesterday. She introduced herself, and passed along the person to talk to about care homes. That was a help this morning." Changing the subject, not unreasonably.

"I might have had a word. Or dropped her a note, more accurately." Cyrus had, in fact, made a flying visit to Trellech after lunch yesterday, and he'd managed to catch Rhoe still in her rooms. It had given Mabyn a chance to gather herself. Cyrus too, she thought. He had, in fact, put on his cloak of being entirely in control, jovial and good-hearted.

Which he was. But she couldn't help thinking of him yesterday, of the way he'd tilted his chin after they'd kissed. His blush, at realising what the peony meant. The cautious way he'd not pressed.

She wasn't ready for that. She was sure he wasn't either. But she was beginning to be quite curious about what it would be like when both of them were. They'd spent much of the morning just talking quietly. Some in bed, side by side. Eventually, in the sitting room. Nothing about Council matters, bar both of them having to answer a pair of journal messages each. Just the comfortable natter of what they were currently reading, that wasn't solely about the next problem to solve.

It made her start, when she heard the cough, and what must be a repeated, "Mabyn?"

"Yes, pardon?"

"You were thinking about something." Cyrus said it with an easy good-natured wave of his hand. He didn't ask, though, what precisely. "Lionel was being intimidated by my sister. Nothing new."

"Not intimidated, exactly." Lionel held his hands up. "Not entirely sure what to make of her, though."

"Well, that puts you in good company." Cyrus was decidedly amused and in a fey mood now.

"Rhoe doesn't care what people think of her. She cares that she's doing what's needed. Most people, particularly in the upper social circles, aren't sure what to do with that." Mabyn nodded at Nora. "Not a bad model, if you want it. Or Gemma, who's taking after her that way."

Cyrus beamed, as if that were a grand compliment. "It's been interesting to see." he said. "Rhoe was different, well, when she was Alexandra."

"Wait, what?" Nora blinked. "Are you telling me that you all change names now?"

"Not that often. I mean, not in that way. She's a sworn priestess, remember? Has been since before her marriage. Though that doesn't make that much difference here. She took a new name when she made those oaths. She says it's a help at the Temple, actually. People who know me well enough to spot me realise the resemblance, but in passing, on forms, in a hallway, it's much less fussy. And people prevail on her less to get just a few minutes of my time." He waved a hand. "Anyway. She's Alexandra Pelagius, now, when she needs to do something fussy in the non-magical community. She's on a couple of committees where there's interaction. Public health obeys no boundaries. She puts on the name like she puts on the proper frock."

Nora frowned. "You said I could - if - I mean."

Mabyn saw where she'd gone, immediately. "Assisting at the Temple of Healing, those sorts of committees, is a perfectly acceptable and useful thing for a Lady of the land to be doing. And necessary for someone to do well, honestly. Or, as we said, some sort of teaching. I have some ideas about that, though you'd want to learn more yourself, and plan to hire on one or two other teachers."

Nora blinked. Before she could say anything else, Cyrus stepped in. "First things first. I think we'll be able to make far more progress on the land. I did some exploring this morning, and I'm sure Eustacia laid in some tokens - charged, not particularly well-made, in the grand scheme of things. Scattered where she could, so they're mostly close to the house, focused on the moat. Very convenient to throw things in, a moat. And they're similar enough to the one she tried to place in Nora's rooms that we can use that as a link to identify where they've got to."

It made Nora half-laugh, despite the serious turn of topic. "What - what does fixing it involve?"

"With your permission..." He made the request to both Lionel and Nora, simply by how he angled and pitched his voice. "I would like to invite the Penelopes to assist. It would be a decent training exercise for their apprentices, tracking down what's been added to the landscape that shouldn't be there. If we get the whole current crop in, it shouldn't take too long. A few days. I'd like to get all the items, and samples to figure out how to negate what leeched out in the water and soil. That will be a longer process, we'll need to consult others."

"My permission?" Nora blinked. "You ..."

Lionel pointed out, "Yours as much as mine." He straightened his shoulders. "I - it seems early to say this, but also as if it's the right timing. If the Council Members feel sure they can resolve things from here, I want to make it formal as soon as we can."

Mabyn hesitated for a moment, but Cyrus waved a hand for her to speak her mind. "Lay out your thinking, please, Lionel?"

"It's the house I love. I always have. I've got ideas about more of it. The public rooms, something that respects the history, but is also practical. I - if you'll have me, I'd like to keep my rooms, Nora. Or perhaps different rooms. But live in the house, at least until you - well. A family, if you choose."

"If I don't choose, we're going to have this problem again, in not terribly long." Nora pointed out. Mabyn had worried she was going to come over all prickly and defensive, but that wasn't the case. She let out a breath. "I - I love the place. The view out my window. The oak." She gestured off in that direction. "I want to figure out how to tend the land. Properly."

She hesitated, twisting to look at Lionel more directly. "I feel like - I feel like I have a brother, and I never had one before. Of course, I want you to stay. It's your house, you've made it a home. I don't know what the future's going to bring, only...." Then she glanced up, as one of the maids was coming over.

"Master Darius Gallagher has called by, Council Members, your lordship, mistress." There was a slight bob of a curtsey. "What message should I take back?"

Nora, amusingly, had gone bright pink. Ah, indeed. They did both have the new magical journals, now Mabyn thought of it. Younger people were apparently making a habit of writing in them, as her generation had written letters. A different sort of writing, and harder to burn in a fury when a romance went awry. On the other hand, clearly these two had been in some communication beyond the dinner invitations.

"Nora?" Mabyn leaned back. "Is there anything you'd like to tell us?"

Nora glanced from one to the other and laughed. "If you all don't mind, may Darius join us? Or do we have things to discuss that he shouldn't hear?"

"Oh, I think we've managed most of those for now." Mabyn smiled at that. "And if you - mmm. If you are considering his company in a long-term sort of way, better begin as you wish to go on."

Nora nodded. "Emma, would you ask Master Gallagher if he would like to join us, and if so, escort him over and then see about another place setting for tea?" The maid bobbed and went off. Once she was well on the way, Nora cleared her throat. "We've been writing, as well as the suppers. Is that a problem?"

Cyrus shook his head. "Not at all. We didn't know if you'd take to anyone we invited that way, but it was certainly one of the thoughts behind the guest list. If not someone there, perhaps someone they knew. It would be ridiculous to be upset when that worked out. There are..."

Nora nodded quickly. "He's said his family might have some concerns. And when everything was even more nebulous, it seemed ridiculous to bring it up. But now you're more sure it can all be sorted."

"We have work ahead, months, still, probably." Cyrus said. "But I am a lot more clear on what needs to be done, and a fair bit of how to approach it."

By the time Darius came around the corner of the house, they were relaxed, and Lionel had just told a story about one of the renovations. Darius was somberly dressed, and he came over, making a slight bow at Mabyn and Cyrus. Then he bowed to Lionel, finally added a bow and a smile at Nora. "I beg pardon, but the maid assured me I was welcome to join you?"

"Please, have a seat." Cyrus said, easily.

Before Darius moved, he focused on Lionel. "My family and I were very sorry to hear about your mother." When Lionel raised an eyebrow, Darius nodded at Nora. "Nora mentioned it. I'm sure it's very complicated, but also, I gather means that there might be some resolution for the land?" Lionel nodded, smiling enough to make it clear he'd taken no offence.

Nora smiled at him as he sat down. "We were - well. Discussing some options for the coming months."

Darius nodded, then glanced around the table, as if he weren't sure which of them to focus on. "Nora and I have found ourselves enjoying each other's company. And she's so widely read, and in ways I am not. Yet."

Mabyn found that 'yet' entirely charming, though she was predisposed to think romance a pleasurable if novel joy at the moment.

Nora beamed at him, and Darius went on. "But my parents and aunts and uncles are cautious. They don't wish to have me make commitments to someone in a tenuous position, not of the community. It's the legal profession, people do judge. And it would affect Papa's chambers, as well."

Cyrus nodded. "You have your family to think of, as Nora has her own plans. And there is no need to rush anything either."

"We had been talking about - there are some additional steps Cyrus is, um, is the word optimistic about?" Cyrus nodded, and Nora continued, more smoothly. "If in the meantime you are a regular visitor here - with proper supervision, if that would make you or your family feel better - things can progress from there. There are various summer events, of course."

Darius let out a breath of relief, glancing at Nora. "I would appreciate your advice, all of you, yes. But there isn't a rush. I'd want, I mean, if we go forward with this, Nora should establish herself properly in her own right. Though of course I'd be delighted to escort her."

"Not the summer solstice Council gathering, I think, though if you wanted an invitation, I think we can arrange that easily. Better for Lionel to be her escort to the Council keep." Mabyn was weighing out the details. "But the parties around that, or the Midsummer Faire, perhaps?"

That led to a bit of cheerful conversation about upcoming events and the different implications particular invitations might hold.

CHAPTER 40
MABYN'S FLAT, WEDNESDAY, JUNE 29TH

In the end, it took Cyrus and Mabyn a month to figure out how to get a night alone, somewhere other than Baddock Hall. They'd had evenings in each other's company, but it felt entirely too naked in the wrong way to attempt to spend a night in one bed or the other. Things were still unsettled in the house, even with Eustacia installed properly in a good care home. It had meant nestling in together on the sofa, and an increasing vocabulary of small touches in passing. Kissing, certainly. But they had kept their clothes largely in place.

The land was beginning to recover, at least. They could all feel it, even Lionel, and especially after the Penelopes had been so successful. Lucy Doyle had called them 'drops of harm', and said plucking them out of the landscape was like saving a dog from thorns. They hadn't been able to get them all. Some of the charmed stones had got buried in deep muck or the moat, but they'd been able to work with that. The house already felt brighter, and last week's rain had behaved much more as Cyrus had expected.

And of course, there had been all the summer solstice events. The Midsummer Faire had been a great relief to all of them, a bubble of enjoyment and pleasure. They'd arranged a private tent where Lionel could retreat from commiserations about his mother and questions about when he was marrying. And Nora could get a break from people courting her, or deciding if she was worth their time.

Nora was actually handling the flurry of social obligations surprisingly well. She wasn't afraid to admit something was new to her, and it came across as charming and interested rather than naïve. Of course, Darius and Lionel had been attentive escorts, and Darius had enjoyed comparing customs with her in particular. Nora had had dozens of questions after the Council's Summer Solstice ball, with the formal dances and all the other events.

No one had commented on the fact Cyrus was escorting Mabyn. No one, that was, except for Gemma, who'd turned up to meet them at Baddock Hall with flowers from her garden for Mabyn's hair and Cyrus's buttonhole. And for Nora and Lionel, of course, but Cyrus knew she'd made her point.

He'd managed to get two hours for lunch with Rhoe, as well. She'd let him dangle, trying to figure out how to explain what he and Mabyn were reaching for. After letting him fumble through it for a good five minutes, Rhoe grinned. "Bring her round for supper when we can all get free." She'd promptly presented him with her schedule for the next month, and he knew she approved after they'd had a glorious free-flowing lunch.

The question, though, was what precisely he and Mabyn were. Colleagues. Friends, he felt it was safe to say that. Partners in the work, that felt increasingly comfortable every day. But they were not yet lovers. Not in that sense. So when Mabyn suggested they go back to her flat in Trellech after that week's Council meeting, he agreed, and packed a bag. Cyrus didn't know what he wanted, precisely, but he could take a hint. Especially after Mabyn had said things might run late, don't expect them back until the next day, just so much necessary discussion this week.

And now here he was, in Mabyn's flat, in her bedroom, waiting for her to change into something in her dressing room. His things were in her guest room, and he'd changed into a dressing gown and pyjama bottoms, and now he felt completely unprotected.

The room was at least fascinating. There were soft lights shaded with stained glass. He wondered, for a moment, if that was as much for the magical qualities of the pigments as for the beauty of the light. Not just stones, either. There were potted plants and trails of ivy on every shelf. The whole space had a quiet about it. Like the healing baths, but not so touched by the divine. This was a human space, whatever else it was.

Right now, though, that quiet was broken by Mabyn humming under her breath, tunefully. He placed it as she came in as one of the summer dances, from the Midsummer Faire, before he got a good look at her. Her hair was loose, flowing down her back. Her gown was made of the sort of silky fabric he no longer knew the name for, in a pale blue like fog. She looked like a queen, entirely in control of all she surveyed. It took his breath away. Then, there was just a flicker of something in her eyes, and he was standing.

"Come, sit, please." He didn't know how to name what he'd seen, but Mabyn was terrified. Self-possessed, glorious, and scared, all at once. He took both her hands in his, feeling the flicker of her pulse under his fingers, and bringing her to sit beside him on the bed. "It all came rushing in, didn't it?"

Mabyn nodded, her hair shifting like a curtain. She took a breath, then glanced sideways at him without saying anything.

"You know we don't need to do this." Cyrus had his own complexities about this, she had to know that.

"You've been very patient." Her voice cracked. "You must...."

Cyrus rolled his eyes. "Oh, of course, Aubrey would have been like that. I'm sure he didn't care what you felt about it. Do your duty, let him have his pleasure. Good grief, the man was an idiot a dozen ways round. No, scratch that. Hundreds. Thousands."

Something in his tone made her crack. There was a sucked in breath, and then she was shaking, leaning against him. He barely had time to get an arm around her waist to hold her more steadily. She wasn't crying, not exactly, but it was a tremendous release. He suddenly wanted, more than anything else, to bring her to that point in pleasure. To show her what it could be like when someone paid her the attention and affection that was her due.

Eventually, she rubbed her cheek on his shoulder. "I'm a mess."

"You're human. And - you didn't have a wide experience, did you?" She'd never come out and said it. But he was long past suspecting she came from the sort of family that had comments about purity and cleaving only to your husband.

"No." She swallowed, half-hiccoughed. "You?"

"Only had eyes for Tanith, so - no. And I've done without more than my hand this long. I promise if I get too frustrated I'll go excuse myself, tend to my pleasure with hand and charm, and come back and not make that your problem."

"Aubrey..." She hesitated. "Blast. Why does he have to be part of this?"

Cyrus had thought about that, quite a bit on his rides the past fortnight. "Because you and I, we have history. Some of it good, some of it bad. You've not told me all of it, and it's fine if you never do. But I can tell he's the sort who was selfish. Wanted you available whenever he liked, didn't care what you felt, rolled over and snored as soon as he was done. All the mess and fuss, and nothing for you."

"Mess and fuss and roaring." Mabyn agreed.

"All the noise." Cyrus waved one hand. "I was thinking how quiet it was here. Like Rhoe's baths, but much more human. Something I can touch." He chose the words deliberately, beginning to feel this come together like a ritual. He knew exactly how each word and gesture built up something larger and splendid, but also something that was made real in magic.

He'd been a different man when he was Tanith's lover and beloved, in ways he hadn't even begun to realise yet. Something in that caught Mabyn. "And you?"

Cyrus couldn't sneak anything by her. He could make light of things, but that was wrong. Both of them should have better than that. He'd spent so long glossing over everything around being intimate with someone. The intimacies of being a parent or a brother were entirely different. When he didn't respond immediately, Mabyn shifted to brush his cheek with her fingers. She didn't press at him, just made it clear she was right there and waiting.

"I don't know who I am now, in bed. In ..." He let out his breath. "In loving."

Mabyn nodded. "We can't put aside everything we know from the past. And Nimue knows, I don't want this to be by rote. I do know the theory of how it might go, if it's good. I read novels, including that sort. But it's not the sort of thing where you follow the recipe and get the same result every time."

"Art, not craft or science." Cyrus agreed. "And..." He shrugged. "Ritual by yourself is predictable. Reassuring, comforting, often. But it's nothing like collaboration."

She snorted. "Of course you'd think of it like that. I - well. I suppose that gives me somewhere to start. It was competition for Audrey, but I've had hundreds of happy hours in a stillroom or laboratory with other people. Being together, the dance of it."

Cyrus shifted, reaching to cup her cheek and draw her into a kiss. This, they had done before, enough times that he'd stopped keeping count now. Each still ran lightning bolts through him, of surprise and joy. He let his hand slide down her shoulder, to her back, while his other began, slowly, to loosen her gown.

When he pulled back, he said, "I am thinking you should be the one to decide what you wish to try." He let his gaze travel down her body. "You do not ride horses, I know, not often. But you can ride a man astride. Find your own pleasure, leave my hands free to help."

He could feel the shiver up her back, the flicker of her skin and a moment of tension. He'd surprised her and he wasn't sure how she was taking it. Then Mabyn was looking at him, her eyes wide and exceedingly blue. "You'd let me?"

Cyrus chuckled, then let himself laugh in delight. "Let

you? Let you decide how you wish to delight yourself, how I might lend my earnest assistance? Oh, yes. I will let you." He arched his shoulders. "Bed, Mabyn. Let's see what we enjoy."

There was something about rearranging the space that made a difference. It wasn't much, just pulling the blankets back to the foot of the bed to be handy later. Pillows stacked where he could lounge back, or she could grab one to lean on, or change the angle of her knees.

By the time they had sorted all of that out, her gown was hiked up, fabric draping off her hips, and she was breathless with kisses. And, to be fair, the ridiculousness of sex if you let yourself dwell on it too long. So much fuss about the angles and directions and how things might fight together.

He, mind, was ragingly hard, and he was sure she was quite aware. She kept moving her hand in a broad arc, as if to avoid touching him, even when she finally settled on her side, beside him. Mabyn had gone shy again, and this was where they needed a gentle touch.

When it came down to it, he had the words. "May I?" He wanted to touch her, too. He needed to, it was fire burning in his veins and making his breath catch, to have her this close. But he had that instinct of needing to go this way, this moment. And above all, he would trust his instincts.

"Whatever else we do tonight, it is about wanting. I want you, you can feel it." He let his fingers bring hers to touch, and then he arched with it, the pleasure of it, the anticipation. All the desire was building up in him. Nowhere near cresting, he was older now. He could be gloriously patient with it, build things up into temples of hedonism.

Her fingers stuttered, but as he let her see what she was

doing to him, just by that one touch, she shifted her hand. Her fingers closed, holding, getting the proper measure of him. Like she would some new piece of Materia she'd just been given for the first time.

She didn't stroke, she didn't tease. She was there. Herself. That, more than the touch, stole his breath and his wits. When he could focus on her, he was sure his eyes were wide and wild, because he could see it echo in her.

"May I?" he asked again, and this time, he brought his fingers to touch her. Her breast, then baring it to his lips, his mouth. His fingers slipping down her hip to pull up her robes, to begin to explore her in turn. He'd taken such care, that morning, to trim his nails, to buff the callouses from his hands. All the intricate preparations to make every piece of this as smoothly done as he could offer.

When she finally moved to straddle him, they were both flushed. Cyrus had taught her the pleasures of the potions that would ease his way in, the lubricants and oils. When she finally knelt up above him, he steadied himself, and waited. The moment lasted forever, like the height of a wave before it came crashing down. Then she was around him. Her head went back, like his had, her body clenching then relaxing. He could see how she used all her skills to take a breath, to let the tension, the newness be a gift rather than a burden. The way, all those years ago, she must have thrown herself into the Council Trial.

She was not remotely like Tanith, except in her delight. And in her curiosity and the brightness she brought to all of it. But she felt different from his memory, her weight, her curves, her knowledge of her own body in all the other ways she had. Before he finally gave himself over to his own pleasure, Cyrus soaked all of it in, wanting to let it wash over him again and again.

When they were both replete, damp with sweat, she let herself fold down against him, her body pressed against his. Mabyn barely managed to pull the blankets up, and then she nestled against him, and she was asleep almost immediately. Entirely trusting that he would let her be quiet.

EPILOGUE
BY THE OAK, THURSDAY, SEPTEMBER 29TH

Mabyn let out a long breath. It felt, finally, as if things were on the right track. It had been a long summer full of hard work, occasional Council urgencies and emergencies, and a cascade of complications in sorting out the land magics. She was, honestly, tired. There had been harder - and much worse - years in her life. This past six months had been gruelling, complicated, delicate. But also rewarding.

Finally, last week, they thought they'd untangled the last of the major damage. It would take time for the land to come back, for the magic to flow as freely as it should. But yesterday morning, Darius and Nora had seen a star hare at the edge of the field. They were drawn to magic, but skittish at the best of times. It was a tremendous omen.

Nora couldn't keep away from the land. She'd learned to ride well and surely enough that she could do a circuit around the grounds every day. She'd pick some new direction and loop so that she rode through most of the property every week. Sometimes Cyrus joined her, sometimes Lionel did. Sometimes, like yesterday, Darius did. It had settled into a comfortable pattern, but one that Mabyn knew would need to change again.

She felt Cyrus's presence before she consciously heard him. He was good about giving her a little warning, a tiny brush of magic, but she often sensed him even before that. The feel of him, the way other people always knew where the sun was, or their favourite tool or book. She'd never had her sense for Materia act like that for a person, and she'd been afraid to ask. Maybe it was something he wore or carried, rather than himself. They could test it, sometime, when they were in her flat, and properly alone.

There had been some of that. Enough, even, to begin to convince Mabyn that there was a reason people came back, again and again, to sex. She'd never quite lost sensual pleasures, the joys of a long bath with a good book, an exquisite meal, the feel of silk or fine linen against her skin. But to herself, she admitted she'd never expected to find sex anything other than an obligation. A pleasant obligation, perhaps, rather than a painful one, but she'd never expected someone else to take her places her own fingers and charms could not.

With Cyrus, there had never been any question of her own pleasure. Not since that first night, with its stops and starts, all the awkwardness of figuring out how things might work between them. He'd always, resolutely, made sure she was honestly enjoying herself. He'd called her on it a few times, when she'd made a gesture of pleasing him when she wasn't sure she was in the mood.

Now, he came up behind her, but didn't touch her until she turned to him and held out her hand. "We should, I suppose, talk about the future."

"The star hare decided me. And the pass of the estate I

made this morning. There are still things Nora should learn. We certainly shouldn't abandon her to it."

"We won't. But she does not properly need us here all the time. We could come for tea or supper, or something like it. Every week, twice a week?" Cyrus stretched. "I admit, I miss my flat. I miss Trellech's bustle. And there's three new projects wanting more of my time."

"How did that conversation go yesterday, about Mackenzie and Sons?" She'd only got the gist of it from the briefing at yesterday's meeting. Something about some less than savoury magic for personal gain, found in a warehouse in Trellech.

"The Penelopes are sorting out what they actually did, and they'll be reporting next week. Unless something dramatic happens."

"In which case sooner." Mabyn knew how that went. "Tricky, with the other warehouses so close." She shook her head. "And I've more waiting for me. Besides the Alchemy and Materia discussions."

Cyrus nodded, then he slipped his arm around her waist after a momentary check, allowing her to decline if she wanted. He did it so gently, wordlessly, but it was a brief ritual, often repeated. Something about it gave her space and made her want to turn into his touch more and more. "And us?"

"That's the question, isn't it? A hair under three months to solstice." She hesitated. "Where do we go from here? Separate flats, meeting up as we can?"

Cyrus considered. "I'd been considering giving mine up. The upstairs flat is a tad noisy, even with charms. Bright Young Things, it's not the noise exactly as much as the ambient attitude. They'll sort themselves out, but I'm not sure I need to be in earshot."

"I have space. If you don't mind the books. We could make over the guest bedroom into a study for you." It was, perhaps, time for her to shake things up too. "And you've a valet, don't you?"

"Did. His mother's ailing, he's asked for - well. A month or two's leave if it's as quick as it probably is going to be. But we don't need to sort space for him just yet."

"All right." She considered. "Three months together, until solstice. Then we'll see whether we want to move into a larger flat, with space for whatever staff we need? Or whether we clutter up your family home instead, or something else?"

"I think that sounds grand. Enough time to be a bit of an adventure. And you can always send me off to Gemma if you like. Not that she'll notice unless I tell her I'm handy."

Mabyn snorted. It was very practical of them both, really. "So the other question is, do we keep our privacy until then, and make a show of it and let the gossip roll? Tell a few more friends?"

"Well. We should figure out the shape of what we're telling them." Cyrus snorted. "Mind. I suspect Isembard and Thesan guessed. Or my imp of a daughter mentioned something. He was looking at me curiously last night."

"Consulting with Garin, or someone else?" Mabyn couldn't help wondering, though Isembard had seemed a bit more comfortable with his position as an ally to the Council the past year.

"Alexander asked him out to consult - they were looking at that patch on the keep wall, whether it needs further reinforcement. Complex problem, apparently, they had to replace a wood beam in the storehouse, and apparently it was a load-bearing enchantment or near enough. Nothing disastrous. I mean, we're scarcely likely to have a dragon diving from above, not in this century. But it should be fixed."

Mabyn shook her head. "I, what was I reading. Nora actually put me on to it, a treatise about protective marks in Tudor era buildings. Not from our people, but it had some quite accurate examples and analysis. I'll send it along to him when I find it on my desk."

"Alexander, or Isembard?"

"Both. They can wrangle over it. Do them good." Mabyn shrugged. "Anyway. What was he doing when he was looking at you?"

"You know they married rather quickly once they decided they were going to." Cyrus drew out the last vowel, thinking out loud.

"Four months. Though, as Thesan pointed out, it would have meant waiting at least another six if they didn't choose the winter, and they decided they didn't want to. Teaching schedules being what they are. We don't have the same constraints."

"No. But I find ..." He shrugged. "Part of me would like to make Lady Jenifry and Aubrey's family very annoyed in ways they can't do much about. Treat you like a queen for all to see."

"Queen, is it?" Mabyn tsked. "That would disqualify me for the Council, right off."

"Treat you like one, not make you one." Cyrus grinned at her, something boyish about him suddenly. She loved those bursts, where he let all the protective walls he'd grown over the years come cascading down in a glorious release. "You're overdue, anyway."

"I am not at all sure I can tell you no." She hesitated, and felt his hand shift a little, steadier at her hip.

"Don't want to, or can't? The second one's a problem for me." Now his voice was a low rumble.

"Don't want to." Mabyn let out a puff of breath. "Though I suppose we ought to try me telling you no sometime. Until I realise I can." She held up her free hand. "I'll pick small silly things. And tell you after what I'm doing. Fair?"

"Fair. It's like all the drills, learning to do ritual work. Or duelling. Put the practice in, or you can't trust it later."

"And there is a later, for us. I mean."

He moved, leaving his right hand on her hip. He pivoted so he could look her straight in the eye, taking her right hand in his left and bringing it to his lips. "As much later as we can. I rather hope decades." He grinned, suddenly. "I am still so far behind on that reading list you gave me."

"You don't have to read the whole thing, you, you." She shook her head, laughing. It was twenty pages of books she'd found stuck with her, over the years, culled from her reading journals. "Pick the ones you like."

Cyrus laughed. "I like a challenge, a learning challenge."

"Yes, but if you have your nose in a book, what am I to do with the rest of you?"

"Good thing we have time to find that out as well." He leaned in and kissed her nose, the kind of youthful exuberance that delighted her. "Right. Walk, supper, and retreat to your rooms?"

AUTHOR'S NOTES

Thank you so much for joining me for *The Hare and the Oak*. My thanks as always to my most excellent editor, Kiya Nicoll, as well as to my early readers, all of whom made this book immeasurably better.

I've loved Cyrus since he first showed up - barely named - next to his sister in *Carry On*, and even more since his appearance in *Sailor's Jewel*. (This is the one to read if you want more about the 1901 Atlantic voyage that is referenced several times.)

Mabyn appears briefly at the end of *Eclipse* but the mentions of her there made me want to know more about her life. It was a joy to see them find each other. If you'd like a bit more about Gabriel and Rathna Edgarton, *The Fossil Door* is the story of their romance.

I've known for some time that I wanted to write a book focusing on members of the **Council**, who took on responsibility for the larger land magics in 1484, at the time of the Pact. All of them are exceedingly competent, and even the kinder ones can be extremely ruthless and single minded in pursuit of their oaths. (Cyrus and Mabyn are both definitely on the kinder end.)

As this book makes clear, the 1920s are a rough time for the **land magic**. While Albion wasn't a direct battleground during the Great War, plenty of men and women came back shaken and hurt in ways that affected their magic as well as their minds and bodies. The Council is only beginning to understand the range of impact that is having, and how to ensure the land magics continue appropriately.

The other big piece of this book is that one of my early readers has pointed out for a while now that we really needed a book that demonstrated what happened when someone pushed too hard on an **oath**. By design, oaths made to the Silence (i.e. those anchored by the Pact) are not meant to be fatal. The goal is always to make you so scared you can't proceed with doing something that would break the oath. It's very effective that way, if also unyielding.

However, many people only rarely swear on the Silence. Think of it like being in a courtroom or hospital operating room. For some people, that's their day to day life, but for most people it's something that happens only very occasionally (and you might prefer never.) As noted in a couple of my other books, the Guard and Penelopes make these oaths frequently, as part of their professional duties. So do judges and magistrates, the Council, and in some cases others.

In Eustacia Baddock's case, she obviously pushed past both the oath to the Silence she made when she became Lady Baddock, and past the binding oath that Cyrus and Mabyn required of her, to avoid interference. It did not fully trigger (in terms of consequences for her long-term well-being) until she did something that could not be easily taken back, making sure the charmed stone was placed in Nora's room. We don't see her reactions in that span of time, but it was likely something akin to progressive debility, and the longer she didn't reverse her course, the more terror pressed in on her, and the more she wasn't able to react.

Let's get into the specific notes for this book...

The brief mention of someone walking down the street and **spotting their double** has happened a number of times, but there was a news story about this in 1926, and of course I had to use it as a passing reference.

One of the joys of research is getting to poke around and look at actual **census records** and figure out what information would be available. As Cyrus notes, the 1901 census includes name, age, place of birth, but doesn't include parents. People are listed by household, which means they could connect Nora to her aunt, but not necessarily know more about the relationships. Fortunately, Cyrus does have access to other records.

I also wanted to write a character who, while magical, had not lived in a **magical community.** There are magical folk throughout Albion, of course, with many living in the larger population centres (Trellech and London are the largest, but there are a number of other communities in other cities.) Manchester, though, doesn't have a core community in the same way. My thought on that is that the neighbourhoods where that might have happened had rapid change due to the rise of factories and other industrial production, with some people moving elsewhere.

Plenty of people in Albion live alongside non-magical folks, with perhaps a few advantages (a more reliable kettle, they get slightly fewer infections, their milk stays good a few days longer, their chimneys are less smoky), but without being very noticeable. I'd wanted to write someone from this background for a while, and writing Nora was a fun chance to explore an outsider's take on some things the magical community just takes for granted.

Nora and Mabyn talk about **ghosts** at one point. Ghosts definitely do exist in Albion, though they're not nearly as widespread as ghost stories suggest. Most old houses do have stories, but they're more often caused by lost troves of coins or other metal objects that have accumulated magic than by actual ghosts. One of these days, though, I'll write about an actual ghost.

Cockfighting chairs are in fact a real thing. I stumbled across one in other research (figuring out the furniture that is something of a plot point in *Fool's Gold*), and had to reference them somewhere.

They're as described, a chair that you could sit astride (if you were wearing trousers, anyway), with a folding ledge for a book, betting slips, or other paper items. If you wanted to sit with your back supported, you turned the chair around and put the reading ledge down. Either way, there was a small compartment under the seat for pens, paper, and of course your betting slips, cards, or other amusements. As Mabyn notes, they fell out of favour when cockfighting became illegal, because it is very difficult to claim you weren't watching an illegal match when you had purpose-made furniture handy.

I was delighted to set this book in **Suffolk**, for a personal reason and for an equestrian one. My father was born and grew up in Ipswich in Suffolk (a handful of miles south of Baddock Hall), and I've visited the city a couple of times (though not at all recently.) It's a large port city, and while I didn't want to focus on the city for this book, I had a delightful time exploring the fauna and flora of the area.

The **Suffolk Punch** is a local draught horse breed, always chesnut (in that spelling, as Lionel points out), and they are absolutely gorgeous to watch. (Check out YouTube or other sources for videos.) They're considered an endangered breed, but they are smaller than other draught horses, hardy, and generally very good-tempered.

The rest of the notes for this book all have to do with magical theory, folklore, and related topics, so I'm going to group them somewhat thematically.

One thing I'm committed to in the **depictions of magic** in my books, is the idea that there are many different forms of magic. Some work better than others for certain situations, and some absolutely have more social support than others. But it's a big and varied world out there.

Think of magic a bit like music: some kinds don't fit well together, lots of people have their own personal preferences and tastes (especially about what they're interested in spending a lot of time with). But there's also room for different combinations, approaches, or for an individual to have skills in a number of different styles or techniques. Cyrus and Mabyn both have their own approaches, and so do other people. One thread through the book, of course, is trying to figure out what might work for Nora, well enough that she can pick up the land magic obligations.

Similarly, there are a variety of options for **shapeshifting** in Albion. Some people learn to shift (see *Magician's Hoard* for more about this - one of my working chapter titles for that one was "shapeshifting 101"). Others have a family tendency, such as the berserker legends, while others are living with a curse or other external magical situation.

This leads to a variety of different approaches. The garden exploration that Cyrus sets up is a little more rooted in a formal ritual approach (though modified to be more flexible and free flowing, suitable for a 'see what calls you' goal.) The ritual they do in the workroom is an older form, one anchored in elemental attunement. I imagine it as having origins in the grimoire traditions of the Western magical community in the mediaeval period. The actual method he uses, though, has been revised and refined over the years for a variety of reasons.

On that note, there are many ways to maintain the **land magic obligations**. Every one of the landed holdings has their own particular rituals (most commonly around spring equinox, May Day, summer solstice, harvest, and often winter solstice), but the specific vary a great deal.

Each person has their own preferences - someone who is an expert in ritual magic is going to go at those rites differently than someone who prefers materia or incantation or who has a strongly elemental approach. There's lots of ways to make a joyfully festive occasion, but some are going to be more to your taste or skills than others.

Which is, of course, why we get Cyrus riffing on **Shakespeare's** "There are more things in heaven and earth than are dreamt of in your philosophy" which is from *Hamlet*. (I am not yet committing to what Shakespeare may or may not have known about magic, though being magical would explain some things about the obscurity of his background at various points in his life.)

As Mabyn notes, some fairly famous examples of magic aren't their sort of magic, to say the least. **Isobel Gowdie** is a well-known tale from Scotland, talking about her turning into a hare. There are various song versions of this text. Two I love are on Maddy Prior's *Year* album as "The Legendary Hare", and Fay Hield's "Hare Spell" on her *Wrackline* album.

Likewise, as Mabyn comments, the **fairies at the end of the garden** aren't the Fatae at all. This is a reference to the Cottingley Fairies. They were much later confirmed to be a hoax, but were very compelling to Arthur Conan Doyle, author of the Sherlock Holmes stories, among other things. Mabyn does reference a few of the Fatae seen and referenced in other books, including the Belin (seen in *Goblin Fruit*) and the custos dragons (one of whom appears in *Fool's Gold*).

Finally, there are a number of different personal approaches. **Hag stones,** a stone with a hole in it, have a number of different pieces of folklore attached, including the ones Mabyn mentioned. They've been seen as magical and special in a number of contexts, especially when made of particular stones like the flint one Mabyn has had.

If you've read this far, check out my mailing list for more about tidbits of research, extras about characters (I have one planned for this book), and other goodness. And I am hoping to spend some time with Gemma in a book of her own down the road.

Happy reading! (And read on for an excerpt from *Point By Point*, due out in May 2022)

EXCERPT FROM POINT BY POINT

November 1926

"Give me something better." Edward Morris flicked the pages back across the desk at Lydia. They were marked up in red ink. That part didn't bother her. She expected it, even welcomed it. He didn't waste ink on people who were hopeless. Or time.

Today, he'd called her in for notes on the last three pieces she'd turned in. None of them were breaking news, all of them were longer investigative pieces. She was no good at the puff pieces about fashion or ladies societies - even if some of those were every bit as cutthroat as any business conquest. Lydia had known her heart wasn't quite in the series of pieces about new approaches to apprenticeships. She'd dutifully done in-depth interviews with a dozen people, all learning desperately needed magical trades. Individually, they were all fine.

Fine. Not passionate. Not enlightening. Not a call to arms or action, to change the world.

"I assigned you to those." Edward flicked his fingers at

the papers again, and this time a little puff of magic pushed them closer to her. "I expected a spark. Kindling."

Lydia's head came up. That was the problem, she hadn't had a better idea. "Sir." She couldn't argue, he was right.

"What would you do if you could?"

She hadn't expected that. Morris wasn't a man who invited suggestions, as a rule. He ran the Trellech Moon as an absolute dictatorship, which meant he held everyone from the journalists to the print-setters to the cleaners to the highest possible standards. All the time. He was demanding, driven, but he drove himself harder than anyone else.

He did not, however, ask for ideas.

She'd had a few she'd discarded. They were the kind of thing that would take time, reporting time she wouldn't have for other things. She hadn't been sure if he'd pay her salary. It was one thing to do that for a week or two, for a story that was fine. It was another thing to do it for a month or more.

"Come on. You've done good work in the past. That one about injurious apprenticeship clauses. Complicated and more risky than you told me up front, but a good piece." He hadn't praised it like that, then. She'd contracted an apprenticeship with the harmful terms, ridden it out for a week, before she'd brought the weight of the Dwellers at the Forge to bear. That hadn't come out in the final piece, but she'd been able to use it to get proper advice from the Ministry, from the Guard, from several other sources, about how to spot an unfair contract and what to do if someone you cared about ended up in one.

"Sir." She leaned back. "It would take a while. A month minimum, probably three, longer if I found anything especially good. And it would mean I'd not be available for other reporting."

He raised an eyebrow. "Stunt reporting, then? Getting yourself fully in the midst of everything? What do you have in mind?"

The idea had hit her a month ago. They'd been talking, up in the upstairs lounge at the Dweller's club, late into the night. Most of the more hotheaded of their lot had gone off somewhere, for more labour debates and it had been Lydia and a handful of others. She'd been draped across one of the chairs, her food dangling off the arm, when it had hit her.

Now, she gathered her thoughts, working hard to make them line up in an orderly manner. "Sir, you remember that business with the Research Society and Lord Sisley, a year ago or so." She hadn't reported the story.

"Not all of that came out at the time." Morris grunted. Which was another admission. "Why?"

"What's happened since? Not to them, though a follow-up is due. The people who lost power. But - who stepped into that power? Or who's tried to?"

Morris tilted his head. "Good enough question. But how do you propose to find out." He waved a hand at her. "You don't come from those circles."

"And they wouldn't trust a reporter who did." She knew her place, as well as anyone. Then she said, carefully. "Might know someone who could get me entry in the right places. Maybe. I'd have to do some background research, and see if he's up for it."

She suspected he wasn't. Only maybe she wouldn't need Galen to do much. Come to a few parties. Be posh. She was fairly sure he was in practice being posh these days, the family business interests were steadying out again, and the estates were doing better.

"Might doesn't get you a story." Morris flicked his fingers, and there was another little puff of air. "What's your plan?" What he wasn't asking, precisely, was how long she needed to put something together.

Lydia had a better answer for that. "Three days - starting today - in the morgue for background." It was still only ten in the morning. "Hope I can catch the person I want to ask tonight, if not that might be a day or two." She looked up, meeting his eyes directly. "Thursday afternoon." Three days and a couple of hours. She could do late nights, that was fine, to pull together all the notes she'd find.

He glanced at his diary, open on the desk beside him, and scribbled a note in. "Half-two, this office, Thursday." She'd have half an hour to convince him, he always went off for the editorial discussion of the afternoon's paper and notes on the next day's stories at three.

"Sir." She nodded. He crooked his finger, and a piece of paper flew from a stack on the bookshelf on the far wall, right into place in front of him. He scrawled a note, with the curving initials at the bottom. "Take that to the morgue."

Lydia knew a dismissal when she got one. And honestly, that was at least five minutes more time than she'd expected. She nodded. "Sir." Then she picked up her satchel and walked out through the desks, managing not to whistle for joy until she got halfway down a flight of stairs at the other end.

Ten minutes later, she was tucked in at an elderly table, down in the basement, where all the old files were kept. The clerks were bustling around, finding things for other reporters, but she knew to stay out of the way. They each had their own patterns and paths, and magic help anyone who got in the way.

After a minute or two, the senior clerk sat down next to her. "Master Wilson." Lydia nodded respectfully. There was no sense making him annoyed. For one thing, she'd rather not. For another, it would make her working life impossible. "Himself was generous. What's your query?"

By which Lydia knew he meant the subject, the topic. "Two things, interrelated. What happened to the people who went down in that whole mess with the Research Society last year. Lord Sisley and all. And second, who's moving into their places now."

"Evans. Over here." That summoned a middle-aged woman, glasses perched on her nose, her hair back in an untidy bun. Lydia had seen her before, but had never actually been introduced. She appeared promptly, pulling a notepad out of a pocket in what turned out to be an apron around her waist, that blended into her dark skirt.

"Sir?"

"Pyle here needs your brains. Sisley and the aftermath, you'll want to look at who took over in the Research Society, and the quiet resignations file. And then..." He reeled off a series of names. "Alder, Wrightman, Lewis, Fitzwilliam, and, there's one more."

"Sutton, sir."

Master Wilson grinned at her. "Just so. Go to." He then turned back to Lydia, confident she would. "Mistress Evans is here from half-eight to half-five, hour for lunch at noon. You have her time until lunch on Thursday, but you are not important enough for overtime. See you remember."

Lydia had to smile at it, but then she did her best to be properly serious. "Of course, sir. And I know the rules. One envelope at a time, don't mix things up, check them in and out with her."

Master Wilson nodded. "Her desk is there." He gestured four desks down, in pride of place. It was the productive sort of slightly untidy: several piles of files were out, but they clearly had purpose. "Pencil only, we can't risk ink spills."

"Of course, sir." Lydia waited for him to say something else.

He just nodded once, and got up, going briskly over to another of the desk. Lydia waited until he was gone, then drew out her notepad, three pencils - already sharpened - from her pencil case. By the time Mistress Evans came back, she was as ready as she was going to be.

"Which first?"

"Quiet resignations, please, Mistress Evans."

"Ev." The single syllable came out clearly enunciated, a moment before a very sizeable folder was put in front of her. "Quiet resignations, last three years."

"Beg pardon?"

"Call me Ev. Are you Pyle, or something else?" Her voice was brisk but cheerful enough.

"Lydia, please. Though Pyle's fine if you'd rather."

"Not the most euphonious short names. Lid. Pile." She shrugged, amused at the wordplay. "What next?"

"Research Society, please, and then the names. I expect I'll have a better idea once I've got through this." Lydia tapped the folder with the envelopes.

Ev left her alone, going back to the filing cabinets. Lydia quickly lost herself in the work, going through each folder and scribbling down notes. By the time she came up for air ninety minutes later, her stomach was rumbling and she desperately needed to resharpen all of her pencils.

She waited for Ev to look up and then caught her attention. When the older woman came over, Lydia cleared her throat. "Not to be a bother - where can I sharpen my pencils?"

"You've twenty minutes to lunch. Would another pencil do you?" It would and did. Twenty minutes later, Lydia brought her satchel with her, checking all the files back in to Ev's desk, and waiting while they locked everything up. She then ducked out with a "Back at one." and went to the cheapest cafe she knew. It was a good quarter hour walk, but it gave her the chance to check in with a couple of sources along Club Way, the various staff who were out and about at this time of day on all sorts of errands. They picked up interesting information, some of which they were willing to share.

At two minutes after one, she was back at her assigned table, and hard at work again. At twenty past five, she was tidying her notes up. She'd gotten most of the way through the quiet resignations folder, she'd have to pick up her pace tomorrow if she could. And she'd be up all night reconciling her notes. Assuming, of course, that she could get hold of Galen for the other part of her plan. All the research in the world wouldn't help if she couldn't do that.

When she caught Ev's eye, she nodded. "I'll need that top envelope in the morning, and might need to go back to the whole thing when I've looked at the rest. More pencils."

Ev nodded. "You can come to lunch with us tomorrow, if you want."

Lydia expected it would be a bit pricier than she wanted. They got a steady salary down here, unlike her piecework by the story. But on the other hand, knowing more about the clerks down her could be only to the good. "I'd like that. Thank you."

That done, everything handed over, she took herself off to the Dwellers. She could scrounge something from the kitchen there, almost certainly.